UNLEASHING
the
STORM

As always, there are so many people to thank for helping us take this book from idea to finished product.

Our agent, Roberta Brown, for all her support in ways too numerous to count.

Our editor, Shauna Summers, for her continued guidance, patience and belief.

Pam Feinstein, who's been our fantastic copy editor through two books in the Storm series, and to the Bantam Dell Art Department for the always fabulous covers.

A big thank-you to Lara Adrian and Jaci Burton, who are always there with advice, jokes and margaritas whenever we need them. Your friendship is very treasured.

A special thanks to Susan Grant for sharing her pilot expertise and knowledge of aircraft operation.

For Alison Kent, who always listens and advises, and to our blog buddies over at Writeminded for the daily fun.

Last but never least, for Zoo, Lily, Bryan and Brennan, for letting us slip into our ACRO world for long periods of time at the expense of forgetting the real one exists— and for always believing.

"Ma'am?"

She blinked, realized she'd been so busy in her own world that she hadn't heard anything Tom had said, and the way he was watching her, like he didn't enjoy being ignored, made her a little jittery.

"I'm sorry. What did you say?"

"I asked if maybe I could move in? Get started working."

His voice, powerful and compelling, rolled through her like a muscle-deep caress, and she wondered if his effect on her was a result of her growing need or if he always talked with a rough, erotic edge.

"Right." She started up the drive toward the guesthouse, and motioned him to follow. "I don't know how familiar you are with Rainbow Ridge Sanctuary...."

He settled into an easy, long stride next to her, and the warm breeze brought his scent to her, a powerful mixture of grass, woods, and sun-warmed man no one else would have smelled unless they'd been on top of him. Which, she thought as she glanced at him, sounded like a nice place to be right about now.

Yeah, spring fever was kicking at the barn door, and it was only a matter of time before it broke out at a dead run.

Tom...there was something different about him, an earthy animal magnetism she'd never encountered. After eleven years of suffering for a few weeks a year, she knew her body, and she'd been sure she had a couple of days to prepare for this, but it seemed as though Tom's presence had brought the fever on early. Fighting it seemed pointless.

Clenching her fists at her sides, she threw her head back, let her heart rate double, let it flush her body with blood that had heated up a couple of degrees. Her nervous system sparked like someone had struck a match to it, and every nerve ending tingled with hypersensitivity until her skin was on fire.

It had begun.

Also by Sydney Croft

RIDING THE STORM

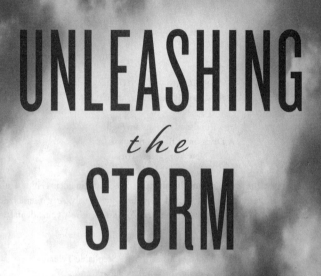

UNLEASHING
the
STORM

SYDNEY CROFT

DELTA TRADE PAPERBACKS

UNLEASHING THE STORM
A Delta Trade Paperback / March 2008

Published by Bantam Dell
A Division of Random House, Inc.
New York, New York

Delta is a registered trademark of Random House, Inc.,
and the colophon is a trademark of Random House, Inc.

Library of Congress Cataloging-in-Publication Data
Croft, Sydney.
Unleashing the storm / Sydney Croft.
p. cm.
ISBN 978-0-385-34081-6 (trade pbk.)
1. Supernatural—Fiction. 2. Animal communicators—Fiction. I. Title.
PS3603.R6356U552008
813'.6—dc22
2007029275

Printed in the United States of America
Published simultaneously in Canada

www.bantamdell.com

BVG 10 9 8 7 6 5 4 3

CHAPTER
One

Kira Donovan would be dead by now if Ender needed her to be, another victim of his steady hand and expert marksmanship, which were part random gift of nature and part honed by years of training.

He lay in familiar sniper position, on his stomach on the broad, grassy slope overlooking the farm, mentally lining up one perfect shot after another as the woman he'd been sent to persuade walked in and out of the dilapidated barn without a care in the world.

The woman born as Charity Connelly was going to require a hell of a lot of training to bring her up to spec. And she was going to have to stop wearing those shorts and T-shirts that showed off too much tanned, curvy flesh too, because that was much too distracting for everyone involved. Ms. Freakin' Doolittle and her merry band of animals were going to have a rude awakening.

He sighed, put his forehead down against the cool earth and breathed in the scent of nature that always seemed to be a part of him, no matter how hard he'd tried to get away. And even though he so didn't want this assignment, he was here, and he had a job to do. And his jobs always got done.

Speaking of done, what hadn't been was the beautiful woman he'd picked up last night, someone who shared his tastes in bed and his penchant for no-strings relationships. That had to be the real reason for his hard-on.

They'd just gotten to the handcuffs portion of the evening when he'd received the call from work, something he couldn't ignore. And when Dev, the head of the Agency for Covert Rare Operatives that employed him, and Ken, his direct supervisor, had laid out the plan to him, which meant taking the red-eye from the Catskills, New York, compound to bumble-fuck Idaho, Ender had just shaken his head in a combination of irritation and no-fucking-way.

"Why me?" he'd asked when he arrived at Dev's office. Because he'd worked for five years as one of their top Convincers, the guy who brought home the big catches. He liked being able to go in and pick off the men and women who'd already been briefed to some degree about the agency's dealing in Special Ops of a very different kind, was always prepared for one of these rare-ability types to go off the deep end, but never had much more than a casual, passing acquaintance with them.

He did not want to be one of the people who actually had to recruit the talent.

"You've got patience," Ken said.

He snorted. "Patience when I'm waiting for the right shot, yes. My patience where new recruits are concerned is severely limited, and if you mean patience where women are concerned—well, I just went from bad to worse."

"You've got the background for the cover. You grew up on a farm," Ken continued.

"Shit," he'd muttered, because he'd put his shit-kickers away when he left the farm, and the horse, when he was sixteen, and never looked back. Hitched around the country for a year doing odd jobs, whatever he could get his hands on—same went for women—and finally, when he hit seventeen and got his GED, he hit the nearest recruiting office. He wanted different—college—something. And the Army had given him that, Delta Force and Covert Ops even more. His parents had given consent, grateful that he'd finally called to tell them he was still alive.

He finally appealed to the head of ACRO. "Come on, Dev. You've got plenty of other guys who could handle this one—guys whose job it is to do this. What the hell do you need my talents for so early in the game?"

Dev had smiled, and with his usual straightforwardness, simply said, "Because if she can't be convinced to join us within forty-eight hours, you're going to have to kill her."

Ender had grabbed the file and left the office without another word. Ken hadn't wanted a trail—needed a quick in and out because of the target's highly specialized and unforeseen increasingly urgent needs, and the fewer people seen on and around the farm, the better. So it was good-bye Ender and hello Tom Knight for the next forty-eight hours.

If he had his way, the job would be done in twenty-four. Whatever it took, no holds barred, he was going to drag Kira the animal whisperer kicking and screaming into ACRO, or he'd carry out his alternate orders. From what information he'd gleaned from her files, she might actually enjoy being tied down, especially during this time of year.

If it could only be that easy, a seduce and convince special, normally Wyatt Kennedy's favorite means of persuasion. An ACRO operative who specialized in deep undercover ops, Wyatt was convinced that ninety-nine percent of women would roll with just the right kind of persuasion, and the other one percent would require a tranquilizer gun.

Ender had both plans covered.

Mixing business with pleasure had never gotten in his way before, and from what the first contact person, a psychic who'd gone undercover at the sanctuary, had reported, it might be the only way to get Kira on board. ACRO's psychic had claimed that Kira's spring fever was a major issue and, according to Ken, utilizing Kira's insatiable need for sex during this time was supposed to be part of Ender's master plan. An open invitation.

Now he pushed up from the ground and headed down toward the barn, taking the main route that led from the driveway. Bag slung over his shoulder, he looked like a man who'd walked in from the one Greyhound bus stop in this one-horse Idaho town, without many possessions or cares.

Still, Kira came out of the barn and headed right in his direction like she had a homing device on him. He hadn't spotted any cameras, but he'd been told she was paranoid.

"Can I help you?" she asked, her voice brisk, businesslike and not at all like the soft tones he'd figured on. Immediately his own needs gained quick interest and let him know they'd demand to be heard sooner than later.

God, she was pretty—naturally pretty, all long, light brown hair and full, pouty lips, wide amber eyes and a body to freakin' die for.

"Hey, I'm Tom. Your new man for hire," he said, and yeah, he'd let her work him in more ways than one, if she was game.

He hadn't used his real name in years, preferred the anonymity of "Ender" and the images it conjured up, especially at work. It kept most of the assholes, and everyone else, at bay. Because, at heart, he never was a social kind of guy, and things were not going to change if he could help it.

He approached her, palm out, and she hesitated, the skittish side he'd been expecting showing through. Finally, she extended her hand, her palm rough from work, her shake strong and sure.

"Hello, Tommy," she said.

"It's Tom," he said, then cursed inwardly and shrugged. "But, whatever, it's all good."

Yeah, real fucking slick.

She didn't smile, but the corner of her mouth pulled up slightly. "You're right on time."

"I try to make that a habit," he said, became aware of something sniffing his ass and turned to find a goat staring at him. It didn't look happy either.

"Do you also make it a habit to spy on people?" she asked, and he turned back from the animal to her.

Son of a— "No, ma'am," he said.

"So you just decided you wanted to stare me down for an hour and a half, then?" She'd folded her arms over her chest, and he let his eyes skim her breasts before meeting her gaze and smiling.

"I got here a little early and wanted to take a nap. Didn't want to bother you or anything. And then I saw you, walking back and forth from the barn and, well..." He shrugged. "Shit, I'm a red-blooded man, Kira."

That part was more than true, and standing this close to her, inhaling the scent of apples and honey and cloves that surrounded her, despite the other, more pungent smells close by, was killing him.

She narrowed her eyes at him, and he held his breath because he couldn't screw this up this soon. Something was wrong—very wrong. He'd never been spotted, not like that. He'd been hidden, camouflaged, and he was good enough at that to know that she'd gotten her information about his watching in some other way than stumbling on it herself.

When the goat poked him in the back again, everything suddenly became clear.

●

Kira watched Peeping Tom for a long moment, allowing Cheech time to sniff him out. The little Nubian goat was a great judge of character, and if he indicated that Tom needed to be watched, then that's what she'd do.

And frankly, she'd watch him anyway. She'd never been one for the rugged, outdoorsy type, but something about Tom grabbed her in places no man had grabbed for a long time.

Not since her last spring fever.

Now that May had come again, the yearning had begun, the

fierce, primal burn that permeated every cell and told her she was days, maybe hours from the insanity that would consume her for upward of four weeks.

She'd been getting antsy, had been unable to concentrate on simple tasks. And simple tasks in the presence of males . . . forget it. It was definitely time to scope out potential partners and give her battery-operated toys a rest. She'd figured her other hire, a dark-haired, brawny hottie named Derek, would be the first mate she took this season.

But now, as she studied Tom Knight, with his piercing blue eyes and sun-streaked blond hair that was too long for a military cut and too short for a surfer, she began to think he might be more fun until he wore out. High, chiseled cheekbones, firm mouth . . . yeah, he may not be her type, but during this time of year, all men were her type, and besides, she wasn't looking for happily ever after.

There'd never be one of those. Not for her. Not for someone people thought was psychotic if they didn't believe she could talk to animals, or were terrified of if they did believe. Because she didn't just talk to animals. She understood them, communicated with them through words and body language and scents, but mainly, mental images and sensations that transcended most human understanding.

And the other aspect of her gift, the part that was more of a curse, well, people *really* didn't understand that. Hence, the moves. The name changes. The prayers that her latest relocation and identity would be her last.

Cheech gave Tom a head butt and then, with a low bleat, told her he'd keep an eye on the man. The goat seemed to think it was strange for a human to lie on the ground the way Tom had, and Cheech wasn't going to trust him any time soon.

"Ma'am?"

She blinked, realized she'd been so immersed in her own world that she hadn't heard anything Tom had said, and the way he was watching her, like he didn't enjoy being ignored, made her a little jittery.

"I'm sorry. What did you say?"

"I asked if maybe I could move in? Get started working."

His voice, powerful and compelling, rolled through her like a muscle-deep caress, and she wondered if his effect on her was a result of her growing need or if he always talked with a rough, erotic edge, as though urging a woman toward orgasm.

"Right." She started up the drive toward the guest house, and motioned him to follow. "I don't know how familiar you are with Rainbow Ridge Sanctuary…"

He settled into an easy, long stride next to her, and the warm breeze brought his scent to her, a powerful mixture of grass, woods and sun-warmed man no one else would have smelled unless they'd been on top of him. Which, she thought as she glanced at him, sounded like a nice place to be right about now.

Yeah, spring fever was kicking at the barn door, and it was only a matter of time before it broke out at a dead run.

"I know it sits on roughly forty acres, and that there's a public and private side." He looked over his shoulder, frowned at Cheech. "Is that thing going to follow us everywhere?"

"Just you. He's suspicious of strangers."

"Great," he muttered, turning his attention back to their surroundings. "I'm guessing this is the private side."

She nodded. "The people who own the sanctuary live on the front twenty acres with the exotic animals. Fifteen or so volunteers help out over there, and they charge a nominal admission for people to visit. Down here"—she waved her arm in an expansive gesture—"we take care of the domestic animals."

He slowed to avoid stepping on Peepers, a crippled mallard duck she'd rescued last year from a kid who'd grown tired of his Easter present. "I thought you were in charge of the whole place."

Nodding, she bent to run a finger over Peepers's smooth green head, which put her at crotch level with Tom. Heat billowed from him, heat and seductive male scents, and oh, she needed to be alone with him. Soon.

"I'm the manager," she said hoarsely, and straightened. "So I do the hiring, and I oversee all the animal care and training. I live down here with you and Derek."

"Derek?"

"He's my other hire. You two will share the upstairs part of the guest house. The bottom floor is mine." She thought she saw a flash of irritation in his eyes, but it was gone so quickly she might have imagined it. "Is there a problem?"

He shrugged and ignored Cheech when the goat gave him a head butt for the sheer pleasure of it. "I was under the impression I was the only hire."

They started walking again, his boots crunching gravel, his tread lighter than she'd have expected as they navigated around flocks of farm fowl and three sheep that refused to give way. Tom didn't miss a beat, moved with her to give the animals a wide berth, and she tried not to focus on the way his lean thighs flexed inside well-worn and well-fitting jeans with every step. Or the way the muscles in his bare arms looked strong enough to effortlessly pin her beneath him.

"Two of my guys quit suddenly a couple of weeks ago. One of them went on vacation and never came back, and the other got up one morning, packed and left before I knew he was gone."

The kind of labor-intensive, low-pay work they did in a place like this had a tendency to weed out all but the most dedicated animal lovers, but it had still been odd to lose Jack and David like that, and in such a short span of time. Especially since they'd been around last year during her time of need, and they'd seemed happy to stick around for this one.

Maybe she shouldn't have cut them off when she'd no longer required them. Then again, she knew full well the consequences of trying to maintain a relationship outside her fevers.

"I hired Derek to replace one," she said, "and you to replace the other."

They arrived at the guest house she'd partly remodeled with the money she made under the table here at the refuge, and she mounted the rickety steps. "Watch the banister—it's pretty well shot."

"I can probably fix it," he said, going down on a knee to pat one of the three dogs lounging on the porch. When Cheech clattered up the steps and demanded attention, Tom scratched the goat's brown back.

"That's okay—Derek already offered. I guess he's a carpenter in his spare time. He's going to paint the house as well, as soon as he gets some time."

"As long as it's under control," Tom said. "It's always good to have someone handy around."

She bit her lip. Tom had no idea how handy *he'd* be to have around. In more ways than one.

"You and Derek will always use the back-entrance stairs to the upper floor, but I'm taking you in this way so you can see the place and meet the kids."

"Kids?"

"The house critters. Mostly rescues I can't allow outside without supervision."

She opened the door, and fur exploded as cats scattered and dogs came running.

"Fuck. Me."

Tom stood there wearing a shocked expression she doubted people saw much. He quickly recovered and plastered on a neutral mask, but his sharp, focused eyes took everything in. She got the distinct feeling he was cataloging the furniture, the animals, the entire dwelling in his mind.

"Is that a lynx?" he asked, as they walked inside and shut the door, only to be surrounded by several happy dogs and one extra-large cat.

"Yep. That's Rafi." She crouched on her heels to scratch the lynx behind the ears. "He was on a butcher table, about to be skinned alive for his fur, when he was rescued." Her stomach churned, as it always did when she thought about how close he'd come to an excruciating, lingering death. "The people who rescued him from the fur farm only had enough money to buy him and one other cat. The rest..." She trailed off, unable to talk about it.

She straightened, waved the animals away, and they bounded off like a bunch of kindergarteners released for recess. "So this is where I live. Nothing fancy. Thrift store furnishings." She gestured to the left, where the only pieces of furniture, a stained blue love seat and a tiny television she never watched, made the room seem bigger than it was.

"Living room there, dining room to the right, my bedroom and den in the back. Those stairs ahead lead up to your room, but like I said, you'll use the back entrance." She took a key off the rack on the entryway wall and handed it to him. "The door on the right is yours. Derek is on the left. You'll share a kitchen and a bathroom. Sheets and towels are in the wardrobe next to your bed, which is a twin, so don't expect to have any comfortable nights with guests."

"Comfort isn't usually a concern."

He swung his gaze back to her, blatantly taking in her body from her lips to her thighs, as though the mention of a bed had made him picture her in his. She could certainly picture being there, could imagine his lean, hard body against hers. The potent energy surrounding him, the aura of power and eroticism, promised that time shared between the sheets would be something to savor.

"Anything else, Kira?"

"Yes. We start work at six A.M. You can break for lunch anytime between eleven and two. We work until around six, but we sometimes go later. You and Derek can each have one weekend day off. Work out between yourselves which day you want, Saturday or Sunday. I work both. If you need to run to town for anything, groceries or whatever, you can take my truck parked out back. Just ask first. Ditto with my computer. You can use it, but ask. And there's no Internet connection."

"Why not?"

Because Big Brother watches your every move. "I like my privacy."

He gave her the usual you're-a-nutcase look, and then rubbed the back of his neck. "Is that all?"

The words, spoken in a flat and emotionless drawl, sounded innocent. But she suspected that inside he was bucking her authority as fast as she could throw it at him. This man did not like being told what to do. How odd that he took this kind of job—when he'd called this morning about a position, she'd been pleased with his credentials, but now she had to wonder if his farm background, typically a male-driven trade, made him a little edgy when a woman called the shots.

So it was with great pleasure that she said, "There's one more thing. Under no circumstances will you consume meat on this property or in my presence. I'm a strict vegan, and while I won't begrudge you eggs and dairy products, I will not tolerate the offensive consumption of animal flesh by humans at this refuge. Understood?"

A vein popped out on his forehead and began to pulse. Though there were no other outward signs of his annoyance and unease, she could smell the potent mixture coming off him in waves.

He smiled, hefted his bag high on his shoulder and said, "That's cool." And then she watched his fine backside while he took the stairs three at a time, as though he couldn't wait to get away from her.

But she knew better. Because along with the other smells, she'd caught the scent of lust, pure and simple.

Closing her eyes, she allowed the tantalizing aroma to invade her senses and trigger systemic responses she should be trying to suppress—for a couple of hours at least, because after that, there would be no suppressing anything.

But Tom . . . there was something different about him, an earthy animal magnetism she'd never encountered. After eleven years of suffering for a few weeks a year, she knew her body, and she'd been sure she had a couple of days to prepare for this, but it seemed as though Tom's presence had brought the fever on early. Fighting it seemed pointless.

Clenching her fists at her sides, she threw her head back, let her heart rate double, let it flush her body with blood that had heated up a couple of degrees. Her nervous system sparked like someone had struck a match to it, and every nerve ending tingled with hypersensitivity until her skin was on fire. Deep, frequent breaths brought crisp scents and life-giving oxygen into her lungs, and she could almost feel each individual cell distribute the fuel to the pleasure centers that had begun to swell and pulse and crave what only a man could give her.

It had begun.

CHAPTER
Two

Kira was a ballbuster. Again, unexpected. Ender, who didn't do unexpected unless the surprise came from his end, planned to get up to speed immediately and get back to the comfort of being the cleanup end of the job. He also planned on eating a nice juicy steak, or two, right under Ms. Greenpeace Tree-Hugging Doolittle's nose. And he was going to enjoy every bite too.

But this Derek thing was going to be a problem—a big one. And Kira had a lot to learn about whom to trust.

Paint the house, my ass.

That phrase, and its ultimate meaning, was one of Derek Martin's specialties. Ender's too, and he'd never had a problem admitting it. When Derek and Ender were members of the same Delta Force unit ten years earlier—a team Derek had eventually quit—Derek used to tell Ender that his father had coined the phrase, which really meant to kill a man, when he'd worked for Jimmy Hoffa. Ender couldn't be sure if it was the same guy until he came face-to-face with him, but his gut told him it was.

Derek wasn't anywhere to be seen when Ender found the empty bedroom meant for him, went in and shut the door behind him. It was hot as hell up here, and when he opened the windows in a useless attempt to catch a breeze he heard the sounds of children laughing. He looked out to see a busload of preschool-aged boys and girls running through an open field to get to the main part of the refuge, and he sighed. Like this job wasn't enough trouble already.

Kids, animals and women. Someone owed him big-time.

Using the small device that hooked into the button on the front of his jeans, he made reluctant contact with the Comms Division of ACRO, lowered his voice and spoke rapidly.

"Bryan, I need you to pull the W2s on the two guys who worked here before me. Names are listed in the psychic's report."

"Why? What happened?" Bryan asked immediately. Ender was sure the guy never slept, but as head of Communications, he couldn't afford to. He also heard muffled female giggles in the background.

"I'm betting they were executed. By the guy who I'm going to be working with," he said.

"Sucks to be you. Stay tight, bro."

Yeah, sucks to be me.

He slipped his mini-scope and knife into his pocket—the small pistol he always carried would be discovered by that goddamned goat sniffing around him—and slid out into the hallway. He opened Derek's locked door easily enough and did a quick scan of the area.

No weapons, but he didn't figure the guy would be stupid enough to leave them lying around. But he did immediately hone in on something shiny and metal sticking out from the bed. Careful not to touch anything he could leave prints on, he pulled on the blankets until he saw the handcuffs lying against the sheets, and his blood ran hot and cold at the same time.

If anyone was going to use handcuffs on Kira, it would be him. Because he had no doubt in his mind that Derek planned on using stronger restraints, and more, when he kidnapped her—these were just for fun.

It was time to get his ass down to the barn. He'd wire the room for sound and video later, because his plan had already taken form.

He went down the stairs, swearing under his breath the entire time. He hit the barn from the back entrance, taking only a second to create a distraction that would ensure Derek leaving him and Kira alone for a few minutes at least.

He heard Kira's laugh, saw Derek helping her balance—yeah, right—on the ladder that led up to the loft. He took a long look at her legs, the casual way Derek had his hand on her hip, and he knew he wasn't getting out of there before giving that guy a good old-fashioned piece of his fist before he killed him. Literally.

All's fair in love, war and the world of rare operatives.

"I've got you," Derek was saying, his voice a combination of big city, old money—too well cultured to be a farmhand, and Ender wondered why Kira wouldn't have picked up on that.

Kira climbed down from the ladder and Derek kept his god-damned hand on her hip. That is, until she spotted Ender and moved away from Derek's touch. Derek turned and frowned at him for the briefest second before putting on a fake glad-you're-here-man smile.

"Derek, this is—"

"Tom," Ender said, at the same time Derek said, "Tommy," and continued smiling. It didn't reach his eyes, and from what Ender remembered, it never had.

Kira looked back and forth between them, and Ender noticed, with no small satisfaction, that her gaze settled on his when she spoke. "You two know each other?"

"Farming community's not that big," Derek said, and Ender grudgingly gave him points for the nice catch. Interesting that he chose to admit that they knew each other at all. It was a way Ender would've preferred not to go. But he'd run with it.

Another operative in the mix always made things more interesting.

"Good to see you again," he said to Derek before turning his full attention to Kira. He was finding it hard to think straight or concentrate on anything but her, like she was throwing scent around or something. From the way Derek looked at her, he could tell the guy was feeling it too. "Are you going to get me up to speed?"

"I figured Derek could show you around this evening," she said, and *fuck, no,* that was not going to happen. Not when, according to the urgent file the psychic had put together, Kira's spring mating ritual was about to begin and there was one too many choices of mates.

"Cool. But first, want me to take care of the horses that broke loose? Unless they're supposed to be wandering," Ender said.

"I thought you tied them well?" Kira asked Derek.

"Shit. I did," Derek muttered.

"Well, you need to get them back. And then you might as well finish repairing the fence on the west side of the compound before it gets dark," she said. "Tommy can finish helping me around here."

Ender bit back a smile, because Derek would be gone most of the evening and there was nothing he could do to protest without arousing suspicion. Especially when Kira had already turned her attention firmly to Ender, giving off a powerful vibe that made his balls tingle.

Oh, yeah, he was going to help Kira. Right out of her damned shorts.

"Sorry about that. I've got it covered, boss," Derek said. He walked past Ender, gave him a nod that meant *I'll kill you the first chance I get,* and Ender watched him get into a truck and drive off in search of the errant horses.

"Guess it's just you and me," he said, and Kira smiled at him in a way she hadn't at Derek. He wasn't sure why that mattered so much, but it did.

KIRA HAD WATCHED DEREK saunter out of the barn, taking his fierce sensuality with him. Still, he was nothing compared to Tom, whose seductive, primal pull electrified her, spun her off balance and left her grabbing blindly at the air for a handhold.

She'd never experienced anything like it, and she trembled with the massive exertion of restraint she had in place right now.

"You certainly settled in fast," Kira said with a casualness she didn't feel. She propped one foot on a bale of hay to tie the loosened laces of her bright pink hiking boot. "Quite the eager beaver."

Tom smiled, likely the first genuine smile she'd seen since they'd met. He also stared at her legs and butt for the hundredth time. Thankfully, men were predictable.

She got the impression, though, that Tom had a few curveballs up his sleeve, and she'd be an idiot to underestimate him. Then again, she'd gotten that same impression about Derek. Both men exuded confidence, power and raw sexual energy, and both shared a quality she rarely encountered in humans: a subtle, almost gamey scent she could describe only as danger. She'd bet her last dollar—which she'd be down to soon—that they'd both spent some time in the military.

Or prison.

She cocked her head and studied Tom studying her. "Ever been in jail?"

"Nope." He reached down to pet Morris, one of the barn cats, who had been rubbing on his denim-clad leg. "Why?"

"Just wondering." She watched him a moment longer, wishing his big hand was stroking her instead of the cat. Heat worked its way through her veins at the thought, and before she pounced on him in a lust-induced fit, she glanced up at the loft.

"I need to store this riding gear. Would you mind handing it to me and keeping the ladder steady?"

"Like Derek was doing?" he asked, his steely blue eyes glittering in the sunlight that streamed in through the dirty windows.

She smiled. She'd known exactly what Derek had been doing, and she hadn't minded. She'd long ago stopped trying to fight the animal instinct that came over her at this time of year, the frenzied desire to mate often and urgently.

Never had any single man been capable of satisfying her during what she thought of as her *heat cycle*, and now it seemed that with two virile men within reach, her prayers had been answered.

"Yes," she said, "like Derek."

She grabbed a few frayed nylon halters and started up the ladder, which desperately needed to be replaced. When she'd almost reached the top, she tossed the gear onto a pile she'd started there.

"Okay, I'm ready for more." She turned, and the ladder wobbled.

Tom swore and grabbed the ladder, his big body tensed, the muscles in his arms flexing. "Let me do this."

"You're too heavy."

"If I had a dime for every time a woman said that to me..."

She laughed, because she'd love to feel his weight on top of her and decide for herself whether or not he was too heavy. "Just hand me the bridles, smart-ass."

Grinning, he did, then braced the ladder as she placed them in an old wooden chest. "So, uh, do you want the whips and riding crops?"

She wrinkled her nose. "Yes. I'm going to lock those things up here where no one will find them."

"You don't use them?"

"Never. Horses will cooperate without being beaten."

He reached for a crop, a thick-handled stick with a leather paddle at one end, and slapped it in his palm. "They are good for... other things." His voice was deep and dark and so sexy she wanted to melt into a warm puddle and let him lap her up.

"Like what?" she asked, aware that she was stirring up a hornet's nest, and she could only hope he'd sting her.

One tawny eyebrow arched, and a wicked smile turned up his sensual mouth. Bracing the ladder with one hand, he stretched upward with the crop until the soft strip of leather touched her skin just above her boot. A shock of desire shot straight from her ankle to her crotch, where moisture began to pool as he slowly traced circles higher and higher on the inside of her leg.

His gaze caressed her leg along with the riding crop, and then his eyes caught hers, darkened to a stormy blue as he pushed the stick up to stroke and tease the leg opening of her denim shorts.

"This is wrong," she said, her voice sounding a little winded to her ears.

The flap of leather slipped beneath the material, and pleasant tingles dispersed over her suddenly inflamed flesh. "Why's that?"

She bit her lip when the tip of the crop tickled the crease of her sex. "Because you aren't using it right."

That wicked smile of his became even more so, sending a hot rush of blood surging through her body. He pulled the stick from her shorts and slapped her lightly on the back of her bare thighs. She nearly groaned.

"Better?" he asked.

Better? She had no idea how to answer that, because her need had deepened, focused so her world had become her body and that of the man standing at the base of the ladder.

"Again. Harder."

The leather cracked across her skin. The sting of pleasure shot straight to her sex.

"Better?" Tom repeated, his voice husky.

Her restraint dimmed, flickered, then finally snuffed out.

Impulsively, she shimmied down the ladder to stand facing him on the bottom rung, which put them eye to eye. Crop in hand, he watched her with half-lidded, inquisitive eyes. She could feel his heat, could smell his arousal, which was obvious in the bulge in his jeans.

"Better," she murmured, "would involve a lot fewer clothes."

Unconcealed hunger burned in his gaze, and she got the feeling that under any other circumstance he wouldn't hold back, but in the middle of the day in a barn where anyone could walk in—not to mention the fact that she was his boss he'd met barely two hours before—he was conflicted.

Conflict was not something with which she had an issue. Not during this time of year when she'd be perfectly fine having sex on a football field during halftime.

"You saying you want to drop in the hay and go at it right here?"

"Dropping into the hay would take too long."

She didn't have time to blink before he surged against her, pressing her back against the ladder rungs. His mouth came down on her throat, and she threw her head back, let his teeth rake her skin. One of his hands tangled in her hair, holding her for his demanding lips, and the other, the one clutching the crop, dropped to her ass as he pulled her mound against the hard ridge of his cock.

A low groan rumbled in his chest when she raised one leg to hook the back of his thigh with her calf, putting her aching sex in contact with the seam of his jeans. His fingers drove into her shorts' leg opening, the callused pads skimming her wet folds.

Desire quickened her blood, and her heart pumped so hard it hummed in her ears. God, even his light touches were killing her. She couldn't imagine how he'd feel inside her, his thick length stroking swollen, stretched flesh and sensitive nerve endings.

Grasping his arms, she dragged him as close as she could, until she could feel his nipples harden and rub against her chest through layers of clothing. She wanted to rip his shirt off with her teeth and take the hard nubs between her lips to taste them. She wanted to taste all of him, but only after she found relief for the fever that had made her skin stretch tight, her bones ache, her head cloud.

Arching her hips, she rocked her sex into him, creating a rhythm that had them both sweating and panting, burning up from the friction. He kissed a fiery path up from the hollow of her neck to her ear as she slipped her hand under his T-shirt to explore the muscles of his back, which jumped under her fingertips.

Splintered wood bit into her spine, but she didn't care. She needed Tom inside her. Needed him to take her over and over until neither of them could see straight, until she felt normal again, if only for a few hours.

She bit his earlobe hard enough to make him suck air through clenched teeth, and then she told him exactly what she wanted—and how often.

Groaning, his breathing ragged, he reached between their

bodies and cupped her breast, flicked his thumb over the sensitive nipple.

"You're the boss, ma'am," he said, and she wasn't sure if she wanted to rejoice or be afraid, because she suddenly knew that this man might be the one she'd been searching for all her life.

The one who could satisfy her when no one else could.

CHAPTER
three

Christ, Ender was going to take her right against the ladder, in daylight and in the middle of the open barn, and there was no use worrying anymore about that. He wasn't letting this opportunity slip through his fingers.

Focus, man. Focus. "You always this forward?" he asked, watched her breathing quicken as she ground against him.

"Yes. Do you have a problem with it?"

"I have no problem sleeping with you. I just want to make sure I'm not putting my job in jeopardy."

"I'm not paying you for stud services. Those need to be strictly voluntary."

"And here I always thought volunteer work was overrated," he said as she tugged hard at the zipper on his jeans. She stared down at his cock, then looked into his eyes and back down to his cock, and yeah, *Who's your daddy now, Kira?* Her hand circled his dick roughly and he growled. "Ah, fuck."

"Yes, that. Now," she said, stroked him while she looked at him with those wide amber-colored eyes and smiled. He wondered when he'd lost control of this situation, even though he knew a man never really had any control when he was fucking.

Still, he'd never been this bad.

"Hey, wait a minute," he murmured in a moment of clarity. "Gotta come prepared." He dug in the pocket of his loosened jeans and pulled out a condom, put the wrapper between his teeth to tear, since his other hand was busy up her shirt tugging at her nipple.

Her reaction could only be described as violent. She hissed, actually hissed, and knocked it out of his hand. "No."

"I don't play with shit like that."

"I'm on the pill."

"I don't care," he said, bent to pick it up and she yanked him back to her by the front of his shirt.

"No," she said again. She nipped his ear again, harder this time as her sex ground against his cock.

"Kira..."

"I'm on the pill and I can't use condoms," she said, her voice low and throaty, and she wasn't going to relent.

She was probably allergic. And if he didn't take her, she'd move right to Derek, would develop an intimate rapport that might shut him out. It was a move he couldn't afford to make, especially since instinct told him that Kira hadn't slept with Derek as of yet. Besides, this wouldn't be the first time he'd taken his life in his hands.

"I need you, Tommy," she purred into his ear, her scent rising around them, the smell of sex and lust and everything in between. In seconds, his only focus was the woman in front of him, the beautiful, horny woman he wanted to take over his knee and spank, the one he wanted to cuff to the ladder and make her beg for him. Nothing else mattered, not the job, not ACRO, nothing except getting inside her pants and inside of her.

His head swam, like he had some kind of transient vertigo, and every one of his senses heightened, almost to the point of pain, and told him to pull away simultaneously. Told him that she was more dangerous than anyone at ACRO knew.

She nuzzled him, everything moved in slow motion and he knew there was no escape as every fiber of his being screamed with the urge to mate. To make her his and his alone.

Dammit. He turned her so she faced the ladder, used the whip on the back of her thighs one final time before he told her, "Drop your shorts."

She complied quickly, sticking her perfect round ass out, and he kicked her legs apart roughly.

He didn't bother pulling off any of his clothes. Instead, he grabbed her hips and entered her hard as she held on to the ladder for dear life.

A low keening wail rose from the back of her throat. He gripped her hips as her pussy contracted around him almost immediately, a series of multiple orgasms ripping through her that made his world rock, and still she wasn't finished. She pushed against him with an intensity he'd never had from any other woman.

Normally, he wouldn't have allowed that, would've had her bound and helpless and he'd be taking her on his terms. But his cock was prisoner to her and it didn't seem to mind a damn bit. She was taking him for a ride and his balls throbbed from the pressure.

"I think she's still in the barn..." A woman's voice rang out, too close for comfort, followed by Derek's. Ender wasn't one to put on a show for anyone, but he didn't, couldn't care. Something about Kira's scent drew him to her like he'd never been drawn before. She moaned his name, offered her neck to him, and he heard her gasp when he bit deeply, holding her for his mating like a stallion covering his mare. He knew she'd taste as good between her legs as she smelled, wanted to pull out of her, spread her legs and lick her until she screamed.

Yeah, he was going to do that soon. But the voices drew closer.

The rough denim of his jeans rubbed the backs of her bare thighs, her shirt rode up and they rutted, her orgasms still coming one right after the other again, and still she didn't stop. Her ass rubbed against him, her rhythm urging him deeper, faster, gave him no choice but to spill inside her with a muffled groan against her neck.

A thin sheen of sweat covered her tanned skin and the last thing he wanted to do was pull out of her. Good thing she felt the same way, because she wasn't letting go. She turned her head, a wide smile on her face, and when she opened her eyes and gazed at him, the wild, desperate look was gone.

She just looked content as hell. And sexy. He was already in more trouble than he'd bargained for and he was only two hours into this mission.

Derek's voice became louder, calling out for Kira, but still, Ender didn't rush pulling out of her. When he did, he barely had time to tuck himself back into his jeans before Derek called again. For a second, Ender stayed where he was, facing Kira so she could pull up her shorts and fix her shirt with a slight bit of privacy.

"Thanks," she said, gave him a quick wink.

"Not a problem. And now I'd really better get to work," he said. He grabbed the riding crop that he'd let drop to the floor and trailed it up her thigh before tucking it under his arm. "I'd better take this. You don't want to let it get into the wrong hands."

"Kira, I was looking for you." The woman whose voice he heard earlier came in, Derek close on her heels. "I found Derek tying up the horses and he said you were here."

"Sorry, I was up in the loft," Kira said. "Tommy, this is Deb. She's our resident animal nutritionist. She takes care of feeding all the exotics. Deb, this is Tom, our newest farmhand. He just started today."

"Oh, hey, Tom. I'd be happy to show you around town later on when you're finished up here. There's not much to do around here, but there are a few spots I'll bet you'd be interested in," Deb said. She was small and blond and cute, but not his type.

He held out his hand, gave the polite, good ole boy nod and watched Deb assess his face and body. "That sounds great," he said, knowing he'd never go.

Still, Deb smiled, flipped her hair, and he bit back a laugh when Kira grabbed Deb's upper arm and shepherded her away.

Ms. Doolittle was more possessive than he'd thought she'd be. Good to know.

Satisfied, he turned and walked past Derek, just close enough for the guy to smell Kira on him like a badge of honor. Derek tilted his head and glared at him, and Ender bared his teeth and let a low growl escape from his throat.

Derek backed away first, muttering about fence posts, and Ender turned to pack up the rest of the equipment Kira wanted out of sight.

Score one for me, asshole. Literally.

When he'd first read the file on Kira and her animal instincts last night before he left his house, he figured that someone had slipped in the part about her spring fever to get a rise out of him.

It was no joke, not the way, when he'd used the crop on her, her eyes had gotten that slightly glazed look that only a major jones to get off could do. And yeah, he'd be more than happy to turn her over his knee and give her a spanking, make her comply with any and all of his whims. And that's how he was going to work her for this job—get through to her.

If she was this easy to seduce, the enemy would have a field day with her. In the wrong hands, Kira would be a menace to any society, and then some, and ACRO wanted to make sure that she was firmly in their camp, and only a threat to those who threatened the United States', and her allies', security and safety.

Hell, he was going to have to recommend that ACRO keep her under lock and key during her spring fevers, not to mention keeping her ... serviced. Until then, servicing was his job, and a job he planned on doing better than well.

Once night fell, he'd take care of everything else.

TUESDAY 8 P.M. EST

Devlin O'Malley, head of ACRO and all her operatives, sat at the head of the conference table, rubbing his fingertips along the smooth oak while trying not to tune out the two men who sat across from him, arguing over who would get possession of Kira once Ender delivered her into ACRO's eager hands.

Henry Stockton, the Paranormal Division director, a man who had been at ACRO since before it was even called ACRO, coughed. He'd only recently stopped smoking, but it hadn't been soon enough. Six months ago, ACRO doctors found cancer in the man's lungs after one of the psychics alerted Dev that something was terribly wrong with the older man. So far, treatments had gone well.

"She's an animal whisperer. Basically, an animal psychic. Which means she belongs in my division. With the *psychics*," Henry argued.

"Where, no doubt, department heads are arguing like you two over who would get her," Dev said.

And Henry concurred. "Mostly the Medium and Telepath departments."

"Doesn't matter," Jason Templar, the Special Operations director, said. "She's physiologically extreme."

Dev nodded, though they had no idea how extreme she was. The Science Division had expressed concern that through her unique physiology, genetics and diseases could be modified. In the wrong hands, that could spell disaster.

"No matter how psychic she is, her ability doesn't affect human minds or actions. She's an RSO," Jason finished.

"Sure," Henry scoffed. "Just like Remy."

Dev sighed at the mention of Remy's name, because he couldn't go through this argument again. Remy had a connection to the weather that was almost too extraordinary to believe, and his control over Mother Nature had only grown stronger since he'd arrived at ACRO and gone through the proper training.

The lines between what made a person fit into which of the agency divisions were not always clearly drawn. He'd just gone through this with a new recruit, an excedosapien who happened to be mildly clairaudient. Both Para and Excedo Divisions wanted the guy, who had ultimately gone to Excedo, though Para could borrow him.

And Henry was still fuming over the loss of Remy to the Rare Special Operative department.

"You two do realize that Kira will be assigned to the Animal Division."

"She still needs a home division."

Dev's laptop beeped, and he swiped his fingers over the touch pad. Because he was tired it took slightly longer than usual to absorb the message from ACRO's parameteorologist, Haley Holmes. She'd narrowed down Itor's secret location for their massive weather weapon to three possible locales.

It was good news, but with hurricane season starting next month, it wasn't good enough.

He realized Jason and Henry were still arguing, and he ground his teeth. "Enough. Write up your arguments and submit them to me tomorrow."

"Sounds good."

Jason's hostile glare at Henry sizzled over Dev's skin. Those two would never see eye to eye. But then, Jason rarely saw eye to eye with anyone, and Henry had been set in his ways since he was born.

Jason left, but Henry remained seated.

"You have more to say?" Dev asked.

Henry shifted in his chair, the creak of fabric on leather louder than it should have been, and Dev knew his near future involved a splitting headache. "I want my division to finally get a fair shake. Ever since you started bringing in rare-ability types—"

"I'm aware of your views, Henry."

Henry and a handful of others had opposed Dev's expansion of ACRO from the exclusively psychic operation it had been under his parents' direction. He accepted the validity of some of the arguments.

Bringing in excedosapiens and RSOs had created several problems he couldn't annihilate no matter how hard he tried. The two types had a tendency to cause a lot of trouble and could be hard to control. There was also the perception that the RSOs received preferential treatment, given their extreme rare abilities and notably small numbers in comparison to the agents in the Paranormal and Excedosapien Divisions.

On the other hand, the addition of excedos and RSOs had made ACRO the most powerful agency in the world—secret or not.

Henry's BDUs rustled as he shifted again. "You know I have great respect for the work you and your parents have done."

Dev inclined his head. "But?"

"But maybe ACRO has grown too big and unwieldy for one person. A few of us have been talking, and we think it might be time for you to take on partners."

"I see. You want ACRO to be run by a board of directors."

"It would ensure all voices are heard—"

"Because I'm not fair enough to hear all voices?" Dev asked softly, and he felt a distinct change in the room's energy.

"I didn't say that. And you would, of course, remain on as president..."

"How generous. You *few* have this all figured out." Dev pushed to his feet, braced his hands on the table and leaned forward. "I'm about to prove how fair I am. See, I'll forget you ever brought this up. And you? You'll leave right now, by way of your own two feet. Trust me, that's more than fair."

He heard the quiet shuffle as Henry left the conference room, shutting the door behind him. Dev pressed the panel under the table, the code that would open the door that led to his private office, where he refused to hold meetings, refused to let many people in at all. He needed a refuge in this place.

He needed to calm down. He was tired, mentally, physically—but more than that, he was tired of the director's shit. He'd taken this organization too damned far in eight years to stop now, but sometimes he wished he was back in the military where it was more than okay to settle disputes with a few good punches. But there weren't many options for a blind pilot in the Air Force. Which was why his sudden, amazing ability at CRV—Controlled Remote Viewing—had earned him a quick paperwork shuffle to NASA and its mind-bending program after the accident that killed his flying career ten years ago.

His parents had been disappointed. Again. They wanted him

out of the military altogether, wanted him with them at ACRO. He'd refused. They had plenty of help.

But while everyone was busy feeling the leftover peace and love from the Stargate program, the outside world fell apart, competing agencies opened and someone took his parents out, execution-style, in their mansion in Syracuse, Dev's childhood home.

The hit was ordered by an agency much bigger than the FBI or the CIA. In Dev's mind, it was definitely Itor, although the other two agencies had their reasons for also wanting his parents dead. That alone was enough to shove Dev firmly away from the government and into ACRO's fold.

Today, when the government and the military came to him for help, they played by his rules. Dev had tightened security until it squeaked, expanded the ACRO divisions to include rare operatives his parents never dreamed of—he took in those rare men and women who limped in from the military or wherever, like refugees who'd lost their homeland; he embraced them, trained them. Saved them. All they had to do was pledge loyalty to ACRO.

Those were the easy ones—the desperate ones, the ones who didn't mind joining the land of the freaks.

The others did not go down easily. Or quietly. And those were the ones they needed most. He needed to make the old guard around here understand that change might not always be easy but more often than not it was for the best.

He let his mind wander over Henry and Jason again—each a more than perfect candidate to be the leak—a leak they needed to plug, and fast. He'd just learned that one of his operatives had died in China, and the only way that could have happened was if the mission had been compromised. From the inside.

There were very few people at the agency he could actually trust without fail, and one of them was gone, in the field, probably fucking his goddamned brains out as per orders.

Dev wasn't ready to share his suspicions with his assistant, although he knew Marlena would do whatever she could to help him get to the bottom of things. If nothing else, she'd go out of her way to help take his mind off the intrusion, if only for a few minutes.

He smiled briefly and buzzed her in without another thought. Coming might not focus him, but it never hurt.

TUESDAY 7 P.M. MST

Kira stepped out of the shower, glad to have washed the day's farm grime from her body, not so glad to wash away Tom's scent. She loved how he smelled, loved the way he'd looked at her, touched her. She'd taken a lot of lovers in her life, most of them during the weeks of desperate need that made her life a living hell, but while all had served their purpose, none had excited her as much as Tom had.

She couldn't wait to do it with him again—not because she'd needed to, but because she wanted to. These weeks might be hell, but they allowed her to spend a brief amount of time in a man's arms, to take joy in human contact most people took for granted. When strong hands stroked her skin and warm lips caressed hers, her loneliness dissolved, if only for a few precious moments.

Her bedroom door squeaked open, and Babs, a Weimaraner who'd been at the refuge since before Kira arrived almost two years ago, trotted inside and jumped on her bed.

"Hey, girl." She ruffled Babs's ears. "You didn't happen to notice if Tom and Derek finished their chores?"

One of the men must have come inside the house, because Babs had been near the barn when Kira had come in for her shower. A mix of images flickered through her head . . . Babs, digging at a gopher hole, then jumping into the back of Kira's pickup, then Derek opening the upstairs door and letting the dog through. Derek had apparently finished with the fence repairs.

She dressed in cargo shorts and a T-shirt, not bothering to do anything with her wet hair but put it up into a high ponytail. She padded into the orange and gold kitchen that was all but a shrine to the seventies, and turned on the radio on the windowsill. Bouncing to the oldies, she pawed through the cupboards. Neither Tom nor Derek had taken her truck today to go to the store, so she'd prepare a big dinner, and if they wanted to share, they'd be welcome.

She scrounged up enough tofu and fresh veggies for a decent dish that would feed three, and with practiced hands, she sliced, diced and tossed the ingredients into a wok.

The animals migrated to the kitchen to beg—asparagus was always a favorite with the dogs—and soon over two dozen pairs of eyes surrounded her. Rafi jumped up on the old stand-alone dishwasher at the end of the counter and swatted playfully every time Kira walked past him.

She sang out loud about gypsies, tramps and thieves as she set the table with mismatched thrift store dishes. When she finished, she dug through the fridge for the pitcher of lemonade, and then turned to the crowd. "Will one of you go get the boys?"

It was unnecessary to speak; the animals understood her in other ways, but talking kept her sane when sometimes she felt anything but. She formed an image in her head of the upstairs bedrooms, and Babs, ever the responsible helper, ran off, her nails clacking on the wooden stairs behind the kitchen. Tom might not recognize the message, but Derek, after just a couple of days, had figured out that when a dog scratched on his door, Kira wanted him.

No one came. Grumbling to herself, she turned down the heat on the tofu, asparagus and tomatoes, and headed upstairs. Babs sat between the doors, her ears droopy, her expression dejected, like she'd failed a mission.

"It's okay, little Babby-Sue. Go back downstairs."

She knocked on Tom's door. No response. She tried Derek's. The door squeaked open. He stood in the middle of the room, talking on a cell phone, his voice hushed and harsh. His frustration filled the room with a bitter odor. Feeling like an intruder, she turned away.

"Kira. I'm sorry. I didn't see you there."

She turned back to see Derek stuff his phone into the pocket of his jeans. "I thought you might want some dinner."

"Is Tom invited?"

Odd question, but then, her spring fever affected more than just her. Men picked up on her body's signals, reacted to them, if only subconsciously, and she'd expected some tension between the two eventually. "He's still working, but he can eat when he comes in." She paused. "Why?"

Derek grimaced. Silence stretched.

"Derek? What is it?"

"It's just..." He sighed. "You need to keep an eye on him."

She let out a slow breath and stepped into the room. "There's more to the farm thing, isn't there?"

He nodded. "We were in the Army together. That's how we really know each other."

Interesting, but not surprising, given the military vibes she'd gotten off both of them. "Why the secrecy?"

"I was trying to protect him." He looked down, scuffed his boot on the hardwood floor. "But then I realized you're the one I should protect. He's not...stable."

"Yeah, well, most people don't think I'm very stable, so you need to be a little more specific."

Derek scrubbed a hand over his face, which was rough with dark stubble. "I don't want to get the guy in trouble, so I can't say much, but don't get too close. And don't believe anything he tells you. Anyone with a dishonorable discharge...well, be careful."

Great. Her first mate of the season, and he was probably a homicidal maniac. "I appreciate the warning, but I can take care of myself."

Derek's mouth eased into a friendly smile. The one that had taken away her breath before she met Tom, whose rare smiles made all her erogenous zones scream for attention.

"I'm sure you can." He studied her with keen eyes that always seemed to take her measure, as though he liked to stay one step ahead of everything. "Do you have any kind of self-defense training?"

"A little." A lot, actually. Back in the days when she trained police and military dogs, the handlers had been nice enough to give her private lessons.

"That's good," he said, but his displeasure wafted to her on a raft of scent. Maybe he'd wanted to give her lessons himself. "Show me what you can do."

He threw his arm out toward her, his fingers stretching for her shoulder. She didn't hesitate, seized his hand and twisted hard. Heart pounding, she thrust down in a wrist manipulation technique she'd practiced with a cop named Wayne. Swiveling quickly, she enveloped his elbow with her other hand and jammed it downward. He grunted, and she smiled as she restrained him, his body bent at the waist, his arm twisted awkwardly behind his back.

"Nice," he murmured, the admiration in his voice mixed with surprise.

And then it was her turn to be surprised, because before she had time to get cocky, he jerked her forward. His fingers snared her wrist, and he stepped behind her, wrenching her arm up her back hard enough to make her wince, but not enough to be painful. Much.

Damn, he was strong. But then, she'd seen him lift the back end of her truck up and out of the mud in which it had become mired. Well, she'd seen it through Cheech's eyes, but still . . .

Derek held her immobile with one hand, wrapped his other muscular arm around her neck and pressed his chest to her back. Cramps tweaked her biceps, and her throat felt a little tight as it funneled her rapid breaths through it.

"There's always a countermove," he said, his voice rumbling against her ear in a rich, seductive tone that struck her as sounding practiced. He rocked his pelvis against her, driving his erection into her hip. Dropping his arm from her throat, he let his hand drift down her chest, over her breast, to her waist.

Message received.

He wanted her, would be willing and able should she want—or need—him soon. Warmth oozed across her skin, and when he released her, she spun away before her body could react further to his arousal. She didn't *require* sex for a couple more hours, but she came equipped with a self-preservation switch that activated her libido in the presence of an aroused male, effectively forcing her to accept all mating opportunities that presented themselves.

Had she been in the room with Tom, she'd welcome the chance to take him down to the floor, but sleeping with Derek now would only intensify the tension between him and Tom, something she didn't want to deal with yet.

"Wow." She wiped her palms on her shorts simply because she needed to do something with them. "That was impressive."

Extra-impressive, given that Wayne assured her the hold she'd used was difficult to break. Wayne, who had held her often enough. Who had definitely done his civic duty to protect and serve her several times during one of her spring fevers. Who had been the one to warn her when the warrants for her arrest had suddenly been reinstated.

"Don't sell yourself short. You know your stuff." Folding his arms across his broad chest, Derek watched her with dark eyes that had gone nearly black with desire. "Can you break out of restraints?"

Heart still doing double-time, she jammed her hands on her hips. "I've been asked a lot of strange questions in my life, but Derek, you're going to some new places here."

He grinned. "I could go to more new places, if you'd like."

"Men," she huffed, but her drama lacked conviction. At this time of year, she was receptive to all flirtations.

"I'm only looking out for you." He moved to his dresser, took a pair of handcuffs from the top drawer. "Let me show you something."

"Ooh! Cool! I've been cuffed before." She narrowed her eyes at him. "Why do you have handcuffs?"

"Personal reasons."

"Whatever floats your boat, I guess."

"Hold out your hands." In two fluid strides, he closed the distance between them. "Why have you been cuffed? Or do I want to know?"

"Personal reasons." She winked, hoping he'd buy the lie. The truth, that she'd been arrested more than once, was something she liked to keep to herself.

"Hold your hands like this"—he turned her wrists—"it'll make the cuffs looser once they're on." He snapped them into place.

"Am I interrupting something?"

Tom's voice, calm and cool, floated into the room. Kira grinned and looked over her shoulder at him. "Derek was just giving me some tips on how to make cuffs more comfortable."

"I'll bet." His mouth curved, but if his smile was genuine, she'd eat a burger. Raw.

"I came to see if you two wanted dinner— Oh, crap! Dinner! It's burning." She shoved her wrists at Derek. "Take them off." His smile didn't fade, but his gaze never left Tom's.

Men. Morons.

Once free, she darted out of the room. "Come on, boys. Dinner's ready. You'll love it. Sautéed asparagus with curried tofu and tomatoes." She rolled her eyes at the two men who stood there watching each other like rival roosters.

Babs, who hadn't gone downstairs, gave her a look that said it all.

Males are dumb.

CHAPTER Four

Ender ignored Derek's smirk, patted Babs on the head and turned to follow Kira. The whole never-turn-your-back-on-the-enemy thing was overrated. So was Derek. And sometimes, turning your back gave the enemy enough time to screw up, or to show them that you didn't give a fuck.

But Ender did give a fuck, and it looked like Derek was planning something for tonight. And with the way Kira acted this afternoon, and again in Derek's handcuffs, he ran a real risk of getting the rug pulled out from under him.

He could almost guarantee that Derek had called in backup. Almost. But this was the delicate balance involved in an Operator who acted as Convincer and killer.

On one hand, he needed to keep Kira safe and out of the enemy's grasp. But she'd already lost two farmhands, and killing Derek right now, which would be his first, most natural instinct, would cause too much suspicion on her part. Then again, it could bring them closer together, force her to turn to him for protection.

Part of his plan also involved discovering just what uses Itor had for her. He'd get that out of Derek later. And then he'd kill him. Because killing him too soon would bring out the dogs, literally. I-Agents had a virtual worm implanted in their brain that transmitted back to the home compound, let them know that after twenty-four hours of no brain activity an agent had died.

Ender needed a little bit longer than twenty-four hours, and he had a plan to buy him that time.

The kitchen was hot as hell even though the sun had already started to go down, the heat from cooking raising the temperature enough so that Ender wished he could strip down to his shorts and take a long swim in the lake that ran along the back of the property.

He moved close to Kira, close enough so she needed to touch him to move past him, the bare skin of her arm brushing his, and he waited to see if he got the same vertigo-like sensation he had earlier out in the barn. When he led with the wrong head. There had been nothing in the files about a latex allergy, or any other, and she hadn't even bothered to check to see that the condom was lambskin. Although with her militant animal rights stance, that wouldn't have gone over well anyway.

He inhaled, taking in the freshness of her skin, the honey-cloves mix that drove him up a wall, and his dick stirred, but that was a normal response.

Babs wouldn't leave his side, a gray, Velcroed, touch-seeking bundle of energy. "Bet she's a beauty when she runs," he said.

"Feel free to take her anytime you want. She can always do with more exercise," Kira said. Derek sidled to the counter and took the hot dish out of her hands and brought it to the table.

"Tommy, can you grab the lemonade, please?" Kira asked.

Tommy. Fuck me. "Yes, ma'am."

Putting the sedative in the drink took all of three seconds in between giving the lemonade a final mix and pouring it into the glasses. Ender took a sip first, then drank about half his glass because Derek watched him suspiciously. Finally, the guy followed suit.

Ender took the seat on the far end of the large, antiqued farmhouse table, back to the wall. Derek sat diagonally across the table from him and smirked when Kira slid into the seat next to him, leaving Ender alone. Like Ender was supposed to give a shit. This wasn't the dating game, but if it was, he would've already been far in the lead.

He sat back in his chair, stretched his legs out under the table so they locked around the legs of Kira's chair possessively. Even pulled it enough toward the table so that both Kira and Derek noticed.

He sent a good ole boy smile Kira's way, and yeah, her eyes lit. Then she flushed slightly and started dishing out heaping helpings of something that was supposed to resemble food.

"What is this?" he asked.

"It's asparagus, tomatoes and curried tofu. You'll love it."

He looked at the pile of tofu and vegetables in front of him, knew nothing in there was going to satisfy him well enough—he was going to need some red meat, and soon.

Maybe Deb would be good for something, after all.

"Kira, this is amazing. Makes me think about coming over to your side," Derek said as he dug in enthusiastically.

Ender snorted and Kira looked over at him.

"You don't like it?"

"Tofu's not really my thing," he said. He grabbed a piece of bread from the plate in the middle of the table and loaded it up with margarine.

"Most people usually try it, just to be polite," she said.

"I'm not most people," he said, took a bite of bread and washed it down with lemonade.

But Kira wasn't going to give up. She just looked at him with those wide amber eyes that reminded him of a contented panther lying in the afternoon sun and then she looked back down to his plate.

"I went to an awful lot of trouble," she said.

"Didn't ask you to. Ma'am."

"I'll take his share," Derek said, as he continued to shovel in the tofu-curry crap.

"You're not welcome to anything of mine," Ender told him,

then let one bare foot linger against Kira's calf under the table even as Derek turned to her and dabbed at some tofu-shit that had spilled onto her chin.

"Let me get that," Derek said. Ender upped his foot action against her calf, satisfied when he got a response from her.

Kira seemed to be enjoying the whole two-men-vying-for-her-attention routine. Which meant it was time to rotate the game right back on her.

Easy enough. He didn't have to pretend to play hard to get because he *was* hard to get. His longest relationship of note was forty-eight hours in Fiji on a private beach with a married twenty-four-year-old heiress who didn't mind the fact that he fucked her brains out and didn't remember her name half the time.

"So, where does Deb stay?" he asked, figuring two birds with one stone and all that, then reminded himself he probably couldn't say shit like that out loud around Miss Militant Vegan. Kira's eyes widened slightly. Derek just shook his head. "What? Did you want a piece of her?" he asked Derek.

"You haven't changed a bit, have you, Tom?"

"I think Deb will get in touch with you if she's interested," Kira told him.

"I think she's interested." He stabbed his fork into the tofu and took a few reluctant bites as per his plan, ignoring Kira and Derek as they chatted about the day's work and the refuge and chores to be done the next day.

He looked up when he heard a small crash, saw Derek's lemonade spilled across the table. One of the cats leaped to investigate, but Ender grabbed the animal and mopped up the mess fast. That's all he needed was to hurt her babies.

"Derek, you look kind of pale," Kira was saying as she leaned to touch Derek's arm. Derek groaned in response and looked at Ender, his eyes fuzzy. He mumbled, "Ender," but it came out more like "under."

Ender pushed his own plate of tofu away and grunted. "Something's wrong with this shit."

"It's not shit. And I'm fine," she pointed out.

"Yeah, for now." He put his head down on the table and Babs licked his face. "Christ, get this mutt away from me."

Babs completely ignored him, probably because she knew he didn't really mean it.

"I've got to go upstairs," Derek mumbled, pushed away from the table unsteadily.

"I'll help you," Kira offered, but Ender was already behind Derek. No fun if the guy fell down the stairs and broke his own neck. He made sure he put an extra sway in his step.

"Do you really think it's the food?" she asked him.

"How do you feel?" he asked as he made a show of grabbing his stomach like he was doubling over in pain.

"I feel fine," she said as she stood. She took two steps and he noticed that her gait was slightly off, that she held on to the back of the chair a little too tightly. But she wasn't nearly as bad as Derek.

Speaking of, there was a clatter on the steps as Derek lost his footing. Ender grabbed him and half pushed him up the stairs, even as Derek lost consciousness by the time they reached the top.

"Everything all right?" she called upstairs.

"It will be once this crumble crap gets out of our system. Dump it," he called, and then he smiled when he heard her mutter, *"Fuck you."*

He shoved Derek through the door of his bedroom, got him to the bed and checked his pulse. Guy was out cold, and would be until morning. Which gave Ender plenty of time to decide his next move.

He reached into Derek's pocket and pulled out the cell phone he knew Derek had. It would be password protected, of course, but Ender had never known Bryan not to break a password.

He took out his own cell and connected the two, dialed a line to Bryan and beamed the information from Derek's phone to Bryan through his. Didn't even have to talk to the guy—the magic of spy-shit capabilities. Within the hour, Bryan would let him know the times Derek would need to check in to Itor, and the special codes Ender would need in case he'd have to be the one to do it for him.

Normally agents only had to check in once every forty-eight hours, if not less. Things like making a suspicious phone call could severely compromise any undercover operative's mission, and he doubted Itor worked any differently than ACRO with that pattern.

Once the file transfer was complete, he wiped the cell clean of his prints out of habit, stuck it back in Derek's pocket and did a quick sweep of the room to make sure nothing had changed, especially the small monitor he'd rigged earlier that day.

More spy-shit. Ender preferred good, old-fashioned guns.

He shut Derek's door behind him, just in time to hear a loud crash come from the kitchen. Dogs began barking and Babs was on her way up the stairs to get him when he blew by her.

"I've got her," he said, and wondered when the hell he'd started talking to animals.

KIRA LOOKED DOWN at the mess of dishes she'd dropped and wished she could peel herself off the side of the fridge. Her feet seemed to have stopped working. Her sense of balance had also become a casualty of whatever had affected Tom and Derek. Maybe the curry had gone bad.

And dammit, she couldn't feel her face.

The sound of pounding footsteps rattled in her head, and she smelled Tom before she saw him.

"What happened?" He skidded to a stop before he plowed into the dinner dishes and the dogs helping themselves to the scraps.

"I'm feeding the dogs," she said, and blinked because her vision had gone fuzzy. "I think the curry went bad. Need to throw it out."

Tom bent to pick up some of the plates. "Could have been anything. How much lemonade did you drink?"

"Lemons don't go bad, silly." She bit her lip. "Well, I guess they do . . ." She dragged herself along the fridge toward the spice cabinet. Feet still wouldn't work. "I only had a sip."

He craned his neck to peer up at her. "A sip?"

"Uh-huh. One teeny drink. A sip. If I had a dictionary I could look it up for you. Sip."

"It's okay." Holding a pile of dishes, he stood and moved toward the sink.

She took a step. Her legs went, but her body stayed. A wave of dizziness sent a flashing swirl of spots in front of her eyes, and she slumped to the floor, her back scraping the kitchen cabinets, her legs sprawled before her. Immediately, six dogs climbed into her lap.

"Shit." Tom dumped the plates into the sink and hurried to her side. "Kira? You okay?"

She blinked up at him, not entirely sure what he'd said. And wow, he had the bluest eyes. Four of them. Cool. "I'm crawling with dogs."

"I can see that." He settled down on his heels, lifted one of her eyelids with his thumb and peered into her eye. "Have you taken anything today?" He dropped his hand to her wrist, pressed some fingers against her pulse. "Any medication? Alcohol?"

"Nope. No, no, no." She waggled a finger in front of his face. "I can't. I'm like a dog."

He swore again. He sounded so sexy when he swore. "You're not making any sense."

"Dee, oh, gee. Clean out your ears. Dog. My, um…metabolism. It's like I…" She searched for the word, but she came up with things that didn't fit. Like "typewriter." And "hayfield."

"Process?"

"Yes!" She clapped, startling Brutus, a three-legged yellow Lab lying across her thighs. "You're so smart, Tommy Knight. Deaf, but smart. One of my cats is deaf. She's not very smart, though. She's over there."

Kira tried to turn toward the utility room where Miss Priss liked to sleep, but her head just lolled to one side, so everything in the kitchen tilted and swayed in a psychedelic swirl of color. Groovy.

Tom's hands framed her face and brought it around so she was looking at him. "You said something about your metabolism. What was it? Might be good to know."

"Um...my body. It processes stuff weird. Drugs. Chocolate. I don't catch human diseases. No colds. No flu. I got Parvo once. I have to go to the vet." She frowned. "Did I say that out loud?"

She shouldn't be talking about any of this, but her mouth kept opening, and words kept falling out.

"I'm, uh, going to put you to bed now."

"Mmm, bed." She let her finger trace his lips. "What time is it? Should I be horny yet? Because I don't think I am. Maybe you could touch me and find out."

"God, I hope you don't remember this tomorrow," he muttered.

"I remember everything." She tapped her temple. "Like an elephant. I like elephants. They talk slow, though. So slow. They think humans are stupid. Probably because they are."

"Come on."

He slipped an arm behind her back, but froze when her newest acquisition, a German shepherd that had been trained for police work but had been retired due to excess aggression, rumbled low in his chest, baring his teeth.

"Luke," she said, wrapping her arm around the growling dog's neck and hugging him to her side, "it's okay. Tommy's helping." Her gaze felt jerky as she dragged it back to Tom. "He smells danger on you. You do kinda reek of it. It's like a mix of gunpowder and...something else. Cheese, maybe. No, not the word I was looking for."

"Okay, Kira, I need you to focus. Can you tell Luke to not tear my arm off?"

"Oh, right." She gave Luke a stern stare. "Do not tear Tom's arm off."

Luke pouted and glared at Tom as if the dog planned to win the next round but grudgingly gave him this one.

"Good boy." Tom shooed the rest of the dogs away, and then before she knew it, she was in his arms and being carried down her hallway and to her room.

She snuggled against his chest, inhaled his scent, a pleasant mixture of grass and soil, sun-warmed skin and gunpowder. No cheese, for sure. But there was something else beneath it all, beneath even the subtle fragrance of the sex they'd had earlier . . . a wafting thread of anxiety and fear. Was he worried about her?

"That's so sweet, Tommy," she said, wrapping her arms around his neck to bury her face into the curve of his shoulder.

"What's sweet?" He pushed open her bedroom door.

"I don't remember. But it feels good to be held. No one holds me. It's all I want, you know. Someone to hold me. Understand me. Love me."

He missed a step, probably hadn't seen the throw rug on her hardwood floor. When he deposited her on her bed, she immediately burrowed into the covers. "Do you have pajamas?" he asked.

Pajamas? "I think I sleep naked." She yawned and rubbed her face on her pillow, settling in to pass out. "I'll bet you do too. If we slept together, we'd be naked. Skin on skin. And hot. So hot . . ."

The sound of his harsh curse floated above her somewhere, melted into a swirl of soft farm sounds. Poor Tommy and his four blue eyes. She'd have to have sex with him later.

When she could open her own eyes.

TUESDAY 11 P.M. EST

Annika Svenson thumbed through the two dozen wigs in her closet until she found the perfect one. Long. Jet black with a blue streak at the temple. The polar opposite of her short silver-blond hair, which she'd grown out over the last few months to touch her shoulders, even though keeping it short meant an easier time with wigs.

Next, she pulled a gold lace camisole off a hanger. A cropped black leather jacket came next. An ultra-low-slung, supershort leather skirt and combat boots rounded out the goth biker-chick ensemble.

Creed wouldn't know what hit him.

It was Tuesday night, and the ghost hunter would be hanging out in the dive biker bar on the edge of town, someplace she'd gone inside of only once, a year ago, to drag out a drunk operative who had been talking too much. She felt comfortable anywhere, though, especially when dressed for the occasion, which she would be.

Besides, tonight was all about pleasure, and as Creed had shown her several times since taking her virginity last year, pleasure could be had anywhere. Including a dark corner booth in the back of a tavern. Or on the seat of his motorcycle in a parking lot.

She hadn't wanted to admit how much she loved their games, but if Creed didn't believe that she was one hundred percent into something, he wouldn't do it. He might take control when it came to sex, but everything he did was about her pleasure. He was so good to her, and a tiny part of her knew he deserved better than her. The larger, more selfish part wanted to keep him for as long as he'd be happy with a strictly sexual relationship.

Blood humming with excitement already, she pulled on a flimsy pair of black underwear that should tear with little difficulty. She considered a bra and then tossed it to the floor. Fewer clothes meant easier access, which was important when one was in a public place or too horny to take things slow ... or both.

She'd just returned from a six-week assignment in Belgium, and she was more than ready to climb aboard Creed and ride him until he collapsed. To leave a ring of black lipstick around the base of his cock. To wash it off later with a fistful of soap in the shower.

Not that they'd ever made it to a shower, or even a bed.

She'd held on to her cherry for twenty-one years, and since Creed popped it, she'd been eager to make up for lost time, and he didn't have any complaints. Which was good, since he was possibly the only man in the world she *could* have sex with. The only one who was immune to the massive power surge her body gave off at orgasm.

Her body flushed with heat at the thought of Creed taking her to climax over and over. Already her sex ached, her internal muscles clenching as though preparing for the erotic intrusion of his thick, tattooed shaft. Though really, could he be considered tattooed if he was born with the markings?

She shrugged, because it didn't matter. She'd licked every one of the things that covered the entire right side of his body, and tonight she'd give him something to lick. Something besides what throbbed between her legs.

She'd had temporary tattoos professionally applied to her left leg, hip, arm and neck.

Yeah, he wouldn't know what hit him tonight when she walked into the bar. She wondered how long it would take him to recognize her, especially if she used an accent, one complementing any of the twelve languages in which she was fluent. Brown contacts would disguise her blue eyes.

She just hoped Creed's stupid tagalong ghost wouldn't interfere again. That bitch had ruined more than one night with him, and Annika was seriously tempted to shock the *earthbound spirit*, as he called her, right out of the earthbound world permanently. Even when they did manage to get in a good fuck without Kate's interference, Annika had a feeling Creed paid for it later, though he never talked about it.

Then again, they didn't talk much at all. Creed tried, like she needed some sort of mushy emotional connection or something, but no way. She wasn't some insecure twit who thought a man *completed* her. Gag.

A tingle of electricity skittered over her skin, reminding her to hurry up and get dressed and quit thinking about pillow talk and creepy, overprotective ghosts. Tonight she was getting laid, ghost or no.

CREED SAT ON A WORN STOOL at the bar, two women on one side who'd been trying to gain his attention all night without success and a biker on the other.

He'd just downed his second shot of Jägermeister and was

motioning to the bartender to pour him a third, when his skin began to grow sensitive to a sudden change in air pressure around him.

He shifted so he could see the front door better and tried not to get his hopes up.

ACRO was starting to kick into high gear this time of year—it had been a long winter in Upstate New York and spring fever was taking over fast.

For operatives not out of the country, it had been a long, cold season. But Creed had finally found the warmth he'd been wanting for years last September at Dev's family mansion.

Even now, just thinking about that experience, an unpleasant shiver shot straight through his spine that had nothing at all to do with the memories of making love to Annika in that house. He shifted in his seat, knew that if she were here she wouldn't be able to hide the look of concern in her eyes at his sudden reaction.

They'd discussed it the last time they'd been together, when Annika mentioned she was worried about Dev. That something was bothering their boss.

Even though it chapped Creed's ass to play second fiddle in Annika's life, he'd never let Dev down. Dev had known him his entire life, and Creed had far too much respect for the man to let anything happen to him.

His skin tightened again, the line between pleasure and pain narrowing, and he forced himself to turn away from the door. But when he caught sight of it opening, he couldn't look away, and his entire body sighed in relief as the woman with the long, dark hair sauntered directly up to him, her short leather skirt showing off the greatest pair of legs he'd ever seen.

It took everything he had not to grab and kiss her. Instead, he leaned back on his stool and just watched her.

"Hey, baby," she said, her voice low and seductive. "Love your tats."

She'd put a hand out to trace the intricate pattern covering the right side of his face and neck, and he would've gladly stripped right there in the middle of the bar to let her continue her trail of touch down the entire right side of his body.

"Yours aren't bad either," he said.

"I have more," she said, bared a shoulder provocatively, until the guy sitting to his right—a member of the Hell's Angels—began to enjoy the show a little too much.

Annika always liked it when Creed played along as long as possible. It made her feel like she actually had a shot at fooling him. But he wasn't about to let a man whose nickname was "Meat" come anywhere close to the woman he loved.

Not that he'd mentioned the love thing to Annika, because she'd freak.

"She's with me," he said to Meat, who reluctantly turned back to his beer. Creed focused his full and proper attention on Annika, wished she'd take out the contacts so he could watch the normally icy blue of her eyes begin to soften when he touched her.

"How long have you known it was me?" she asked.

He let the corner of his mouth tug up in a smile, the way it inevitably did whenever she came within fifty feet of him. It might be the electricity she carried with her that alerted his body to her presence, but he wasn't complaining. "I always know it's you, baby," he said, pulled her so she stood in between his spread thighs. "Let's get out of here."

"I'm not sure . . . do you think you're man enough to handle me?"

"I know I am." He'd been hard from the second he'd sensed her, and when she'd walked through the bar, her familiar strut yanked all his chains in so many different, exquisite ways.

His cock molded hard against his soft leather pants and the entire right side of his body pulsed.

"I don't know if I can wait that long," she said. "Why don't we just stay here?"

"Here?"

"I already checked out the storeroom—it's not locked," she said.

She ran a hand across the tattoo on his neck, her palm lingering across his throat, and the fact that she could kill him with her pinky turned him on, maybe more than anything. He didn't mind handing the reins over to the beautiful twenty-one-year-old with a body like sin and a mind to match.

If he relented right now, he'd be shivering under her touch within minutes in the storeroom, or in the alley, or on the back of his hog in the woods, but tonight that wasn't going to be enough.

Tonight, he wanted a bed. Because he wanted a lot of different positions, and he wanted Annika where it wouldn't be easy for her to just walk away when she was done. Because as many times as he'd tried to talk to her, she ended up stopping him by forcing him to use his mouth for things other than talking. And then she'd leave town on assignment.

She'd been away for six weeks this time. Kat was pissed that he hadn't even tried to be with anyone else—she knew it meant Annika was special to him. She was right, of course, and there was no reason to try to deny it.

"Come home with me, Annika," he murmured, his thumb stroking her nipple through the thin fabric of her camisole. "Come home to my bed."

"It'd be hotter here," she countered, and at her long, cocky look, he nearly lost his resolve.

"My house," he said firmly, put a hand around her upper arm in an attempt to steer her out of the bar.

"No," she said loudly, her voice carrying over the jukebox music and generally raucous patrons of the bar. Which made all of them stop and stare.

Most everyone here knew Creed. He was a hard man to miss because of his height and the tattoos. He was always being approached and asked the name of his tattoo artist, and he'd tell them that he'd gotten them done out of the country. Which, technically, wasn't a lie.

He just didn't mention how far out of the country.

"Problem?" the bartender asked.

Creed looked between him and Annika, who still wore that I'm-determined-to-win-this-round look he knew so damned well, and he let go of her arm.

"Nothing that's going to get solved tonight," he said, right before he walked out, sans Annika.

He kicked his Harley roughly into gear and revved it twice, his normally calm demeanor shot to hell. Even Kat's attempt to soothe him wasn't going to help him tonight—nothing but Annika in his bed was going to make it all better.

CHAPTER *Five*

Ender was restless—woke with the blankets half off his naked body and a thin sheen of sweat covering him and he knew he wouldn't go back to sleep. There were a few things that could cure that restlessness instantly, things Kira could help him with if she wasn't passed out, so he limited his options to outdoor activities he could do alone.

He'd never slept much anyway. A few hours of REM would do, and the ability to achieve that state quickly, and with maximum effectiveness, had been drilled into him from his first days of Delta training.

He flipped open his cell phone, brought up the feed of Derek's room and Derek's image, splayed across the bed in the same position Ender left him in hours earlier.

Derek's strength might top his, a fact he grudgingly admitted to, but Ender's metabolism allowed him to drink the same amount of the drug as both Derek and Kira with minimal effects. He'd get a brief, mild high, the same as he would with double or triple the dose of what he'd used, or even stronger drugs. And the good people at ACRO had certainly tried them all with him when he'd been brought in, freshly released from the brig and hating the entire fucking world.

That hadn't really changed.

He slid on a pair of shorts and a T-shirt, left his feet bare as he padded to Kira's room, opened the door quietly and slid inside.

The various animals lifted their heads in greeting, a few wagged their tails at him and looked back at Kira, like they were worried.

She'd shifted in her sleep, was facing the door, lying on her side, her head resting on her arm. Totally freakin' naked.

He hadn't been able to get a good look at her in the barn or earlier when all the animals were jumping around. But now, with the moonlight through the windows, he was able to take it all in—the fact that she was tanned golden all over, the dark pink of her nipples framing two of the best-looking breasts he'd ever seen, the slim waist and the curved hips leading to long, shapely legs.

What time is it? Should I be horny yet? Because I don't think I am. Maybe you could touch me and find out.

He approached the bed, put two fingers to the pulse on her neck and counted. Again, a little faster than he'd expected, faster than it should have been. He used the light from his cell phone to check her color—pink in her cheeks and lips, breathing wasn't labored and there were no signs of distress.

I don't catch human diseases. No colds. No flu. I got Parvo once. I have to go to the vet.

He made a mental note for ACRO to check out her metabolism and realized his own pulses were now running too high. He turned to leave the room and got distracted by the floor-to-ceiling bookshelves, something he hadn't given himself a chance to check out earlier. On the middle shelves, the most easily reachable, was a collection of Shakespeare plays that rivaled his own. He pulled out *Macbeth*, his favorite, saw that her copy was also well-worn. Written in too, with passages underlined.

It didn't mean anything. He shoved the book back to the shelf and left the room without a backwards look, headed down the steps to the outside. Because something was up.

Once his feet hit cool grass, he expected to feel better. When he didn't, he knew something else was wrong.

He'd never wanted psychic abilities, but sometimes they'd sure come in handy.

He moved swiftly toward the back of the barn, letting his instinct guide him. Something threw a shadow across the back wall and he moved in a way he'd never been able to describe, not until the people at ACRO taped him in action and he realized that he moved so fast, he was barely a blur on the screen.

Whoever it was wouldn't know what hit him, and Ender didn't hesitate for one second to get the guy into his death grip. He looked him in the eye for one second and was reminded again about who he was and why he was here.

With a snap, the neck broke and he let the guy's body slump to the ground. He searched the pockets, knew he'd find nothing except the gun that was going to be used on him, and on Kira.

He'd made Derek nervous enough to call in backup. A nervous operative always made mistakes, stupid ones too, but this could work in Ender's favor.

This was also going to move things along much more quickly than Dev had predicted, but between Kira's spring fever and Itor's agents coming out of the blue, it couldn't be helped.

Kira had bonded with him—she'd taken him without hesitation, as if she couldn't help herself, and he'd known out there in the barn that everything the file said about her was true.

At least you got to her before Derek.

He was still restless, and thinking about Kira's body taut against his didn't help. He dragged the body roughly through the wooded area that backed up the barn and tried to shove him up under one of the old tarps that covered the cords of wood.

Two other bodies were in the way. The two missing farmhands, most likely guys who never did anything worse than spit tobacco and screw the farmer's daughter. He peered more closely at them for cause of death and saw that their necks had both been broken cleanly—with very little effort, based on the state of the bodies.

Derek.

They'd been dead for a couple of weeks—with the smell of compost and manure out here, the decomposition of rotting flesh would've been easy to miss. His fresh kill joined the other two men and he re-covered them with the tarp. He'd bury them later so the animals didn't come into contact with them. That was sloppy on Derek's part.

He glanced up at the main house to check that all the lights were still off. He wasn't worried about Derek—the guy was going to sleep through until morning. He wasn't as sure about Kira, but figured he had at least a few more hours alone.

Something brushed his back, and he turned swiftly, figuring it was that goat again. But thankfully, there was no sign of the tattle-tale creature. Instead, one of the more beautiful horses he'd seen earlier whinnied and stomped in front of him.

Nothing more beautiful than a female when she's looking for attention.

"Come here, baby," he murmured, and she complied, head down, and nuzzled against his chest. He brushed his hands over her neck, then put his head against it and breathed in deeply.

He missed this, no matter how much he told himself he didn't. Maybe if it had been more of his choice to leave the farm all those years before, things would've been different.

But tonight, right now, there was no difference between the boy he'd been and the man he'd become. His muscles stretched, taut under his skin, his pulse raced steadily, and he knew what he needed. He gave the nag a firm pat on the rump, and she took off, eager for the game. He was right behind her, cutting through the night air until his skin was damp with sweat and the trees were a blur, ran until he couldn't think or feel anything beyond his own limbs flying and the natural, desperate high he craved.

THE TINGLE THAT WOKE KIRA made her shiver between her sheets, even though her skin felt hot to the touch. She groaned, rolled to a cool spot in her bed and looked at the clock. Just after ten. Five hours since she'd had Tom. *Five hours.* She must have been exhausted, because her body never let her go more than four.

A slave to the tight pull between her legs that was worse than usual thanks to the extra hour she'd slept, she groggily swung her feet to the floor, yawned. Her head swam. She pressed her palm to her forehead. Sex withdrawals. Right on time. She needed to hurry.

She stood. Frowned. Looked down. She was naked. Not normally anything to cause concern, since she slept that way, but she didn't remember getting undressed.

She didn't remember much of anything after dinner.

Her body didn't care about what her mind remembered or didn't remember. It hummed with hunger, throbbed with need, and she decided she'd solve the memory mystery later.

Quickly, she threw on a pair of shorts and a tank top, and padded out of her room. A dozen dogs and cats sleeping in various places on blankets on the floor lifted their heads to watch her with exaggerated hopefulness, like she was a total sucker.

"Nice try, guys," she whispered. "Not time to eat."

She crept up the creaky stairs, her pulse already pounding in anticipation of having Tom inside her. At the landing, Spazzy, a wire-haired terrier mix, lay at Tom's door like a sentry. For a moment, she thought Spazzy might have the same issue as Cheech, but when she reached down to scratch him between the ears, the sensation that flashed through her wasn't one of suspicion. Spazzy liked Tom. And Spazzy had also seen him go outside in shorts and bare feet.

Odd. Tom wasn't a smoker; she'd have smelled that. Maybe he'd gotten too warm. The old house didn't have air-conditioning, and the rooms overheated on sunny afternoons.

She hesitated at the landing, cast a glance at Derek's door. Derek, who had warned her about Tom. Who had flirted with her, had liked her cooking. Who didn't seem to want Deb like Tom did. She closed her eyes, sucked in a deep breath, pushed away the strange pinch of jealousy that tweaked at her for the second time today. She had never been territorial when it came to men. How could she be, given that she couldn't limit herself to one man per season?

None of that mattered right now. She needed sex, and she needed it now. Derek might not mind her climbing into bed with him out of the blue, but she already had a connection with Tom. She could save Derek for later. For when Tom wore out or he decided he'd rather have a stacked blonde.

She hurried down the stairs and stepped out onto the front porch, grateful for the cool breeze that rippled the fabric of her baggy sweat shorts and that seemed to shrink her tank top to her aching breasts.

Find Tom.

The dewy grass tickled her toes as she headed toward the barn. She didn't need the bright light from the nearly full moon to guide her—she could find the barn blindfolded—but it helped her keep an eye out for Tom, who was nowhere to be found.

Lifting her nose, she inhaled, seeking his scent. Now that they'd mated, his fragrance had become a beacon, stronger than it had been before, and she should be able to smell him if he was nearby. She caught a lingering impression—he'd been this way recently.

Frowning, she stopped at the stack of hay bales that had been delivered yesterday and that needed to be hauled into the barn. A T-shirt lay draped over one corner. Horse snorts and sleepy chicken trills and the sounds of animals moving about in stalls collided in her ears, but no footsteps.

She glanced back toward the house, cursing. Derek might be her only option right now. But dammit, sleeping with him would only cause problems this early in the game. Dinner had been mildly amusing, the way the two men had been so blatantly competitive, but in all seriousness, the rivalry was a bad sign. Clearly, neither was the type to share, and she had no time or desire to deal with jealousy or posturing or idiotic alpha-male chest pounding. And unfortunately, Tom and Derek seemed to be as alpha as it got.

Hands on hips, she looked into the distance, into the forest behind the farm, up the hill toward the exotic animal acres, in the field to the west.

The field where one of the horses frolicked, seemingly chasing a man. A man who moved like an Olympic sprinter. She blinked the sleep out of her eyes. There was no way a human could keep up with a horse. No, her eyes *weren't* playing tricks on her. The man was Tom, and he was running a race with Shamal, her little gray Arabian mare.

She inhaled sharply, her mind trying to make sense of what she was watching. Did Tom possess some sort of animal gift like hers? Was he somehow genetically enhanced? She wouldn't put it past the government to try something like that. Especially with soldiers.

The graceful power of his body mesmerized her, drew her, made every cell quiver until they felt ready to burst, and she suddenly didn't care if he was Robocop. Heat washed over her until her clothes felt sticky and confining, and she stripped out of them, spread them on the bales of hay. She threw back her head and let the night breeze cool her, caress her naked, tingling skin.

When she looked up again, Tom was heading back, following Shamal now as she cantered in a beautiful, easy stride. It was hard to believe that at one time the horse had been so starved she'd been only hours away from death.

Kira climbed up on the bales of hay and stretched out, stomach down on the clothes, wanting a view of Tom as he jogged in, wanting to be ready for him.

She lifted her hips slightly, slid her hand down her stomach, dipped her fingers between her legs and found that she was definitely ready. Her juices already ran hot and heavy, matching her breathing, her pulse, her desire.

Burying her fingers to the second knuckle inside her core, she stroked herself. Her blood surged, and she knew she wouldn't last long once Tom entered her. Heck, she was on the verge now. She imagined her thumb circling her clit was Tom's tongue, that her fingers were his…it had been so long since any man had done more than simply screw her, and she craved the attention.

Tom's attention.

He drew closer, her breath grew more rapid and, reluctantly, she slid her hand from between her legs and admired the way his sinuous, effortless lope brought him to her quickly. As he slowed, she reached for him. "Tom."

A blur of silvery, shadowy motion hijacked her vision. Pressure and a pinch of pain shot through her. She barely had time to blink, and then the pressure and pain evaporated. The hand that had been crunching down on the back of her neck was gone, balled in a fist beside Tom's thigh.

"Fuck! Kira, what the hell? You scared the shit out of me."

She pushed up to her knees and brushed bits of hay from her cheek that had been smashed into the bales of hay.

"Yeah," she muttered, moving her hand to rub the back of her neck. "Ditto."

His sharp, angry scent mingled with the sudden musky scent of arousal. Her lack of clothing had registered.

"What are you doing?" His voice, already slightly labored from his run, now sounded a little low and rough. "Why aren't you sleeping?"

"Why aren't you?"

He swore, ran a hand through his hair. "I needed to burn off some energy."

She twisted around to sit on the bale, planted her feet on the edges and spread her legs wide, letting the cool night air ease her where she burned. "So did I." Boldly, she palmed her inner thigh and stroked her way to her sex. Using the tips of two fingers, she found her bud, swollen, hard, slippery. "I hope you didn't burn off too much."

His audible swallow rang in her ears, almost as loud as the hum of blood rushing through them. "No, ma'am."

She'd never masturbated in front of a man, but thanks to the extra hour, her need had doubled, and the more aroused he was, the more semen he'd spill. Besides, inhibitions flew the coop when she was in heat. When her cycle was over, she'd be humiliated and full of regret at the things she'd done, but right now she didn't care.

Biting back a moan, she slid her two fingers, one on each side of her clit, up and down, and then added a grind with her hips.

"I've imagined your tongue doing this," she said, and the way he watched her, his gaze like blue fire, set her blood alight like her veins contained gasoline.

"I've imagined the same thing." He took a step toward her, and though she was dying to let him do what she suspected he was going to do, she couldn't wait any longer.

Quickly, she shimmied down the hay pile. She strutted up to him, drew a finger through the sheen of moisture on his bare, muscular chest. "Another time. Right now I need you inside me."

"You aren't afraid to ask for what you want, are you?"

She shuddered at the sound of his voice, at the heavy scent of her arousal, and his, at the way his nostrils flared as she dragged her hand down through the light dusting of chest hair. "Never."

Spreading her fingers, she flattened her palm over his abs, took in the way they bunched beneath her touch. A wave of dizziness spun her head, and there was no more time for foreplay.

Greedily, she yanked down his sweat-dampened shorts. His cock, dusky and marbled by thick veins, curved upward so the tip nearly touched his stomach, and beneath the magnificent length, his sac drew tight before her eyes. As she rolled her spine straight, she let her cheek brush his erection, let the velvety skin caress hers. The way his breath caught and his body went taut brought on another wave of dizziness and desire. Oh, she wanted to take the time to taste him, to suck him until he begged her to let him come, but the dull ache in her womb had worsened.

Damn that extra hour.

"Now, Tommy," she whispered.

Before he could move, she swung a leg up, wrapped her arms around his neck, and clambered up him like he was a tree.

He barely had time to grasp her butt to support her before she lowered herself onto his cock and impaled herself deep.

"Jesus, Kira," he growled, and, oh, God, his voice alone ... her climax blasted through her.

She screamed with the intensity of it, with the sweet, sharp pleasure that went on and on. Searing flashes of light exploded behind her eyelids, and she writhed against him, felt him lift her up and down, drilling into her core. The incredible strength it would take to do something like that barely registered because all that mattered was finding relief that orgasm couldn't bring.

Not her orgasm anyway.

"Come, Tommy, please ..."

She fell forward, burying her face in his neck. The stroke of his shaft against her pulsing inner walls brought her to the edge again, and she dug her nails deeply into the ropy muscles between his shoulder blades. He was so strong, so raw, and she could only bear so much. Groaning in exquisite pleasure, she ground against him. A shudder went through her, appreciation for the hard body holding her softer one. The sensation of skin sliding against skin fogged her brain until all she could do was feel.

And the things she felt ... fire where their bodies joined, her juices flowing down his cock, his tawny chest hair rubbing her hard nipples ... God, she'd never get enough.

She tightened her secret muscles around his shaft, squeezed so hard she felt his pulse in the sensitive ring of tissue at her entrance.

"Oh, man," he panted, and he swelled inside her, his release so close she could feel it coming.

"Tommy, fill me ..."

He grunted, rammed upward so hard she nearly lost her grip, and then his hot wash of seed spread through her insides like the caress of a million tiny fingers, and she came apart again. Flexing so violently she felt a pop in her spine, she bucked against him, let her channel clench and milk every drop he could give her.

Slowly, the sexual haze receded, and she eased back on her gyrating hip motions that made Tom's body jerk reactively.

"Thank you," she said, her voice quavering, and he merely nodded, his breathing still coming in panting rumbles.

Her legs felt rubbery and liquid as she let them slide down his magnificent body, let his semi-erect cock slip from her sex. He watched her, his eyes hooded and not giving anything away, but she got the impression he didn't know what to make of her. No one did, no matter how hard she prayed to find someone who could.

When her heel caught on a baling twine, his hand flashed out to steady her, and this time his gaze took on a slightly protective gleam. Now might be the perfect opportunity to set some ground rules for the safety and best interests of all involved.

"Look," she said, as she retrieved her clothes from the hay bales, "we need to get a few things out in the open."

He arched an eyebrow and pulled up his shorts. "And those would be?"

"You are never, ever to come into my bedroom unless I invite you. Don't even knock unless there's an emergency." She slipped her tank over her head. "And just because you're servicing me, don't think that gives you any special privileges around here."

He nodded, and she swore one corner of his mouth twitched in an amused smile before it twitched right back to Mr. Grim Face.

She pulled on her shorts. "And last, but not least, don't think sex equals a relationship. You don't own me, you have no claims to me, and you have no say in my life. I do what I want, and I see who I want. And, of course, the same goes for you."

Now he didn't look amused at all. In fact, his lips pulled into an even deeper frown, though no other outward signs that he'd even heard her were visible. "Yes, ma'am."

"Good."

Slipping past him, she headed toward the exotic-animal pens to make her night rounds.

Hopefully, if she needed Derek—or anyone else—soon, Tom would remember what she'd said about seeing whom she chose. She'd also set some of her limitations, something she'd learned long ago she needed at this critical time. A tight rein on her life, especially during the spring, kept her world as controlled as possible, a vital element since the fever made her vulnerable.

A tight rein also kept her alive.

*   *   *

The C-130 leveled off, bouncing in the turbulence. Dev kept one hand on the yoke to steady the plane and prepared to go home.

"Dream Catcher, this is Ghost Control—we've got Deltas lookin' for a ride home." The controller on the radio issued lat and long, and Dev checked the charts.

"Ghost Control, this is Dream Catcher. Roger, copy your coordinates. We'll see you in thirty," Dev said. He gave a nod to his copilot and banked the empty plane around, reversing course. The unusual order piqued his curiosity—and his sense of foreboding. Somewhere, something had gone wrong if his crew was being tagged for a last-minute pickup.

They entered a cloud deck, and immediately the ping of rain on metal echoed in the cabin. The craft shuddered and jolted in the light chop, and then the mid-level clouds thinned out, and they were in the clear.

"This weather's shit," Monty observed.

"What weather? It's smooth, blue, and what else can you ask for?" Dev shot Monty a concerned look, because the guy had been stressed out lately. Trouble at home; he'd married too young to a woman who hadn't adjusted to military life. He saw storms everywhere now.

"Yeah, whatever," Monty muttered, and they flew in silence until the purr of the engines lulled the residual tension out of the air.

Their descent took them through more clear air, but Monty grumbled about clouds and Dev decided the copilot needed a serious decompression session when they got back to base.

It was ridiculously good weather, but for a brief second, on final approach, Dev's vision clouded and then returned. He blinked, but shook it off, because ahead the runway beckoned, smooth as shit and glinting beneath the Afghan sun. He pulled back the throttles. Oh, yeah, this landing was going to be a beauty . . .

Monty shoved the throttles up again. "What the fuck are you doing? Pull the fuck back! Don't you see the fucking explosions?" He grabbed the yoke and pulled back, his eyes wild.

"Get your hands off my controls!" Dev yelled. "What the hell is wrong with you? I've got a perfect landing!"

The cockpit came alive with lights and blaring alarms, low-altitude warnings, and...what the fuck? The whole craft had gone mad, the copilot had lost his mind, was fighting for the controls. They were going to crash.

Dev unbuckled himself and lunged, slammed his fist into Monty's face. The other man grunted and fell forward against the instrument panel. Panting, Dev regained control of the aircraft, eased her in toward the runway.

The next thing he remembered was the heat, blistering his skin. Burning fuel seared his nasal passages and lungs, and even in the midst of the chaos, he knew he'd never forget the crackle and creak of superheated metal.

SLOWLY, DEV BECAME AWARE of his screams, almost inhuman. The nightmare hit out of the blue, and thank God he'd chosen to spend the night alone. He'd even sent home the guard dog Ender sicced on him before he left for his mission last night, an excedo with superstrength nicknamed Trance because of his hypnotic stare and powers of persuasion that went beyond the norm.

He'd known the stress would get to him, whether it was tonight or tomorrow or next week, knew it was going to wake him up, make him relive each and every painful memory.

At times like this, he liked to blame everyone but himself—the old guard at ACRO, the military...hell, Mother Nature herself for the weather that hadn't even caused the crash at the LZ.

Pilot error. It would've shown up right in the black box. Should have. He knew Ender was good, but even he couldn't have made pilot error disappear. And still, Ender was the one who was court-martialed, put in lockup for two years with the worst of the worst after the crash investigation.

Ender, who still blamed himself for everything—accused of the most horrible of crimes. He was supposed to have spent the rest of his life in jail. Would have, if Dev hadn't joined ACRO and gotten him out. And still, Ender resisted heartily. *Didn't want any fucking favors from you,* he'd spat from behind the bars of the solitary confinement cell where he spent twenty-three hours per day. Even now he refused to admit that he'd been the one to save Dev's life. Told Dev to his face that he *had no problem killing friends, so why would he save someone he barely knew.*

Dev never bothered telling the military that Ender could've escaped anytime he wanted to. The fact that he never bothered to was something that concerned Dev the most.

It's the leak at ACRO that's doing this to you.

There was most definitely a mole at ACRO—whoever it was had wormed his or her way into the deepest recesses of the organization, had made themselves privy to all pertinent information and had nearly gotten Remy, Haley and Wyatt—all ACRO operatives—killed several months earlier.

And the weather machine was still out there—although it hadn't been confirmed, Dev could feel it in his bones. Itor had something big planned.

It was the one and only reason he'd sent Creed and Annika to his old family house in Syracuse. The ghost that had mysteriously haunted him for years as a teenager, the same one that had come back on the terrible night Dev crashed his C-130 into the side of a mountain, and again nearly four years ago, was still there, banished to a portal inside the deserted mansion.

"It was a fucking badass in real life and it's looking for revenge," Oz, his former lover and the most powerful medium ACRO had ever seen, had told him when they were still just teenagers. "It's trying to find that way through you."

At the time, Dev hadn't known or cared why the entity sought him out specifically—he'd grown up with psychic parents and otherworldly crap all around him and all he'd wanted was normal. Which he'd been until his plane crashed ten years earlier and his second sight came through loud and clear. After that, he'd wanted to know more about the spirit.

The spirit wanted Dev—craved him—promised to reveal seductive truths about Dev's past, about enemies current and future—even about Itor Corp. Things that Oz always convinced him he was better off not knowing. And Dev hadn't ever wanted to hear what it had to say when he was a teenager, had blocked it out with Oz's help and banished it from his being.

When he'd summoned it four years ago, it had been for a specific purpose, to try to locate an agent lost in Itor territory, and again Oz had to rescue him. Oz had exorcized it from Dev, was strong enough to lock what he'd deemed as a truth-spirit seeking redemption into a special portal in Dev's childhood home.

And then Oz had left him—a huge blowout over Dev sacrificing himself for the greater good of ACRO. Dev never thought he'd even attempt to use the spirit again, but the leak at ACRO had him backed into a corner.

Yes, the spirit definitely knew things crucial to the success of ACRO. This time, Dev wanted to hear—needed to, although he wasn't sure if he was ready to pay the price.

Creed claimed that the ghost was still there—free from the portal it had been banished to, but not free from the actual four walls of the house itself. Which meant it was still controllable.

Dev hadn't been able to bring himself to make the trip there yet, even after all these months. He'd thought about calling his former lover, laying it all out on the line, but in the end figured he was better off going it alone.

One A.M. and he wasn't nearly ready to return to bed, figured a swim might relax him.

He stripped as he walked down the stairs, tripped when he got to the bottom of the flight on the first floor and clung to the banister tightly, his heart hammering in his chest.

He *never* tripped, not even when he'd first lost his sight, and certainly never in his own house. Not when nothing was moved an inch without his okay. And even if it did it wouldn't matter—his second sight was always there.

He checked the area around the bottom step. Nothing. He'd gotten tangled in his own feet.

Let it go.

Naked, he slid open the glass doors and let the night air swirl around him. It smelled like rain, tasted sweet like the summer, heavy like his favorite brand of port. There was a definite storm brewing to the west.

Remy and Haley must be having a field day. That thought at least got a small smile out of him. His two operatives worked quite well as a team—Remy controlling the weather and Haley the only one who could control him.

His own cock stirred, not that it ever took much anyway, but the thought of rough, hot sex was almost too much. There were people he could call in for that specific purpose, people who wouldn't talk to him or ask questions. ACRO trained Seducers well in that area, and whether they were in the field or helping out one of their fellow employees, they lived up to their names.

But tonight he needed to be alone.

He dove into the water, kept icy enough to chill the worry right out of him. His head pounded as he stayed under as long as he could—he kicked hard and came up at the other side of the pool, his feet easily touching the bottom of the shallow end.

He pushed up out of the water and walked toward the house. When he felt a hand touch his back he turned, even though he knew no one human was there.

He struggled to breathe as he grew light-headed. Because it was happening again.

You can't control everything, Dev, it whispered.

He backed up in the direction of the house, his second sight trying to cover him in all directions. But his calves bumped one of the lounge chairs before he could stop himself and he sat down hard.

A warm hand touched him again, middle of his shoulder blades, traced a path down his spine, and he sat motionless. The touch was soothing at first, comforting, meant to lull him into a false sense of security. The stroking got harder, more forceful, a two-handed caress from strong fingers that tried to knead the tension from his muscles.

He fought the urge to scream, bit his lip instead, so hard he drew blood.

You invited me, Devlin. And I'm here to stay.

No, this couldn't be happening. Creed told him that the spirit remained in the house—free of the portal but not free.

But there was no denying that the spirit had escaped Dev's childhood home and found its way to Dev.

God, he was in trouble. His mind immediately shifted to the one man he knew could help him, and he felt the spirit wipe away the single tear that rolled down his cheek.

CHAPTER
Six

The sound of growling woke Kira. Bloodcurdling snarls, followed by sudden, urgent barking. She sat up, looked at the bedside clock. Two-thirty A.M. She'd have awakened soon anyway, her body needing to find Tom.

Thumping noises in the hall made her jump. Angry male voices.

She leaped out of bed, threw on the same shorts and tank she'd worn earlier and opened the door. Derek and Tom stood in the hallway. They faced each other, teeth bared, doing some impressive growling of their own. Behind her, the dogs were nosing her legs, eager to join the action, but she stopped them with a quick mental command.

"Son of a bitch," Derek snarled, red spittle from his split lip splattering on her floor. He took a menacing step toward Tom. "Nice trick with the fucking lemonade."

"You're just pissed you fell for it." Tom kept his angry gaze on Derek as he took his own step forward. "Kira, get back. Lock yourself in your room."

"Kira," Derek said in a low, simmering tone, "come here. Remember what I told you about him? I'll protect you."

The scent of danger, of hatred, of blood, made her stomach churn. Dear God, these men weren't engaging in a minor testosterone-induced dispute over territory. This was life or death.

"Don't do it, Kira," Tom snapped, and she looked between the two men, confused and more than a little frightened.

Around them, a dozen dogs watched, some whimpering, others crouching, hackles raised. A black shadow slipped past; Luke, creeping through the crowd of spectators, low to the ground, his lips curled in a silent snarl.

"Luke! No!"

Too late. The shepherd lunged, sank his teeth deeply into Derek's calf. Shouting, Derek twisted, brought his fist down on Luke's head with such force that the dog sank bonelessly to the floor.

"Bastard!" she screamed, and then Tom was there in a blur of motion, had Derek in a headlock.

They both slammed into the wall across from her. Somehow, Derek broke free, spun Tom and put his fist into Tom's back so violently that Tom grunted and his knees buckled. Tom hit the floor. Derek smiled, sent a roundhouse kick into Tom's ribs. Tom flew into the wall with a sickening crunch.

Oh, God. Kira slipped behind them, gathered Luke into her arms, checked his breathing. Still alive. Relief washed over her, until Derek shifted his weight to throw another kick. Inside she screamed at him to stop, but nothing came out. Her heart hammered. Her teeth chattered. She gripped fistfuls of Luke's fur as she watched Tom roll and sweep his legs out.

Derek crashed to the ground. Tom's fist slammed into Derek's jaw, and blood splattered the walls.

"That," he ground out, "was because you touched Kira." He pounded Derek again, the slap of fist on wet skin sickening. "That was for fucking Sergeant Jones's wife while he was getting killed." Another punch. "And that was for working for Itor."

Derek silently wrapped his hands around Tom's throat. Tom struggled for a breath, brought his leg up hard between Derek's. Derek shouted in pain, must have released his grip just enough, because Tom shouldered the other man's arms away, and then, in a motion so fast she didn't see it until it was over, he smashed his hand into Derek's throat.

Derek made a half gasp, his eyes wide, shocked. Then they glazed over, and his chest stopped moving.

Panting, Tom fell back on his hip, sat there watching her as he caught his breath. He said nothing, just gazed at her with hooded, impassive eyes. He looked exhausted, but she knew if she moved—for her room, for the phone, for anything—he'd drop her in a heartbeat.

In her arms, Luke stirred, and she closed her eyes, let his thoughts wash over her. He was confused, somewhat hungry and pissed as hell. She wanted to smile, but there was a dead man bleeding all over her floor, and the man who'd killed him was staring at her like she might be next.

"How's the dog?" he rasped, and she blinked.

"Why? Are you going to kill him now?"

He didn't answer. He merely stood, winced and prodded Derek's body with his foot.

Swallowing sickly, she helped Luke to his feet and pushed him back when he looked like he might still want a piece of Derek. She got to her own feet, stood there on shaky legs. She glanced at her bedroom door, wondering how fast she could get inside and get the door locked. Maybe she could escape out the back window.

"Don't even think about it," he said.

"What—" She swallowed again, tried to get the lump of terror to go down. "What happened? Why did you kill him?"

He fisted his hands at his sides, looking from Derek to her, saying nothing. She inhaled deeply, needing to know where his emotions were. The danger scent had faded, but a new, sharper one sank into her lungs and sent her pulse into a pounding throb. Her body was answering his, even if the scent of lust rolling from him had come about from an adrenaline rush and a battle. Unbelievable. He could kill her right now, and her body wouldn't care as long as he had sex with her first.

"Answer me," she snarled. "This is my life—so, damn you, answer me!"

He stood there, all dark and menacing, and a chill ran through her because she knew she wouldn't like the answer he was going to give her.

"HE WAS GOING TO kill you, Kira," Ender said finally, barely recognized his own voice. But it was something about the way she stood there, looking so brave and strong, that stopped him from being a total asshole. Instead, he showed her the handcuffs Derek held, the tranq gun stuck in the guy's back pocket with a large enough dose of ketamine to take down a few horses.

It was a lie, of course. Derek's plans went far beyond killing her, but she was on a need-to-know basis, and right now, she didn't need to know anything but what he told her.

She looked between him and the body, no doubt reliving the fight scene inside her mind. Her hands shook slightly, and she fisted them while she stared up at him. "Who are you?"

There were so many ways to answer that. *A killer* was the first that came to mind, followed shortly by *The guy who fucked you like an animal earlier,* but she already knew both those things. That's not what she was after.

He'd have to settle on something she'd like and give her a little of the truth—a combined plus. "I'm the guy who just saved your life."

She snorted, not buying it. No way, not after she'd spotted him running earlier, the way he'd fought Derek.

"Am I supposed to take you at your word?"

"Yes."

"I don't understand any of this," she said, wrapping her arms tightly across her chest. "I don't think I want to." She nodded down at Derek's body. "What are you going to do with him?"

"I'll take care of it," he said. "But you'll have to come with me."

"Are you crazy? I'm not going with you to bury a dead body."

"Actually, it's not just one. I've got four to bury, but it shouldn't take long."

"Four?"

"I found your two missing farmhands," he admitted.

"Oh, my God," she whispered, and swallowed sickly. "Jack and David . . ." She leveled a dark, angry gaze at him. "And what about the third body? You just picked up an extra one for good luck?"

"Something like that."

She shook her head and stepped back, as though easing toward her bedroom door. "Who do you work for?"

"As of yesterday, I work for you."

"Not anymore." She stalked to the end of the hall and grabbed the cordless phone from the table against the wall. "Get out. I'll give you a head start before I call the police."

He almost laughed. She was all show, no action. She had no one to call, and the police weren't an option. For the next couple of days he was going to be Kira Donovan's entire world.

He left her staring at an empty palm as he slid her phone into his pocket.

"How did you do that?" she demanded, but her voice shook beneath the bravado.

The good-ole-farm-boy act was over. Done with. For everyone's own good. "I work for an agency called ACRO. They know all about you. They want you to come to work for them."

He didn't have the touch for this shit, the special, touchy-feely, everything's-going-to-be-okay-baby attitude the rest of the agents who did this job had. Besides, his ribs fucking hurt where Derek had ripped into him, his kidneys ached and he'd be peeing blood by morning. He was going to lay it on the line to her, tell her what she needed to do. Noncompliance was not an option.

If it is, you're going to have to kill her . . .

"Why do they want me?"

"Because they know you're an animal whisperer. They want to develop your skills, take you off the market before someone else grabs you. Someone far more dangerous than my organization," he said.

She glanced over at Derek's body, then back to Ender's face.

"And you work there. As what? A thug? A killer?"

"I'm an operative," he said.

"Is that what they call it?" She shook her head and narrowed her eyes at him. "Why are you so fast? They experimented on you, didn't they? Some sort of crazy government research."

"Trick of the moonlight," he said, but she pushed her palms against his chest, put all her weight behind it. He didn't give her an inch.

"Bullshit. Tell me what you are."

Dammit—he'd always hated that question, never knew quite how to answer it. Dev had always gotten a good laugh out of the fact that Ender never lumped himself in with the special-ability types. Then again, he hadn't known there was a name for what he was until he was recruited into ACRO eight years earlier.

You're an excedo, Dev had told him.

I'm a killer, he'd answered back, and Dev had shaken his head and taken him into the ACRO fold despite major resistance.

He'd just thought he was some kind of freak. Still did in many ways, but it didn't bother him. A lot of the rare operatives loved to moan and gnash their teeth, a woe-is-me attitude toward the special gifts nature had bestowed on them.

As far as he was concerned, if Mother Nature wanted to throw something extra his way, he was all for it. She'd bestowed on him super eyesight and the ability to move at cheetah speed. A human blur. Super eyesight and speed were the best of all combinations, in his opinion, static gifts that he put to good use on a regular basis. That and a bigger-than-average cock, also put to good use on a more than regular basis. Because sometimes nature insisted that it was time to just slow down and enjoy the ride.

Now, of course, was not the time to slow shit down. It was time to start convincing Kira of what she needed to do to stay alive.

"I'll explain more as soon as I take care of a few things," he said. His time, his schedule. No one else's ever.

"I'm not working for anyone but myself, especially not some mysterious agency that sends thugs to do the recruiting."

"You don't have the luxury of that choice anymore," he told her, the words coming in a low growl.

"What, like it's your way or the highway?"

"More like, it's my way," he said, baring his teeth slightly, because he was so done with this pre-convincing shit.

"You're an asshole."

"What's your point?"

She stared at him and slowly shook her head. "You can tell the CIA or NSA or whatever to go fuck itself."

He snorted. "ACRO's not government."

"Military? Derek said you were Army. He said you'd been dishonorably discharged."

"Derek was correct about that. Probably the only thing he was right about since he got here," he told her.

His own Delta Force days were more a blur than anything, a way to legally pass the time and burn off the constant, extra energy he always possessed. A way to stay out of trouble. Lots of excedos led a nice, productive life of crime, and true to form, Derek had gone down that road for a while before joining Itor Corp, a smaller agency of rare operatives that regularly went head to head with ACRO.

"What did you do to get a dishonorable discharge?" she asked.

"Don't ask questions I can't give you answers to, Kira. Answers you don't want."

"Here's an answer I'm sure *you* don't want—I'm not joining your agency. Ever. And there's nothing you can say or do to convince me. I've lived through worse than you," she said. "Now you need to get the fuck out of here before I call out my dogs." But her voice lacked a certain conviction even though he was pretty sure she meant what she said.

Something else was wrong.

He stared at her, the tank-top strap falling off one shoulder, the hastily pulled-on shorts, her hair loose around her face and shoulders. And there it was—the need was back in her eyes. He could tell she was torn between hating him and wanting him.

Join the club, honey.

She wrapped her arms around her chest, squeezed her legs together tightly like she was trying to keep from reaching out and grabbing him. Even her jaw tensed, and she closed her eyes momentarily, swayed a little like she couldn't control her own body.

"Let me take care of what I need to," he said. "We'll talk more about this in the morning. When you've calmed down. When you've gotten your needs met and you can think clearly."

"No. I can't stay here with you tonight," she said. "I have to go find . . . someone. Seeing how you killed my backup."

"You're not leaving my sight."

"Then you can come with me and watch."

"And give you an opportunity to escape or get help? I don't think so."

"I have to, dammit." The need was burning bright in her eyes, and she shifted from foot to foot. Part nerves, part lust. "Tommy, you need to let me go."

The way she called him *Tommy* reverberated straight to his dick. "You need *me,*" he said. "And I'm all yours."

"I'm your prisoner," she snapped. "I can't trust you. And I don't."

"I don't trust you either. That didn't matter the last two times, and it can't matter now. I know how to help you."

"You don't know anything about me."

"That's where you're wrong. Very wrong," he said.

She hesitated briefly, the adrenaline almost visible around her, before she took off out the back door, and in a dead run through the empty field behind the barn. She had to know it wouldn't do her any good, but he gave her credit for having the balls to try.

He was on her within seconds, tumbling her to the soft earth and pinning her underneath his weight. For a minute, he just lay there, his face inches from hers, letting the hard planes of his body feel every soft curve of hers, reveling in the fact that she didn't try to struggle.

The adrenaline from the run seemed to have taken the edge off her craving slightly, but the heat from her body began to rise all around him, scorching through his T-shirt and making his skin prickle.

"Want to play This Is Your Life, Chastity Belle?" he murmured roughly against the side of her cheek.

"No," she spat out through gritted teeth. Her eyes shot fire at him. "And it's *Charity*, you asshole. But you knew that."

He grinned, because yes, he had known that. "Too bad. We could talk about the fact that you're much more used to wearing handcuffs than you let on to Derek. The fact that you've been arrested at animal-rights rallies."

"Big deal. Protesting the unethical treatment of animals is something I have every right to do under the Constitution," she said.

"What about lighting fires at slaughterhouses?"

"Never proven."

"The sinking of the whaling ship?" he asked, watched her eyes grow slightly wider, half panic, half lust taking over, and the dizzy feeling he'd gotten earlier was coming back strong. "You know you're on the government's terrorist watch-list."

No, she didn't know. He could tell by the way her mouth fell open, her full, pink lips parting in a way that left him breathless.

He stared from her face down to the graceful column of her neck, thought about the fine bones that ran along the side of her trachea, knew it would take only the pressure from one of his fingers to finish his job quietly and cleanly. Humanely. So easy to end this job now, probably was the right thing to do, because his gut told him that Kira didn't have a cooperative bone in her body when it involved anything other than her heat cycle.

"You're all alone in this great big world, Chastity. So many people looking for you. The government, the police, the men who tried to take you away in a van outside of Memphis," he said, and she whimpered. "Who's going to take care of you now? Your animals can't protect you forever."

"Stop calling me Chastity. And don't call me Charity either. It's not my name anymore."

"Why? Did you change your name legally?" he taunted her. "Oh, right. No way to do that when you're a wanted woman."

"At least I'm not a killer," she said.

"Not that they've proven. Not yet. And time's running out." His fingers itched with the urge to do something, but he stayed motionless on her, his elbows propped on the grass and pressing her immobile arms against her own body, his thighs a deadweight on hers. His cock strained against his shorts, throbbed against her with a life of its own, something he couldn't have stopped no matter how hard he tried.

Her heart beat against his, faster than when she'd first taken the drugs. Her metabolism, and her urges, were headed into maximum overdrive.

"Are you going to turn me in?" she asked.

You wish, honey. Especially if she knew the alternative.

"What if I did? Would you let a police officer take you, right there in your jail cell, with all the guards watching?"

"It's happened before." She shuddered and closed her eyes, and when she opened them, her gaze clung to his, pled with him. "Don't do this to me. Please, Tommy, just stop it and let me go."

"I can't."

"You won't."

"Same difference."

She'd started to panic, turned her head from side to side, and it wasn't his imagination that she was starting to gain strength. It wouldn't be enough to buck him, but things were intensifying.

He wasn't going to kill her tonight.

"How about I take the choice away? Will that make it better?" he asked.

"No," she whispered, but he didn't believe her, could smell her scent, her raw desire rising up in the night air. "You don't understand my needs. They're too much for one man to handle. You'll never be able to keep up with me."

"I think I'll do just fine. As long as you obey."

She shifted under him, tried to stop herself from rubbing against him. "Obey? I don't obey anyone or anything but my needs," she said, and Jesus, she was actually, honest-to-God purring while she lay trapped underneath him.

"You're going to have to start if you want to stay alive," he said, but his words had stopped registering with her.

"Don't move. I like your weight on me," she murmured, and the low rumbled purring started again in her throat, vibrated through his entire body. She groaned throatily and thrust her hips against him.

"*Obey* is the key word here. Don't think I won't take you over my knee, Kira." His voice was rough with that promise, throbbed with a lust that shot straight through her. "Don't think you won't love it—bare-assed, submitting to my every single whim."

She sucked in a sharp breath through her teeth because, dammit, she needed him, wasn't going to be able to stand it much longer if he didn't take her every way he possibly could, and soon. It didn't matter who he was or what he'd done. All that mattered was the way he made her feel.

She never thought she'd need a killer to save her life.

"I've got to get out of here," she whispered, clawed frantically at him, tried to tear away. But the combination of his skin on hers, his scent, the inherent command in his voice . . .

She wasn't going to make it.

"I'm the only one who can keep you safe now. Keep you, fuck you, satisfy you," he murmured, his fingers brushing between her legs deftly, not lightly, the way she liked to be touched.

"God, yes."

"Going to let me help you?"

"I hate you," she moaned, even as she arched up against his erection. "Do it. Do it now, Tommy."

"One thing." He grabbed her wrists and pushed them above her head. In one swift movement, she found her wrists handcuffed together. "You're not the one giving the orders anymore."

"Bastard," she said. At least, she tried to say that, but her ears heard something more like, "I don't care," because right at this moment, she didn't. Later, she'd care a whole lot, but now she needed him.

"Now that we've got that settled..." His voice, a rough caress, made her skin tingle. He drew the callused palm of his hand down one arm stretched above her head, then down her side, to her hip, and every inch of the path his hand took sizzled.

She wriggled, worked her legs out from under his so she could wrap them around his waist. The hard length of his erection rubbed her through the fabric of his sweat shorts in just the right place, made her groan, but it wasn't enough.

His fingers slipped beneath her waistband, and then he released her cuffed arms and pulled away enough to strip her of the shorts. The soft grass tickled her bare skin as she let her knees fall open. Cool night air caressed the very place she wanted Tom to be, but he just sat there on his knees between hers, his eyes glittering in the moonlight. His chest heaved, his gaze burned her skin where it landed.

A muscle in his jaw twitched with the force of his clenched teeth, and she inhaled, found the harsh scent of anger beneath the more potent aroma of lust. A battle raged inside him, and terror sliced through her like a cold blade. What if he wasn't going to do this? What if he left her to suffer and die in the field?

"Tommy?"

She reached her cuffed hands out for him, tried to sit up, but he pushed her back down with one forceful hand to the ribs. His other hand gripped her thigh, spread her wide, and she breathed a sigh of relief as he backed up, put his mouth between her legs like she'd been wanting him to do since they'd met. Angling her pelvis to meet him, she melted at the first gush of hot breath that enveloped her sex.

His fingers parted her swollen flesh, opening her completely to his invading tongue. She struggled to suck in a ragged breath as she shivered with the deliciousness of his eager licks, and though this wasn't what she needed, his talented mouth dared her to argue. She lost the dare. Her body would just have to wait a few minutes longer to get what it craved.

"I've thought about how you'd taste," he said, in a low, guttural voice, and she whimpered, arched against his mouth. He sucked her throbbing nub between his lips, pulled hard, and she had to bite her lip to keep from crying out. "Jesus," he panted. "It's like a fucking drug."

He dragged his tongue up her center, lapped at her juices like he'd die if he didn't get enough of her. Two fingers thrust smoothly into her slick entrance, and his thumb pushed up on her clit as his tongue flicked over it. Sliding his fingers in and out, he found a rhythm that made her writhe.

"That's it," he said, his voice vibrating deep inside her sex. "Fuck my hand."

She moaned. "Yes, Tommy, yes."

Oh, damn, he was good at this, and she reached for him, gripped his hair to hold him there even though he wasn't going anywhere. The cold metal cuffs sent a chill up her belly from where they rested against her hot skin.

Still easing in and out with his fingers, he reached for the cuffs with his other hand. He dragged her wrists down, breaking her hold on his hair, and then she gasped when he used the chain between the steel bracelets to stroke her clit. The action forced her to spread her thighs wider to prevent the cuffs from digging into her skin, but the feel of the cool links rubbing her most sensitive flesh...she was out of control, mad with the need to come. She heard herself begging, "Please, please, oh, please," but he drew out the torture, flicking the chain up and down, around, finally pushing one link around her clit like a cage. His tongue tapped the exposed, sensitive nub, and she came off the ground, digging her toes into the soil for purchase.

It was all too much, and when he replaced his fingers with his tongue, thrusting it inside her, she couldn't prevent a throaty wail of pleasure from escaping. He circled her opening, plunged deep, stroked her inner walls until she wanted to scream.

His eyes had been closed, but he opened them as he dragged the flat of his tongue back up through her wet folds. The sight of him pleasuring her with his mouth as he watched her reactions threw her over the edge. Thrashing wildly, she closed her eyes as always at release, and threw her head back to howl at the moon.

She came hard, pumping herself against his face for what seemed like hours as his talented tongue took her higher and higher. Her legs shook, her breath burned her throat and, finally, just as she worried she might pass out, her orgasm melted away. Her muscles felt rubbery, but the tension inside remained, seemed to have worsened now that Tom's lust had grown, and hers had only been held off.

Tugging at his hair, she tried to pull him up so he could give her the rest, but he tore away and pushed to his feet. She blinked, confused, as he dug into his pocket.

"Just looking for the keys. I swiped the cuffs off Derek."

She shook her head. "Don't care. Just finish." She crawled toward him, but he stepped back.

"We're done. I have work to do."

"No," she breathed. "No! You can't do that to me!"

He stared at her like she'd gone insane as she clawed at his leg, attempting to grab a fistful of his shorts to yank them down.

"What the hell is wrong with you? I just gave you what you needed." He wheeled away and bent to grab her shorts.

A haze of red clouded her vision. Panic and rage and lust squeezed at her like a vise. Her blood, already running hot with primal need, now boiled, seared into ash everything that made her human.

Snarling, she leaped. Landed hard on Tom's back, took him down like a lion on a wildebeest.

CHAPTER
Seven

Ender knew he'd been off balance when he'd attempted to walk away from her, was dizzy from the second he'd put his face in between her legs and felt the undeniable urge to stay there for days, screw the rest of the mission.

Off balance, yes, but something else was wrong, evidenced by the way he'd been taken by surprise *and* taken completely down by a tiny stick of a woman who couldn't weigh one-ten soaking wet.

"Fuck," he grunted as she tumbled against his injured ribs and sore kidneys and grunted again as she dug her claws into his chest and scrambled on top of him to straddle his hips. He could fight her, but shit, he'd be fighting an animal, because Kira had left the building. Even her eyes had changed, had gone luminous, feral, like the harsh growl rumbling near the surface of her throat.

There wouldn't be a fight—he'd just have to kill her. And he wasn't ready to make that choice yet, not until he was able to see for himself just what in the hell was really happening here.

She moved like a cat, tore at his clothing with her cuffed hands. Her position pinned his shorts, allowing only the head of his cock to poke up from the waistband. Apparently, that was enough. She lunged forward, slammed the cuffs against his throat so the chain cut into his windpipe, and in the same motion sheathed him inside her.

"Need. Sex." She snarled, baring her teeth when he grasped her arms to take pressure off his throat, dug her nails so deeply into the sides of his neck that he winced.

Her body moved like it was possessed, her quick, shallow thrusts impeded by the shorts keeping his cock partially clothed.

Maybe he should have given her another orgasm, but shit, he'd been in a hurry, had things to do. And he hadn't wanted to be a slave to her pheromones or whatever the fuck it was that clouded his mind and made his body answer hers.

"Kira, pull down my shorts," he said, his voice rough and low thanks to the chain-link collar she'd made for him. "It's not going to work this way."

But she'd stopped listening, her movements getting more frantic, especially once she realized she wasn't getting what she needed from him.

He turned his neck slightly, so his trachea wouldn't take the brunt of the chain, pulled his hands away and reached down to free himself from his shorts. He gagged, choked, the world spun from the pressure on his neck and, fuck, he wasn't so kinky that he got off on asphyxiation. But as much as he struggled, his reflexes, his speed, didn't seem to matter—like the life was being sucked out of him, and he forced himself not to panic.

He exerted what seemed like an inordinate amount of energy to get his hands back under her wrists at the same time he slid fully inside of her. That seemed to satisfy her, because she groaned, released his neck, and he responded with a grateful gulp of good, clean air. And even though he didn't want to, was pissed as hell, the part of his body that never gave a shit about his other emotions pulsed inside her, his hips rocked upward and he knew Kira was going to take what she wanted, with or without his consent.

He wanted more too, wanted to feel himself pushed deep inside her heat, because it was so fucking good when they rutted together. And when she moved forward, he was able to sink fully into her with a loud, satisfied groan.

"God, Tommy, God," she whimpered. She'd thrown her head back, closed her eyes and smiled as he let her wet heat rub him in all the right ways.

So fucking good.

He grabbed her hips for leverage as she arched back, her cuffed wrists pressing his rib cage as she came. He followed soon after, came with enough force that he sucked air through his clenched teeth as she collapsed against him, sobbing.

She was fucking sobbing. He'd never, ever understand women. She rolled off him, curled up in a ball as her crying quieted, and his breath came in harsh gasps. He'd have the impressions from the chain across his throat for days.

He moved his hand in front of his face, pleased to see the silver blur. His excedo skills were still there. Just not when Kira had him so deep in her rut.

A man's never safe when he's fucking, Dev always said, and Ender had always laughed, told him, *I'm always in control.*

But this, this wasn't control, not with her spring fever increasing in a violent cycle that promised to last two weeks, if not longer.

They'd find ways to service her at ACRO safely. Privately. She wouldn't be his concern anymore once they got to the facility. None of them ever were, and this wouldn't be any different.

Ender took the keys from his pocket and unlocked the cuffs from her wrists. After he backed away, she sat up, hunted for her shorts. Once she'd pulled them on, she pulled her knees up to her chest and looked at him where he continued to lay sprawled on his back on the grass.

"Are you all right?" she asked.

He ignored her question. "Twenty-one hours," he told her instead. "I'll give you twenty-one more hours here on the refuge. Until midnight tomorrow night."

"Then what? Either I join you and your agency or you kidnap me?"

"Something like that," he said, shifted on the ground to find a more comfortable position. He'd heal more quickly than the average person, but he still felt pain just like everybody else. "By tomorrow night, it's not going to be safe for you to stay here. You'll put everyone's lives in jeopardy. Including your precious animals."

"Stop trying to scare me."

"I thought I'd already succeeded in doing that, Kira."

"Screw you," she said, pushed up off the ground and stood over him. With the moonlight streaming behind her she looked almost unreal, too pretty and too pure to be anywhere near him, despite what had just happened.

"You just did, honey," he said, his voice harsher than he would've liked. But his patience had finally worn through. "I'm trying to tell you the truth, but you're too pigheaded to hear it. This is much bigger than you are. I can only hold off the men Derek worked with for so long. I'm not Superman."

"Yeah, could've fooled me," she muttered. "And you never told me what you are. You know everything about me and I don't know if a single thing I know about you is true."

He swore softly, grabbed for his shorts and shirt and dressed quickly before standing. "That's the way I like it. And you've got the day to decide if you're going down easy or hard."

"Aren't you worried I'll escape?" she asked, absently rubbing her wrists where the cuffs had been. He was pleased to see that the red marks were already fading, and no bruises were apparent.

She hadn't even struggled against the steel bonds. He wondered what it would feel like to be that out of control, and realized she'd given him a real taste.

He reached out, grabbed her wrist and brought her hand to his crotch. Then he smiled. "No. I'm not worried, honey. You seem to know what side your bread is buttered on."

He'd planned on walking away then, leaving her jaw-dropped and sputtering mad in the middle of the field. He had work to do, and by his calculations she needed sex approximately every four hours.

He turned his back, but she called after him. "Just because your dick's big and you can bring me to orgasm doesn't mean you're going to be able to keep me satisfied. Asshole."

He didn't turn back to face her. "I've never had any complaints."

"Yeah? Well, guess what, Mr. Big Shot Bionically Enhanced Operative. I don't need orgasms. Not when I'm in a heat cycle. Don't you think I could take care of things myself if it were that simple?"

He sighed, finally turned to face her. "Then why are you craving my dick every four hours?"

"Your agency didn't hire you for your brains, did it? It's all about *your* orgasms. My body gets what it needs from your fluids, like any good animal does." It was her turn to smile now, and damned smugly too. "So we'll just see how up for this job you are. In the meantime, I hope you've got a backup plan."

He wanted to ask her what happened if she didn't get what she needed, but didn't want to give her the satisfaction. Still, she knew. She walked up to him, her eyes gleaming.

"If I don't get what I need, I die. Mate or die, Tommy. Like I said, I hope you're up for it, because my life is on the line." And then she marched past him, toward the main house, as every muscle in his body tensed.

Son of a bitch. He needed to get back into control, hit the ground running again and find some way to bring this forty-eight hours to a satisfactory close. "Kira, wait," he called. She stopped, her shoulders tightened but she didn't turn around to face him.

Instead, he closed the distance between them, ended up in front of her. "It's a lot to take in," he said.

She nodded, crossed her arms in front of her and looked somewhere over his shoulder before settling her gaze on him. "Are you saying you'll give me more time?"

"I can't do that. Wish I could. But here's the deal—in twenty-one hours, no matter what else happens, I'm out of here."

"And I have to go with you," she said.

"No, you don't. But what I told you before is true. Your life *is* in jeopardy." He spoke slowly, carefully, wanting his words to sink in but not wanting to use intimidation this time. "If you don't leave with me, you're going to be killed. And that's something I can promise you will happen."

"So I can stay here and take my chances or leave with you to-morrow night?"

"Yes."

She laughed, but it came out harsh and bitter. "That's not much of a choice."

"We never have much of a choice, Kira, no matter how much we try to kid ourselves."

She nodded slowly. "And you'll be, ah, around for me all day tomorrow?"

"Yeah. I'll be around for you," he said.

She turned and took a path that would lead her toward the barn instead of the main house, while he limped there instead. He'd take care of Derek, make a comms report to Itor using the codes Bryan had gotten for him. He knew trying to convince Kira to leave this fucking place before she was ready, if she was ever ready, was worthless. He was going to use tomorrow to get his freakin' perspective back so he could do the job he was sent here to do, no matter which way things went down.

RYAN MALMSTROM DISCONNECTED his comm link to the man who had just pretended to be Derek Martin. Whoever the guy had been, he'd done an admirable job with the impersonation, but Ryan was an expert in voice recognition and languages, and no one could fool him.

The consequences of being caught in a lie firmly in his mind, he e-mailed his Itor supervisor, a soft-spoken, stuffy Brit named Andrew, letting the guy know that everything on the animal whis-perer assignment was rock solid, that Derek had checked in as scheduled. And then Ryan signed the e-mail as Steve Kurtz, be-cause that was the name Itor had given him upon recruitment. All Itor agents took new names and identities.

Of course, Itor had no idea ACRO had given him a false identity as well, had named him Curtis Hancock and had planted him in the civilian world to make waves until Itor took notice and recruited him.

Such was the life of a secret agent.

A knock at the glass door of his tiny cubicle startled him, and he turned to see Gabrielle, a stunning blond psychic with a heart of titanium. She didn't wait for permission to open his door. "Have you heard from Victor?"

He shook his head. "He's not due to check in for another day."

She sniffed, shut the door. No thanks, no acknowledgment, no fuck you. Bitch. It wasn't his fault her precious Victor, a Dreamer who got off on giving people nightmares that caused heart attacks, hadn't completed his assignment in Israel.

A green flashing symbol appeared on his computer, and he opened the file sent by someone a lot higher up in Itor than anyone he'd met, and cursed at the photo on the screen. A photo meant to titillate. Yeah, right.

His boss at ACRO had cooked up a full meal deal when he created an identity meant to lure Itor to Ryan, and that identity included an extreme BDSM fetish. The more depraved a person was, the easier to control them through their desires, and Itor thought they had him under their thumbs. Small gifts, like the picture on his screen, were supposed to make him happy and hard.

They made him want to take Itor down from the very top to the bottom, to erase every one of the sick bastards from existence, especially because he knew the picture was only the beginning of today's *gifts*. Tonight they'd send him a woman. Hopefully, this time a willing one, because he couldn't afford to fake illness again to get out of a potentially nightmarish situation.

Yeah, these fucks needed to go down. Unfortunately, doing so would take time and a hell of a lot more freedom than he'd been given. He didn't even know which of Itor's six main sites he'd been taken to. All he knew was that the sites were located outside the United States, all in different countries, which ensured that the destruction of one would in no way cripple the agency.

Their paranoia didn't end there. Until new agents proved their allegiance, constant surveillance kept them in check, and regular interrogation and intrusive psychic procedures kept them honest.

Fortunately for Ryan, his gifts went well beyond the ability to learn any language in a matter of hours and crack language-based codes. He could also portion out his thoughts, something many psychics could do on a limited basis to fool other psychics, but that he'd taken to an exceptional level.

Instead of separating a single thought from his mind and circulating it like a shield that guarded his true thoughts, as most psychics did, he could create entire scenes, histories, stories. He would then arrange them inside an imaginary force field surrounding his mind, where it effectively blocked all attempts to penetrate. Anyone sifting around inside his head came away with innocuous images of his childhood, some bogus college recollections and perverted depictions of his false sexual fetishes.

The ability made him the only ACRO agent capable of infiltrating Itor.

His true talent, though, the one ACRO and Itor hired him for and that complemented his talent for language, was his ability to use any mode of electrical connection to step inside another person, to see, briefly, through that person's eyes.

Which was why, when he'd been speaking with "Derek" a few moments ago, he'd seen a few fleeting images of animals, a bedroom and the speaker's foot. Had the guy looked in the mirror, Ryan might have recognized him. Then again, he'd not met every ACRO agent, not even close. And it was possible the guy wasn't ACRO. He could be a free agent, or even someone from a U.S. government agency.

What he had learned, though, was that whoever's eyes he'd been looking through had been resistant to his presence. Probably not on a conscious level, but the guy's mind had definitely not wanted Ryan there, and the images had been disjointed, fuzzy and unremarkable.

He wished like hell he could contact ACRO and find out more, but communications with his agency had to remain limited and be carefully arranged with no deviations from standard operating procedure. Anything else could put his assignment—and his life—at risk.

Besides, his assignment wasn't to assist any of the dozens of ACRO missions taking place around the world. His objective was to gather intelligence, and since he was the first to have gotten in—alive and as something other than a prisoner anyway—he had to let the small fish go and stay focused on the trophy tuna.

It was a mission that could potentially last for years, and one that could get him very dead after long hours of painful torture. No fucking way was he ever going to be tortured again.

So yeah, whoever that guy had been on the phone, if he was ACRO, he was on his own. Ryan had bought him some time with his false report to Andrew, but the dude had better keep his ass covered. The other Itor agent sent as backup hadn't checked in, so the next time "Derek" called, Ryan would have to report the impersonation.

And Itor would descend on the target in force.

CHAPTER
Eight

WEDNESDAY MID-MORNING

Annika stalked into Dev's office, her head pounding for a lot of reasons, but the raging hangover topped the list.

"Rough night?" Dev asked over the rim of his coffee cup, and she didn't bother to ask how he knew. Anyone who considered his blindness a handicap underestimated him big-time.

"*Rough* is putting it mildly."

After Creed had left her spitting mad at the shithole bar, she'd slammed nearly a dozen shots of tequila, flirted with as many guys, who couldn't come close to comparing to Creed, and then when one got a little too friendly, she'd reacted badly enough to start a brawl. A brawl she'd also ended.

"I've been trying to get hold of you since last night. You haven't answered my calls." She tossed a key onto his desk. "And you changed your locks."

He cocked an eyebrow and put down his cup. "You broke into my house ten times before I gave you a key, and you're saying you couldn't get in?"

She snorted. Yeah, she'd found ways into his supersecure

fortress of a house, mostly by frying his security systems, but every time she broke in, he thanked her for finding a weakness and then fixed the problem so no one could gain entrance the same way again. His house was now impenetrable, and he knew it.

"I finally had to make an appointment to see you."

"*You* made an appointment?"

"Well, no. But I thought about it." For all of two seconds. Then she showed up at Dev's office and stared at Marlena until the other woman huffed and buzzed her in.

The computer next to him beeped, and he ran his fingers over the touch pad before asking, "What happened last night that you needed to see me so badly?"

"Nothing much, really. Just some asshole totally dumped me in this dive. Left me alone like an idiot with a bunch of psycho strangers."

Dev breathed a lengthy, tolerant sigh. "You were assisting CIA operatives on missions when you were nine, Annika. You were a world-class assassin at the age of fourteen. You can shock an entire room full of people into unconsciousness with a single touch. So I know you aren't asking me to believe you were scared and helpless."

She felt her cheeks heat, because yeah, that line wasn't going to work and she shouldn't have tried. Dev never let her get away with anything other than the truth. But the truth, beyond the fact that she'd simply not wanted to be alone, wasn't something she wanted to share. They'd talked about her past, her childhood, the things she'd done in the name of national security and world peace. They discussed things she never opened up about to anyone, but her sex life had been largely ignored, probably because, ick, it would be like talking orgasms with a parent.

Not that she knew what a parent was, since the CIA couple who raised her from the age of two had gone through the motions to give her a pseudo-normal childhood, but had never succeeded. Not when the word *love* had never been spoken. And not when games like hide-and-seek were played with Tasers, and "family" camping trips turned out to be exercises in survival. And how many parents not only taught a six-year-old how to play poker, but how to slit a throat with the king of hearts?

"Why did you change the locks, Dev? What's been going on with you lately?"

"It's a private matter. I don't want you involved."

Private matter. Hurt winged through her. He'd locked her out of his house, and now out of whatever was going on with him. "Whatever it is, I can help. I want to help."

"Out of the question. This is something I have to deal with on my own. The fewer people who are involved—"

"Who are they?" Jealousy lashed at her. Control had been drilled into her from an early age, but restraint had always been an issue, and she didn't know how to handle an emotion she'd never experienced. "Why do you trust someone else but not me?"

Throwing back his head, he closed his eyes, and she knew why he'd been avoiding her. He didn't want to have this conversation. "Annika, you have to let this go." He dropped his head to spear her with a fierce stare despite his blindness. "Now."

"Fine," she snapped. "Then send me on an assignment. Get me out of your hair. Obviously, that's what you want."

Another tolerant sigh stirred the papers on his desk, fueling her anger. She wasn't a goddamned child.

"You know the rules. Everyone takes downtime following a mission, and you need it."

"How the hell do you know what I need? Well, you might know if you'd deigned to see me last night. You might know how the only guy I've ever slept with totally dissed me like I'm not good enough for him." The sting of tears burned her eyes, which pissed her off more, because Creed wasn't worth a single tear. It wasn't like there was anything between them. She ground her teeth and clenched her fists in her lap. "Doesn't matter. It was nothing but sex anyway."

"Some asshole was using you for sex?"

We were using each other.

"It's more complicated than——"

"*You're having sex?*" he asked, as though what she'd said had only now sunk in.

"Dev. Hello...I'm not a kid anymore."

A fact he'd apparently not confronted even when he'd learned about her private lessons with a Seducer when she turned eighteen. It had only made sense that she learn to kiss, to touch, to blow a guy's mind as well as his dick, should the situation arise, if she was going to be a convincing agent. Since she hadn't been able to have sex to gain the experience on her own, Seducer training filled in the gap.

Dev had acknowledged that fact with dignity, grace and only a little cursing...but when she went for her next lesson, the Seducer, Adam, had all but slammed the door in her face. To this day, he paled when he saw her, and she wondered what, exactly, Dev had said to the poor guy.

"What's his name?" Dev demanded.

Annika almost smiled at the big brother act, because even though she didn't have a brother, she imagined one might sound a little like Dev right now. Sure, she was upset at having been locked out of his life all of a sudden, but now she knew it wasn't because he didn't care about her.

"Do you tell me the names of everyone you sleep with?" The list would read like a phone book. She couldn't count the number of times she'd gone to his house and had to hang out by herself until he finished with whoever he had in bed at the time.

He cursed, long and loud. "Look, I don't think it's a good idea for you to be in a relationship right now."

"What do you mean, 'right now'?"

"You're young——"

"I'm almost twenty-fucking-two!"

To his credit, he looked a little uncomfortable as he shifted in his seat. "Physically."

"Oh, so, what? You're saying I'm emotionally retarded?"

"I'm saying that you didn't have a normal upbringing. You

could be vulnerable to some bastard who doesn't understand you." He shot her a pointed look. "Or who wants you for one thing and you mistake it for something else."

"Oh, God. You're reading way too many chick magazines. Sex isn't love. I get it." And her mistaking sex for love was so not the problem here. The problem was that Creed was an arrogant asshole who thought he could tease her and then leave her high and dry. He'd rejected her, when all she'd wanted was sex. It wasn't like she was asking for a damned commitment. What the hell was his problem?

"Just do me a favor and stay away from men for a while, okay? Especially the son of a bitch who took advantage of you."

She wanted to tell him that Creed had done nothing of the sort, but a glance at her watch told her she was late for the martial arts class she taught on base to operatives, so instead she stood.

"Then send me on an assignment. Anywhere. Anything. I need to get away." She needed to be needed. And since Dev clearly didn't need her for whatever supersecret bullshit he was dealing with, a job would take her mind off things.

"Annika—"

"*Please.*"

Silence stretched, and then Dev gave a slow nod. "I'll see what I can dig up."

"Thank you."

"Don't thank me. I'm not doing you any favors. You need the break." He sighed. "I can never say no to you."

"You spoil me." And she wasn't so spoiled that she couldn't see that. He'd always been good to her, even when she didn't deserve it. "Dev?"

"Hmm?"

"Why didn't you put me down?"

His eyebrows rose half an inch, probably matching hers. She'd been as surprised by the question as he was, because although she'd always wondered, she'd been afraid to ask.

"You were sixteen when you came here. A kid. I wasn't going to kill a kid no matter how dangerous you were."

He was such a softie. How he managed to run an operation like ACRO with a soft streak like that was beyond her. "You still didn't need to keep trying to reel me in. You could have caged me in a dungeon and let me rot. Killed me on my eighteenth birthday. It would have been the smart thing to do."

Especially after what she'd done to him and several other ACRO agents.

They'd kept her locked in a training cell, and after she'd seriously injured a couple of her handlers, they'd resorted to speaking with her through the comms system, and tranquilizing her for medical appointments. Dev came daily for weeks, trying to talk her down, but she hadn't believed anything anyone said to her. Finally, she settled down, tricked them into thinking they'd won.

And when Dev came into her cell to talk to her face-to-face, she'd sent enough volts into him to knock him across the room. She'd escaped, had run out of the training building and into the main compound, where alarms were blaring and operatives were swarming. They'd surrounded her, dozens of them. She'd put up her electrical field so no one could touch her, and she could have gone through the crowd that way, except that something had held her immobile.

Later, she'd learned her capturer was a telekinetic named Dawn, but even without the invisible hold, Annika doubted she'd have moved.

The people circling her were just like Dev had described. She'd lived her life with the CIA believing she was unique, a weapon with no function except to kill. But to her right a man was bouncing balls of fire off his fingertips. To her left, a woman levitated a foot off the ground. The woman in front of her unzipped her black flight suit and stepped out of it . . . and instantly blended into the background like a chameleon.

Annika had stood there, openmouthed, gaping at the group, and when Dev pushed his way through the crowd, limping, his arm at an awkward angle and blood streaming from a gash in his scalp, she released the power she'd been holding. Dev had nodded at Dawn, and suddenly Annika was free.

Dev had held out his hand, and without a word, she'd taken it, allowed him to lead her to his office, where, after he'd been stitched up and his shoulder dislocation repaired, he'd explained again what ACRO was about, and how she would never be used the way the CIA had used her.

He'd rescued her that day, had saved her life when he'd had every right to take it. She owed him, and though she was angry at being shut out, she couldn't be an outright jerk.

In fact, she should probably tell him that if he needed anything, she would be there for him—but then, he knew that.

And obviously it didn't matter to him.

WEDNESDAY 6:30 P.M. MST

Deb was good for something, although if she'd been expecting anything from Ender in return, she'd have been sorely mistaken. *Sore* being the key word, because he'd suddenly felt the overwhelming urge to hang a shingle around himself that read Stud Services Inc. And he was damned tired of drinking water and Gatorade.

He'd had to endure Babs, the Weimaraner, staring at him with her head tilted and a look of *You're gonna get it,* as he'd cooked right on Kira's stove the two huge hamburgers with real freakin' meat Deb had snuck him. And then he'd stuffed them into his mouth after he shoved them between the only bread Kira seemed to own, some sprouted wheat shit that almost made him vomit. But he needed the protein, and dammit, so did she.

"Don't start with me," he told the dog. "Because you have no idea what I'm dealing with. Oh, hell, you're a female. Maybe you do."

Babs stood and wagged her tail, and he groaned.

He'd been staying busy around the farm, keeping track of Kira and making sure nothing else was going on behind the scenes. Itor would never hit during the day anyway—too many people, too many tourists.

And, like clockwork, every four hours Kira would look at him, the desperation in her eyes hard for him to miss now that he knew exactly what it was all about.

He wondered why the hell it bothered him, the fact that he could've been any stud servicing her, that she just needed sex, not sex from him. *No ties that bind forever* had always been his motto. But ties that bind for a few hours, well, sure, those were the best kind.

The kind that almost took you out last night, asshole.

Maybe that was it. His ego had taken a nice hit, the bruise that ran across the front of his neck a painful, visual reminder, and he was doing everything in his power to live up to his boast, to prepare for when she whispered against him, *Come on, Tommy. Take me, right now. I can't wait.*

Like a living, breathing dream, except his dick was so sore he was afraid, for the first time in his life, that it might actually fall off from overuse. Talk about taking one for the proverbial team.

He'd survived wars. Bullets. And sex was going to be the thing to kill him.

And suddenly, he knew the reason why Dev sent him in alone on this one. Nothing to do with his hard heart and everything to do with his sex drive and his rejuvenative powers. But shit, Dev had underestimated this one, and so had everyone at ACRO. Not that they'd have had any way of knowing that Kira needed more than sex for survival. That was a nice little bomb she'd dropped in his lap last night. Mate or die.

He'd made sure she'd been mated with, all right. His pride stirred more than a little, because he had to admit he'd done a damned fine job of keeping her satisfied over the past twenty-four hours. Being an excedo did have its perks.

His meal had energized him slightly. He checked his watch, saw that early evening had come up more quickly than he'd realized. He had just enough time to make a quick sweep of the area before Kira needed him again. She'd pop a vein when she smelled the hamburger on him, and for the first time that day, he was actually looking forward to seeing her.

CHAPTER
Nine

WEDNESDAY 9 P.M. MST

It was Kira's favorite time of the day. After sunset when the refuge volunteers had gone, and the exotic part of the sanctuary was alive with the sounds of nocturnal animals becoming active.

She made her rounds, checked the critters with health issues first. Inside the small building used to house animals under veterinary care, a severely malnourished black bear still struggled to survive, but the other dozen animals that had suffered at the hands of humans were doing well.

She only wished she could say the same. How could her life have gone bad so quickly? Yesterday she'd been happy. As content as she could be anyway, given that she was wanted in several states and had been entering into the seasonal cycle that made her life a living hell. Now, twenty-four hours later, she'd seen a man killed, had learned her farmhands had been slaughtered, had been taken hostage by a thug who wanted her to work for his secret thug agency, and then she'd practically forced said thug to have sex with her.

Swallowing a groan, she stepped into the wolf pen and played with the dozen wolves and wolf-hybrids, let them tell her about their day. The easiest of the nondomestic animals to communicate with, wolves were so open to learning and sharing.

Unlike a certain male human she'd attacked for sex.

This time she did groan, sank onto a boulder and let the wolves surround her. She had no idea what had happened, had very little memory of the events following the oral sex. All she knew was that desperation had seized her, and then she found herself on top of Tom, milking his orgasm for what she needed. Flashes of her actions punched her brain in tiny, painful blows.

She'd leaped on him. Nearly choked him with the cuffs. Snarled like a demon.

Never, ever, in her twenty-seven years had she been so out of control. Not when she diligently planned every aspect of her life in order to avoid desperation and a loss of restraint. To avoid the sickness and pain that came when sex didn't.

And now the strangeness surrounding her had thrown all her careful planning into chaos, had turned her life upside down and left her spinning and as powerless as a turtle on its back. Tom certainly hadn't helped things by taking her prisoner and taunting her.

To be fair, though, he'd revised his ultimatum, had at least given her the illusion of having a choice. Go with him and live, or stay and die. The part of her that liked to breathe wanted to go. The stubborn part of her, the same part that didn't trust anyone who even hinted at being military or government, wanted to stay and prove she could make it on her own. Even if staying meant leaving on her own terms later. She'd done it before.

Confusion ate at her. She'd fed all her house animals and left notes for the owners, just in case. But no matter what she decided, she'd still have to deal with Tom, would have to actually speak with him shortly. Her time was almost up, and they'd left things open-ended and awkward last night.

It was clear that he'd been clueless regarding the seriousness of her sexual needs, and oddly enough, he seemed to be trying to make it up to her. Their matings since the incident in the field had been silent, but he'd been attentive, had taken the time to make her come over and over.

He'd stayed with her after the first time, like he wanted to talk, but she'd fled. Her emotions had become a jumbled mess...she hated him for tearing apart her life, yet her confusion over how she'd taken him like an uncontrolled beast stabbed at her like the tines on a pitchfork. He could have stopped her, but she wouldn't have made it easy, and he'd have had to hurt her. Obviously, he didn't want to hurt her, or he'd have done it already.

Or maybe his bosses had wanted her unharmed. So they could harm her themselves, experiment on her, like what happened in movies. And what if his agency was the bad one, and Derek had belonged to the good one? What Derek had said about the lemonade had sparked a memory, and after putting two and two together, she realized her curry had not gone bad, that Tom had drugged them. Besides, she had no proof that one word Tom said had been the truth, and she'd smelled meat on him during their last mating, so really, she shouldn't suffer guilt over anything.

Feeling inexplicably better, she bid the wolves good night and headed toward the big cat pens.

At the entrance to the fully enclosed area that housed nearly fifty cats ranging from ocelots to tigers, she paused. The throbbing had begun, and she'd need Tom again in a few minutes. She hung her head and closed her eyes, because dammit, she'd give anything to have another man right about now, one who wasn't so scary, who didn't bury bodies as easily as he breathed. Maybe she should have tried to run for it today, tried to sneak out with the visitors.

But if he was right, if he was her only hope...she couldn't risk running. Not even to find someone else to service her.

One thing was certain: She wasn't joining his stupid agency. Once the threat was over, maybe she could return here. If she was still in danger, she could assume yet another name and find work elsewhere. She was an expert at starting over, had been ever since she'd been forced to leave her dog training business after some men had piled out of a van one day and tried to drag her inside.

Her dogs had saved her, but at a high price—a dozen had been killed. She'd had to go on the run, because the men came back two days later, and suddenly the police, who had lauded her as the best trainer of police dogs in the world, had suddenly decided to arrest her.

She'd had no doubt that the government had been behind the van incidents, as well as the sudden police turnaround. She'd been arrested too many times for disturbing the peace and for suspicion of being an accomplice in violent animal-rights crimes. But now, after what Tom had said, she wasn't so sure about who had tried to grab her.

The sound of a tiger chuff brought her back into the present, where her body was craving Tom, but if this was the last time she'd ever see her babies, she needed to spend time with them first. Besides, he would be keeping a close eye on his watch and would find her, if he wasn't already nearby. She sniffed the breeze but caught no trace of him, which meant little; he could be upwind.

"Hey, kids," she said, as she stepped inside the main entrance and then carefully closed the gate.

A black jaguar stretched up the chain-link fence next to her in greeting, and she stuck her hand through the feeding slot to scratch his belly. Smiling, she passed the lynx and cougar pens, giving everyone an affectionate pat. She entered the two lion and liger—lion/tiger hybrids—pens to play with them for a bit, and then she visited the refuge's three Siberian tigers.

The two females, Anya and Nika, immediately settled into deep, rumbling purring as they brushed against her hips, knocking her around the pen with their gentle enthusiasm. Anya playfully hooked her paw around Kira's calf and pulled, nearly dumping her on her butt.

Across the pen, Pasha, the big white male, paced. He kept his head low, his eyes locked on Kira. One lip lifted in a half snarl.

"What are you doing, boy?" she asked, and he didn't answer.

Pasha often didn't. Fiercely intelligent, he'd always been difficult to read, one of the few animals she'd encountered who could block her probing mind.

Anya and Nika began a wrestling match, and Pasha roared. He took a step toward Kira, his sharp teeth flashing in the overhead refuge lights.

"You think you're tough, huh?" She bent at the waist, caught his gaze and held it, something no one should ever try with a big cat.

Pasha snarled, crouched.

She took a slow, stalking step toward him. He growled low in his throat. She growled back.

"You don't want to mess with me, baby," she whispered, and this time she got a response. A vision. A picture of her trapped beneath him, his mouth closed around her skull.

She wheeled around, took three steps, and then suddenly she was on the ground with seven hundred pounds of tiger on top of her. Rancid, hot puffs of breath washed over her face as Pasha opened his mouth around her head. Hard teeth bit into her scalp, but the pressure, though intense, didn't hurt.

You win, Pasha. But I'm getting faster. I got an extra step in tonight.

The big cat made some snorting noises and released her head, but he held her down just because he could. She felt a mouth close around her foot, and another around her arm. The affection, respect and gratitude all three cats felt for her shimmered across her body, made it tingle in the way it always did when animals communicated their emotions.

The tigers sensed her worry, and were, in their tiger way, trying to comfort her.

She sent all the love and comfort right back at them, because she had no idea what the future held for them, and they needed support more than she did.

Lying there like a big chew toy, she glanced at her watch, surprised that she'd spent over two hours saying good-bye to her babies. Then again, the tension crackling inside could have clued her in to the time. She closed her eyes, concentrated on holding back the throbbing need that would, in a moment, force her to seek out

Tom. Heat built in her veins, desire stretched through her like a deep, sexy moan. The scent of sun-warmed skin and grass tickled her nostrils as her body remembered his smell. Wetness bloomed between her legs as it prepared to mate, and ravenous hunger clawed at her.

The beast wanted to be fed.

CHAPTER *Ten*

WEDNESDAY 11 P.M. MST

Twenty hours and counting, and Ender found himself flat on his back on the bed in his overheated room in the old farmhouse, staring up at the ceiling. He wanted to be on the road before midnight. Midnight was when the security that surrounded the refuge pared down considerably, leaving two lonely guards on either side of the large plot of land. Since the refuge didn't officially close until ten, and some nights even later depending on foot traffic and tours that got waylaid looking at the more exotic animals, he wasn't worried that Itor would come in much sooner than that. Many animals preferred to hunt their prey under the cover of night, and he was no exception.

No, he had other things he was worried about. Like if Kira had made her choice yet. He hadn't been able to get a read off her all day, his brain effectively turning to mush when he was in her presence and turning off when he was inside her. At that point, he was powerless to do anything but let everything else wash away but the feel of flesh on flesh.

Had *he* made *his* choice was the bigger question, and one he refused to answer. Instead, he hoisted himself off the mattress and threw his belongings into the bag he'd brought with him to the refuge yesterday. After studying his gun for a second, he loaded it, unlocked the safety and tucked it into the bag's front pocket. The bag hung at hip level, the pocket perfect for easy access without calling too much attention if his hand rested there. Now he just needed to find her.

Their last mating, as she liked to call it, was a little over four hours ago, and he'd been surprised that she hadn't come into the house to get him by now. He'd told her where he'd be and normally she was on him before he had a chance to go looking. And while nothing tripped his internal alarm, his gut still tightened and his gait took on speed. He used the cover of dark and a backwoods path that only the workers used, to arrive within seconds at the more secluded part of the refuge, the place where Kira told him she always ended her days.

The wolves lifted their heads and began a mournful howl as he sped past them, his radar honed for Kira. He was almost at the end of the line of the large habitats when he saw her, inside the cage with the tigers. With the biggest of the big cats lying on top of her, mouth open and teeth bared.

For a second, he froze in place, afraid that a move on his part could startle the black and white beast whose jaws were too close to Kira's neck for his comfort. His hand moved slowly to the gun in his bag, and the only thing stopping him from taking the tiger out immediately was the fact that Kira would probably never forgive him.

Since when did he give a shit what anyone thought about him?

Forgiveness was the last thing he'd ever needed. And this would be a perfect opportunity to do his job with a captive audience.

What the fuck was happening to him? He'd thought maybe the lack of protein had screwed with his head, and while he did feel stronger after eating the burgers earlier, his mind was still not fully his. It hadn't been since he'd caught wind of Kira.

His hand steadied on the grip of the gun when both the tiger and Kira turned their heads toward him. He nodded, waited for her to give him some kind of signal, something, any way to help her, when suddenly she hooked a strong leg around the tiger's back. He tensed, the tiger snarled and let itself flip onto its back and Kira just rubbed a hand over its stomach as it lay, belly up and purring like some kind of fucking house cat.

She smiled over at him and he got a sudden, intense hit of just how unbelievably special this woman was.

All he could do was shake his head at her and turn away so she wouldn't see the relief on his face. He took his hand away from the butt of the gun, let the bag drop to the ground. He let his legs sink to the soft earth and he lay on his back like the tiger, stared up at the stars and let Kira finish whatever it was she was doing.

Within minutes, he heard the soft clink of a cage closing, a low, collective growl from the big cats that reverberated through to his soul, and saw Kira standing over him.

"What the fuck was that all about?" he asked. She smiled down at him, her skin damp from exertion, her eyes liquid amber under heavy lids. Her full lips remained slightly parted, the tip of her tongue peeking through her teeth. For the first time in all of this, he wanted to sweep her mouth with his, and he tore his gaze away. The tank top she wore emphasized her full breasts, nipples already hard with excitement, and she still wore the shorts he'd been pulling off of her all day. In the barn. By the old well. In the kitchen. And in the small bathroom reserved for the tourists. They'd nearly taken the sink off the wall with that one.

"Are you jealous? Do you want to wrestle with me, big boy?" Her voice was throaty, sounded slightly out of breath as she placed her feet on either side of his hips and lowered herself onto him, too reminiscent of last night for comfort.

"I'm not a boy, Kira. I thought I'd proven that to you by now," he said quietly, his body tensing against hers as she brought her hands to run along his shoulders, up his neck and then through his hair. He smelled her, the need, the want thoroughly imbibed by his nervous system until it cut away his vision for anything else but her.

He reached behind his neck to grab her wrists and push them away, down to her sides. She growled, deep in her throat, brought her hands back up and tried to lie on him, but he used his speed to grab and pin her to the ground, much in the same way he'd seen the male tiger do.

She arched against him, her ass rubbing demandingly against his crotch, and he pressed her, not so gently, into the dirt. Jesus Christ, his heart was still racing, even though she was safely out of the cage and in his arms and for a second he buried his face in her hair, smelling the scent that was uniquely hers.

As much as he wanted to know what choice she'd made, he wanted this moment more.

"What took you so long?" she was asking, palms down and still pushing against the ground and against him at the same time. He finally let her, eased himself back until she was up on all fours. His hand drifted around to her waist, slid along her flat abs to unbutton her shorts and yank them down. She lifted her knees slightly off the ground so he could drag the fabric past them, and left the shorts to tangle around her ankles, keeping her legs locked in place as his fingers began to stroke her. He kept his other hand steady and heavy on her lower back, grounding her, while she lifted her head and groaned, pushed back against his steady rhythm.

This was the first time he'd teased her all day—he'd learned his lesson effectively last night, but now ... now he wanted to play, didn't want a quick end.

"Are you okay, Kira?" he asked.

"Yes. Oh, yes," she murmured. He pulled her shorts off her ankles and spread her legs wider. He bent his head to taste her again, letting his tongue dip into her sweet wetness, licking, sucking her clit, using her hips to push her against him in order to get deeper inside of her as her orgasms started to roll through her. She came against his lips, his teeth, over and over until he realized he could die happily, just like this.

For a second, he wondered what it would be like, what *she* would be like, when she wasn't in a heat cycle, and pushed that thought out of his head. He wouldn't be around for that.

She wouldn't want you anyway.

He nibbled her thigh, reluctant to part with what he was doing to give her what she needed. But her breath had started to come fast, and her head hung low and he knew this was a test of trust.

He knelt behind her, brushed his erection between her soft folds. She shivered, let out a laugh laced with relief. No matter how many times he'd taken her today, his dick sprang to life from the dead whenever he was in range of her pheromones.

He took her with one long stroke and her pussy contracted around his cock greedily. He bent forward so he was on all fours too, his body covering hers as they rocked together, hard and fast, their groans mingling with the howls that surrounded them in the dark.

His orgasm took him by surprise—he'd been concentrating on her so much, he hadn't realized how close to the edge she'd brought him. He lifted his head toward the sky, let out something akin to a howl as the blood coursed through his veins, and he felt more alive than he had in a long time.

He rested his forehead against the bare skin on her upper back, where her top had risen up, while he tried to put his mind in working order. After a minute, he released her hips, rested on his knees. She straightened and stretched while he watched the scattering of muscles on her slim back flex.

She was so much stronger than she looked.

She turned and he handed over her shorts, stood to pull his own jeans up. He checked his watch: 2330. Too close to midnight for comfort.

"You're leaving?" she asked, her eyes on his bag. He nodded, lifted it and put it on his shoulder. He let his hand rest casually against the outside flap and waited a beat.

His throat went dry when she didn't say anything else, just zipped and buttoned her shorts and tucked in the tank top. Then she looked back at the cage that held the big cats. They were resting, a big pile of fur together by the large rocks in the far corner.

"I can't," she started, and his palm tensed against the cool gunmetal.

He'd slipped his hand inside the pocket, his subconscious taking over because it knew his conscious mind was too full of thoughts, of sex, of Kira, of everything, to do the job it needed to do. The part of him that was trained not to give a shit about anything but the job would take her down without a moment's hesitation.

Doing it quickly wasn't going to make it hurt any less. "So you're staying?" he asked, and fuck, why was he still stalling for time?

"I can't leave the animals unprotected," she said, her eyes begging him to understand. "I want to go with you. I'm just not sure. I believe you when you say that I'm in danger, but who's going to protect them?"

He drew in a deep breath, letting the oxygen flood his lungs, but he didn't move his hand off the gun. "If I call in backup now, your choice to join my agency goes out the window," he said. "And I can't afford to keep you here that long."

"Do you think they'll be safe?"

"I think you're the main target, so I don't think they'd waste their time here. But I can't promise that." *Can't promise you shit.*

He reminded himself that he'd already made her promises, and let his trigger finger curl, as he had so many times before, around the pistol's hard, worn trigger guard.

One shot, straight through the heart, would kill her instantly. Where that would leave her animals was none of his concern. Where that would leave him should be none of his either.

"I haven't agreed to join your agency," she said.

"I know."

"And you're not going to force me to join?"

"Have I forced you to do anything you didn't want to since I've been here?" he asked, flashed back to her holding him by the throat against the grass. His free hand moved to his neck, which still bore light bruises, and he wondered if he'd saved her life last night for no good reason.

He could let her run on her own, give her time to escape, hold off Itor. But that would be like giving the fox to the hounds. She wouldn't have a chance, didn't know how to hide herself properly. And every spring, she'd be open to anyone's suggestion.

"No, you haven't forced me to do anything I didn't want to." Her voice was soft, thoughtful. God, he wished she wasn't watching him like that.

According to Dev, she was far too dangerous to leave alive. Her potential as a biological weapon of mass destruction was too real a threat. That's what he needed to concentrate on . . . his job.

"I need to know your choice," he said, his voice oddly soft.

She opened her mouth, and he knew her answer was still no. Before she could utter a word, he heard a low, menacing chorus of growls coming from the tiger pen behind her. She turned to them and then back to him and his hand stayed steady on the metal, his heart rate slowed.

"What's happening?" she asked, her voice a whisper, and he didn't know if she was asking him or the animals. He surveyed the area, didn't sense any danger.

When he looked toward the tigers, he noted they were staring directly at him. *Shit.*

"The animals say I'm in danger," Kira said. "That there's someone here who wants to kill me. Tommy, who's here?"

Ender took full advantage of the situation, trying not to let his voice show his relief that there might be another option. Still, he refused to pull his hand off the trigger. "It could be people from Derek's team. I've told you that they're coming."

She bit her bottom lip and moved toward him. The animals' growling got louder. "When I get settled someplace new, will I be able to get some of my animals? Babs and Spazzy and . . ."

"Yeah. I'll make sure of it," he said. "What does this mean, Kira?"

"Keep me safe, Tommy," she said. He let out a long breath, and only then did he take his hand out of his bag. He flexed it by his thigh.

Technically, his job wasn't done—she hadn't agreed to join the agency, but he could get her to that point. A few more hours wouldn't matter.

"We've got to go. Now," he said. He heard howls in the distance, as if the other animals were getting in on the act.

"We can take my truck," she said, pointed to the blue pickup parked across the field. "The keys are already in the ignition."

"Let's go." He took her arm and ran with her to the vehicle. But as they approached, the pungent smell of gasoline hit him, and *fuck*, maybe the animals weren't growling only at him. "The gas line's been cut."

He pulled Kira behind him, scanned the area and saw nothing. This was not good. If Itor had taken the time to do that, that meant they'd done something to disable each and every vehicle left here overnight.

"What happens now?"

"We go on foot," he said.

"I'm just going to grab my bag. Is it all right to go into the cab?" she asked.

They wouldn't have wired the car to blow—Kira was much too valuable for something like that. "It's fine. But I thought you said you weren't sure you were going to leave with me?"

She pulled a bright pink backpack from the backseat of the truck. Yeah, *that* was going to camouflage well. "I always have a bag packed...just in case I have to run."

"That happens often?" he asked.

"Often enough."

Speaking of enough... "We've got to get the hell out of here and fast. I've got some BDUs I'm going to ask you to change into so we can move unnoticed during the day, but for now, keep up as best you can."

"And if I can't?"

"I'll carry you." He took her by the upper arm and led her into the woods behind the refuge. He saw the tears running down her cheeks, knew there was still more than a little resistance in her gait, but she'd just saved herself. And maybe, somehow, she'd saved him a little too.

CHAPTER
Eleven

THURSDAY 4:30 A.M. MST
Men with guns are bad. Tell others. Warn us.

The coyote paced, watching Kira—but mostly Tom—with suspicion. They'd startled the creature near a stream, and when Kira had called out with her mind, it had nearly tripped over its own feet. Domestic and captive wild animals were rarely surprised when they learned a human could communicate with them, but completely wild animals sometimes reacted badly. Fortunately, of all animal species, wild canines tended to be the most open and curious.

The coyote sniffed the air in all directions, then turned back to Kira. *Men bad.* She felt the sentiment more than saw it—she usually needed direct contact for images—and then he slipped into the darkness broken by the light of the full moon.

"I think he'll warn us if he sees more humans."

Tom nodded, glanced at his watch. "Let's take a breather. Get hydrated."

They'd stopped an hour or so ago to have brief but intense sex against a tree, but after more than four hours of moving almost nonstop, she was exhausted and not ashamed to sink down on the ground and rest. The cool Idaho night air felt good against her sweat-dampened skin, and despite the multitude of scratches from branches and bushes, she was glad Tom hadn't yet insisted that she don the BDUs he'd mentioned. She wondered how the clothes would look with her pink vegan hiking boots.

She gratefully took the water bottle he'd dug out of his bag. "So what happens when we get to this agency of yours?"

She'd been asking him questions since they left, but he hadn't done more than grunt, so she didn't expect much.

To her surprise, he looked out over the gurgling stream and said, "You'll probably be shown the animal facility. Then you'll be taken to the training quarters to be assigned trainers and a room."

"*If* I join. Which I won't. Ever."

"Doesn't matter. Whether you join or not, that's what'll happen. Everything at ACRO is strictly structured, and the training program is especially so. Anyone even considering joining has to go through the same process, has to stay on base. It's for the safety of both ACRO and the recruit."

"Great," she muttered. Sounded even more military than the military, and the urge to run, to escape Tom and his agency, struck her again. If her season hadn't started, she would have, but leaving now meant certain death. "I still don't understand any of this. Like, why is Derek's agency trying to kill me?"

He glanced at her, and then looked away. "Because they'd rather see you dead than in our hands."

"Why? Why am I so important that it's better to kill me than let another agency have me? Because if anyone thinks I'll train animals for war or some crap, there's no way."

"That's not what we want you for."

When he didn't offer any more in the way of explanation, she sighed. "So what'll happen when we get to ACRO and I need you? How will that work? Do they know about my situation? Will they understand?"

His fingers tightened around his water bottle, and she scented a note of irritation coming from him. Maybe she was asking too many questions, but dammit, this was her life.

"It won't be me, Kira."

"Oh."

She snapped her mouth shut, both hurt and embarrassed. Of course she shouldn't have expected Tom to be there for her later, but...

Idiot. I'm such a freakin' idiot.

Her face burned, and she was suddenly grateful for the early morning shadows. And why did his answer bother her anyway? Why should she feel even a small measure of hurt? Tom had made it clear that his job was to get her out of here alive. Nothing more. His life would probably improve considerably once she was out of his hair and rolling around with someone else.

Oh, God. What if...? "Will there be someone? They won't let me die, right? Not after all this."

Her voice had gone shaky and high-pitched and she didn't care, because panic had set in. Panic that she'd have to mate with some-one—maybe multiple someones—she'd trust even less than Tom. Panic that she might have no control over getting what she needed when she needed it.

The memory of the jail cell two years ago was still too fresh in her mind.

Tom didn't look at her. "ACRO has people who can deal specifically with your situation."

"People who just have sex? What kind of crazy operation do you work for?"

"Trust me, it'll make sense soon." He finally swung his gaze around to her. "And the Medical Division might even be able to come up with some sort of cure. A way to deal with your spring fever without sex."

"Really?" Her heart soared before she could bring it back down to earth, where it wouldn't shatter from the inevitable fall. "They could do that?"

"Maybe. I don't know."

For a moment, she let herself dream of life after a cure. She'd long ago given up on any hope that she'd have a normal existence, but if Tom's agency could give her that...

"I'd be able to do so many things," she breathed. "I could have friends. Maybe a family. Oh! And sex during the entire year."

Tom frowned. "You don't have sex except during your fever?"

She shook her head. "I learned a long time ago that my situation doesn't bode well for relationships. As soon as my season starts, women turn on me because their boyfriends and husbands paw at me. And whatever guy I'm dating thinks my sex drive is cool for a couple of days, but then, when he can't keep up . . . well, let's just say it isn't pretty."

Not pretty at all. During the years she'd been on her own, she'd had her vehicles and houses vandalized, painted with the words *slut* and *whore*, had been threatened, attacked, refused service in stores and restaurants, and much more than she'd ever shared with anyone.

"All of my relationships end in a lot of pain." Usually, though, the pain was one-sided. All hers.

"Why relationships, then? Why not just screw around? Have fun?"

"Because I screw around with strangers enough during the spring. With all the weirdos out there, why risk danger more than I have to? And the last thing I want to do is make people think I'm more of a whore than they already do."

"No one at ACRO will think you're a whore."

"No matter how many men are sent to service me?" she asked quietly, and she caught another whiff of irritation.

He stood abruptly, dug some water purification tablets out of his bag and added one to each of their bottles. "We need to move out." He took the bottles, sauntered to the stream and filled them.

"You didn't answer me."

He tucked the bottles back into his bag. "No matter how many," he said tightly. Then he hefted his bag and hers onto his shoulder and held out a hand to help her off the ground. "Now, let's go.

THE EARLY MORNING IDAHO DARKNESS posed no problem for Ryan, not when he was thousands of miles away and looking through the eyes of an excedosapien with natural night vision. The I-Agent, Jarrod Warren, spoke softly into his headset, letting Ryan know his every move.

First-mission jitters. Why Itor had sent in this rookie as secondary backup was a mystery, but then, Itor often did things that left Ryan shaking his head. Too many generals and not enough grunts made Itor more disorganized and more top-heavy than ACRO, which led to conflicting orders, rescinded orders...total chaos at times.

"Where's your partner?" Ryan asked, and Jarrod looked off toward a barn he hoped looked better during the day than it did at night.

"I don't know. Gina was standing right there by that haystack."

Unease settled in Ryan's gut, but he had no idea why. The disappearance of Jarrod's partner, an experienced pyrokinetic, probably meant that ACRO had arrived on scene at the animal refuge and was cleaning up. Had they also grabbed the animal whisperer and taken out the second Itor team? He wouldn't know; he wasn't Team Two's comms handler.

"I'm going to find Gina," Jarrod whispered, and Ryan sat back in his office chair, allowing his mind to absorb the sights Jarrod took in—like the shadow in the corner of his vision. Ryan heard a grunt, and then suddenly he was looking at the starry sky. Jarrod groaned, blinked repeatedly until a female face descended.

Annika?

The blond woman smiled, and yes, it was Annika. He'd know that frosty grin anywhere. There wasn't a single male at ACRO who wouldn't love to melt the bergs that flowed through her veins.

Of course, no one would dare try. Even those who might be willing to risk their lives to her dangerous talents wouldn't think of trespassing on their boss's territory. Everyone knew Dev and Annika had a thing, and only an idiot with a death wish would screw with either one of them.

Annika cocked her head and stared into Jarrod's eyes—Ryan's eyes—and his heart rate doubled. The things she could do to him, pleasant and unpleasant—God, maybe at the same time—icy sweat broke out on his forehead. He couldn't feel what Jarrod was feeling, but he saw what the other man saw, could feel the intensity in Annika's gaze.

"Where is the animal whisperer?" she asked, her voice tinny through the headset's static. "Is there another team?"

"Long gone," Jarrod moaned, and suddenly the view went fuzzy.

Blinding flashes of light burst behind Ryan's eyelids. He cried out and blasted backward in his chair. Everything went black, and he had to blink a few times to bring his own vision back into the light.

Annika had just shocked the shit out of Jarrod. Ryan shouldn't feel sorry for an Itor agent, but he did. A lot of Itor's operatives thought they were playing for the good guys.

Taking a steadying breath, he pushed his intercom button. Team Two's comms handler answered.

"I lost my team," Ryan said, hoping the other man would say the same. Laughter boomed in his ears.

"My team is in pursuit of the animal whisperer. She's being protected by only one ACRO puss. We'll have them both in a matter of hours."

"I'll inform Mr. Blake." Ryan hung up and clenched his teeth. He prayed whoever had been charged to protect Kira was good—the best—because Team Two had experience and not a small amount of insanity going for it.

Kira and her agent could be in for the fight of their lives.

CHAPTER
Twelve

Creed kicked open the door to the main conference room with one heavily booted foot and entered, bringing with him a buzz of energy that disrupted every mind in the room, except Dev's, scattered their psychic senses like marbles and left them shaking their heads to clear them.

Creed's physical appearance didn't help—even to those who knew him, he came across as more than a little shocking. A broad six feet, five inches, long dark hair tied at the nape of his neck, and piercings that ran up his left ear, his chin, a labret through his eyebrow, a ball through his tongue—Dev didn't want to know if there were any more hidden ones. Add to that the tattoos that covered the right half of his face, neck and body giving him a yin-yang appearance that unnerved even the most jaded of ACRO operatives. Forget people from the real world.

The head-to-toe black leather also added a nice touch.

Creed ignored everyone to hone in on Dev, just as Dev knew he would. And Dev felt an instant twang of relief on seeing the younger ghost translator—the first time anything or anyone had taken the edge off since last night when the spirit made its appearance.

"You're early," Dev said.

"I thought we weren't calling in ghost hunters anymore after that last incident with the Bell Witch," one of the older psychics sniffed, referencing the spirit that Creed supposedly descended from. Dev made a mental note to send one of the male Seducers, or two, to her house later that night. She needed something to improve her outlook.

"I made the appointment with Devlin, not the other way around," Creed lied, just the way Dev had asked him to. "A private appointment. And leave the Bell Witch out of his. That bitch doesn't need any more press."

"You're always supposed to go through your supervisor before calling a private meeting with Devlin," Henry said.

"Bite. Me." Creed sent another burst of energy out that Dev felt like a shot in the chest. The guy didn't even realize he did that, and none of the ACRO staff had been able to figure out how to help him control it. Until then, Dev figured it was a secret best kept from Creed.

"Enough. Meeting's over. And I'll go over protocol with Creed myself." Dev waited until the only energy he felt in the room was Creed's, then motioned to the bigger man to follow him down the hall and into Dev's private office.

The Ghost Hunter department at ACRO had been there almost as long as the Clairvoyants, but it was a rarely used asset. Most of the operatives assigned there were kept busy disproving hoaxes, and it was on one of those missions, twenty-nine years earlier, that married Ghost Hunters Dave and Martha McCabe had discovered Creed.

At first, the crying decades earlier coming from inside the Tennessee cave the famous Bell Witch supposedly haunted had gotten the seasoned, and cynical, ghost hunters more than a little excited.

They weren't sure what to think when they'd come across a squalling baby who'd been left naked on a scratchy wool blanket in the middle of the cave instead of the ghost of the Bell Witch. At the time, it had seemed like an amazing gift, since the McCabes had long since stopped trying for children, having been unable to conceive after many heartbreaking years. Martha had scooped the baby up and immediately felt the energy buzz tingle her skin at the same time she noted the small, swirled tattoo that covered the infant's entire right side, from head to toe and a few places in between. But she didn't care.

Upon further investigation, the McCabes learned that the baby had lain there for hours, because no one in the town wanted to enter the supposedly haunted cave. And rumor had it that the baby was a direct descendent of the Bell family, left there to appease a ghost that was due to make an appearance within the year to the family's surviving members. A human sacrifice.

The McCabes had taken the baby home, named him Creed and didn't worry about the Bell Witch nonsense. Even when they began to experience poltergeist activity from the minute the baby entered their house, it was all more of a blessing than a curse.

Creed told his parents later, when he was old enough to speak, that he wasn't a descendant of the Bells, but a descendant of the actual ghost herself. He wasn't sure exactly how he knew that. He just did.

Creed also wasn't sure it was the Bell Witch who haunted him, but he knew it was the ghost of a Native American woman named Quaty. He called her Kat just to annoy her, since the good people of Tennessee always called the Bell Witch Kate.

Creed had confided to Dev years earlier, *The bitch won't let me get close to any woman for longer than it takes to have sex and roll over.*

But Dev had felt Creed's strange, wonderful energy from the second he'd been in the same room with the infant. Dev had been seven years old when the McCabes were visiting his parents, and had encountered the buzz through his brain.

Dev had asked Martha if he could touch the baby because he'd been fascinated by the tattoos. And while his fingers traced the contours of Creed's face, he'd actually felt someone put his hands onto him, not hard, but with enough pressure for him to know that if he'd planned on hurting Creed, he was going to be up against something bigger.

Creed had remained at ACRO long after Dev left for the Air Force, was still working there when Dev returned to take over ACRO. He was one of the better-adjusted operatives despite the drag on his love life, and one of Dev's most trusted ones too, next to Annika and Ender.

Couldn't ask for more from an operative—any help, be it living or dead, worked in Dev's book.

"Close it down and don't let anyone in," Dev told Trance, who was waiting outside his office, once he ushered Creed inside ahead of him.

"I'm on it, sir. I just swept your office clean. Nothing found," Trance said.

"Have you heard anything from your friend?" Dev asked, even though he already knew the answer.

"Nothing, sir. But you know how Ender hates check-ins," Trance said easily.

Yes, he knew. Fucker could block his mind better than anyone. "Let me know the second he deigns to notify us that he's still alive," Dev said.

He walked into his office and let Creed pass him before he shut the heavy door. And then he turned to Creed, who'd been busy pacing the room because he never could sit still, even when commanded.

"Does this have anything to do with what happened at the mansion?" Creed asked as soon as the door shut.

There was no use lying. Creed would figure out that the ghost he'd wrestled with was the same one now haunting Dev, a ghost who had a deep need to share something with Dev, although that had always come at a price.

And now he'd begun to pay the price again.

"Yes," he finally answered. "It's here."

"I never let that spirit out," Creed muttered to himself. "I made sure of it. It was trapped there."

"I know you didn't let it out," Dev said.

"Then how..." Creed stopped. "You knew this was going to happen."

"No, I didn't think it was strong enough to leave the house. I never would've had you free it from the portal if I'd thought that."

"So now it's free to fucking roam. Have you involved Ani any more in this?" Creed demanded, and Dev was taken back for a brief second.

Ani? "No, I haven't involved Annika since she returned from the house. And if I had, that would be my goddamned business. Are you going to help me or not?"

Creed didn't miss a beat. "Of course. But you've got to give me more information."

Dev hesitated briefly, but his senses told him this room was safe. As had Trance. Whoever the mole was couldn't get into his mind unless he allowed it, and right now he was shut tighter than a steel drum and just as reinforced. If someone could get into his mind now, he had bigger problems and no way to solve them.

He turned his back to Creed as he unbuttoned his black BDU shirt, the same one that all the rest of the ACRO operatives were supposed to wear on base. Dev wore them in case someone from Itor broke in and tried to kidnap him. Camouflaging with one's surroundings was a lesson Dev had learned from the military and still took very seriously.

He pulled the shirt off his shoulders and wondered for a brief second if Creed would be able to see it, if it was still there.

But he knew it was. And knew that if the dermography scrawled between his shoulder blades hadn't faded by now, it wasn't a good sign.

When Dev had CRVed it last night, the writing looked the same as it had years earlier, the same broad script, the same four letters, all of it invoking the same feelings of helplessness and fear he'd tried to avoid.

Mine.

Creed sucked in a sharp breath, and Dev waited a beat before pulling up his shirt and buttoning it. When he turned, he was in charge again. "Can you help me?"

"You're going to need someone stronger than I am," Creed said, and Dev realized he was chanting, *Don't say it,* in his head, over and over. But Creed pressed on. "You need someone who can see the dead. You need to call in Oz for this one."

"No!" Dev hadn't meant for that word to come out in a shout. When he spoke again, his voice had a normal timbre. "That's not an option."

"I hate to be the one to tell you this, but I think it might be your *only* option."

"There's got to be something you can do."

"It doesn't want to deal with me. Might be that Kat is pissing it off or something, but it needs someone stronger to take it in hand. Someone who was born into this shit."

"You were born into this shit."

"Not like Oz."

No, no one was like Oz. "Do you know where he is?"

"You mean you don't?" There was definite surprise in Creed's voice. He didn't know what had happened between Oz and Dev. None of them knew. None of them ever would either.

"No," he said simply, heard the defeat in his own voice. "Will you get him? See if he'll come to ACRO?"

"Leave it to me."

As Creed walked out of the office, Dev half collapsed in the leather chair behind his desk. He hoped he hadn't made a mistake by bringing in someone from his agency for help on something that wasn't strictly an ACRO matter. Then again, if Dev was destroyed, he could end up taking the entire agency with him, the one his parents had built from the ground up, starting with some of the original Stargate members after the military declared the project null and void.

The old guard at ACRO was never going to be happy about the way he ran things here. But Dev knew that in order for ACRO to survive, to stay ahead, they needed to employ more than just psychics. They needed strength and power, and if that meant a little instability at times, then so be it. A small price to pay to keep the world at large safe.

*   *   *

THURSDAY 3 P.M. MST

Kira had spent a lot of her life on the run, but Tom Knight gave new meaning to *Don't stop till you drop.*

They'd set a brisk pace for another three hours after the coyote encounter, heading, as far as she could tell, east into the morning sun. They'd taken breaks for water and granola bars, but the breaks weren't long enough. Finally, at around seven in the morning, Tom pulled a tiny portable tent from his bag. After he'd seen to her needs and they cleaned up in the stream they'd been following, they'd slept until she required him again.

Heat licked over her skin at the memory of how she'd awakened him, her mouth sliding up and down over his cock until he swelled hot against her teeth. He'd allowed her to mount him, to seat herself fully on his hard length, but then he'd pinned her wrists to her belly with one hand and used the other to grasp her waist and rein in her movements.

A simple, purely animal form of dominance, his grip had dictated the tempo, the depth of her thrusts, and just when she didn't think she could take the restraint anymore, when she began to whimper and struggle, they'd come together in a combustive surge of pleasure that left her pleasantly immobile for several minutes afterward.

Now, hours later and ready to collapse right there on the side of the mountain, she felt her blood heat with the need to combust again. Soon.

"Kira? Do you hear that?"

She broke out of her sexual haze just as a black bear burst onto the trail ahead of them. It snarled, its teeth bared and shiny with drool that dripped from the corner of its mouth. Tom had drawn a gun from God-knew-where, and ice careened through her veins.

"Don't shoot him," she whispered. "Back away slowly." She tugged him with her.

Concentrating, she sent the bear thoughts, pleasant images of salmon runs and fields of berries. Anything to distract it and send it in search of easier prey than humans.

Disjointed, broken pictures and scents came back to her, musky rage, bitter fear, blood, a larger, angry bear...this youngster had been attacked, was still confused and looking for a way to take out its fury.

It swung its head and ambled forward.

"Can't you talk to the fucking thing?"

She met the bear's gaze. Angst rolled off it in pungent waves. "No."

"Then what good is your damn gift?"

The bear growled, curled its lips back from sharp teeth. "Hush. Fire your gun, but don't shoot him. Scare him."

"Shit." He aimed at a rotten stump and fired. Dead wood exploded, showering the bear, which roared, but turned and lumbered off.

Kira breathed a sigh of relief, and Ender swung around to her. "Why couldn't you talk it down?"

She rolled her eyes. "Just because I can communicate with animals doesn't mean they'll listen." At his blank stare, she crossed her arms over her chest. "Look at it this way: You might be able to communicate with an angry mugger bent on taking your wallet, but will he listen?"

"He'll listen to the sound of his throat being ripped out."

She huffed, and he chuckled as he returned his weapon to his bag. "Yeah, fine. I see your point. Are all animals like that?"

She shrugged. "Some species are worse than others. Wolves are great communicators. And big cats. Lions are really open to cooperating. Tigers are a little more testy."

"What are the worst?"

"Badgers. They are the most stubborn, hardheaded, obnoxious..." She cocked her head and studied him as he scanned the area as if he expected the bear to explode out of the brush again at any moment. "Kinda like you."

"You don't know me."

"Was my assessment wrong?"

"Well, no."

She shot him a smug look. "And I didn't even need to use my cool animal superpower to know those things about you."

A breeze rippled his sandy hair as he shook his head in what she suspected was exasperation. "Lady, I've met a lot of special-ability types in my career, but you have to be the first that's so well adjusted."

"That's gotta be the first time anyone ever used *well adjusted* to describe me."

"Yeah, well, the people I deal with are used to hiding their abilities. They deny them, or don't have control of them, or they have this bitter I'm-a-freak thing going on." He looked at her as if she were an animal species he hadn't seen before. "Not you. I've never seen anyone so comfortable in their own skin."

"Oh, don't be thinking my gift isn't a royal pain in the ass sometimes," she said, remembering just the other night when four of her dogs had jumped on the bed to wake her, complaining about one another like a bunch of five-year-old boys.

"Life is a royal pain in the ass." He motioned for her to sit, another fifteen-minute break for him to collect his bearings and her to rest her aching feet.

As she stretched her arms over her head, her muscles failed to relax, instead tightening. Everything tightened, her breasts, her abs, everything but her sex, which throbbed with a soft fullness.

Tom sat on the ground a few feet away, his back to her, his attention focused on the dense woods around them. His black T-shirt cut across defined muscles she'd never tire of admiring. One sleeve was bunched up around his biceps, and all she could think about was running her tongue over the hard swell.

Yeah, she'd do that.

She crouched, let her breathing grow shallow but slow. She went to her hands and knees, moved silently toward him, stalking. Her inner thighs rubbed together as she moved, heightening her already intense need. Pausing, she sniffed the air. Trees and soil and man . . . her heartbeat bumped up a notch.

She couldn't stop the faint purring noise that rumbled up from deep inside her chest as she approached, and Tom shifted so slightly no one else would have noticed, but she knew she'd been detected.

Her pulse pounded as she brushed her mouth across the back of his neck and then nibbled her way up to his ear.

"You don't have to seduce me, you know. I'm a sure thing."

She sucked on his earlobe, and he moaned, tilted his head to grant her better access. "You could try playing hard to get every once in a while." She nipped him, taking no special care to be gentle.

"I am hard to get," he growled.

Smiling, her teeth still attached to his lobe, she wrapped her arms around his waist to pet his erection through his pants. "Oh, you're hard, all right."

He reached over his shoulders, grabbed her around her rib cage, then, in one smooth motion, he brought her forward while he lay back, and she found her face in his crotch. She felt his face in hers. In seconds, he had yanked down the BDU bottoms he'd finally made her wear, freeing one leg and leaving the pants bunched around the ankle of the other.

"Do you think you can hold off the main event for just a minute?" he murmured against the sensitive skin of her inner thigh, and she nodded, though he couldn't have seen.

His tongue slipped into the leg opening of her underwear, teasing and probing as one finger tunneled into the other opening. The tip of his finger stroked the crease of her leg, and she wriggled to create more room for him to play. His smile tickled her skin and sent an involuntary shiver running through her body.

The warm, musky scent of arousal filled her nostrils. Eagerly, she tore open his BDUs and released his cock. It jutted upward, jumped as she pressed a lingering kiss to the shaft. No man she'd been with had ever been so well endowed, so ideally shaped for her feminine passage and hot buttons. Always before, orgasms were hit or miss during intercourse. But with Tom, she came every time, several times, often from nothing more than penetration. It was as though his body was made for her, and it was time to reward him for that.

Raking her fingernails over the skin of his inner thighs, she flicked her tongue downward. She lapped at his balls, listening to the sound of his breathing as it came faster. His cock strained against her cheek, a rod of heated marble, and under her tongue, his balls swelled, the skin covering them growing taut, lifting them to her mouth.

"Jesus, Kira...oh, *yeah*." His groan rumbled through her sex, releasing a gush of moisture his tongue dipped into. She squirmed, tilting her hips to allow him better access.

She fisted his erection, feeling his pulse beating in her palm as she brought the head to her lips. Creamy drops of pre-ejaculate beaded at the tip, precious little pearls she shouldn't waste. But it had been so long since she'd even wanted to know any man so intimately, and her mouth watered with the desire to taste him.

A sound of desperation erupted from him as she traced his velvety cap with her mouth, applying his essence there like lip balm. She sipped at the tiny slit until he began to pant, and then she twisted around to smile at him. Slowly, seductively, she ran her tongue over her lips, licking his fluid from them. His flavor, wild and tangy, gave her mouth a buzz, and when she saw how he was watching her, so captivated that he'd forgotten what he was doing between her legs, her entire body buzzed with yearning so intense she quivered.

"You're killing me," he rasped, and then he paid her back for her little game by locking his penetrating gaze on her as he stretched the crotch of her panties aside and pierced her core with his tongue.

He didn't take his eyes off her as he worked her, and as she began to peak, she dropped her head between his legs, drew his sac into her mouth and let herself scream around it.

"Oh, God!" he shouted, the echo bouncing off the mountains as her release thundered through her, her muffled noises vibrating through both of them.

Even before the last spasms melted away, he grasped her panties and gave them a frantic tug. "Playtime's over."

A sound—a distant yip—brought her head up with a soft growl. Tom froze.

"What is it?" he asked quietly, as several more yips joined the first, some very near.

"Coyotes. They're warning us."

He swore. She scrambled off him, her body shrieking in frustration because her orgasm had only intensified her need. Tom came to his feet like lightning, a gun in one hand, his other tucking his cock back inside his BDUs. He winced as he buttoned up, and she knew she wasn't the only one feeling the pain of sexual withdrawal.

"Tom—"

"Stay here," he said sharply, and started to move off, his gait a little stiff.

"Tom, wait. You have to hurry."

He nodded, and she hoped the urgency in her voice told him just how much he'd have to hurry. She needed sex. Soon.

ENDER HAD BEEN THE LAST ONE to know there was trouble. He'd been too lost in the way her mouth had been doing things no woman had ever done to him, the way she tasted when she came, the way his balls had been on the verge of exploding far too soon. And yeah, it was going to be damned good...

The low growl that had come from her throat hadn't sounded like the end of her orgasm, but he'd been so busy thinking about getting into her, his body conforming to her needs and actually aching for her after four hours, he hadn't realized her response was in answer to another, more sinister sound.

He'd sent Kira away with that coyote she claimed knew of a safe spot for her to hide, but there had been a brief moment of hesitation in her stance. He figured it had more to do with needing sex than actually being worried about him, and felt his anger mount at even worrying about her feelings.

Shit, he needed to get himself together. Maybe killing these Itor agents would help.

He'd waited until Kira had gotten out of sight, as swiftly and silently as any operative he'd ever worked with, and then he moved, just as quietly but far faster, to meet the men Itor had sent after her.

Two men. Itor always sent them two-by-two, while ACRO preferred teams of one in the field with constant backup in the form of psychics. Ender refused to turn his mind over to them, and this time, he hadn't even let Dev in on his plans.

Being a freak in the real world was a funny thing, and both agencies knew that if you wanted to stay in the game—and thrive—then you didn't send in huge teams of operatives and create a spectacle. Neither agency could be sure who was watching them, waiting to snap a picture or capture an operative and turn them and whatever superability they might have over to the public for scrutiny, and in turn expose them all.

No, under the radar meant more dangerous missions for all operatives, and this was turning out to be worse than usual.

He waited, stock-still, half-hidden in the foliage like a good sniper, and assessed the danger headed his way.

Two men—one excedo with as yet unknown powers, and one unknown entity. Possibly a mind-fucker.

A nudge to his thigh made him turn his head slowly, until he was staring down at a black bear crouched on all fours as if at the ready. Ender knew that if the bear stood on its hind legs, man and beast would be eye to eye.

You here to help, buddy, or am I going to have to fight you too?

The bear cocked his head, and Ender swore it gave him that same exasperated look Kira continued to give him. He turned back to the men, watched as the excedo ripped a large, thick branch off a nearby tree like it was a mere twig, and knew he was dealing with another Derek. Or worse.

Itor had been experimenting with their excedos, especially the ones with superstrength, giving them massive doses of steroids to enhance their natural abilities. The combination resulted in men who doubled their strength—and doubled their rage until it became uncontrollable. Animals. The drugs ate away at their minds until some of the operatives had to be put down. This man who stood ten feet from him was one of them. Ender could see it in his eyes.

The other guy still gave no indication as to what he was. Times like this, having a little bit of psychic in him would come in handy.

He pulled his gun into position slowly so as not to upset his new furry friend, locked the scope and prepared to take out the second guy first. The devil you didn't know was always the more dangerous. He pulled the trigger with the confidence of someone who'd done this enough to know he was spot on target.

He'd also done this enough to know that something had gone terribly wrong. The bullet, which sped toward its mark, slowed as it got within ten feet of the man.

He's got a force field. Not a very well-known skill, but it told him that the man was telekinetic. And Ender knew he was pretty well screwed.

The man turned, smiled, pointed as he casually moved out of the way and the bullet hit the tree behind him. Ender saw him mouth, *Go get him,* to the excedo even as the gun ripped out of Ender's hand.

Ender didn't bother pulling his second. Guns weren't going to work until he got rid of the telekinetic, which meant snapping his neck.

"We're on," he said, because, hell, might as well start talking to the animals too. But before he could take a step out of his hiding place, he was slammed quickly and efficiently to the ground.

The bear growled, low and controlled, rose on its hind legs and allowed enough distraction for Ender to get his shit together and regroup. The bear lunged and he heard a yell as excedo and animal rolled over each other in a fight to the death.

Had to leave me with the hard one, he thought, seconds before he found himself flying through the air. He remembered what Wyatt taught him in that workshop Dev made him sit through last year—something about partitioning and not being able to use too many powers at once without draining one or both. But there was something else, something about the speed of light, and in order to beat the telekinetic's mind and penetrate his force field, Ender would have to do something completely foreign to him.

He'd have to slow down.

He honed in, using his beyond-normal eyesight to keep watch on the man's face so he could detect when he was going to fling his powers. He'd give something away, no doubt—a slight rise of the eyebrow, a push of the lip, a crinkle of the nose. Everyone gave something away.

"Jesus, get him off me." He heard the excedo's bloodcurdling scream and the telekinetic smiled, no intention of trying to save his supposed partner. Ender shifted his attention to the massacre for a second, in time to see an arm hanging out of the bear's mouth, and shit, steroids were no match for nature.

"It doesn't matter—she can send all the animal friends she wants to help, but we've already got her," the man said.

Focus, Ender. Fucking focus. He's got to be lying. But the guy's face gave away nothing, an impenetrable mask of hatred even as Ender's gut began to ache.

"She was calling your name as we took her away," the man continued, and Ender stayed crouched on all fours, not attempting to move. "I wonder how long she's going to last before she begs one of the men to fuck her? From the research I've seen, she'll die without it."

How long had he been separated from Kira? It had to have been an hour, at least, and she'd been in need at that point. An hour later, she'd be climbing the walls. Two and beyond—he didn't want to think about that. Thinking about that had been what got him into this situation in the first place.

"You could actually be quite useful to us, if you care to join."

"No thanks. I've seen how you treat your agents," he answered finally.

"Him? He needed to be put down. I was just waiting for an excuse. I'd been hoping you'd put him out of his misery, but this is actually far more fun," the man said.

"Where did you take Kira?" he asked, and Jesus Christ, the bear turned to look at him and he knew, dammit, knew for sure that Kira was safe. This was crazy. He was going bat-shit crazy, and he was getting back to civilization as soon as possible.

Then again, he'd been surrounded by animals all of his life, some fiercer than others, but all primal, just the same.

"I'd tell you, but then I'd have to kill you. Then again, I plan to do that anyway, because you don't seem the cooperative type," the man said.

Come closer, you bastard. Give me one more shot.

He knew it was coming, saw the subtle twitch in the guy's left eyelid, so when he was slammed onto his back again he was able to land easier.

The guy held a gun in one hand, a knife in the other, and when Ender tested his theory about moving slow, his arm felt like it was being pulled through molasses. It served the purpose of giving the man false hope, and now Ender knew for sure his plan would work. It also earned him a deep slash across his biceps that was going to hurt like a mother while it healed.

"Now you die," the man said. And Ender was not going to mind proving him wrong.

When the guy leaned in to him, gun drawn for the kill, Ender put his hands around the man's throat. Normal human speed, but for him, it was nearly painful to move at that pace. His muscles didn't understand it, his ligaments screamed for speed and the guy's eyes widened in surprise as Ender snapped his neck.

Of course, Ender got a surprise of his own as the last of the guy's telekinetic energy flung him easily over the precipice and down into the dense woodlands below.

KIRA'S EVERY INSTINCT HAD TOLD HER to go with Tom, partly because she didn't want to lose track of him, not when she needed sex so desperately, and partly because she wanted to help. In the end, though, she knew he was right, and reluctantly she'd followed the coyote into the woods. She'd nearly jumped out of her skin when the bear they'd encountered earlier emerged from some brush behind her. Apparently, he'd followed, his curiosity piqued once the initial shock of running into them had worn off. It had been easy enough to convince him to watch after Tom. The price had been two candy bars from her backpack and the suggestion that the men Tom had gone after might have more.

When neither man nor beast had returned an hour later, she considered going after them. But no, if Tom came back and she wasn't here, it might already be too late for her.

She paced some more. And when, two hours after Tom had gone, the pain began, she knew she had no choice. She had to find him.

She had to find anyone.

Nausea swirled in her stomach as she stumbled in the direction Tom had gone. Her legs grew more shaky with every step. Even her vision had started to blur. She careened off a couple of trees and lost her balance, hit the forest floor in a tangle of brush.

"Tom!"

Crows erupted from the trees around her, and she wished she could speak with Aves more than she could. She tried to push to her feet, but her legs gave out. No problem. She'd crawl. Thorns and pine needles dug into her palms, and cramps seized every muscle. Oh, God, she hadn't been this sick in years.

She shuddered, tasted bile. "Tom," she croaked, because her throat had gone dry and scratchy, and merely breathing had become agonizing.

Every foot forward became a struggle, and finally she could no longer crawl. Trembling, she curled up against a tree and sent out feelers to any nearby animals. *Please,* she begged. *I need help.*

A chipmunk skittered toward her from beneath a fallen tree. He chattered, scolded her, then flicked his tail and watched her with suspicion. Closing her eyes, she sent the little guy a picture of Tom, sent him Tom's scent. Sent a lot of images the poor thing didn't need to see, but her mind was swirling with panic and pain, and delirium had turned her into a quivering blob of hormones.

A hawk screeched overhead, and the chipmunk scampered away. She had no idea if the tiny rodent would be able to find Tom, or if it would even try. And if it did find him, would Tom know to pay attention?

Belly cramps doubled her up, and her skin, so hot it had to be burning the foliage beneath her, prickled with unbearable stabs of needlelike pain. Her bones felt like they were rubbing together, splintering.

"Hurry, Tom," she gasped. "Mate or die."

CHAPTER
Thirteen

THURSDAY 7 P.M. MST

Ender shifted back into consciousness like a switch turned abruptly on. The sunlight was nearly gone and he stared into the dark mass of trees high above him and wondered how Dev could stand waking up to total blackness.

He ignored the pounding in his head and concentrated on flexing the muscles in his legs first. He couldn't tell if his toes were really curling or if that was just wishful thinking, because he'd fallen a hell of a long way. He finally resorted to pinching his thighs, and when he was sure he felt that, along with the throb in his arm that reminded him of the knife wound, he sighed with relief. Slowly, he moved his neck from side to side, and as full consciousness settled over him he became aware of the rocks he was lying on. They dug into his spine and he was never so grateful for any feeling in his life.

A movement to his left startled him because he was sure those two Itor agents were long dead. And if there were more, he needed his body to be ready. Immediately.

Just as the shadow came closer, he jumped to his feet in one fluid motion, adrenaline rushing through his muscles and throbbing through his veins, and he came face-to-face with the bear who'd killed the enemy for him. And it did not look happy.

It roared in his face and he roared back, more from surprise than anything else. The bear wasn't backing down, and just when he'd prepared to use his newly rediscovered skills to get out of the way fast, he realized what the bear was doing.

It wasn't pissed—it was protecting him—again. Because the blood from his own wound had brought out the scavengers, and he heard the low-timbred growls from behind him. He turned his head to see more than one wolf, teeth bared and growling into the night, and shit, Ender was no match for this.

Thankfully, the bear didn't seem to want his help. Ender backed away and began his climb up the cliff. Once he had sure footing, he started to move. Blood dripped down his biceps, but he ignored it. Because, like Kira, his body was screaming for sex. He'd been gone nearly four hours.

He yanked himself back over the ledge, and once on firm footing, he took off. Seven miles and fifteen minutes later, he was back within range of where he'd left her, and discovered that either she or that damned coyote had wiped the trail clean. Excellent thinking, except for the fact that she might be dying and he didn't have time to waste tracking her.

When he felt the tug at his boot and looked down to see the chipmunk there, looking up at him expectantly, he didn't bother to groan out loud the way he wanted to. Instead, he actually said, "*Hurry*," out loud, and the thing scurried away, leading him through the underbrush and to the deserted cabin that kept Kira safe and sound.

Well, safe, but she appeared to be far from sound, lying on the floor. She was wet and dirty, and it looked like she'd been out searching for him when she collapsed and had been dragged back here by some of her friends.

He was on his knees next to her within seconds, everything else forgotten but her. "Kira. Shit, Kira honey, can you hear me?"

Her head moved to the side and a low moan escaped her lips. A thin sheen of sweat covered her body and the pulse at the base of her throat was thready against his two fingers.

He roughly pulled her cammy pants off even as he released his cock, which seemed to spring to life at just the thought of her, and he spread her legs.

"Kira, I'm here. I'm going to help you," he murmured as he slid inside her and got an almost immediate response, her legs reflexively banding his waist to lock him down.

"Tommy, please hurry. Hurry," she panted, and sometimes having superspeed really did have its advantages. He came within seconds of pumping his hips, and when he spilled inside of her, she groaned, her eyes opened and her breathing eased.

He touched her neck again and she moaned softly at the contact. Her pulse was stronger, but still weaker than he would've liked. She needed more of him, and he needed to clean them both up, plus suture his wound or risk a major infection.

He gathered her carefully in his arms and walked her outside and toward the sounds of water he'd heard earlier. The wide, smooth stream was sheltered from the breeze by a mountain of rocks on one side and by trees on the other. He dropped his bag at the edge of the stream, toed his boots off, with her in his arms, and continued on.

He'd gotten blood on both of them, and he walked, him still basically fully clothed and her wearing just the shirt he'd given her, into the cool water. That began to revive her even more, and she actually smiled up at him.

"Hey," she whispered.

"Hey yourself," he said.

"I thought—" she started, and he put a finger to her lips.

"I'm here now."

She nodded, her eyes still slightly unfocused. "Did you get the men who were following us?"

"Taken care of. Thanks for sending in the furry backup," he said.

"Is Cheveyo okay?" she asked.

"You named the bear?"

"He already had a name," she said, and he shook his head.

"He seemed to be doing fine when I left him."

"Good." She nuzzled his neck and he realized his own pulse was racing—part fear, part adrenaline. He was too attached.

"You're warm," he said when he realized she was staring at him.

"If I go too long without sex, my body temperature soars. It's going down now. But I'm going to need more. Soon," she said, and even though she didn't avert her eyes from his as she said it, he knew she wanted to.

"You'll get more. And then we've got to move out, make time."

"Okay," she said.

"Can you give me a few minutes now, or do you need me?" he asked.

"I can give you a few minutes, but you're not going anywhere, are you?"

"I'm staying right here," he assured her. "Can you stand?"

She nodded, and he let her go so she stood in the waist-deep water in front of him. She didn't take her eyes off him for a second, and he didn't blame her. The way she'd looked when he'd found her was terrifying enough—he didn't want to know what kind of toll it had taken on her body.

He stripped off his shirt and waded to where he'd left his bag, the water rippling around him as he moved.

She was right by his side. "You're hurt."

"I'm fine."

"Fine doesn't require stitches," she pointed out. He didn't argue any further, let her clean his wound, first with water cupped in her hand and then with the peroxide from his medic kit. He could see in her eyes that she was going to need him again within minutes, but just touching him seemed to calm her enough to wait.

With her eyes still on him and her hands on his back, he quickly used the black thread to close the wound. He healed faster than most people, and the stitches would help that healing process along. A shot of antibiotics and he was done—that was something he'd normally forgo and take the risk, but he couldn't afford to get sick now, not with Kira needing him.

She caressed his back with one hand and undid the buttons on her BDU shirt with the other. He could smell her urgency as she moved to his pants, which were still unbuttoned, and pulled them down under the water. He stepped out of them and she tossed them onto the dirt bank and dunked herself under the water, rubbed her face to get rid of the dirt. Then she stood again in the waist-deep water, her skin luminescent in the soft moonlight that managed to peek through the trees.

It was so quiet—he'd never heard it so quiet—and his mind slowed and everything else was forgotten except the way her nipples tightened as she watched him and he watched her.

He'd never gotten to just watch her, appreciate the curves of her body and the way she moved, lithe and sexy. So uninhibited when she was in this state.

"You're staring," she said.

"Yes."

"Do you like what you see?"

His throat was dry, and he blamed it on the day's events, not her. It couldn't be her that made him feel like a stupid schoolboy. He nodded instead of answering her directly.

"Come here now," she said, and although he bristled slightly at the command, he moved toward her anyway.

She needed the control—he got that, but shit, this wasn't going to be easy.

"You don't like it when I tell you what to do," she said, and he just stared into her eyes. They'd already turned golden and his arm snaked out to grab her waist and pull her tight against him.

"I don't like anyone telling me what to do," he growled. "Never have, never will."

She accepted that, the corners of her full lips tugged up and he knew he was in for it. "Then I guess you don't want to put your mouth on my nipples. Because that's something I want right now," she whispered. He raised her by her hips so her breasts were level to his mouth and he suckled one nipple and then the other until her moans filled the night air, until her back arched and she was chanting, *"Can't wait, can't wait."*

KIRA'S BODY THRUMMED WITH NEED so intense she figured she should glow. Tom had revived her, but hours would pass before her body fully recovered, before her muscles regained their strength, her temperature normalized and her organs stopped cramping.

It had never been this bad.

Hopefully, Tom hadn't noticed how ill she still felt, because she didn't want to be babied. She wanted him raw and wild, like the landscape around them, like the scent of battle that still clung to his skin and drove her crazy.

He'd fought for her and won, and she was more than ready to express her gratitude.

"Can't wait." She wriggled down his slippery body until his erection slipped between her folds and rubbed her clit. *"Can't. Wait."*

Fingers digging into her butt cheeks, he lifted her, settled her opening over the broad head of his cock. His movement, smooth and sure, might have convinced her he was okay, but the nearly imperceptible grimace at the corner of his mouth told her otherwise. Blood oozed at the edges of his arm wound, the stitches torn by the flex of muscles beneath his skin.

"No." Palms planted against the hard wall of his chest, she pushed roughly and dropped her trembling legs back down to the riverbed. Her body screamed in protest, but it would have to wait until she made it to the Volkswagen-sized rock that jutted out of the water a few yards away.

"What the hell?" Tom grabbed her arm, but she slipped out of his grip and stumbled downstream.

Sharp stones bit at the soles of her feet, but she didn't care. "I won't hurt you."

"I'm fine—"

Her legs gave out, and she slipped beneath the water. Strong hands yanked her up, and she sputtered, coughed, still clawing her way toward the rock.

"What are you doing?"

He sounded angry now as he held her tight against him, his cock nudging her center, and all she wanted to do was ride him until she passed out again. "The rock. Take me to the rock."

Muttering obscenities, he carried her there, steadied her when she couldn't stand on her own feet. His skin glistened wet in the moonlight, and she shivered with the desire to lick every inch, to dip below the waterline and take him in her mouth like she had earlier, but not tonight. She was too weak, too in need, and with a pang she realized that she'd never be able to swallow one of his orgasms. Semen was too precious during her season. And by the time the fever ended and she had the time to make him come the way she wanted to, he'd be long gone.

"Take me." She lay back on the rock, welcoming the bite of cold, wet stone against the raging heat of her skin.

He looked at her as if she'd gone insane, but she'd grown used to the expression, had decided she liked being able to surprise this man who didn't ruffle easily. Moving in, he lifted her thighs around his waist and sank into her, the lubrication from his earlier orgasm easing his entrance. Slow, gentle, exactly what she'd tried to avoid. His palms slapped the stone on either side of her head as he held himself over her so they touched only below the waist.

Remaining motionless, he gazed down at her. "I'm sorry I was late."

He didn't wait for a response, probably didn't want one and the conversation that might ensue. Instead, he rocked against her, his cock stretching her wide, pushing deep where she needed it. His balls tickled the sensitive spot at the base of her sex, and she shifted her hips, angling so his shaft stroked her clit in exactly the right place.

The river gurgled around them, swirling and frothing where their bodies locked intimately. Cool water lapped at their skin and relieved the intense heat that formed from the friction of their joining. The hoot of an owl rode in on a breeze that smelled of pine trees and spring berries. She closed her eyes, let the primal beast inside mate with her lover, with nature.

As though he felt the same primitive tug, he slammed into her with the force she'd wanted from the beginning. Each thrust drove her out of the water a little more, made the waves lick her clit until she was ready to scream. Her breath caught in shallow gasps that burned in her throat, and she closed her eyes, on the precipice of a release she knew would take her apart physically, emotionally...and beyond.

She wasn't ready to be alone in that, needed Tom to see the truth, all of it. Tightening her legs around his waist, she dug her heels into his buttocks. He grunted, ground against her because she wouldn't let him pull back to thrust. If she could hold him there inside her slick heat, where every ridge and bump on his textured cock caressed her sensitive tissues without even moving, she'd be happy forever.

"Kira," he rasped, "let me come."

Opening her eyes, she looked deeply into his, saw the feral gleam there, the one that revealed so much about him simply because of how hard he tried to hide it. Man and beast battled inside him, and she wanted the beast, the wild side of him that acted on instinct and didn't let human conventions interfere with what he really felt.

"Dammit, Kira. Stop fucking around. You need this."

As if to prove his words, her body bucked, wanting to break free of her restraining willpower, but she ignored the way every cell had tightened to the point of pain while they waited for the rush of hormones he could give her.

"I do." She dug her nails into his shoulders, raked them down his back, and he hissed through clenched teeth. "But what do you need, Tommy?"

He dropped down to his elbows so his chest hair rubbed her breasts, and his nose touched hers. "I need to keep you alive."

For your agency. She didn't say it, didn't ask, didn't want to hear it. It was the truth, but she wanted the other truth right now, the one he didn't want to admit.

"What else?" She arched up, loosened her grip on his waist so she could ride him in short, shallow strokes, not caring that the hard bumps in the rock tore into her spine. Her climax hovered too close, too hot. "Do you want to know who I really am?"

A guttural sound ripped from deep in his chest, and he tried to drive his hips hard, but she clamped her thighs together, holding him captive inside her.

"Fuck."

"I'll take that as a no." Her words came out as a moan, because his struggles had been enough to take her to the very brink. Quivering with the need to come, she grasped his face, and when he would have reared back—so stubborn!—she held him firm until he stopped trying to jerk away. "You need to see."

She released her vice grip on his waist but kept her palms pressed against his cheekbones. He lunged forward, taking her over the edge, and she battled the impulse to close her eyes, to conceal what she'd always hidden, what no man had seen.

Explosions scattered her insides, tore through her in a series of bursts that brought her off the river rock. She clenched her teeth, struggled to hold open her eyes as her orgasm ripped through her.

"Yes, Tom," she gasped. "Oh, yes."

He drove into her, his breaths coming in ragged pants, and surprise flickered in the depths of his eyes as he gazed into hers.

"Oh, man," he said, and it was her turn to be surprised, because he whispered, "*so beautiful,*" and then dropped his forehead against hers and came, his hot semen filling her and triggering another powerful orgasm.

When she came back to earth, her mind could only reel at what he'd said. He'd seen the way her pupils constricted and elongated into slitted cat eyes and had still thought she was beautiful.

Not a freak.

But then he withdrew, much too quickly, like he needed the distance, though he didn't go anywhere. The sudden loss of their connection crashed over her as though they stood in an ocean surf and not a gently rippling river.

"Are you okay?" he asked gruffly, and she nodded, clenched her internal muscles, desperate to prevent the stream from stealing his seed.

Silently, he gathered her in his arms and carried her to the shore, where they dressed as rapidly as possible, though she still moved like a slug, and he had to help her put on her socks and boots.

"So, um, what really happened out there?" she asked, and she saw in his eyes that he knew she was talking about the bad guys. "How many were there?"

"Two."

"And you're sure they're...ah..."

His gaze slid to hers, the fierceness there stopping her heart. "They won't come after us again."

She tried to keep her imagination from running wild, but his wounds, the blood on his clothes that couldn't all have belonged to him, the lethal knife he carried...Criminy. Her mind took her to horrific places, and her heart started again, in painful, spastic bursts. He seemed to know, covered her hand with his in a rare tender gesture.

"Kira, you did good. You sent help for me, and you hid like I asked you to. And you've been so strong. I know men who would have fallen apart by now." She clung to his praise as he finished tying the laces on her boots and stood. "We have to move. There'll be more I-Agents, and we've got to put some miles between us and them."

She nodded, unsure how she'd be able to make it a few feet, let alone a few miles. Tom took away the question, though, and after he gathered his bag and her backpack, he loaded her over his shoulder and headed downriver.

THURSDAY 9 P.M. PST

"Your mother's here," Oz said. He stared directly at the beautiful blonde who sat across the table from him, her big blue eyes wide and transfixed on his.

"She's here? In this room?" Her voice had a slight shake to it, her lip quivered and it was time for him to bring it home.

"She's standing right behind you. Her hand is on your right shoulder. Can you feel it?" he asked, and after a second she nodded. Because the power of suggestion was a wonderful thing and ninety-nine percent of people couldn't feel a ghost touching them at all unless it really wanted them to. And if that kind of contact happened between the living and the dead, the living person was in big trouble.

"I feel it," she whispered dramatically, and he fought the urge to roll his eyes.

Kiki Karlson was one of Hollywood's most notable and well-paid actresses, living in a house high in the Hollywood Hills, and she was shelling out thousands of dollars for this parlor-trick shit. Even if she discovered what he was telling her wasn't the exact truth, she wouldn't care. Everything about this woman was fake—hair, breasts, nails. So yeah, he'd tell her what she wanted to hear.

People in general did not want to hear the truth—that most entities who hadn't crossed over were not good-natured, I'll-be-on-your-shoulder-forever, fucking Casper the friendly ghost coming for a sweet visit. No, in his experience, most ghosts or shades or haints wanted revenge. Wanted to be alive instead of caught in the shadowy realm between life and the Other Side. And they'd do anything to make the living feel their pain.

Of course, this was only his legacy—he wasn't sure if other psychics who saw the white-robed, beautiful figures were lying or not, but for some reason he'd been given the gift to see the worst of the worst. It hadn't instilled a whole lot of faith for mankind in him.

So instead of truths, he gave his clients this circus-freak shit. Traveling from house to house whoring his wares. He guessed it was better than whoring, but whoring had felt a hell of a lot better.

Kiki would let him screw her if he played his cards right.

"She said she loves you. That she's always watching over you," he said.

"Is she all right? Happy? Does she look beautiful?"

"She's very happy. And she looks beautiful."

"She doesn't look the way she did when I found her?" Kiki asked, the tears beginning to run down her face. "I hate thinking about that night..."

"The murder is behind her, Kiki," he said. "She's dressed all in white. No scars."

"Is it all right if I put my hand over hers?" she asked. Oz looked up over Kiki's shoulder at the ghost with the long, snarled, white hair, a constant grimace pulling her lips back to reveal rotting teeth. Her eyes held that inhuman look Oz knew well, and he watched the blood drip from the gaping hole in the spirit's neck onto Kiki's beautiful white shirt. The hand that grasped Kiki's shoulder was a claw, withered and bony and just waiting for Kiki to touch her. The thing nodded at Oz, begged, *Let her do it, let her open the door,* and Kiki looked at him just as expectantly.

"It's better that you don't," he said.

Bastard, the spirit mouthed.

Tell me something I don't know, he answered, watched it disappear through the mirror it came from and knew he had to get out of there.

"She's gone," he said. He stood abruptly, because he sensed another disturbance in energy, a human, not a ghost, and he knew he had to get home.

He took the shortest route to his house, his motorcycle echoing in the hills, calling to the ghosts that haunted the witching hours. Some of them would follow him home and get pissed when he told them they couldn't stay. But that wasn't his concern right now.

Dev was. As always, even though he hadn't seen the man in three full years and counting. Now that was about to change. He'd be getting a call soon—most likely from Creed, not Devlin.

Oz and Dev had gotten together when Dev was seventeen and Oz was nineteen, broke up when Dev left for the Air Force Academy at eighteen. Oz worked at ACRO before and after Dev took the reins at twenty-eight, and the two had reconciled. Five years later, Oz left the agency after helping Dev put down the ghost that had been bothering the man since Dev had been a teenager. A ghost that neither Oz nor his spirit posse could get through to—a ghost that only wanted Dev and would do anything to control him fully.

At the time Oz left Dev, he'd told Dev that he would not come back to help him with the spirit again, that if Dev brought it out again, it was his to deal with.

There was no way Oz could stick to that promise...not when he knew Dev was in trouble. Oz didn't know who the man behind the ghost was, but this time, he would make sure he found out—and that he banished the ghost once and for all.

CHAPTER
Fourteen

Kira woke, her stomach slightly queasy, her head throbbing. Last night had been a close call. So close that when the sun came up and Tom had let them stop for sleep, she'd wakened him for sex three times, even though her need hadn't been that great.

He'd taken it like a trooper, though, had given her what she needed, even doing all the work because she'd still been too weak to do much besides lie there in the little tent like a blow-up sex doll. The poor guy had to be exhausted; she knew he'd spent half the day prowling the area to make sure they were safe.

A blast of desire robbed her of her breath at the memory of how he'd start off sleeping as far from her as the tent walls would allow, but then, in his sleep, he'd rolled against her and grown hard, setting her on fire inside and out.

Her body trembled at the sudden fierce need that gripped her. She reached behind her, but her hand came down on the thin canvas floor. She rolled over. Tom was gone.

An instant, terrifying band of pressure tightened around her chest. *He's probably just watching out for bad guys.* She repeated the words in her head as she pushed to her hands and knees. Her thighs and arms felt watery, barely able to carry her weight.

"Tom?" She swept aside the door flap and crawled outside. Panic made her gut clench. "Tommy?" Oh, God, where was he? She came to her feet, swayed like a baby taking its first steps. *"Tommy!"*

Then he was there, from out of nowhere, and she was in his arms. "I'm here, Kira. I'm here."

She wrapped herself around him, tried to hide her tremors. "I wasn't worried," she said, knowing he didn't believe her, but wanting to convince herself. She felt like such an idiot. A clingy, demanding idiot.

She hated being so dependent on anyone, especially when her life was at stake and she had no control over whether she lived or died.

But Tom had controlled things pretty well. He'd put his life on the line to save hers, and he'd done it without flinching. The knowledge stripped her to the bone, flayed her emotions wide open, so everything else he'd done to infuriate her didn't matter. She'd always been more a creature of emotion than logic, and his saving her life had opened her up to feelings she needed to tamp down.

She could fall for this man.

His hand caressed her back in slow, soothing circles as he nuzzled her hair, pressing tender kisses against her scalp. He was so funny that way, how he could be gentle and attentive, and then at other times freeze her out with indifference.

"I know you weren't." He tightened his arms around her, and she melted against him. "Do you need me again?"

She nodded, despite the fact that they'd mated just two hours ago. He swept her up, crouched low, and carried her into the tent.

He laid her carefully on the floor and unbuttoned his pants as she stripped off hers. They'd slept in their clothes; Tom had told her to stay as fully clothed as possible at all times, in the event that they had to move out quickly.

Kneeling between her legs, he mounted her.

"Wait," she said, even as he slid home. "Could we...maybe...?"

"Take it slow?"

"Mix it up."

He cocked an eyebrow at her, and her cheeks burned. She shouldn't have asked. Sometimes he was willing to add foreplay, but afterward he was always much more distant than after the times when he took her quickly just to give her what she needed to survive.

"You mean, like, handcuffs?"

A pleasant flush broke out over her body at the memory of what he'd done with the cuffs the night he'd tackled her in the field. But she'd also had too close a call with death last night to want to be helpless in any way.

"No...never mind. Forget I asked."

Still sheathed inside her, he reached for his bag. He rummaged through it, and when he nodded to himself, she knew she was in trouble. "Perfect."

He pulled the riding crop from his bag, and she gasped. "I can't believe you kept that."

"You never know when one could come in handy."

Excitement shot through her, because for all the sex she'd had in her life, most of it had been about feeding her body. Never her mind. She'd never taken the time to play.

Tom eased out of her and scooted back, still on his knees. When she tried to sit up, he pushed the tip of the crop against her sternum and forced her to lie back.

"Stay."

Breathless with anticipation, she did as he'd ordered, and then kept an eye on his face as he trailed the leather flap down her abdomen. He hesitated when he reached her mound, but when she cut her gaze away to watch what he was doing, he slipped it lower, between her dewy folds.

He began a leisurely exploration with the leather flap, coaxing a moan from her.

"You like that, Kira?"

"Oh, yes."

"Has anyone ever used a whip on you this way?"

She looked up; his gaze slammed into hers, and somehow, she knew her answer was more important to him than he'd ever let on. "Never."

She caught the subtle softening in his eyes before he looked back down to what he was doing with the crop. "Good. That's good."

The rub of the soft leather grew firmer, faster, and blood began to roar in her ears. Her clit throbbed, but each pass he made through her slit barely skimmed the aching nub. When he withdrew the thing, she whimpered—until he moved closer, turned the crop around, and used the hard, leather-wrapped handle to stroke her instead.

"Spread your legs wider," he commanded, one palm putting pressure against her inner thigh until she let her knees fall open. A low sound of approval came from him, and he licked his lips as he moved even closer. She thought he would put his mouth where the crop was, but instead, he drew the handle down to her entrance. Her breath jammed in her throat. Would he—

"You're soaked," he murmured. "Dripping."

Oh, God, she knew that, could feel moisture flooding her sex, right there where he was rotating the tip of the crop, caressing the sensitive circle of nerves at her core. Pleasure streaked through her, and it nearly peaked when he plunged the handle inside her.

"Tom!"

"Do you want me to stop?" Tom began an easy, sensual rhythm, *in, out, twist*. "You've fucked my cock, my hand, my mouth, now this ... do you think you can come?"

The thrill of what he was doing was too much to allow for an answer. Instead, she ground her hips to meet his thrusts, mindless at the feel of the slick friction, the erotic pleasure that sliced through her clit and made her clamp down on the tool she'd always thought of, and despised, as a means of delivering pain.

She squeezed her eyes shut, concentrating on the sound of Tom's breathing, rapid, ragged, concentrating on the exquisite sensation of being penetrated with a weapon wielded by a man who knew the best way to use it.

"Let go, baby," he whispered. "Let me see you come."

As though she'd needed his permission, her nerve endings exploded, and her orgasm surged through her like she'd been set aflame. Tom did something—angled the handle just right—and before the first climax had waned, another caught her by surprise, tackled her and didn't let her go.

He withdrew the crop, and while she still pulsed, he entered her with his rock-hard cock. The delicious stretch of her tissue had her coming yet again, and on his third stroke he released inside her with a groan.

Worn out, sated and feeling like a pampered cat, she prepared for him to pull out immediately, as always. But this time he lay on top of her until they stopped panting, and then he rolled to his side and took her with him, his cock twitching inside her.

He watched her, his eyes bloodshot, the dark hollows beneath emphasizing his fatigue.

"You're exhausted." Letting her gaze linger on the angular planes of his face, she ran her fingers through his hair, pushed it away from his forehead. "I'm so sorry."

"This is nothing. I've been through worse."

"You've been forced to have sex every three hours instead of four?"

A smile quirked his mouth and she suddenly wanted very much to kiss him. Impossible, she knew. Something told her that doing so would send him into icy-distant mode.

"I never thought I'd believe there was such a thing as too much sex. I'm sore as hell." His smile faded, and then he did withdraw from her body, leaving her feeling empty. As he sat up next to her, he shook his head. "How do you deal with it?"

She reached for her underwear and pants. "It's not horrible as long as I've got everything planned out and mates arranged."

Outside, birds chirped, probably seeking their own mates, some for life. Regret and sadness brushed her heart. A life mate and family was something Kira desperately desired but could never have.

She pulled on her clothes as Tom buttoned up, and then she drew up her knees and wrapped her arms around them.

"It's when things go screwy that it gets bad."

"Bad how?"

Shifting to avoid the sharp edge of a rock beneath her, she nibbled on her bottom lip, unsure how much she should tell him. He hadn't judged her so far, had been nothing but accepting of everything he'd seen. What would he think when he knew how bad things had been for her? Then again, it didn't really matter. Once they arrived at his agency, she might not see him again. He'd certainly made it clear that he wouldn't be the one servicing her.

"It's like a drug addiction. If prior arrangements aren't made, then the moment I get sex, I start thinking about how I'm going to get it again. I do things . . . I mean, I've had to proposition strange guys in bars."

Unable to bear seeing a look of disgust on his face, she averted her gaze, concentrated on the pine needle one of them had tracked inside. "Do you have any idea how desperate I have to be to do that? To walk up to some stranger and ask if he wants to screw me in the alley?" She shuddered. "At the time, it doesn't matter who they are or what I have to do. That's how this affects me. I just need it. Afterward, I feel dirty and sick."

"You shouldn't. It's not your fault."

She snorted. So easy for a man to say. "Tell that to the towns of Great Falls and Albany and Jasper."

"Is one of those where you were jailed?"

"You tell me. You seem to know my criminal record better than I do."

"I know your official record. I'm guessing the time you were raped in the jail cell was strictly off the books."

Nausea bubbled up in her throat. "I wasn't raped."

"Bullshit. You needed sex, and I'll bet men lined up to take advantage of that."

The memory rattled around inside her skull, the same sound as cell bars being shaken. She wanted to curl up in a ball at the thought of how she'd been arrested for disturbing the peace in a bar where she'd gone to find someone to service her. The interested man's girlfriend had caught them and all hell had broken loose. As a newcomer in the one-stoplight town, Kira had been the only one to go to jail, and she'd nearly gone insane in the cell.

She'd thrown herself against the bars, begged one of the officers for sex, had degraded herself like never before or since.

"They lined up—" dear God, they'd watched as each man took his turn "—but you know what it's like to be around me when it's time. They couldn't help it. And I begged."

His curses blistered her ears. "Dammit, Kira, you needed one man. The rest of the bastards had no business going near you. How many were there?"

"Four," she whispered, "but one only watched."

Ice spread through her insides. She'd pleaded for sex while they laughed, called her a slut, whore—and worse. Eventually, her pheromones wore them down, and the one who smelled like cigarettes and hot dogs shoved her face into the wall, lifted her skirt and entered her. Afterward, she'd slid down the wall and sat on her heels as she sobbed.

The sound of the door squeaking open a few moments later had filled her with dread. Then came footsteps, the clink of a belt buckle, the warm hand of the second officer as he yanked her off the floor. She hadn't needed him, had pleaded with him to come back in four hours, but he'd hit her so hard her vision had blurred for an hour. The third man followed, and they'd taken their turns all night. By then, she hadn't cared because she didn't know how long she'd be locked up, and she had to take every opportunity she could.

"They let me go in the morning, early. Probably didn't want the next shift to find out what happened. When I got home, my house had been vandalized. The girlfriend from the bar, I'm sure." She sighed. "I packed a bag that morning and hitched a ride to Idaho with a trucker who was more than happy to take sex as payment."

"Where did this happen?"

"It doesn't matter."

"Oh, yes, it does," he pressed, and the tone of his voice, low, edged and jagged like the knife strapped to his thigh, made her shiver.

"I just want to forget, Tom. Please. I know that sounds pathetic—"

"Fuck that," Tom muttered. "You're so strong, Kira. What you went through would have broken most people."

"Strong?" She shook her head. "There were times when I tried to go without sex, just to let myself die. But I was weak. When the sickness and pain took over, I gave in. I keep telling myself that if I die, no one will listen to the animals. They won't have a voice. I'm not sure if I'm being weak or selfish or both."

"I'd say neither." Tom was silent for a long moment, and then he reached for what he called his rucksack. "Have you always talked to animals?"

Oh, she could have kissed him for diverting the conversation, but she knew the subject wasn't forgotten. Not for him. She wasn't stupid enough to think he'd seek justice for some chick who was nothing but a job to him, but she got the impression that Tom Knight's code of honor wouldn't allow him to sit back and ignore bad guys with badges.

"Since birth. My parents said the day they brought me home from the hospital, the pets gathered round and wouldn't let me out of their sight."

"Did they think it was weird?" He handed her a granola bar, different from the others they'd been eating, and she checked the ingredients for animal products before she tore open the wrapper.

"At first they thought God used animals to watch over me."

"At first?"

She nodded. "They thought it was sweet how I 'made up stories' about the animals' thoughts and stuff. Then, when the things I told them turned into things I shouldn't know, they suddenly didn't think God had anything to do with it anymore."

"So what, they thought you were possessed?"

"Sort of." She bit off a tiny corner of her granola bar and chewed slowly before answering. "I grew up in the Bible Belt, where people think psychics get their messages from the devil. My parents believe that I speak with Satan through evil animals. I guess way back in my family tree, one of my great-grandparents was burned as a witch for talking to animals, so of course I was a bad seed."

"Must have been fun around your house."

She laughed, because yeah, good times. Her parents had gotten rid of all the pets by the time she was eleven, and her dad shot any stray that came near.

"It was hell. Things really got bad when a neighbor's dog escaped his chain, and when I found him, he gave me an image of a dead body in a ditch. I was fifteen, so I called the police. My parents threatened to kick me out of the house if I told the cops how I knew about the body, but I couldn't lie. The whole town thought I was nuts."

"Did your parents kick you out?"

"Yeah. I had to go live with a friend. And then things got really bad."

"Worse than your parents believing you rub elbows with Satan and the whole town thinking you're one bullet short of a magazine?"

"Your tact astounds me." His lips curved into a pleased smile, and she rolled her eyes. "Yes, worse than that. I was sixteen. And the heat started. I didn't understand it, just knew I needed sex. So basically, after that, I was rubbing elbows with the devil, crazy, the town slut."

"What happened?"

"My friend's family kicked me out of their house, and my parents wouldn't take me in. So I ran away, changed my name and never looked back." Well, that wasn't entirely true. In a fit of loneliness, she'd contacted her only sibling, Peter, a couple of years ago, but he'd told her that Charity Belle was dead to him and to never call again. "In Memphis, a lady who trained drug- and bomb-sniffing dogs took pity on me. Marcia. She was an animal whisperer too."

Kira picked at her granola bar while Tom started on his second protein bar. She had no idea how many of the things he had in his bag, but she'd give him the merit badge for preparedness, for sure.

"She's the person who taught you how to train police dogs?"

"Yes. I took over her business when she died in a car accident."

Marcia had also introduced her to the radical animal-rights and anti-government groups she'd joined. Aside from the yearly mating issues, her life had gone well until her first arrest during an anti-fur protest. After that, strange things happened whenever she was near, things she'd had no part in even though she'd been blamed. Slaughterhouses had gone up in flames. Whaling boats sank. Research labs had been vandalized.

Only since Tom had come into her life had things started to make sense.

Someone had been trying to flush her out. Maybe that enemy agency Derek had come from.

"Will your agency be able to do something about all my arrest warrants?"

He barked out a laugh. "Warrants? Kira, no official agency in the world will ever touch you again. And if you want those cops who hurt you to pay, that can be arranged too."

"I told you, I just want to forget it," she said, and tried to make her voice more upbeat, because she definitely didn't want him to know how much the experience still haunted her, how often she had nightmares about being locked up.

"Yeah, I get that."

She'd just bet he did. He'd probably seen things during his career that would have her wanting to never sleep again for fear of the dreams.

"When we get to your agency, can I arrange for my farmhands to be found? I can't stand the thought of them..." She swallowed sickly, unable to say it.

"They probably already sent a cleanup crew."

Right, because they'd need to get rid of the other bodies. The bad guys. "How long have you worked for them?"

"It feels like forever." He arranged the mysterious stuff in his bag and placed his ammo on top.

"And what, exactly, do you do there?"

"Mostly, I bring in special people like you."

"Mostly?"

He jammed the bag into a corner and moved toward the front of the tent. "Q and A is over. I need to patrol. See if you can get some sleep."

When he started out, she grabbed his arm. "Be careful." He nodded, and she added softly, "And Tommy? I want you to know I believe you."

"About what?"

"Everything. The bad guys. Derek. You said you wouldn't hurt me, and that you'd keep me safe. You have. Thank you."

His entire body went rigid, and then he slipped away. Outside, the birds stopped chirping as though there was a predator in their midst.

It took her a moment to realize the predator was Tom.

FRIDAY 8 P.M. EST

Something was in the house.

Dev got to the bottom of the stairs without incident, tripped over his own feet as he walked into the den, where he spent most of his time when he was home. It was the place he felt the safest. Unbeatable.

Standing, he kept his back firmly against the wall to avoid any unwanted touches, and a burst of cool air brushed his cheek. He put his palms over his face and the touch ran up his bare forearms. He wondered how something could feel so comforting and eerie at the same time.

"Are you prepared to help me this time?" he demanded finally, yelled it to the ceiling as he pushed off the wall and walked to the middle of the room. He stood stock-still, fists clenched, body poised in fight-or-flight mode. Except he wasn't going anywhere. "Answer me!"

"Is that any way to greet an old friend?"

Dev turned toward the voice even as the sound slid down his spine in that achingly familiar way and he cursed himself for not being able to drive certain weaknesses out of his body. Even though he'd been expecting Oz, he hated that he was never able to figure out where or when he'd show up.

"Fuck off," he growled.

"Always a fighter. Can't just shut up and give in, can you? Not even once."

Dev stood his ground even as his world shifted beneath him and he breathed in the familiar scent of musk and whiskey as Oz moved in closer. Too close.

He'd bet his last dollar that Oz still looked exactly the same. Devastatingly handsome. Butch as hell.

"It's been a while," Oz said.

Over three years. But he'd be damned if he'd let Oz know he'd been counting. "This was a mistake. You need to leave."

"You send Creed to find me, drag me here, and now you want to kick me out before things get interesting?"

"I didn't ask you here for things to get interesting," he said, hating to note that the spirit had fled now that Oz was here.

"Yeah, you did." Oz's hand tightened around Dev's shoulder, and warm, sweet breath brushed his ear. "Ask for it again."

Dev jerked away. "No."

"Still pissed at me?"

Silence stretched until Dev finally sighed. "This isn't about the past. It's about saving ACRO."

Oz was standing in front of him, his face inches away from Dev's. As the angry tension dissipated, a new one built, and Dev couldn't help it, reached his hands up to touch Oz's face, the way he'd been taught to do when he lost his sight. He let his fingers wander over the sharp cheekbones, the patrician nose, the full mouth he'd kissed more times than he could count.

Oz took the opportunity to move in closer. Sensual promise

oozed from him, thick and hot. Dev's body answered, hardened, a split second before warning bells rang in his brain, because he was not going to let this happen. He'd been down that road before, and it was bumpy as hell.

Oz chuckled and Dev wheeled away. He moved in a circle, working off both the heat Oz's body emitted and pure instinct, and he knew Oz was doing the same.

"Are you here alone?" Dev asked, even though he knew the answer.

"I'm alone. So are you, by the way. At least for now. I'll make myself comfortable on the third floor. You won't even know I'm here."

"Bullshit." He'd know if Oz was in the same county, let alone the same house.

"What? You want me to stay in your room? It's a better idea, because I don't think you should be alone."

Dev halted, tempted to peg Oz to the far wall. "Don't push it."

"I was serious, Dev. No ulterior motives. I wouldn't be here if I didn't want to help." When Dev didn't respond because he wasn't sure how to, Oz muttered a mild curse. "Want to show me that writing on your back before I go upstairs?"

"Why? You know exactly what it says."

"Yeah, I know."

Dev heard Oz's heavy footsteps leave the room and travel up the two flights of stairs and he realized he hadn't even bothered to use his second sight from the minute Oz entered the den. Like it knew he didn't want to see Oz, or maybe the spirit haunting him wouldn't let him see Oz.

Either way, he was grateful for the moment.

SATURDAY EVENING

Ender heard the bloodcurdling screams before he realized they were his, woke to find himself collapsed over his hands and knees like he'd been trying to pray and fell forward instead. The screams continued even though his eyes were open, wouldn't stop until the images that flashed in front of his eyes were replaced by the soft grass and dirt he'd been lying against.

He'd crawled out of the tent and out across the cool earth as if looking for an escape—from the nightmare. From himself.

"Tommy." Kira's soft hands were on his face, his cheeks, trying to turn his head to look at her. "Tommy, please, tell me what's wrong. Are you hurt?"

Finally, the images faded completely, and he was looking into those deep pools of amber, saw himself reflected there instead of blood and death and destruction. There was no rifle in his hand, just his fingers clawing palm-deep into the cold dirt, but he could still smell the residue of gunpowder and fire beneath the surface of her honey and cloves scent.

"I'm fine," he said, his voice hoarse. He turned and took a deep breath, hoped he didn't vomit right here in front of her, because his stomach still twisted and ached with a knowledge no man should ever have.

"Put your head back down," she urged. "Deep breaths—in through your mouth, out through your nose. That helps the nausea."

He didn't argue, because being told what to do right now seemed to be helping. Some of the mess lifted off his shoulders and he just breathed, letting the night air replace the odors of blood, burning flesh and oily smoke.

You're on the job. And safe, relatively speaking. He'd taken them another full day closer to their destination near Butte, Montana, and he'd woken with the nightmare to see dusk. Which meant it was time to move out again, not break down.

"Water," he croaked finally.

"Do you think you'll keep it down?" she asked.

"We'll find out." He leaned back onto his knees and drank a few tentative sips from the bottle she'd handed him. His stomach didn't protest, and within minutes he'd drained the bottle. "More," he said, and she complied.

"You're burning up," she observed, wiping a hand across his forehead, and he almost laughed.

"I'm fine," he said.

"We're not going to go through this again, are we? You're not fine. What happened?"

He shook his head like he had no idea, but he knew exactly. Dev was having nightmares again. When that happened, they somehow transferred themselves into Ender's subconscious, and he'd wake up screaming at the images Dev saw in his mind.

How Dev knew what happened on the ground around Ender and his team at the same time Dev was busy crashing his goddamned C-130 was something Ender never bothered to ask his boss. Somehow, every single horrific detail, right down to that very last moment, was imprinted in both their brains.

The worst had been when Ender had first gone to prison. They'd been keeping Dev drugged up until then, but as he improved, they'd lightened up on everything and Dev's mind kept reliving the crash over and over. Sometimes it was as often as every single hour. Ender would wake himself and the entire cell block, yelling so loudly he'd lose his voice. Finally, they'd had to put him into solitary confinement, in a cell that was soundproofed. All the way in the basement. Padded walls. Throw the crazy man down there and throw away the key.

Eventually, Dev's mind had eased up, but by then Ender hadn't cared. Had protested when they'd opened the cell door and told him that he could leave—two years, fourteen days and twelve hours later. His hair was down to his shoulders, as was his beard, and he couldn't remember the last time he'd taken advantage of his one hour of daily freedom or the last time he'd bathed. After a while, the guards would usually just poke a hose through the bars and wash everything down.

And still, Ender's excedo skills had remained intact. Had grown stronger, even, as though responding to the underuse by puffing themselves up in preparation, a fact the good people at ACRO had discovered once they tried to strap him down to clean him up.

"Let's get you cleaned up," Kira said when he didn't answer her. She dragged him to his feet and urged him over to the water. "You'll feel better once you're cooler."

He pulled off his clothes as he walked toward the stream they'd continued to follow. He waded in until he could dunk his head and he stayed under the cool water for as long as he could, until his lungs begged for air, until Kira was pulling him to the surface.

He couldn't pretend that what she'd told him about the jail, about what she'd had to do in order to survive, hadn't ripped at his gut. She was just as much of a survivor as he was, and braver than he was. She'd faced up to her past. He had yet to do so, and until he did, he'd be tied to Dev's nightmares.

For a few minutes, they just stared at each other, and he knew another wall in his personal security system had been breached. Vulnerability was something he did not do, especially not in front of other people.

"Maybe if you tell me, if you talk about it, it'll go away," she said finally.

He laughed, a short, harsh bark. "Did telling me about all the men who took advantage of you every year make it better for you?"

"Is that what this is about—you're worried about me?"

"No," he said gruffly, pissed that he hadn't even thought about that as a possible trigger for the damned nightmare. It had always been Dev, mainly because Dev was the person he was closest to. But after spending all this time with Kira...

Shit.

"If you talk about the nightmare—"

"It was just a dream," he cut her off, aware of how ridiculous he sounded. But she didn't call him on it, just continued like she was a seasoned professional.

"Talking about your dream will never take all the pain away. But it helps to tell someone who gets it—who understands how different we are. It helped me." She touched his arm and he jerked away. Completely undeterred, she reached out for him.

He couldn't bring himself to yank away from her hand again.

"I know you're not normal. I've seen what you can do," she said softly.

"I can kill. Doesn't make me any different than any murderer sitting in jail."

"I was talking about your speed. You killed to protect me," she said, and he didn't bother to deny it or elaborate on the many times before that he'd taken lives under the order of defend and protect. And the times he'd done it when there were no orders...

He shook his head, took another dive under the water made murky by the fast-moving darkness ready to take over the dusk, in hopes that when he surfaced she'd be done talking.

Of course, there was no chance of that. When he broke through the smooth, glassy expanse, she was sitting on the edge of the stream, waiting for him.

"When did you know you were different?" she asked, and he cursed this job again. This wasn't what he'd signed on for—none of this—and he was going to make sure Dev got that. Or he was out of this life, out of ACRO.

"We call them special-ability types. Stops people from feeling sorry for themselves." He ran both hands through his wet hair. "I was four the first time I was called on it."

He remembered the day clearly. The sheep were scattering, thanks to a thunderstorm that threatened the plains within seconds, without warning. Tornadoes couldn't have been far behind, and his mother had sent their dog, Boss, out to round up the scared animals and corral them to safety.

"I didn't want him to go alone," he said. "So I ran out after him, before anyone could stop me." He remembered the wind picking up, his mother's yells, Boss's barking as Tom stubbornly pushed forward and outran them all—the sheep, the dog, the truck zooming along the dirt road carrying his father and uncle home from town. It had felt so good, like his muscles finally got the long, burning stretch they'd needed since he'd been born. It was as if he'd finally fit into his own skin.

"I saw the funnel cloud forming, yelled to warn everyone. I didn't know, at the time, that the thing was one hundred and fifty miles away. Saw it clear as day."

"The original early-warning system," she teased lightly. "So you weren't lying when you said you had farm experience."

"Did I seem like I was faking it?" he growled, embarrassed that he'd shared anything with her. Mainly because she was looking at him like he was fucking cute or something, and Jesus, Dev was definitely going to hear about this one.

CHAPTER
Fifteen

SATURDAY AFTERNOON

Creed hadn't left his house all day.

Once he'd called on Oz for Dev, he'd planned on staying at Dev's house until Oz's arrival. But Kat had other plans, had made it impossible for him to stay there—she screeched at such high decibels in his ears that he couldn't stand the pain and Dev had ordered him out. But not before the ghost had cornered him, held him down and tried to finish what it had started last fall at Dev's mansion.

Still, Creed had waited outside the house, slept in his car and made certain that Oz arrived at ACRO and gained access to Dev's house in secret. Then he'd locked himself inside his own home, turned the lights down and lit a white candle, like his parents had taught him, and tried to decompress.

No, the ghost hadn't followed him home, but no matter how many showers he took, he couldn't wipe that snaking sensation off his skin. Kat had been unusually quiet as well. Respectful, even when his thoughts and dreams turned to Annika, but Kat wouldn't answer any of his questions about the spirit currently at residence at Dev's.

He'd just come out of a hot bath, had planned on putting himself to bed, where he knew he'd just toss and turn, when he heard the urgent knocking on his front door.

He rarely had visitors. His house was ten miles away from the main ACRO compound, up a winding hill so he had a full view of the valley below him. His closest neighbors were miles and miles away, his house was shrouded in full green foliage now that the last bits of snow had finally melted. But even though the day was sunny and warm outside, he'd still had to turn on the heat. And he'd lit a fire as well.

He'd checked his temperature in the hopes that he simply had the flu, but it remained normal.

The pounding was getting more persistent, as if someone was actually getting ready to knock down the door. Which was a lot like something Oz would do.

But when he finally answered the door, he found Annika there instead. And he had no doubt *she* would have kicked the door down.

She stared up at him, still on the threshold of the porch, as if stepping over that invisible line would be crossing into dangerous territory.

They hadn't spoken or seen each other since he'd walked out of the bar Tuesday night, and she was still royally pissed. But she didn't start right in on him, was actually restrained—it had to be because he didn't look well. On glancing in the mirror, his normally golden skin had been pale and there were circles under his eyes.

"Are you all right?" she asked.

"I'm better now," he said, and that was the truth. "Come on in."

She hesitated, then put a foot, clad in spring sandals and showing off prettily painted toenails—his favorite color, Vixen, a cross between black and purple—onto the hardwood floor in his foyer.

He didn't push it, turned and headed back into his living room. After a minute, he heard her close the door and her firm footsteps echoed on the floor as she crossed into the main part of his house to see him.

He'd sunk into the couch, a fresh chill washing over him.

"You're not all right, because people who are all right don't have a roaring fire when it's seventy degrees outside," she said. She put a warm hand on his forehead and frowned. "You're cool."

"I'm not sick." He paused, looked her over for any fresh bruises or scrapes and saw nothing. "How was your assignment?"

"Mission complete, as always."

"Good for you."

"I've heard you were on a mission too," she said, and he knew she was lying. She was on a hunt for information, probably wanted to know more about Dev than him and he felt the anger rise inside of him. That, at least, warmed him briefly.

"You heard correctly."

"With Dev?" she asked, and he didn't answer. Kat had skittered out long before Annika arrived—sulking because Creed resisted her touch as well.

"Tell me what's going on," she demanded.

"I can't."

"You're still mad at me, aren't you?"

"Not everything is about you, Annika."

"I know that—and I don't need a lecture from you too. But you walked out on me the other night, so I have a right to be pissed at you."

"Getting you pissed off is the only way to get you to come to my house? Who knew?" he muttered, pulled the blanket tighter around him and wondered if another bath would help.

"Something's wrong with you. I want to know where you were and what happened to make you feel like this."

"Are you checking up on me now? Because I didn't think you really gave a shit about anyone but yourself. And Dev."

Another cheap shot, and her eyes glittered with anger. As much as he wanted to tell her that, yes, he thought her precious Dev was in trouble, he'd been sworn to secrecy. His body still tingled with an unpleasant zing whenever he thought about the spirit's unwanted touch.

He hadn't told Dev just how violated he'd felt. This had been the second time the ghost had attempted to hold him down and touch him—the first time, back in September at the mansion, Kat had arrived just in time.

At Dev's, the spirit had been too strong even for Kat to do much. The only reason the spirit stopped when it did was because it really wanted Dev, and no substitute would do.

"I do give a shit, Creed. Or else I wouldn't be here."

"You're here because you want an orgasm," he said before he could stop himself, and fuck, that wasn't like him at all.

He knew Annika was younger than most women her age, less experienced socially because of her upbringing. She'd been a trained killer for the CIA, hadn't been on dates or to the prom, and he had no right to try to corner her. "Shit, Ani, I didn't mean that. I just...I don't know what's wrong."

Still, even now, when she reached out to touch his arm, he shrank back slightly, hating himself for that reaction.

"So, what? You're so pissed at me I can't even touch you?"

"That's not it," he said, but she'd already started to walk out of his house. "Annika, wait." He moved off the couch, losing his blanket as he grabbed her arm. She swung around and clocked him in the jaw, an automatic response to the threat of capture.

He didn't let go of her arm, even though her left hook was nothing short of amazing. She'd connected with his right cheekbone, and despite the fact that her touch had been a hit, his right side began to tingle in that good way he'd been missing.

"Fuck you," she spat, and then stopped and stared. Because he'd been naked under the blanket and her eyes were drawn down between his legs. He was a big man all around, but that wasn't what held her interest. No, she was drawn to the tattoos that covered his right ball and half his cock, loved to get between his legs and spend time tracing the pattern with her tongue, and Christ, he wanted her there right now.

"Put your mouth on me," he said, and he saw the resistance in her eyes even as she licked her lips. He put a slight pressure on her arm as he spoke again. "Now, Annika. I want you on your knees in front of me. And don't lie to me—I know you want it too."

Her lips parted, her nostrils flared and she sank to her knees slowly. He braced himself for her touch, prayed that he was going to be able to handle it. He wanted Annika to wipe that spirit's touch from him.

She dug her fingers into his hips, licked the tip of his cock and then took him deep into her mouth. He realized he'd been holding his breath when he heard his own long, low groan, and he let his eyes close as she continued to heal him with her talented, warm lips and tongue.

When she grazed her teeth lightly over the ridge at the head of his cock, his right side began to switch temperatures, varying between freezing and hotter than hell. He put his hands on her shoulders, not sure if he could steady himself like that.

But Annika had stopped, was staring at him again. "Has this ever happened before?" she asked, and he was about to answer no, when he realized she wasn't talking about the temperature shifts.

A glance down at his chest and leg revealed that his tattoos seemed to be morphing, nearly moving across his skin, as if the pattern was trying to tell him something.

Annika got to her feet, held his six-foot-five frame steady. "What's wrong? Please, Creed, tell me."

His mouth was dry, his throat tight, and all he could do was let her support him. "Just take me to bed, baby. Please just fuck me and don't ask me any more questions tonight," he said, his voice hoarse.

She didn't hesitate, tugged at him wordlessly until he followed her up the stairs to the loft area that was the entire second floor. Open and airy, with windows overlooking the valley all around and a large, king-sized bed in the middle of the room, it was one of Creed's favorite places to be.

"Too much light," he murmured, and after Annika helped him onto the bed, she found the controls for the curtains and quickly sheathed the room in darkness, rolling down the blackout shades.

He heard her stripping—normally, he'd tell her to slow down so he could enjoy every single reveal of her toned, curvy body.

But now, in the total darkness, all he wanted was her warm flesh on his, and he hoped her electric current was set to high.

"Ani, hurry," he heard himself say.

She crawled onto him, her breasts pressed against his chest, his arousal pressing her belly. "I'm here, Creed."

"Cold. I'm so cold. Can you shock me?"

"You know that doesn't work . . ."

"Try it," he insisted.

But she ignored him in favor of sliding his cock inside of her, where it was hot and wet and it hit him better than any jolt of electricity. Both of them groaned loudly, as she took him to the hilt, his hips came up off the bed and his right side began to warm again, finally.

"Oh, my God—Creed, I can't wait," she cried out, but he was already ahead of her. His balls tightened, his cock throbbed and he released inside of her, clutching at the sheets as the orgasm rolled through his entire body.

He was vaguely aware that she'd come too—hard, her sex milking him dry. But he soon realized that it was as if the electricity he'd felt when he entered her was not going to let either of them off the hook so easily. Because he remained rock hard and she appeared to be in the middle of some kind of amazing, multiple orgasm.

"So . . . good," she groaned. "Oh, God . . . yes."

"Harder. Ride me harder."

The sound of his voice heightened the climax, her fifth, sixth . . . she didn't know. She'd lost count. Creed always made her lose count.

His hands cupped her breasts, and his thumbs rasped over her nipples, which had grown more sensitive since she'd met Creed than they'd been in her entire life. Spasms took her, breakers on top of breakers, and as the waves of ecstasy melted away, Creed thrust upward so fiercely she screamed with the force of it.

"I love when you scream for me." He arched into her again, his cock driving deep and stretching her wide at its thick root, its steely hardness hitting all the right places. "Only me."

Yeah, but was she the only woman who screamed for him? She didn't know if he was celibate while she was off on missions.

She didn't expect it, didn't ask for it, but he'd better not make the mistake of letting her come face-to-face with one of the biker-babe skanks she'd seen him with in the past.

Not that she was jealous. Like she'd told Dev, this was just sex.

And what great sex it was. She smiled and ran her hands over the ripples in his abs and then up, to his chest, which still ran hot on one side and cooler on the other. The tattoos seemed to move beneath her palms, living things that shifted just under the skin, though she swore at times she could feel an outline. Testing, she sent a small shock into the tattooed side of his body, and that made them writhe more, angry.

Still impaled on Creed's shaft, she flicked on the nightstand lamp and watched the designs on his chest, neck and face morph from Native American symbols to faces. Creepy faces with jagged teeth, and narrowed eyes that seemed to look straight at her. If they thought they could scare her... she sent a shock into one of them, and it silently screamed as though in agony before shifting back to the original design.

"What did you do?" he breathed.

"A little shock."

Throwing back his head so the tendons in his neck strained, he closed his eyes. "Not... a good idea."

"You said—"

"I was wrong."

His hand slid up her back to her scalp, and he brought her mouth to his. Slipping his tongue between her lips, he clicked his piercing against her teeth so it sent a rare shock sizzling through her bones. Nothing shocked her, not in the electrical sense, but sometimes Creed's body jewelry acted as a conduit between them—he often said that if one of his piercings touched her when she climaxed, he felt her release.

Which explained why his favorite way to make her come was with his tongue, and she wasn't about to complain.

In a fluid move she'd not believed a body as big as his could master, he rolled her, pinned her to the bed as he plunged deep. He could be rough sometimes, because she enjoyed it, but this was different. Urgent.

Creed grunted and slammed into her, shoving her a few inches up the bed, so her hair brushed the headboard. Every stroke brought her closer to another peak, every one of his panting breaths made blood roar in her ears. She loved the sounds he made, so primal, so raw.

He increased his pace, something she hadn't thought was possible. She clung to him, gripped his shoulders so hard she was sure she'd leave marks. He rode her like his life depended on it, and when he hissed, "I need you to touch me," she wasn't sure what he wanted.

At least, she wasn't sure until she smoothed her hands down his back to grasp his buttocks and pull him as deep as he could go. Even then, he wasn't satisfied.

"Touch me, dammit."

She looked up into his face, a mask of pain she didn't understand, but as her fingers drifted down to stroke the valley of his ass, his expression softened into something like relief. One cheek burned, the other froze—and her fingers met in the middle to stroke it all, to bring the two halves together.

"Yeah," he groaned. "That's it. Make it right again."

Okay, this was new . . . he'd shown her positions and techniques she'd not even dreamed of, but never once had she touched him so intimately, and as her fingertip skimmed the sensitive opening, he gasped, shuddered and released inside her in hot bursts that went on and on and sent her over the edge once more.

Ecstasy took her in an explosion of color and light, and she might have passed out, because suddenly she was aware only of his weight on her, his labored breaths. He was so big, so crushingly big, but just when it seemed her bones would crumple in on one another, he withdrew and flopped onto his back.

Rolling to him, she stroked his chest, the tattoos that now appeared completely normal. "Creed," she said, pushing up on an elbow, "what is going on? Are you okay?"

"I'm fine now." He tucked her beneath one arm so her head rested on his shoulder. "Thank you."

This was too weird. She still had no idea why he'd walked out on her in the bar, but now she was just as confused by his out-of-character, sullen comments in his living room, and then the sudden need—no, demand—for sex. Specific touches. And the tattoos...

"Tell me what all this was about."

"Let it go, Annika."

The fluffy post-fuck bliss vaporized in a mushroom cloud of fury. First Dev, now Creed...they were shutting her out.

"I'm not letting it go. Something bad happened to you. Did someone—or some *thing*—hurt you?"

"I said, let it go."

"You know what? Fuck you." She surged off the bed and threw on her shorts, not bothering with the underwear. "You don't want to let me in on your big secret? Fine. Why don't you tell me why you worked me wet and then left me at the bar like some piece of trash? What, were you embarrassed by me in front of your buddies? You were in a big enough hurry to get me out of there."

He sat up. "Christ, Annika. Is that what you think happened?"

"I don't know what happened," she yelled. "Because you haven't bothered to fucking talk to me!"

"Yeah? How's it feel to want to know what's going on in someone else's mind, but they won't tell you?"

"What the hell are you talking about?"

She swore his tattoos were writhing again, and when he looked down at his hand, at the design that pulsed and glowed there, she knew she wasn't seeing things. He clenched his fist and shifted his dark gaze to her.

"You. I'm talking about you." He grabbed a pair of sweatpants out of the huge oak dresser next to his bed and stepped into them, never taking his eyes off her.

"I tell you stuff."

"Yeah. Pardon me while I reflect on the deep conversation we had about the virtues of fish pudding."

"That's not fair. I hate fish pudding. I did *not* discuss its virtues."

He ground his teeth so violently she heard the grate of enamel on enamel. "No. And you also clammed up when I asked where you'd eaten it in the first place. I don't know a damned thing about you except what everyone else at ACRO knows. You dodge questions and avoid any kind of situation that might lead to intimacy."

God, she'd never met anyone as annoying as him. So what if she hadn't told him her fake parents had fed her only European cuisine? The reason, to keep her more convincing and effective for overseas work, wasn't something she wanted to share.

"Got a dictionary?" She pulled on her shirt, screw the bra. "Because it seems to me that we've been all over the intimacy thing."

"That's not what I mean, and you know it. Have we ever been on a real date? You know, a dinner of more than buffalo wings and a pitcher of beer while you blow me from under the table?"

She bit back a smile at those memories. She loved how he tried so hard to control his breathing while she went down on him in public, loved how he trembled with the effort of not shouting like he always did when she made him come with her mouth. "I have a lot to catch up on."

"Baby, you're caught up on the physical side of things."

An iceberg lodged in her chest as the conversation with Dev about her emotional immaturity came roaring back. "What's that supposed to mean?"

"It means that once you get what you want, you can't wait to get away from me. You won't spend the night in my bed, but you don't have a problem sleeping over at Dev's place. It means that every time we have an argument, you walk out."

"You're one to talk about walking out."

He shoved his fingers through his hair. "Yeah, I know. That

thing at the bar was stupid, and I'm sorry. But that was once. You do it every time."

"Because I don't know how to argue," she snapped. "I never had to. In the world I grew up in, someone pisses you off, they stop breathing. There is no argument." She turned away from his dark gaze and blew out a breath. "And I don't know how to do this." She'd never had a boyfriend and certainly hadn't slept with anyone before Creed. Sex was easy. Knowing what to do afterward, that was hard.

"Do what?"

"This!" She waved her arm around the room. "Me and you. I don't understand the protocol."

"You stop running away. You let me in."

She shook her head. This was way too complicated. She needed another assignment. Bringing in those two Itor agents from Idaho hadn't been nearly exciting enough, hadn't allowed her to slide into the mental place where she was most comfortable: mission-mode. Cold. Efficient. Single-minded.

"Dammit, Annika. Someday you're going to fuck up, or something bad is going to happen to you, and you're going to have to let someone in."

"I have someone."

"Right. The almighty Dev. And what happens when he's busy or unavailable? What are you going to do then? Come find me and fuck the problem away? Your usual MO?"

For the first time in her life, Annika was speechless. Her mouth worked, but nothing came out. Finally she summoned her voice, but when she spoke, it didn't sound like her.

"I don't need this. I don't need you or your dick or your condescending bullshit. If I don't open up to you, maybe it's because the last time I did, you turned me in and got me suspended from missions for six months." That wasn't entirely true; she wouldn't open up to him anyway. "I don't need a fucking therapist, Creed."

"I'm not asking to be your therapist. I'm asking to be more than a closet fuck."

She hated this, hated that their relationship had gotten to this point without her noticing. Hated that what they had might qualify as a relationship at all. "Maybe Dev should have given you the *Cosmo* lecture instead of me." She grabbed her shoes and started out the door, but his soft voice stopped her at the threshold.

"What *Cosmo* lecture?"

"Don't confuse sex with love," she whispered.

And then she fled, just like he said she always did.

CHAPTER
Sixteen

SUNDAY NOON

When they hit Salmon, Idaho, Ender stole a car. He didn't tell Kira he stole it, acted like, *Yeah, this car has been waiting for us all along.* Then he pulled off into the woods, changed the plates and finally phoned his comms contact, Bryan, again.

Bryan officially registered the stolen vehicle within minutes, and Ender and Kira headed northeast to the private airstrip and jet, to take them the rest of the way to the Catskills and ACRO.

All this, and she still hadn't agreed to join. All this, and she was supposed to have been dead days ago. By his hand.

"Fuck." He slammed the car's steering wheel and, next to him, Kira started.

"What's wrong? Is someone following us?" She looked around wildly, checking all the windows.

"No one's following us," he said. Just his past, and shit, Dev was going to ream him. He rolled his neck from side to side to loosen the tight muscles as he pushed the car hard to make up for lost time.

Bryan assured him the private jet would be in place to take them on the final leg of their journey. So far, he hadn't sensed any more

I-Agents, and he wondered why they seemed to have given up so easily.

"So, is there a name for what you are?" Kira asked. She hadn't spoken much at all for the past hour, had crossed her arms over her chest and remained deep in thought. Ender had appreciated the silence, but knew that women, no matter if they were part animal or not, loved to talk.

He gave a long-suffering sigh before he answered. "Yes."

"Are you going to tell me?" she asked, and he thought about telling her no, that he couldn't in case she didn't sign on.

But that was ridiculous, because if she didn't agree to join, she wouldn't be around long enough to tell anyone at all. In many cases, powers could be stripped to eliminate the person as an Itor target or future threat, but ACRO scientists had determined that Kira's specialized physiology wouldn't allow for ability stripping. "I'm an excedo. Excedosapien."

"Are there a lot of you?"

"Enough, I guess. I never took a head count." He shrugged. "Derek was one too. Different abilities. He was stronger, not as fast."

"And you really don't think of yourself as a freak?" she asked.

He thought of himself in a lot of ways, but freak was never one of them. "No."

"Thanks for elaborating on that."

"Kira, look, I just don't want to talk about my life. I never have."

"Are you telling me that there's no one in this entire world who knows about your life?"

"No," he said, aware that he was leaving dent marks in the steering wheel with his fingers. Dev didn't count, because he just . . . knew. Ender had never actually had to sit down and explain anything to anybody. ACRO had tried to force him to see their shrink only once, and after he nearly killed the man, they decided that Ender was better off when his mind was left alone.

"What about your parents?"

"I haven't seen them since I was seventeen."

"So they don't even know if you're alive?"

He wanted to ask why it was so damned important to her, but he already knew. He was the first guy who'd known the truth about her, the first guy who protected her instead of merely fucking her.

Killing her would've been so much easier than this. "I don't know what they know. That life just wasn't for me anymore. I was causing trouble for them. They're better off now."

She nodded, like she got that. And yeah, he could see why she did.

He shifted in the leather seat, realized that his cock was hard. Kira was putting out those damned pheromones again.

"It's almost time," she said, staring down at his lap and sucking her full bottom lip between her teeth. He heard the low growl of approval rumble in the back of his own throat as her hand traveled between his legs, wondered if she could mount him and let him drive at the same time.

"Can you wait another half hour, just so I can get across—" he started, but she tore open his pants with one hand as she freed herself from her own BDU bottoms, and he had a feeling he was about to find out the true meaning of "zero to sixty."

When her hand circled his cock, his foot jerked the accelerator nearly to the floor and he pulled the wheel so far to the right they almost ran off the road.

He cursed, righted the wheel with both hands while she chuckled, her voice low and throaty, the way it always got when her heat became an uncontrollable need.

She stroked him until his breathing was faster than normal, until his split concentration forced him to give himself over to Kira in a much different way than he'd been allowing over the past hours.

He held the wheel steady with his left hand, which allowed Kira to climb on board. He put his right hand on the wheel, because he was going to need both hands for this one, and Kira ducked her head against his neck, her warm breath fanning his skin, her sex wet and hot and rubbing his cock in a way that made him jerk his hips upright against her.

"Impatient, are we?" she murmured.

"Don't play games with me."

"Or what? You'll pull over and spank me for being a bad girl?"

His breath hitched at the thought of taking her over his knee, and she knew it, knew she had the power this time, more so even than when she'd held him down on the ground.

"Mine," she whispered in his ear. "All mine. Say it, Tommy."

"Kira, I . . ."

"Say it. Please, Tommy," she said, and her pheromones must be getting stronger, because as hard as he tried he couldn't resist doing what she asked.

"Yours, Kira. All yours," he whispered, put his head back against the headrest in silent surrender and tried to tell himself that he didn't fucking mean it. That it was all part of the goddamned job.

She pulled her hips back slightly so she could accommodate him in one long, slow motion that sheathed him fully inside of her, and he forced himself to just breathe.

He was sweating and shaking, staring at the road with an intense concentration as the pleasure coursed through his body. She bit him at the tender place between neck and collarbone as she arched against him, held his skin between her teeth as if marking him for life, and he was grateful that this particular stretch of back road was long and straight and deserted.

She cried out, *"Tommy,"* as she rocked against him, and the entire car was shaking from the speed, the floor vibrating beneath his feet, his cock pulsing inside of her, and fuck, this was one of the most out-of-control things he'd ever done. And that was saying something.

And when he spilled inside of her, he eased his foot off the accelerator because he'd started to see stars as his orgasm wracked his body, stronger than ever.

When she whispered, *"More,"* in his ear, he pushed down on the petal again, because, despite the intensity of the orgasm, he was still hard for her, and dying like this wouldn't be the worst way to go.

* * *

Tom pulled into the parking lot of a fast-food burger joint at their next stop, and Kira's stomach rolled when they stepped through the front door. The horrific stench of grilled animal flesh made her taste bile. She should have known not to try. She'd always hated restaurants, couldn't even begin to fathom why people would cook and eat intelligent, sensitive creatures that communicated every bit as well as humans if they would only listen.

"I'll, uh, wait in the car." She backed toward the door. "Just get me a salad. Hold the chicken and cheese."

What he held was her, with a firm grip on her wrist. "I'm not letting you out of my sight."

The hard edge in his voice reminded her that danger still lurked, and that, ultimately, she was little more than his prisoner. Which stung, because after all they'd been through, she felt like they'd become more than that. Partners. Cohorts. Lovers.

Hello, Stockholm syndrome.

"Then we need to go through the drive-thru," she said curtly, and when he would have argued, she added a pathetic "Please, Tommy."

Grumbling under his breath, he gave in, and after a run through the drive-thru, he pulled over in a nearby wooded park. Keeping one watchful eye on their surroundings, he handed her the salad and unwrapped a colossal triple cheeseburger. Once more, her stomach lurched.

"Want a bite?" he asked, and immediately shot her an apologetic look. "Sorry, forgot. Vegan ethics."

Even though he hadn't been snarky, she glared and rolled down the window to let out some of the cooked-animal odor. "It isn't entirely about ethics and morals. I mean, I wouldn't eat animal flesh even if I could, but I can't. It's painful."

"What, it upsets your stomach?"

"Worse. I can't even touch it. Tasting it . . ." She shuddered, remembering the agony, the nausea that brought her to her knees the last time someone at a Christmas party thought it would be funny to slip chicken into a dish that was supposed to be vegan. "It's like how some psychics get impressions by touch."

As though he was bored with the conversation, he looked out the side window, all hooded eyes and lazy grace, but she knew better. The danger scent he threw, as a cop car rolled slowly past, was a dead giveaway.

"You're talking about psychometry," he said, still focused on the outside.

"I'm impressed."

She eyed him with newfound appreciation that wasn't really new, because she always appreciated looking at him. Especially when he turned that hawklike gaze on her, like he was doing now that the patrol vehicle had disappeared.

"I've dealt with a psychic or two."

Interesting. She'd have to ask more about his work. Of course, she'd tried, but he hadn't been very forthcoming.

"Well, it's like that. When I come into contact with meat I feel—and taste—the animal's terror and pain. I experience everything it suffered before and during its death." She shuddered again. "Imagine waiting in a chute or a cage you can't break out of, and smelling blood and death ahead of you, and knowing you're going to die. I feel all of it."

"That explains the slaughterhouses that went up in flames," he said quietly, as he wrapped up his burger and shoved it back into the bag.

She fell in love with Tom Knight right then and there. It was too much to hope that he'd gone veg, but at least he respected her enough to not do something in her presence that pained her, both physically and emotionally.

"I wish I could take credit for the slaughterhouses," she said in a voice tight with emotion she hoped he didn't hear, "but doing something like that would have drawn attention I couldn't afford."

He chowed on a handful of fries and washed it down with his Coke. "If it's not you destroying all the research labs and whaling ships and crap, then who?" He swore and nodded grimly. "Itor."

"That's what I was thinking. Your bad guys were trying to flush me out, or at least get the authorities to arrest me so they could take me from them."

"Do you see why you need to join my agency? You can't hide from Itor."

"I told you I'd check it out, but you might as well prepare yourself for the fact that I'm most likely not going to join. I won't be kept or used by anyone. I certainly won't train animals to fight in wars or whatever idiotic thing the government wants to do with them."

"But you will give it a chance, right?" If anyone else had used the desperate tone he had, she'd have thought they were pleading with her. Tommy was probably just suffering from hunger pangs.

"I said I would. But don't expect anything more."

"Fair enough." He rolled down his window and tossed the bag of food into a garbage can. "Let's get this done."

SUNDAY NIGHT

It hadn't been easy trying to sleep with Oz being one floor above him, but Dev's exhaustion took over.

He was so tired of fighting.

"Stop fighting me. I've got to get you out of here." The man's voice was a low growl. Tense. Rough. Dev smelled fear and wasn't sure if it came off of him or the man dragging him out of the wrecked C-130.

"Monty." Dev flailed to reach his copilot, but the man's grip was stronger.

"He's gone. They're all gone." The man grabbed him and ran, until Dev heard the explosion and the man covered his body with his own.

Dev wasn't sure how long he lay with his face to the gravel, the ground still vibrating, the air ripe with smoke, flooding his lungs, his eyes tearing. But when he could sit up, he stared into the face of the man who'd saved him. And then he rubbed his eyes and stared some more.

The man in front of him wore a suit of armor, a sword at his hip. His blue eyes were fierce, his features chiseled and strong, his body curiously free of the debris and blood that covered Dev.

The man in front of him was a warrior. A divine champion of justice, a paladin. And just as suddenly, the picture changed and the

warrior morphed into a half man, half animal—a man with a chee-
tah's eyes and fur—

"Who are you?" Dev heard himself ask.

"No one," the man said.

Dev blinked again, and for a second, the world went black. He
put out his arms frantically, panicked and blinded. The same man
came into view once more, dressed in fatigues, covered in black
soot and cammy paint. His eyes were haunted, but he was no less a
warrior.

"I don't know what's happening to me," he remembered saying.

"I don't know what's happening to me," Dev shouted, waking
himself up.

"That's not true."

The voice belonged to Oz, not Ender, the warrior who'd saved
his life that day. It had taken him months to figure out that his second sight allowed him to see the soul within his special operatives,
but part of his gift was being able to spot them. To save them. To
know that the person the rest of the world saw was not the truth.
So Ender saved him and now Dev saved others.

And Oz had also saved Dev's life in too many ways to count.

"Another nightmare, Dev?"

He found his voice, but it didn't sound like his. "Yes. I'm fine
now. I'm fine." Like if he said it enough, it would be true. "I
don't need your help. Never fucking did," he muttered, feeling
punch-drunk. He tried to CRV his room and Oz, but nothing.
Just total blackness, and a ball formed in the pit of his stomach.

"Dev, breathe, all right?"

"I am."

"No, you're not. Shit, your lips are practically blue. Breathe,
dammit," Oz commanded, put a strong hand on his bare back
where the comforter had slipped down.

"Is the writing still there? Fuck, Oz, I can't see."

"You haven't been able to see for ten years."

"You know what I mean." He tried to stand, but Oz caught him,
and for a second, held him tight. "Is the writing gone? What does
it say?"

"Let me check you. Please," Oz said, and Dev was too tired to argue anymore, let Oz's hands run over him. "There's no writing there."

Suddenly Dev's mind flashed to the two of them sitting together, his own naked body curved into Oz's T-shirt and shorts-clad one.

"You're a fucking liar," he whispered, felt Oz smile against his neck.

"At least your second sight's coming back."

"Yeah," he said.

"You can't go on like this," Oz said, and for once, Dev agreed with him. "You've got to let me send it back."

He wanted to tell Oz that he didn't need his protection, his walking-dead routine, but he was tired of lying. So damned tired. "Not yet."

And then Oz spoke, his voice a notch below pure rage. "You never listen. Cocky fucking asshole, taking everything on yourself."

"Look who's talking," Dev said softly. "What? Did I take the job you wanted?"

"You still believe I wanted ACRO, don't you? You know I try not to deal with humans, Dev. I deal in souls. I was never interested in saving the world."

"Maybe because the dead are the only ones who can stand you," Dev said, wanting to strike the killing blow. But Oz didn't give an inch, and Dev suddenly didn't want to play this game of who-hurt-who-most anymore.

"The dead aren't the only ones who can stand me," Oz said in his ear. "And that's probably what kills you the most."

"Fuck you," Dev whispered, sounding desperate, even to his own ears. And he was still in Oz's arms.

"I missed you," Oz whispered back, his voice gentle, soothing. "I didn't want to, but fuck..."

Dev swallowed, hard, but he couldn't get the words out. Instead, he just reached a hand out to Oz, gripped the front of his shirt hard and hoped the other man knew what he meant.

"You've got to let me send this thing away. For good. Shit, you promised me last time, Dev."

"I know. But I need the ghost. You have to make it help me."

"What could be so bad that you'd call that thing out again?" Oz asked.

"Things are happening at ACRO . . . things I can't explain."

Oz was silent for a long moment. "Tell it to talk to me. Tell it I'll share with you everything it reveals. It's the only way to find out what it knows."

"I want you to be safe," Dev protested.

"You need to stop worrying about me," Oz told him, even though every fiber in Dev's being told him that Oz didn't mean it at all.

Dev concentrated on the ghost. "Hey," he shouted. "I'm ready to deal. But you'll need to talk to Oz."

For a few minutes, nothing happened. Then the room went cold, and Dev felt the ghost's presence like a weight pressing in on every inch of skin. Oz's breathing grew rapid, and then he jerked away.

"Oz—"

Oz's palm slammed into Dev's chest as though to prevent him from going anywhere, but no worry there. He wasn't moving, not while Oz sat next to him, his body taut, his skin icy.

"It'll deal, but it's demanding the same thing it wanted before," Oz growled, and Dev felt the cold all the way to his heart. As a teen, Oz had banished the thing before it had a chance to request anything in return for information about Dev's past and future. Then, almost four years ago, it had asked for something Dev couldn't give, not even to find the ACRO agent. The guilt ate at him, and this time, he wouldn't back down.

"Yes," he whispered, and then louder, "Yes. Let it know that if it gives me the information I need, it can have my body. Like it wants."

Dev could feel Oz's fury, a wave of psychic energy that blasted through his brain with enough concussion to snap his head back.

"You'll be fighting for control constantly. It won't stop at your body. You'll be in a battle for your soul."

"I can handle it," Dev said, and Oz cursed. "Now find out what it's wanted to tell me for all these years."

The room grew colder, until Dev's teeth chattered, and the pressure on his body increased, as though he were sinking deeper into the ocean, and then suddenly, everything was back to normal.

"Jesus," Oz breathed. "Oh, Christ."

Dev grabbed Oz's hand and turned to him. "What? What is it?"

Oz pushed to his feet, and Dev felt the loss like a strike to the gut. "Dev . . . just, shit."

"Goddammit, Oz. Tell me!" He'd never heard Oz so rattled, so on the verge of what he could only guess was fear.

"His name's Darius."

"And?"

"Give me a second." Oz was pacing. Dev could hear the footfalls, could hear Oz running his hands through his hair frantically. "He was a Druid priest who worked for the man who ultimately took over Itor."

Dev blinked. He hadn't seen *that* coming.

Still pacing, Oz continued. "Thirty-six years ago, that man, Alek, had Darius tortured to death. It was bad. God, it was bad. He's showing me . . . the blood, *God*."

Oz was rambling now, his words coming fast, too fast, because Dev had a sickening feeling he didn't want to know any more.

"You had been born just days earlier, and Darius died screaming your name," Oz said. "Some sort of spell to locate you in death. His ghost found you, has been watching you since you were a baby, waiting until you were strong. Strong enough to take on Itor, to help him get his revenge."

"Why me?"

Oz stopped his pacing in front of Dev. "Darius thinks you'll want revenge too."

"Because Itor killed my parents?"

"No. Shit." Oz cleared his throat, something he only did when he was nervous, which didn't happen. Ever. "Alek's girlfriend was pregnant—and eight months into the pregnancy, she wised up. Darius helped her escape. He brought her to the United States, to people he'd learned about through secret channels."

Dev's heart started to pound, and an icy sweat broke out on his forehead. "I don't want to hear any more." He scooted backward on the bed, but Oz caught him by the shoulders and brought him forward, his grip strong but trembling.

"Those people, the O'Malleys, adopted the baby to keep it safe," Oz said, his voice grim, as deep as if it had been dredged up from the pits of hell, and Dev had to struggle to breathe. "Dev, the O'Malleys raised you, but your biological father is Itor's leader."

The world spun and Darius slammed into his body with a victorious shriek.

"Dev, stay with me," Oz commanded, but his voice sounded far away. The icy hands of the ghost he now knew as Darius touched his back and Dev understood why Creed had been so freaked out when this ghost touched him.

It was a touch from hell…sexual and so much more. Soul-sucking. "I'm not going to be anyone's puppet," Dev growled, more to himself than Darius, but the ghost seemed to understand, to grip Dev even tighter.

"Good, that's good," Oz murmured. "Dev, we can't wait…I know you want more answers, but—"

"We're not going to find them here," Dev said. "Do whatever you have to do. I trust you."

"I'm going to drive it out—for good."

"Yes," Dev said, his hands on Oz's shoulders to ground himself. "Oz, am I really…Oh, my God…Itor."

"Clear your mind now. We'll figure all that out once Darius is gone."

But Dev heard himself babbling, repeating, "Itor," over and over, until Oz took him by the shoulders and shook him hard.

"Dammit, Dev, we don't have provisions in place for ACRO if

you have a breakdown. You've got to stay with me … you have to fight."

Fight. Yes, Dev could do that. Except his second sight had faded to almost nothing, his skin felt too tight for his body and he was cold. "So cold, Oz."

Oz pushed him back to the bed, spread his hands on Dev's back, and a searing heat came through his palms that made Dev hiss. The floor beneath the bed shook with a force that their combined weight wasn't responsible for.

When an invisible hand caressed his cheek, he shivered harder and fought Oz's hands.

"He's mine. Do you hear me? He's all fucking mine," Oz said, his voice low and controlled.

"Oz, please," he moaned, because he wasn't sure what the hell was going to happen. He didn't know whether or not Oz's possessive display was just an act for the spirit, and he wasn't sure he cared if it was.

The caress became a rough slap, first on one cheek and then the other. Dev struggled to get up on all fours, groaned as Oz pressed his back harder and harder, thankful he'd shut down his CRV because he didn't want to see this, not the way his body bowed to Oz's or the way the muscles in his former lover's shoulders flexed.

Walls shuddered, ceilings creaked and something fiercer than the wind and ten times more pissed howled between his ears.

"Concentrate on me," Oz told him, bit the top of his ear hard enough to bring him back to earth momentarily.

He didn't want to come back, wanted to forget Oz and the spirit and just concentrate on himself for once, lose every single sense.

But Oz refused to let him, the tug-of-war for Dev's soul so fierce that Dev realized he'd half collapsed onto his elbows, the spirit scrambling his mind and his body.

"Love you, Dev. Always have. I'll keep you safe," Oz murmured, and Dev knew just how to help Oz get rid of this spirit that threatened to take everything from him.

With an incredible power he didn't think he had, Dev shoved Oz off of him and turned to face him. His second sight was still gone, but he reached out to grab the warm body he knew was right in front of him, pulled at Oz and kissed him, long and hard, until Oz was pushing him back down to the mattress, his aura strong enough to battle with the spirit Dev knew was watching.

Oz didn't care, kissed Dev harder, in a fight for all his attention, and Dev gave in easily, let Oz's tongue duel with his, their kiss part apology, part promise.

He didn't resist when Oz stripped his shirt off, ran his tongue over Dev's nipples until Dev moaned.

"Like the first time," Dev whispered. "Do it just like the first time."

Oz chuckled against Dev's chest. "You were trembling then. So scared."

"I wasn't scared—I was cold," Dev scoffed, remembering his bravado, and the way Oz hadn't been all that gentle but still managed to make it amazing.

It was still amazing, and he yelled that thought out to Oz as Oz entered him, and then his breath caught in his throat, and the enormity of what was going to happen after they finished here overwhelmed him.

Dev could feel Darius quelling with fear as he attempted to fight the bond between the two men...could feel the spirit's last attempt at a fight as it realized it had no hope of battling Oz.

"Don't try to use your CRV. Just picture it, the way it was," Oz commanded.

Oz's cock inside him for the first time, so impossibly hard it made Dev's head spin, put tears in his eyes, and yes, he'd been shaking, a mix of fear and excitement running through his blood.

"The way you remember," Oz said.

Oz murmuring in his ear about how hot Dev was, how much he was going to enjoy it when Oz started pumping his hips, and, oh, his back arched off the bed as Oz angled his cock to hit his prostate over and over.

"This thing can't get into your memories, no matter how hard it tries," Oz murmured.

Dev tightened his legs around Oz's waist and trusted Oz, the way he had when he was seventeen and cried out Oz's name, the first man to ever touch him.

He'd been with many since Oz, too many to count after they'd broken up that first time.

It had been Dev's idea, but Oz had gone along with it, for reasons Dev hadn't even begun to understand until nearly four years ago, when Dev made the horrible, but necessary choice to contact the spirit they now knew as Darius.

"Stop thinking, Devlin," Oz whispered. "Stop thinking and just feel."

Oz pulled out, all the way, and Dev heard himself moan in protest. In seconds, Dev's legs were nearly on Oz's shoulders, and Oz entered him again, first teased him with the head of his cock and then with a deep push that filled Dev in a way no one else ever could.

"Mine," Oz growled fiercely, and something just as impressive growled back, a low timbre that sent a wave of energy through the room. Not evil. Different. And then he felt as if the floorboards would drive right through the mattress.

"Leave him the hell alone."

For now . . . not forever. The high-pitched voice made Dev open his eyes, and he stared straight into Oz's. No CRV. Just pure, god-damned, clear as the day he last flew his C-130, sight.

He needed to keep this moment forever, the look in Oz's eyes, the way his dark hair hung over his forehead, neither too long nor too short. Perfect. Just perfect.

Oz gave a powerful thrust of his hips, sent his cock plunging hard enough to make Dev's eyes roll to the back of his head. Except he refused to let that happen, kept his eyes on Oz's as they came simultaneously, the hot semen bonding the two men—hot and complicated—together again.

*   *   *

MONDAY 4 A.M. MST

Ender put pedal to the metal in order to reach the LZ. By his calculations, they'd be well into the air by the time Kira would need sex again. The flight to ACRO would take between six and seven hours, leaving them enough time to deplane before she'd need servicing again. Once on the ground, he could easily find someplace private before shuttling her off to the training facility.

The thought of dropping her off made his head ache. He blamed the fact that he'd thrown out his hamburger after hearing Kira's story—even though he knew he needed real meat, and fast, he just couldn't bring himself to force it down.

Once Kira got to ACRO, he wouldn't have to worry about any of this. She'd be someone else's problem.

"Are you all right?" Kira was asking, and he realized he'd made it to the LZ, had parked the car and was just sitting there staring out at the sleek private jet.

"I'm fine. Let's go."

"But you've got this funny look on your face. Like you're in pain," she persisted, and she was touching him again. It wasn't sexual, but her hand was caressing the back of his neck, just the same, as if she knew where his pain was.

He stopped arguing, let his head drop forward, and she shifted in her seat so she could work the tight muscles in the back of his neck more easily. Her fingers kneaded his flesh expertly and she was murmuring, "This will help, Tommy," and even though it was nowhere near time to have her again, he still had the urge to lay her down on the seat and have her, deep and hard.

He put his hand over hers and moved it off of his skin.

"Better?" she asked, and no, it wasn't better. And it wasn't going to be better. Not for a long while, and maybe never.

"Let's go." He opened his car door, grabbed his bag and started walking toward the plane, not bothering to make sure she was following behind him.

He ignored the pilot he knew only as Ben, in favor of shoving his gear into the open door. He prepared to board, because they were already slightly behind schedule, when he heard the guy flapping his gums.

"You did the right thing, agreeing to sign on," Ben was telling Kira.

"I'm not sure you understand," she started, but Ender turned, shot her a look, and she shut her mouth fast.

"Did you think I wouldn't get the job done?" he asked Ben, who smiled and looked nervously between Ender and Kira.

"Never doubted it, buddy," Ben said.

Ender's hand shot out, pinning the pilot to the side of the jet by his throat. "I'm not your fucking buddy." He let go of Ben and turned to Kira, who'd gone wide-eyed. "Get in."

He helped her board. Ben had already scrambled in and away from Ender, headed to the cockpit, where he'd no doubt lock the door behind him. If Ben knew what was good for him, he'd leave the two of them alone for the remainder of the flight.

Ender could feel the questions radiating off Kira—the slight panic, the need to escape. But the jet lifted, sleek and solid, and there was no turning back for either of them.

The flight had been long, largely silent, and with the exception of one memorable round of sex in the aisle, in the seats, and against the cockpit door, boring. Tom had seemed agitated, and no matter how often she asked why, the answer had always been the same: *It doesn't matter.*

She'd grown used to his strange hot and cold moods, the ones that made him seem so caring and gentle, and then in the next instant distant and frosty. But this was different. He was on edge, snappish, and he'd scared the crap out of her when he grabbed the pilot by the throat and slammed him against the plane.

Tom was about as predictable as a pissed-off wolverine. Even now, as they exited the plane on the tarmac of the agency he called ACRO, he puffed up and bared his teeth when the driver of the Humvee waiting for them looked at her for a little too long. Seemed like an odd thing to do, considering the fact that he was about to hand her off to the Training department, where, apparently, servicing her needs by someone else had been arranged.

The thought made her chest hurt as they climbed into the vehicle.

"Tommy..." Her voice wavered, and she cleared her throat before scooting forward in the seat to talk to him where he sat in the front. "Are we going there now? Because you said you'd take care of, uh, things, beforehand."

"We're going to the animal facility."

"Oh. Good." He'd told her all about it, and this had been the one thing she'd looked forward to seeing at ACRO.

Sitting back, she took in the compound, the squat gray buildings, the rounded hangars . . . an old military base. Given the state of the surroundings, she expected a cold, lablike facility where the animals were kept—experimented on or some crap—but when the driver pulled into the parking lot of a beautiful, modern building complete with cement sculptures of animals, she gasped. Green fields stretched beyond the structure, and to the right, an equestrian arena and stables that would make the Budweiser Clydesdales jealous took up a couple of acres. Dozens of dogs barked and jumped excitedly in the kennels to the left.

As she stepped out of the SUV, a dark-haired, very tanned man approached, his black BDUs peppered with animal hair.

"Hi," he said, extending his hand. "Kira, right? I'm Zach Taylor. Your supervisor."

Supervisor? His supposition was a little premature, but she merely nodded and drew back her hand before physical contact impacted his libido. It was nearly time to mate again, and her need had already affected Zach in small ways, if the glazed-over look in his eyes was any indication.

Tom donned a pair of sunglasses and relaxed, one hip propped against the vehicle as she smiled at Zach. "You've got a beautiful facility."

"It's yours too."

"Look, you should know—"

"Let's get on with it," Tom snapped, pushing away from the Humvee. "She's supposed to meet her trainers in an hour."

Zach scowled, and for a moment she swore she could see testosterone winging through the air between them. Babs would have sent Kira the usual sentiment, that males were dumb.

"I'd really like to see the animals," she said quickly, and Zach snapped out of it, took her by the elbow to guide her toward the building.

He led them on a tour of the facility, which was more impressive on the inside than the outside. The back half was dedicated to medical offices, where ACRO employed a full-time veterinarian and had another on call. A good portion of the building belonged to kitchens that prepared controlled, healthy diets for each individual animal's requirements. And every animal handler possessed skills similar to hers, though from what Zach told her, she was by far the strongest animal psychic they'd ever seen or had even believed existed.

"*If* I was to join, would I be able to keep some of my animals here?" she asked, as they walked through the immaculate barn.

"If?" Zach shot Tom a confused glance, but Tom's flat expression discouraged questions, and Zach shrugged. "I suppose it could be arranged."

She stopped to talk with one of the horses, learned that his job was to carry security forces along the wooded perimeters where vehicles couldn't go. And he was very excited to tell her about the time he'd been entered in a European jumping competition.

"Why would this horse have been flown overseas?"

"The animals sometimes provide cover for our operatives. Omar was a world-class jumper before a minor fetlock injury took him out of the pro circuit. His participation in a competition allowed one of our agents to get close to a Spanish diplomat with an interest in equestrian sports."

"So you don't train animals for war or to carry bombs into enemy territory or anything, right?"

"Never," Zach said fiercely. "The animals are trained to work with humans, not for them, and they always know the risks involved with every mission."

Interesting.

The rest of the tour proved just as interesting, and all the animals she talked to had similar stories. In the kennels, the dogs practically overwhelmed her with tales of how they'd helped their humans, of how the humans played with them, took them home, gave them the best treats.

There had to be a catch.

"You're wondering if there's a catch," Zach said softly, as he crouched next to her where she was scratching the ears of a fluffy malamute mix.

"Can you read people too?"

He smiled, and her breath caught. The man was devastatingly handsome, in a less rugged way than Tom, who was a few yards away, tossing a ball for a border collie.

"I can only read animals, but I had the same concerns when I came here. ACRO's been good to me. To all of us. Dev even promised that if the little bar we have on the compound ever starts serving food, it'll be vegetarian."

She smiled at that, warmed inside, because suddenly, she was amongst people like her. With the exception of Marcia, Kira hadn't ever related well to humans, nor them to her. And until Tom, she'd never known what it was like to *be* with someone. Someone who knew what she was and didn't care.

This place couldn't be real, and if it was, there had to be a dark side.

"Kira?" Zach's hand ran in slow, soothing strokes up and down her spine. "Are you okay? You seem a little distant."

"It's a lot to take in." The familiar ache began to throb deep in her pelvis, and she exhaled slowly. She needed Tommy.

Thigh muscles quivering as though preparing to squeeze Tom between them, she started to stand, but Zach's palm burned into her back, holding her in place. Her gaze slammed into his, into the blatant lust that burned in his golden brown eyes. Lynx eyes, like Rafi's. And damn, she missed her babies.

"It's true, isn't it? Your spring fever."

She nodded, because denying it seemed pointless. No doubt Tom had reported everything to these people. Then again, they'd known a lot about her even before Tom had sauntered into her life.

"When..."

"Now," she croaked, and jerked away, but again, he held her. She trembled beneath the sensual strokes of his fingers as they worked their way up to her cheek. She needed Tom.

Except, he wouldn't be servicing her now. Maybe she should take someone else. Use this opportunity to force the separation between her and Tom that would come any moment anyway. At least this way it would be her choice. Her terms.

"God, you're beautiful," Zach whispered, and she flushed and turned away because she knew he didn't mean it. Her pheromones had turned his brain to mush.

Her own brain was rapidly growing fuzzy, and her body had come alive with a terrible itch. A burning, gnawing sensation ate at her insides until it felt like only the tightening of her skin kept it all in.

She was strung out, and by all rights should pounce on the male touching her, the one who wanted her even if it was only because her heat had influenced him. But as desperate as she was for a fix, she craved the attentions of another man, with a ferocity that hurt.

Suddenly, she found herself on her feet and hauled up against a hard chest. *Tommy.*

Relief flooded her. The explosion of harsh words between Tom and Zach didn't register; she was too busy rubbing her face on Tom's shoulder, his arm, his chest. She wanted his scent all over her, wanted her scent on him so he couldn't easily walk out of her life.

Her hands slipped beneath his T-shirt of their own accord, and if he didn't find someplace private, she was going to take him right there.

"Please, Tommy," she murmured, and he swept her up. She doubted, though, that he knew what she was begging for. Not for sex.

For him.

THEY NEEDED PRIVACY, and fast.

Kira was rubbing herself against him like one of the big cats she liked so much, and he didn't need her to slam him to the ground and take him in front of Zach and the rest of the crew. Because, Christ, he hadn't had enough protein and probably would be pretty damned ineffective trying to fight her off and this was all embarrassing enough already.

Embarrassing, but hot.

"Keep your fucking paws off of her," he told Zach, who just held up his hands and backed away slowly.

Ender's entire body tensed, with anger and with desire as Kira continued to use her body to give him one big caress—marking him over and over again, and God, he could smell her pheromones rising. And even though Zach had backed off, he could still see the lust for Kira in the man's eyes. It did not make him happy at all.

With a final growl at Zach, he grabbed Kira around the waist and started to walk. The bathroom was the closest place. She'd already wrapped herself around him, arms and legs holding her tightly in place, and he wondered what it would be like to make the first move with her.

Not that he needed to worry about that anymore.

He kicked the bathroom door closed behind them, didn't have time to lock it before she was tugging frantically at his fly.

"Kira, it's all right—I'm here. Hang on." He sat her on the edge of the sink as he worked down her BDUs.

They'd both given up on underwear hours ago.

"Please, hurry," she whispered while she slid her shirt off over her head and he unbuttoned his own BDUs and let them pool around his ankles. Her nipples were already taut, a deep rose color that made his mouth water, and he put his mouth on one, then the other, rolling the hard buds in his mouth. She moaned above him and he sucked harder, knowing they didn't have the time for this. But he loved to make her moan.

He waited to hear her call him *Tommy*. When she didn't, a vague sense of disappointment washed over him, one he couldn't shake even as he entered her fast and hard enough to make him forget his own goddamned name.

Pleasure wracked his body, his legs shook as his cock danced in her heat and she was still so tight, so freaking perfect, that he saw stars.

She clawed at his back through his shirt as if she were trying to make sure there wasn't an ounce of space between them as she bucked her hips against his. He heard his shirt rip, and yanked what was left of it over his head.

"Mmmmm, skin on skin," she murmured. "Love the way that feels."

Yeah, he did too, but still, no *Tommy*, dammit.

He held her hips firm so he could get a better angle to thrust into her, watched as she began to lose control. The sink creaked from the effort, the mirror on the wall shook and he didn't give a shit if the whole place came tumbling down.

She threw her head back, her mouth opened soundlessly as her orgasm overtook her.

He came in short, hot spurts, while her sex contracted around him, as if demanding every last drop. His knees were weak and he wondered if he'd have time to eat something before he took her over to meet the rest of the ACRO team.

He needed meat, but after what she'd told him, he wasn't sure if he'd be able to stomach it well.

She was still nuzzling his neck—he could've sworn she was actually giving him small licks with her tongue, and it felt good. But he pulled back anyway.

"Why didn't you say my name?" he asked, before he could stop himself. Fuck.

"What are you talking about?"

"It's just...you always say my name when you come."

She blinked, and it was obvious she was still in her post-orgasmic state. And then she smiled at him. "I was trying to stay quiet. I mean, you work here—I didn't think you'd want to have people talking about the time there was a woman screaming your name in the bathroom."

He nodded, like it didn't matter. He bent down to retrieve her bottoms and T-shirt, handed them to her before he buttoned his own pants. "Hurry up and get dressed. We're late."

"Was this it, Tommy?" she asked, and fuck—*now* she had to say his name?

"End of the line," he said. He turned away as she washed up, checked his watch and forced himself not to reset the alarm he'd had at the ready every four hours.

Someone else would have to set their alarm for Kira now.

CHAPTER
Eighteen

Squinting in the bright morning sunlight, Kira grabbed Tom's elbow and pulled him to a halt as they exited the dog kennels. "How far is it?"

"The other side of the park." He gestured across the street at a large expanse of grass and flowers dotted with picnic tables. "We'll be there in a minute."

Through the trees scattered around the park, she could see buildings, all too close, and her stomach bottomed out.

"Can we take the long way?" His long pause prompted her to add a quiet "Please?"

Several agonizing heartbeats later, he relented with a brisk nod. They crossed the street and walked in silence along a trail that appeared to circle the park. A half-dozen people greeted them in passing, some in the black military-style uniforms, others in civilian clothing and ACRO badges, and none gave her more than a curious glance. She hadn't known what to expect, but normal, seemingly cheerful people wasn't it.

"Do ACRO employees use the park much?"

"The MWR department puts on a lot of functions here. Picnics, concerts...not my thing, but everyone else seems to have fun."

"MWR?"

"Morale, Welfare and Recreation. I think there's all of one person in that department."

"So you never attend?"

"Nope."

"Do you ever socialize with these people?"

"Nope."

She'd guessed he maintained a lonely existence, but she figured he at least hung out with people who understood him. Heck, that seemed like one of the greatest perks to working in a place like this. She'd spent her entire life watching the world have fun while she stood on the sidelines for fear of getting hurt.

"So I guess I won't see you at the company Christmas party, huh?"

"Does that mean you've decided to sign on?"

"Not even close." She stopped to sniff some purple flowers growing along the trail. "It was a joke, Mr. Talkative."

He kept walking as though he hadn't heard her. His odd mood bothered her. Was he as upset about leaving her as she was about leaving him?

Yeah, right. No doubt he'd be thrilled to have his life to himself again, to not have to babysit her and tend to her needs every four hours.

She, on the other hand, would miss how he tended her. How he smelled of sun-warmed skin and grass, how his gaze heated when he looked in her direction. She'd miss the way he acted all tough and gruff but would take the time to scratch a cat behind the ears. Most of all, though, she'd miss the way he made her feel when he was inside her, like she was the most important person in his life, if just for a few moments.

They rounded a bend, and when they emerged from behind a small group of trees and bushes, she grinned at the sight of a gazebo overlooking a football field–sized pond.

"Ducks!"

She ignored Tom's tolerant sigh and hurried to the edge of the water. Tiny waves lapped at her pink boots as she reached out mentally to the mallards. Their contentment wrapped around her, lessening her anxiety about the facility. Granted, ducks were pretty happy as long as they had food, water and freedom, but here no one hunted them, they didn't worry about predators and they had more than enough people feeding them bread crusts on a regular basis.

"You're stalling."

Tom's voice shattered her inner peace, leaving her stomach in turmoil once more. "I guess I am." She looked up at him, hoping he'd see what she didn't want to admit, and pull her into his arms. When he didn't, she whispered, "I'm scared."

"There's nothing to be afraid of."

Yeah, he'd said as much a hundred times, but he wasn't the one facing God-knew-what. "I don't trust them."

"And they don't trust you." He jammed his hands in his pockets and looked out over the pond, his handsome, angular profile giving away none of his thoughts. "They aren't going to torture you, or cut you open to see how you work. I won't lie to you, though. They will push you to the limit. Past your breaking point. They want to know what you're capable of, and their goal is to develop your gift as far as it will go. But you'll be treated well."

"Great."

He started walking again, and she followed, noted that his pace slowed as they approached a squat brick building ahead. Her gut rolled, and a wave of dizziness washed over her as he reached for the door handle.

"Tom…"

"It's okay. Come on."

They stepped inside some sort of small lobby, and instantly, the air-conditioned breeze eased some of her nausea, but did nothing for her nerves. Her knees trembled, her teeth chattered and her mouth had gone so dry she could hardly swallow.

Two men in black BDUs entered the room from a side hallway that sloped downward. As they approached, she inched closer to Tom, so close she could smell her scent on his skin.

"You must be Kira." The speaker's badge identified him as a trainer named Brad.

Tom stepped forward, to get away from her or to intimidate the other men with his greater height, she didn't know. "I spoke with the training supervisor. She was to have female trainers. It's not a good idea to have males near her right now."

Not a good idea at all, as evidenced by the fact that her pheromones were already affecting the two trainers. Their arousal permeated the air, and she didn't need to look to know they sported erections.

"We're only here to help Kira settle in and get started with some paperwork. Janice and Annika are on the way."

"Annika? Fuck."

"Is that bad?" Kira shot panicked glances at Tom and the trainers. "Tom?"

He didn't take his eyes off Brad, as though the other man was responsible for whatever had pissed Tom off. "Annika can scent weakness a mile off. Don't let her catch wind of yours."

"We can take it from here, Ender." Brad's smile was probably meant to soothe her, but it only made her once again inch toward Tom—or Ender, as Brad had called him. "When did you last have intercourse?"

The only sound that came out of her mouth was a strangled squeak.

Tom angled his body just enough to hide her face, and she could have kissed him for that. "Half hour ago. You've got about three and a half hours. Don't go over."

"With all due respect, this is our field. We've got it covered."

"She'll die if she doesn't get what she needs," Tom snapped. "You know that, right? Have you made arrangements?"

"Assembling volunteers wasn't difficult. We've got three donors on standby."

Donors? Like sperm donors? The other trainer, James, probably thought his announcement reassured her, but it had done the opposite. Panic reached up like a fist and squeezed until she could barely breathe.

"No." She stumbled backward. "No. I can't do this."

Tom held up his hand to stop the trainers from coming after her. "Give us a minute." He took her by the elbow and led her to a chair in one corner, but she didn't sit. "You said you would give this a shot."

"I changed my mind. I can't." He was so close, and it would be so easy to climb up him, wrap herself around him and hold on forever. Or at least until her fever ended. "Take me with you. Just until my heat is over."

"Kira—"

"Please." She grasped his hand and held so tight he winced. "You're the only man who has ever known the truth about me. You don't judge me. You've kept me safe and alive." Tears welled in her eyes, and she blinked to hold them back. "No one has ever accepted who I am like you have. I finally have someone I don't have to lie to and hide from. I'm scared and alone and all I have in the whole world is this backpack and you." She took a deep breath, tried to rid her voice of the tremors. "Tommy, don't make me beg."

For a moment, she thought she'd gotten through to him. He stood there, his throat working on a swallow, his gaze soft and sympathetic. He closed his eyes, and her pulse skittered madly as she waited, but when she felt him stiffen, her heart seized.

His eyes opened, and her heart plummeted to the pit of her stomach. Gone was the man who had protected her, had held her tenderly, had listened to her like she mattered. In his place was the professional, efficient agent who had killed Derek and hunted down bad guys in the woods. This Tom's eyes were ice, his expression hard, and she knew in an instant that the man standing before her was capable of things she couldn't even comprehend.

"You don't get it, do you, Kira? You aren't my problem anymore. The second you crossed the threshold to this building, you became theirs, thank God."

"But . . ." Problem? She had no idea how to finish the sentence she'd begun. Shock had stolen her thoughts.

He dropped her hand and wheeled away, putting a mile of distance in the three-foot span of tile. "I don't have time for this. I have other jobs waiting."

"Other *jobs*." Knowing she'd been nothing but an assignment was one thing; hearing it in his own words was another. Pain shot through her, and she nearly doubled over with the hurt that seared her insides. "More people to kill and other women to screw, is that right?"

"Whatever it takes to complete a mission." He gestured to the two men who had stopped pretending to chat and now watched intently. "Go. It's best for everyone."

Damn him. The air grew thick and still as Tom and the trainers waited for her reaction. She had no idea what any of them would do if she told them to go to hell and then ran out the door, but she guessed they wouldn't let her get far. Tom had warned her that once she stepped foot on ACRO property, she wouldn't be allowed to leave until her training was completed, whether or not she signed on at the end.

She looked up at him, searched for even a hint of the Tommy she'd fallen for, but he was gone. The stranger in front of her had taken over, and that bastard would not see her cry or beg again.

Lifting her chin and squaring her shoulders, she turned away. The trainers flanked her and guided her down the sloping hallway. A strange pulling sensation tugged at her, like an invisible rope stretched between Tom and her, and as the distance between them increased, the more uncomfortable the pull became. The man standing in the lobby might not be her Tommy, might be the cold killer people here called Ender, but her body didn't know the difference, and it wanted him back.

Nothing like that had ever happened before, but she didn't have time to dwell. Brad and James were leading her underground and into a world that scared the bejeezus out of her.

Tom's gaze burned her back, and she wondered if he'd watch until she disappeared, which might be a long time. The hallway went on forever, the smooth walls broken by metal doors with tiny windows. She peeked into one and immediately wished she hadn't.

The rooms were chambers. Full of furniture, decorations, but still too cramped for her comfort. Too cramped and too confining.

Cells.

"Is this—" She swallowed and tried again. "Is this a prison?"

Brad shook his head. "The prison is one level below. These are the trainee quarters."

"Are we free to come and go?"

James knocked on one of the doors on his way past and then waved at the man reading a book inside. "We'll explain everything once we get you to your room."

"No." She stopped in the middle of the hallway and crossed her arms over her chest. "You'll tell me now."

"Kira," Brad began in a soothing, low voice, "let's not make this difficult."

"You're the ones being difficult." She backed up the hall as they moved toward her like stalking cats. "I just want to know if you're going to keep me locked up. I can't be locked up. I need—"

"We've been over this. We have all angles covered."

Idiots. "What if you forget? Or decide to punish me by keeping your damned *donors* away? Or what if some jackass wants to know how long I can go before it's too late?"

James cast a hasty glance at Brad, and she knew she'd hit the nail on the head. They planned to test her limits. Tom had told her as much, but now that it was real ...

She spun around. Three steps later, James seized her arm and jerked her around. She swung. Clocked him in the jaw. He fell back against the wall, but then Brad was blocking her escape, and her feet wouldn't move. Nothing would move. Her arms were pinned to her sides. How were they doing this?

"Kira, you need to calm down. We're not going to hurt you. We'll keep you safe and serviced." Brad withdrew a hypodermic needle from his shirt pocket and uncapped it.

"Let me go," she shouted, because now it was too late to calm down. Images of the jail cell kept flashing in her brain, turning the trainers into cops who wanted to use her over and over.

Terror ripped through her until she shook with it. Rapid, gasping breaths didn't provide enough air, and she grew light-headed. A scream welled in her throat, and she let it loose, if only to get more oxygen.

"Let her the fuck go." Tom's voice, a deep, guttural growl, punched through her scream and panic. When had he come up behind Brad?

She heard running footsteps, knew that people were on the way.

"Ender, we can't. You know that."

"I know you were planning to make her suffer, you son of a bitch." The next thing she knew, Tom was a blur and Brad was against the wall, Tom's forearm across his throat. "Go, Kira."

Released from the invisible bonds, she ran up the hall, gasped when Tom grabbed her hand and dragged her to the lobby.

"Shit," he muttered. "Shit. I am in so much fucking trouble."

"Tommy—"

"Don't. Just run."

They sprinted to the parking lot, and once they were safely inside Tom's vintage Mustang GT500, he peeled out of the lot and through the gate. Tom checked his rearview mirror several times before he slammed his fist into the steering wheel so hard she heard something crack.

"Dammit!" He cursed a few more times, and then looked over at her. "This is just until your fever is over. And then I'm taking you back there, hog-tied and over my shoulder if I have to. Do you understand?"

"Yes," she said, her teeth still chattering. "Thank you, Tommy."

He shoved sunglasses over his eyes. "Don't thank me. Don't you dare thank me."

NINETY MILES AN HOUR ON THE DIRT ROAD that led to his house did nothing to tamp down Ender's anger. It boiled in his veins, seethed in his thoughts, and again he strangled the steering wheel.

He couldn't even look at Kira, and she wasn't saying anything either. Which was good, because he could barely think over the roaring in his own brain.

She'd panicked. He understood why, hadn't even wanted to think again about what happened to Kira in the jail cell, and hadn't been able to *stop* thinking about it.

He'd fucking panicked too when he'd realized how they would test her limits—making her go without sex for as long as she could handle it. *Fuck.*

Inherently, there was nothing wrong with the training and experimentation methods they'd been planning to use on Kira, with seeing just how far someone could be pushed. That's what the military—and then ACRO—had taught him. It was about knowing your limits, learning to deal with them in case of capture.

It didn't matter whether or not he understood the whys of the situation—her panic was enough to send him into a white-hot rage, his protection-mode engaging full force.

They hadn't seen her by the river, when she'd gone without for too long. And he didn't have the time or the patience to explain it to them. Instead, he'd done what he'd been doing for days now—he kept her out of harm's way.

"Tommy . . ."

"What?" he barked, and Kira just pointed to his ringing phone. "Shit." He used one finger to open the flip phone, only to bark, "What?" into the receiver.

"What the fuck are you doing?"

"Don't start with me, SEAL."

Remy ignored him. "Christ, Ender, you nearly killed two trainers. You'd better haul your ass in here."

"I don't need you to tell me what to do," he growled.

"But you will listen to me," Dev's voice rang on the other end of the line. Ender drew a deep breath and closed the phone as he pulled into his driveway.

"Let's go." He got out of the car and strode into his house and she followed him inside. He turned on her suddenly. "Did they hurt you?"

"What? No, they didn't—"

"Are you sure?"

She cocked her head and looked at him and he had a sudden urge to cover himself up. He had to check to make sure he was fully clothed, and then he realized that she was seeing right through him. And for some reason, she liked what she saw.

He picked her up by the waist and carried her to the bedroom and then the bed. By his calculations, she had three more hours until she needed her next mating. He'd have everything figured out before that.

But for now, he grabbed her arms before she could resist and he locked them to the headboard with the leather wrist cuffs he usually reserved for play.

"Tommy, you can't do this."

"I won't leave you for long. I have to go back to ACRO and deal with this mess you've created."

"*I've* created?" She started to struggle and he recognized the panic rising and falling in her chest. He pushed the phone within reach and wrote down the number to his cell.

"I'll be back before you need me."

"I don't understand this. Or you. You cared enough about me to get me out of that place and then you do something like this."

And that right there was enough to give him that final push over the edge of sanity. "Don't you get it? I don't care about you, Kira. I can't care about you."

"Right. I'm just a job. You've made that perfectly clear," she said. And then she turned her head away from him, mustered as much dignity as she could, and he forced himself out the door without a backward glance in her direction.

CHAPTER
Nineteen

Dev sent Remy away, because he knew Ender's next move. Ender would come in and take his reprimand like a man, growl and then attempt to kill a few more people on the way out.

Dev wasn't sure why that made him smile, but it did. He prepared himself for Ender's visit—had to be careful not to let on that his sight was completely restored. He and Oz had decided that, until the mole was caught, it was better to let everyone think it was business as usual at ACRO. Which meant no sight for Dev.

He'd expected that his other senses would lessen, that some sensory perceptions wouldn't feel as heightened as they once had. But the opposite seemed to be true. And when that son of a bitch burst into his office without knocking, Dev sensed something he never, ever got from Ender.

Fear.

"You're back," Dev said, and just because Ender was in pain didn't mean Dev was going to go easy on him. And that pain was even more apparent now that Dev could see the man in full Technicolor and not the muted visions of his CRV.

"Yes." Ender stood in front of him defiantly, his eyes blazing with anger that didn't hide the worry. At least not well enough.

"I hear you're refusing to bring your acquisition back in. I hear that you haven't followed one goddamned order I've given you. I hear that the animal whisperer hasn't even agreed to join. Which means she should be dead."

"Her name's Kira. And she'll join."

Dev nodded, slowly. It had happened just the way he'd figured. "You can't be sure of that."

"She can't be sure of anything until her heat cycle's over, Dev. She needs sex every four hours."

"We have men who can service her safely. Humanely. No one's going to hurt her here. Bring her in."

"I won't do that."

"You don't have a choice; I'm giving you an order. She's still vulnerable, even if she is with you. They're after her."

"She doesn't want other men. She picked me."

"What do you mean, she's picked you?"

"I don't know—something about picking a mate when she's in her heat cycle," Ender said.

Dev turned and walked toward his desk, focusing on Kira's mind while he did so. He got a fleeting mental image of Kira on a bed with a dark gray comforter, saw restraints on her wrists and, despite that, felt Kira's thoughts about Ender.

This was the first time she'd ever picked one mate. Normally, she needed several. And even though she was pissed to hell at him at the moment, she loved him. And that was enough to soften Dev. For the moment.

"Fine. You can continue to be her mate, Ender. But you'll do so here. So we can observe her and figure out the best way to ease her transition."

When Ender finally spoke again, his voice was quiet but firm. "I won't do it, Dev. Do you have any idea what they were planning to do to her at the training facility? I'll keep her safe until her heat cycle's over and then I'll bring her in."

"And suppose it's too late by then? She's dangerous and you know it."

"As dangerous as Remy was, but you didn't think about putting him down unless there was no other choice. Why are you so quick to off Kira?"

"Remy had military training and a power that he alone could control. It would have taken time for an enemy to break him, get him to work for them, if they could do that at all." Dev ran his fingers through his hair, hated to hear Ender calling her by name. "In the wrong hands—or even in the right ones—the animal whisperer is potentially a weapon of mass biological destruction. Itor wouldn't need her consent to use her, they only need her body. You know that as well as I do. Tell me, if she refuses to join, are you going to be able to kill her?"

"It won't be the first time I've had to fuck a woman and then kill her. All part of the job, right, Dev?"

"You didn't answer my question."

"It's something you shouldn't have asked. And why are your nightmares back?" Ender asked.

"I could ask you the same question," he said, heard Ender's sharp intake of breath and saw a man who claimed to call nobody friend with his hands fisted in his jeans pockets pretending not to give a shit. "You still underestimate me. Just because I can't break into your mind doesn't mean Kira's isn't wide open to me. She's concerned about you."

Ender was silent for a long minute, and then his tension, his realization filled the room. "This is about Oz, isn't it? You always get the nightmares when he comes back into your life. I'll kill the motherfucker."

"You'll finish your own goddamned assignment, stop lying to me and figure out a way to bring Kira into ACRO. It'll be the only way to break this bond you've formed with her."

KIRA WAS WHERE HE'D LEFT HER. Ender noted that her eyes were slightly red-rimmed, like she'd been crying. Now all he saw was anger in her eyes, and all of it directed at him.

"I've worked it out with Dev," he said. "You can stay here with me until your heat is over."

"Are you going to keep me tied up the whole time?"

"If I need to."

"Asshole."

"You don't have the right to be pissed at me, Kira," he said. Warning bells bounced inside his skull and he knew he was still skating on the damned edge. Dev knew it too.

"You don't own me, Tom Knight. You can't tell me what rights I have. So. Let. Me. Go. And who knows, maybe I'll find someone else to help me through the rest of my heat."

She didn't mean it—he knew that, but it still cut right through him to hear her say it.

"So you want someone else, then?" he asked.

"Yes. Anyone but you." She jerked her bound hands. "And that kills you, doesn't it?"

"Keep talking like that, Kira, and I swear I'll take you over my knee."

She snorted, as if she didn't believe him. And as much as he wanted to keep her tied up, not deal with it, he remembered all too clearly how not well that had worked days earlier.

He leaned forward and undid her restraints quickly, then stepped aside as she lunged.

This time, he was ready.

He caught her, a bundle of infuriated indignation, and he turned her over his knee, holding her squirming body there easily enough. She wasn't as strong as she was a few days ago, but he didn't think about that for too long. Because he was pissed—at himself for caring, and at her for calling him on it.

Held there, she still managed to turn her head to look at him. "You wouldn't dare."

"Yeah, I would. I promised you I would and I always keep my promises."

She gasped, more with surprise than pain as his large palm took its first whoosh through the air and made contact with her perfect ass. But the slap was through her BDU pants, and he wanted skin-on-skin contact.

He didn't bother to try to pull them down. He ripped them off greedily instead, so he could touch her.

"You are not in charge here, little one," he murmured, even though he couldn't conceal his anger. "I am. And the sooner you learn to deal with that, the better."

"Fuck. You."

He slapped her again and again and as his anger dissipated, so did hers. His palm heated quickly. Her ass turned bright red and each slap took her closer to making her his, which he wasn't sure he wanted but still he couldn't stop himself. Each connection of palm to flesh made his dick harder, and she squirmed and begged, but she wanted it. He knew because she'd started to lift her ass to greet his steady slaps and he felt her orgasm shudder through her body, watched her toes curl and heard the low moan in the back of her throat.

He no longer had to hold her down to make her stay across his lap. But that didn't mean she wasn't still angry.

"Who do you want, Kira?"

She didn't hesitate to answer. "You, Tommy. You know that already."

He stood, taking her with him and flipping her onto the mattress. But she was up within seconds, her face flushed from orgasm and humiliation and anger, and he readied himself for another battle.

"What do you want from me, Tommy?"

For you to stop calling me Tommy. For you to stop giving a shit about me. For this to all go the fuck away. "What do I want? I want my life back, dammit!" he roared finally.

"Which one, Tommy? Which life do you want back?" she asked, and it was the complete and utter wrong thing to say to him. Too logical, and it only served to anger him more. She wasn't the right person to take out his anger on, but she was going to bear the brunt because she couldn't, and wouldn't, stop talking.

He grabbed her by the shoulders, prepared to shake her, to shut her up. He hadn't been prepared to kiss her, but that's exactly what he did, a hard kiss that sucked the air out of his lungs, one that bonded them together more than sex ever would, and still, she was slamming her fists against his shoulders, trying to pry herself away from him even as her tongue met his.

He was losing it. Losing it. And instead of backing away from her, he continued with his mouth pressed against hers in a kiss he insisted had nothing to do with love. Because there was certainly nothing romantic about the kiss. It was one of dominance as his mouth took her again and again—and again, Kira did not back down.

Her mouth held firm against his and she welcomed him—and he was dimly aware that this was the first time he'd allowed himself to kiss her. He'd never been big on kissing—it seemed too intimate, too messy, too full of . . . stars-in-your-eyes entanglements that he didn't think he could ever have.

Why being with Kira had triggered this reaction inside of him was still a mystery. He blamed the pheromones she was giving off, blamed his cock, blamed his genetic makeup. Anything so he didn't have to admit the truth.

He loved Kira Donovan. And there was no room for that to happen in his life.

Her hands held his face, letting him know that she was still fighting for dominance. And when he ripped his mouth away, he let her know that she wasn't getting it.

He took a step back and she remained kneeling on the bed. He wiped his mouth with the back of his hand and she touched her lips with her fingers. His first instinct was to apologize, and that made his anger return full force. His body flushed, his cock jumped and she was climbing him again before he had a chance to think, claiming him until his orgasm was imminent.

"I'm sorry, Tommy. Sorry for getting you in trouble. Sorry for all of this," she murmured, over and over.

She's a job. Your job. Nothing more.

He continued lying to himself while he spilled deep inside of her.

*   *   *

"Kira? Kira, wake up."

She blinked, focused her gaze on Tom's face, staring down at her. A quick glance at the clock showed that nearly four hours had passed since he'd taken her, their mutual anger fueling the frantic pace of their mating and igniting a series of orgasms that wrung her out emotionally, leaving her level for the first time in days.

After sex, he'd thrown on some shorts and disappeared into what she discovered was his exercise room. She'd showered, and then, utterly exhausted after several days of nonstop running and sex, she crawled into his bed and crashed.

"It's time."

Right. Heat pooled in her loins at the thought of sex with him, but for some reason, the fiery, crazy need felt dimmed, was more of a tickle in the background than a pounding nuisance that hijacked her mind and body.

He climbed into bed with her, and she welcomed him, but before he could mount her, she wriggled onto her side, facing him.

"Are you still mad at me?"

"Doesn't matter. It's never mattered when you needed me."

The scent of his arousal stirred hers, and she clenched her thighs to ease the ache there, but the pressure only heightened her desire. "It matters now." She dragged a finger from his throat to his cock. "Because we can't keep going the way we are. I'm sorry I'm making your life so awful."

"We're not talking about this."

"Yes, we are, and you're going to listen to me. I'm sorry I turned your life upside down. I'm sorry I got you into trouble at work. I'm so grateful for what you did...but you didn't have to take me from ACRO. It was your choice, and if you're going to keep punishing me for it, you can take me back there right now."

She'd started to stroke his shaft, but she froze as she waited for his response. She didn't want to go back, but if he didn't feel that keeping her was his choice, he'd forever have an excuse to be angry with her, to shut her out.

The tic of a muscle in his jaw revealed his frustration—with her or with himself, she didn't know. What she did know was that she had better start acting desperate for sex, because something strange was going on with her body, and she didn't want him thinking she didn't need him anymore.

Slowly, she dragged her foot up his leg and hooked it around his thigh so she could pull herself closer, close enough that his erection slid against the seam of her sex. He hissed through clenched teeth, and then she had her answer, because suddenly, he was between her legs, his tongue fully engaged, his lips sucking on her clit, his fingers buried deep inside her.

She groaned, grasped his hair to hold him there because nothing had ever felt so good as Tommy when he was pleasuring her like this. The flat of his tongue stroked upward from her core, then hovered at the top of her cleft, where he pushed the tip into the little hood there. His breath was a hot wash, his fingers magic as three of them filled her.

"Incredible," she whispered, and arched off the bed. He palmed her pelvis, eased her back down and into his mouth.

Ecstasy stole her breaths, her thoughts, her sense of decorum, because she was pumping her sex against his mouth, fucking his hand and tongue and screaming in release.

"Tom," she gasped. "Come up here. Take me. Now."

Taking an agonizing amount of time, he kissed her inner thigh and then slowly worked his way up. "Why?" he murmured against her navel. "Because you need me?"

"No. Because I want you."

His head snapped up, and he fixed her with a hot, probing stare. For a moment, she thought she'd made a grave mistake. But then his mouth was on hers, his kiss urgent and demanding. His cock nudged the entrance to her sex, and she tilted her hips, took him inside where she needed him to be. Needed and wanted, and it didn't matter that she was just a job to him. All that mattered was that she felt safe and, for the moment, cared for.

CHAPTER
twenty

After three days of faking it, Kira knew her heat was over and wasn't coming back.

Maybe the stress of what had taken place at the training facility had ended it early. Or maybe because a single man had serviced her for this long, her body no longer thirsted for something it got from the same male on a regular basis. Whatever it was, the end had become both a blessing and a curse.

Tom had brought her home until her heat ended, and then he planned to take her back to his agency, trussed up like a Thanksgiving turkey if he had to.

That wasn't going to happen.

Tom didn't want her; he'd made that perfectly clear. But she wasn't ready to give him up.

Her needs had diminished, but her desire for him hadn't. If anything, she wanted him even more, and if she had to fake three more weeks of fever in order to stay with him, she would. She craved not just sex, but his nonsexual touches, his embraces, his voice. She couldn't seem to get close enough to him.

Sometimes he didn't mind, or at least he humored her convincingly enough when she snuggled next to him on the couch while he watched that obnoxious O'Reilly guy. Or when she wrapped herself around him while he washed dishes after she cooked vegan meals he actually ate—something that gave her hope for a relationship, since diet was a deal-breaker for her.

Other times, especially when she asked personal questions, he got grumpy, would pull away, withdraw to another room.

She wished he had a pet, because at least then when Tom went all moody-silent, she'd have someone to keep her company.

She also wished he'd open up more, maybe answer when she asked him about the nightmares that woke him up at night, or when she asked about the things in his house. Things like the set of oriental swords on his wall or the beautiful Egyptian tiled box on his dresser.

His collection of books had been a revelation; he hadn't struck her as someone who liked Shakespeare. She'd expected an assortment of military titles, and though he owned enough of those, his Shakespearean literature took up the most prominent shelf spaces.

His house was huge, bigger than she'd have expected and very open. The number and size of windows had amazed her, given his aversion to exposure...until she figured out that the glass was not only tinted on the outside, but bulletproof. A wraparound deck circled the entire house, accessible from two of the four bedrooms, the living room and the dining room. His security system looked like something any museum would envy, and his arsenal of weapons she'd accidentally stumbled upon in the basement could have outfitted a small country.

She didn't tell him she'd found the weapons. He was already on edge because she'd rearranged a lot of his furniture. The last straw had come when he found what she'd done to their bedroom. His roar of "*Kiiiiraaaaa*" still rang in her ears. But geez, a bed should always sit at an angle that would allow the light of the moon to fall across the pillows. Besides, he refused to give up his side of the bed, and she needed to be close to the bathroom. As her body adjusted to the ended heat, she always experienced fluctuations in systemic function, and right now, she had to pee all the time.

Tom had flipped out about the bedroom, which meant that he got all surly and shut himself away in his den, but two hours later, when she interrupted whatever he was doing on the computer in order to have sex on his desk, he seemed over it.

In fact, he'd been relatively pleasant for an entire day since then. He'd even challenged her to a game of Risk last night, and though he handed her ass to her on a plate, he'd grudgingly admitted that her ruthlessness took him by surprise. He'd also said he admired that in a woman.

She was still beaming about that compliment.

"Why are you smiling?"

She looked up from where she sat on a blanket in his backyard, and smiled even bigger. "I'm just happy that you decided to join me."

"I didn't think I had a choice," he muttered, as he sank down across from her. He bent one long, jeans-clad leg up and braced his forearm casually across his knee as he eyed the food she'd set out.

"Oh, stop your grousing. You needed this."

"I needed a picnic?"

"Yes." She handed him an avocado club sandwich with barbecued tempeh. Thankfully he'd taken her grocery and clothes shopping, because he'd had nothing but junk food in the house, and very little she could eat. "You said you never go to your company picnics, and everyone needs to picnic sometimes. Besides, it's so beautiful out here."

She inhaled a deep breath of country air, made sweet by the balsam and spruce trees that surrounded the house on three sides and created a cocoon of privacy. Well, privacy for Tom...anyone approaching from any angle would be spotted by the extensive camera system along the perimeter of his property. Only one corner at the rear of the house was exposed, his land butting up against a vast field full of horses with whom she'd already become acquainted.

"You should see it in the winter," he said. "With snow covering everything, it looks like a painting. Something from a Dickens novel."

"Christmas would be so magical." She could picture it, a giant tree in his front window, deer in the yard ... She wanted to be here for that. Wanted to make love under the Christmas tree, with only the lights and a fire to cut the darkness. For once, she wanted to wake up on Christmas morning with someone with whom she could share breakfast and open presents.

Eventually, she wanted to experience Christmas with Tom and their offspring.

For the first time, she allowed herself to think on the possibility. Before, with no hope of a mate to help her care for them during her heats, having children seemed like a pipe dream. But now ...

"You're doing it again."

She blinked. "What?"

"Smiling."

"Oh." She poured a glass of sparkling cider for her, and a glass of wine for him. "Sorry."

"It's okay. You're beautiful when you smile." A touch of pink colored his cheeks, which looked good on him because he'd been so pale lately.

Avoiding her gaze, he took a bite of his sandwich. "Not bad," he said, after he swallowed.

Thank God he'd liked—or pretended to like—much of what she'd prepared, because she'd been cooking like she was preparing for a winter hibernation. With no animals to care for, she'd been cleaning, cooking and baking—fruit cobblers, nut tarts, cookies. Poor Tom said he was going to gain a hundred pounds.

She doubted that. The man worked out for several hours each day, as evidenced by his ripped body, so iron hard, with layers of muscle on muscle and no hint of fat anywhere.

They finished their meal in comfortable silence, and when Tom was done, he stretched out on his back and tucked an arm behind his head. "Thank you," he said. And then he cocked his head and watched her until she squirmed. "Something's different about you."

Oh, God. If he knew she'd been faking her heat...She broke out in a cold sweat. "What's different?"

"I don't know." He reached out, trailed the back of his hand over her hip, her waist, her belly. "You seem softer."

"Softer?" Pushing his hand away, she said, "You take that back, Tom Knight."

Suddenly, she found herself on her back, pinned, and Tom was stroking her hair as he looked down at her with heavy-lidded eyes that were bluer than the sky above. "Softer."

"I'll show you soft," she growled, hooking her leg over his back like she did with her tigers, and flipped him so she straddled his hips and held him down with her palms on his shoulders.

"You're good," he murmured, circling her waist with his big hands. "But not good enough."

Then she was stomach-down on the blanket, with Tom's knee pressed gently into the small of her back. They'd mated less than two hours ago, and though she no longer needed him, she wanted him. This playful side took her by surprise, gave her warm fuzzies...and was a serious turn-on.

"Tommy? Please...you're hurting me."

Instantly, he lifted off her. "God, Kira, I'm sorry."

She laughed and leaped to her feet. "Sucker."

"You little—"

She didn't hear the rest, because she was off and running. The grass felt good beneath her bare feet, and the wind in her face washed away all her problems. She heard him behind her, and she dodged right then left, the gazelle evading the cheetah. He missed her, cursed, and then suddenly she was rolling on the ground with him again.

"Took you long enough," she panted when they came to a halt at the base of a gentle slope.

He frowned a little before settling fully between her legs. She yielded to him, welcomed his weight. "Yeah, but I have you now."

His erection burned against her belly, and the intensity in his eyes lit her from the inside.

Images of the night she'd tried to run from him at the refuge flashed through her mind. She'd been scared, angry...and at the same time, horny as hell.

This was so similar, and yet so different. There was no fear, no anger. Just a warm sense of rightness and a whole lot of arousal.

"Make love to me," she murmured, and wrapped her arms around his shoulders before she ran her hand down his back, feeling the raw power of the muscles rippling beneath her palm.

His body went taut. "It's not time."

"So?" She arched up, caught his hips between her thighs so the hard ridge of his erection rubbed her mound.

"Two hours." With a long, luxurious sweep of his hand, he caressed her hip, her waist and rib cage, worked upward until he brushed the swell of her breast with his thumb. God, how this man affected her even when she was no longer in season. She loosened up, spread her legs wider to accommodate even more of him.

"Think how good it'll be then," he said. "After we're that much more worked up."

"I don't want to wait." She reached up, cupped his cheek. "You don't either," she whispered.

He hesitated, and then his mouth tightened into a grim slash. "No, dammit." He pushed to his feet. "I agreed to keep you alive. I didn't agree to fuck you at your whim."

He stalked off, and she just sat there, smiling, because despite his harsh words, she knew the truth.

Tom didn't refuse her because he didn't want her. He refused her because he *did* want her—and having sex outside her rigid schedule might just force him to admit it.

GLANCING UP AT THE CLOCK, Kira realized that just over four hours had passed since Tom had thoroughly and luxuriously mated with her in the shower—the things that man could do with soap and a flexible showerhead—and he'd be expecting her to pounce any moment now. She padded through the hall toward the spare bedroom he'd turned into an exercise room, leaving a trail of clothing as she went.

By the time she reached the door, she was nude. Her stomach churned with guilt, but the pulse between her legs canceled out any regrets she might have over deceiving him. She might not be in heat anymore, but her body still grew hot and tingly when she thought about Tom.

The rhythmic sound of pumping weights made her pulse jump—the sight of Tom's muscles bunching and flexing beneath glistening, tan skin would be a picture to commit to memory. Tense with anticipation and a strange nervousness now that her hormones were in control, she opened the door.

Oh, my. She knew he'd be a sight, but he was more than that. Lying on his back on a weight bench, wearing only shorts, he was a thing of beauty. Veins bulged on top of straining muscles as he lowered the weights to lock them in place, and his abs rippled as he sat up and watched her with hooded eyes.

He didn't bother to ask if it was time; he simply stood and shed the shorts. Heart quivering with lust and anxiety, she let her gaze travel from his face to his chest, then lower, over his stomach, hips, to the erection that jutted magnificently from the thatch of tawny hair between his legs.

She ignited. Burned. Needed him like she needed to breathe, and as she moved toward him, she let all her instincts take over. Let them erase her trepidation, let them guide her in the taking of a mate so he'd know without a doubt that he was hers.

Every step stirred her passion higher as her thighs slid against each other and his gaze grew hotter. The pull she'd felt at the training facility, the one that had seemed to call to him, tightened, tugged like a direct line from her center to his.

Mine.

"Are you ready for me, *Ender?*"

Surprise flickered in his eyes, followed by a spark of anger. "Tom."

"They call you Ender at work."

"*You* call me Tom."

Happiness stirred her heart. She doubted he allowed many people to call him by his given name. She stopped so close she could feel his heat, but they didn't touch.

"You aren't in the mood to be ordered around, are you?"

He looked down at her, his eyes sparking with both fire and ice. "No."

"Well, I'm in the mood to call the shots."

"Then we have a problem."

Another case of nerves unsettled her stomach, but she breathed deeply, remembering her goal. Her entire future rode on making him hers.

Planting her palms on his chest, she stroked upward and moved in so her breasts kissed his skin. The scent of his workout, salty, musky, rose to her nostrils, and she inhaled, let his wild, earthy smell invade her senses.

His cock skimmed her belly, and already liquid had formed at the tip, left a cool, prickling trail of wetness across her navel.

He had yet to touch her, engaged as they were in a battle of wills, so she dropped her hands to thread her fingers in his. He cocked an eyebrow, clearly unsure of her intentions.

Leaning back, she bent her knees and tugged him down to the floor. He sank easily to his knees, and when she was on her back with him on all fours over her, she shimmied out from underneath him.

"Kira?"

"Shh." She stood. Left him confused and on his hands and knees. When he would have pushed to his feet, she grasped his hair and stepped into him so his face met the aching apex between her legs. "You know what I want."

Know me. Never forget.

A long heartbeat passed. The scent of his arousal drifted to her, but also the sharper, more acrid aroma of confusion. She doubted he was even aware of why he hesitated, but she knew. She was asking him to bond with her, to learn her scent, her flavor, her touch, so thoroughly that no other woman would ever suffice.

Fire burned in her lungs, and she realized she'd been holding her breath. *Please, Tom*. Then he closed his mouth over her, and she threw back her head as the hot stab of his tongue penetrated her slit.

"Yes," she whimpered. "Oh, Tommy, yes."

"Open for me." His voice was a rough, dominant growl and she wondered when she lost control of the situation, because she immediately spread her legs and drove her hand down, parting her swollen flesh for his invading tongue.

Her juices flowed, warm, thick, and he lapped at her like he couldn't get enough. She spread herself wider with her fingers, grasped his hair with her other hand and arched into his mouth. Closer. She needed him closer.

Chills of pleasure raced across her skin as his tongue danced over her clit, licking, flicking, applying just enough pressure to keep her motionless, waiting for just the right touch. He knew her well enough by now to tease her to the edge and then pull back, prolonging her pleasure and at the same time infuriating her.

"Put it inside me." She lifted her leg, braced her foot against the weight bench so she was wide open, exposed to him like never before.

His tongue swiped her valley once, twice, and then speared her deep. *Tommy*. Her knees went weak, and if not for the firm grasp on his head, she might have crumpled to the floor. He stroked her with his tongue, used it like he would his cock, pumping deep, and then swirling the tip around her sensitive entrance.

"Is this what you want, Kira?" he murmured against her center, his voice buzzing through her labia, his hot breath searing her core. "Do you want me to make you come with my mouth, or with my cock?"

Oh, he was entirely too aware of what she wanted, that her greedy self wanted it all.

Stepping back, she dropped to all fours so she faced him, her mouth a mere inch from his, which glistened with her juices. He watched her warily as she moved closer, avoided his mouth, and rubbed her cheek against his. Rough whiskers scratched her skin, but she didn't care. It felt too good to touch him.

She dragged her lips across his ear, his cheekbone, then nibbled at his jawline, working her way toward his mouth. His muscles tensed as she drew close, and she knew he'd pull back if she kissed him; his kisses were doled out on his terms. Instead, she flicked her tongue over his lips, tasted herself on him.

"Enough." His voice was rough, hard, as he hooked her leg and dragged her around so he could mount her.

She felt the dig of his fingers in her hips, the hot prod of his cock against her buttocks. The carpet bit into her knees.

"Tom, please," she whispered. "Let me love you."

His entire body rocked back. She took advantage of his moment of stunned silence and spun, brought her hand down on his head and sank her teeth into the back of his neck, pressing him back down on his hands and knees, head bowed.

Never had she seen his body go as taut as it was now, the muscles bulging, straining under the skin. His breathing went harsh, deep and even. Battle-mode. He was thinking this through, staying calm even though his body wanted to act.

He could break her hold with little effort, but maybe he felt what she felt, a need to make a powerful connection with this mating.

Slowly, as though gentling a stallion that threatened to balk, she stroked his back, worked her way to his flank and then to his jutting erection. Taking his shaft in her palm, she caressed him until his breathing grew less controlled, until the tight cords in his neck relaxed and then began to tighten again for a different reason.

She released her bite on his neck, soothed with her tongue the indentations she'd made with her teeth. Then she fastened her mouth to the pulse in his throat and let it pound into her. Her clit pulsed in time to his heartbeat, and she squeezed her thighs together to relieve the ache there.

Tom froze, and she knew he felt the connection too, the one that seemed to tie them together via an invisible artery from his body to her very womb.

Mine.

She sucked lightly, wondering if he'd have a hickey on his neck later, and then she kissed her way across his collarbone.

Visions of being with him like this permanently, not just until he took her to ACRO, ran through her mind as she massaged his shoulders, ran her hands down his arms, traced his straining muscles.

"You're so beautiful," she said against the skin between his shoulder blades. "Physically perfect. Powerful. Strong." She smoothed her tongue along his spine, all the way to his tailbone. "What every female wants in a mate."

He groaned, remained motionless as she skimmed her fingers over every part she could reach. Opening her mouth over his hipbone, she bit down. Not hard, but enough to hold him there, to show him without words that she wanted to hold him in every way. She released him, licked the bitten area tenderly.

The sounds of his quickening breaths were like little slaps on her skin, each one making her wild, making her remember how he'd spanked her with the horse crop in the barn, and later with his bare hand.

Creamy wetness spilled between her thighs, because God, she was so ready for him, but not yet. This was about him. She wanted to worship his body and show him what he meant to her.

She moved behind him, and this time he held his breath as her palms squeezed and massaged his buttocks. Her thumbs dropped lower, skimmed the crevice of his ass. The first light touch of her fingers on his testicles made him lurch forward, but she caught him around the thigh with one hand while she put her mouth where her fingers had been.

The musky scent of aroused male heightened her hunger, drew a soft moan from her as she sucked his firm balls between her lips and scraped the tight sac lightly with her teeth.

"Kira...*sweet damn*..."

Insanely aroused by his reaction, she lapped, licked between his legs and up to the smooth, sensitive place behind his balls. When she pushed her tongue into the seam there, separating his testicles, a ragged, guttural groan ripped from deep in his chest.

She could have stayed there all day. Instead, she scattered kisses along the backs of his thighs while his muscles quivered and his breath came in shallow gasps.

"I love how you taste, Tommy. Like danger and sex, like you fought a battle to win me."

A shudder shifted his entire body toward her. She nibbled, tiny love bites across his waist. Then she bent her head, went beneath him, and he whispered her name as her tongue flicked over the head of his brutal erection.

She'd never seen him so engorged, his head so ripe and hot that she could feel the pulse beat against her lips.

She teased, licked, dipped the tip of her tongue into the weeping slit. He arched his back to slip his cock into her mouth, but she angled her head away, rubbed her cheek against it, something close to a purr welling up inside her.

"What's the matter, baby?" The taunt made him grind his teeth so hard she heard the click of bone on bone. "Is this what you want?"

She flicked her tongue along the ridge of the sensitive head, and then took him deep, until he knocked on the back of her throat. He pulsed inside her, spilling a few drops of cum, which she took greedily.

"Oh, yeah," he murmured. "Suck it hard."

She hummed around his length, and he pumped his hips, fucking her mouth. *So good.* She'd never been so turned on from giving oral sex, had never been on the verge of orgasm without a man even touching her. Unable to wait, she fingered herself as she sucked him.

"Kira," he rasped harshly. "You'd better stop. I can't hold it."

She applied serious suction, wanting to drink him in, to take his life-giving seed in the most intimate way possible. He cursed, tried to withdraw, but she stopped pleasuring herself to reach between his legs and tug gently on his balls to hold him. Straining and bucking, he roared out her name, gushing into her mouth.

She loved the sound of his groans, of his rasping breaths. His body began to jerk as his climax faded, and she gently swirled her tongue around his softening flesh, until she felt his fingers trail down her thigh.

He dragged his hand up to her sex, dipped two fingers into her slick core. "I need a minute before I can take care of you."

Then his tongue joined his fingers, and she cried out, because he could take all the time he needed.

CHAPTER
twenty-one

Ender snapped his cell phone shut and leaned back against the old tree trunk on the south side of his property.

He'd made another call he shouldn't have and found out things he hadn't wanted to know. Typical of his life lately. But he knew Kira was panicked about what was happening to her animals, and besides, there was only so much he could watch as she rearranged his whole life and put herself directly in the center. Because what was going to happen when she left?

She didn't see that consequence, obviously, didn't see that she was going to leave behind a big, gaping hole.

But he had things to worry about other than himself.

Apparently, the only one who knew what the hell they were doing at the animal refuge had been Kira. Suddenly Rafi was in a cage because there was no one who could control the pretty lynx, and Luke, the monster German shepherd who'd nearly killed him and then helped save him, hadn't eaten in weeks. Babs was just wandering around listless and Shamal refused to leave her stall.

For a second, he saw his yard filled with dogs and tigers and God knows what else, all of them surrounding Kira.

He imagined Babs snuggling up next to him and realized that

he'd probably lost his fucking mind. This much sex couldn't be good for anyone's brain cells.

Except he knew, deep down, that this much sex wasn't necessary—hadn't been for days. No, Kira's heat cycle was over. He could tell the difference when he took her, the way she was able to enjoy the buildup more, the way she wasn't as frantic, even though she played it well.

Why she was doing so wasn't that big of a mystery—she was putting off going to ACRO. He didn't let himself believe she was faking it to stay with him.

"Hey, I was looking for you." Kira circled the old oak and stood in front of him. She'd confiscated his favorite T-shirt and cut it to fit her. She'd done the same with a pair of his old camouflage shorts and he had to admit, grudgingly, they looked a lot better on her than they ever did on him. "Why are you shaking your head like that? And muttering? You've been doing that a lot lately."

"I wasn't hiding," he said. Man, he was tired. He'd been doubling up on the protein bars to make up for the fact that it had been almost two weeks since he'd eaten any kind of steak or burger, but it wasn't the same kind of fuel at all. He was still dragging. "I've, ah, got to talk to you about something. Why don't you sit?"

She sank gracefully to the ground in front of him, stretching out on the grass next to his jean-clad legs. She rested a cheek on his thigh and he wondered how things had gotten this far, this fast.

He sighed and told her about the phone call to the refuge.

"Tommy, I've got to go back there." She would've been on her feet and on a dead run toward his car if he hadn't put a hand on her arm.

"Calm down, Kira. Please."

"I can't stay here knowing that they're hurting."

"And if you go back there, Itor will have you in no time. How will that help?" he asked. She bit her bottom lip and her resistance to his grip faded. She put her head back down on his legs, tears welled in her eyes, and for a few minutes they both just stared up at the beautiful blue sky.

"What do I do, Tommy?"

"I can't make your decisions for you."

"Did you walk into ACRO on your own terms?"

His head started to throb, and if he thought about it really hard, he could hear the bars of his cell door slamming behind him. "No. I wasn't given that choice."

"Do you regret that?"

"I regret an awful lot of things," he said quietly. "But this isn't about me."

She sat up and faced him again. "If I go to ACRO, they'll let me ship the animals here?"

"Yes. I already talked with Zach about that," he said, and she just stared at him. Her whole face softened. "What?"

"You've been calling the refuge a lot, haven't you? Even though you told me it wasn't possible."

He refused to admit that this was his third call to the damned place. A man had to keep some pride.

She didn't force anything more from him, though, and for that, he was grateful.

"I want to go in on my own terms," she said. "On my own. Without you escorting me there."

"Me escorting you is for your own safety."

"I can make it there on my own."

"Not an option."

"Your car is fast—"

"No," he said and she sighed heavily, but it wasn't with defeat. It was the how-can-I-convince-Tommy sigh.

"I know! I can take Zorro."

"What the hell are you talking about, woman?"

"Zorro," she said patiently as she pointed though the trees. His neighbor's animal was a mile away, and thanks to the protein deficit, fuzzier than it should have been at ten times the distance. He didn't realize that she'd been that far over on his property and he sorely needed to stop underestimating her.

She stood and whistled, and in a matter of moments, the pretty black horse had jumped the fence and was stomping and whinnying in front of them.

"No one will be able to catch me. I'll be there in under twenty minutes."

"I guess you're going to have to get used to doing things on your own," he said finally, knowing full well he'd follow her and the horse in secret, just in case. She'd never have to know that.

"I'm not sure I want to."

"But you just said you'd join."

"Not ACRO. I'm not sure I want to do things on my own anymore. I mean, are there rules against ACRO people being together?"

"You mean, like you and me?"

"Well, I certainly don't mean me and Zach," she said, and he growled without realizing it. "Of course I mean you, Tommy."

"I don't know if I know how to do this," he said. "I've never let anyone in."

"I haven't either," she said. "Maybe we could both try?"

"Try what?"

She rolled her eyes, and dammit if she and Zorro didn't both shake their heads at him. "This. You. Me. Together."

"Are you going to keep rearranging my stuff?"

"Well, yeah," she said.

He nodded, thought for a second about waking up with the sun warming his bed and Kira warming him.

The order to kill her if she didn't cooperate still hadn't been lifted; that was something that broke into his thoughts late at night while Kira lay sleeping contentedly next to him after yet another round of sex.

He'd never *not* followed through on an order from ACRO. There had been times when he had to postpone assassinations due to unforeseen events. Usually his order had nothing to do with killing men or women who were like him.

No, he hadn't done that since the military.

Ender wasn't sure if it was all one big test or not, but if it was, he was hovering precariously along the pass-fail line.

But as he watched Kira communicating with Zorro while she stood in the sun, smiling, her hair tumbling softly down her back, suddenly nothing seemed like a problem. She was going into ACRO on her own terms.

"I'll drive you there. Just to the gate. You can walk in on your own," he said finally. She turned to him and nodded her assent and he knew he had to have her, right here and now.

It had only been two hours since her last feigned heat, and despite the fact that he was tired, he wanted her. Badly.

"Come here, Kira," he said. It came out more like an order, but she didn't hesitate, left the horse and moved catlike toward him. When she knelt in front of him, he pulled her close, kissed her on her full, pink lips, and within seconds he had his answer to the question she'd asked before. This was a real kiss, not one of dominance or anger, but a full-blown, all-out, romantic-as-hell kiss.

Yes, they were going to try this.

"Tommy, it's not time yet," she whispered after he'd pulled back.

"I know. But can't a man have a chance to seduce his woman on his terms?" he asked, went right along with her lie, watched as her eyes began to glow that beautiful golden amber.

"That's never happened."

"Well, it's about to. Maybe you should start getting used to it," he murmured as he pulled her close and kissed her again. It went on and on, her hands around his neck and the two of them rolling around on the ground like they had all the time in the world to lie around and neck. His balls tightened, his gut tensed as his thighs rubbed hers—and how did she always smell so good, like honey and cloves and sunshine?

She'd begun to peel off his jeans before he could stop her— didn't want to, really, until the snort reminded him that they weren't alone.

"Hey, is that horse going to watch us the whole time?" he asked.

She laughed, gave a light whistle, and Zorro bristled for a second before turning his back on them. "He said to tell you that you don't have anything he hasn't seen before. Although you're much bigger than most humans he's seen."

"The horse has seen me naked?" he asked, with a shake of his head. She pushed his jeans down his hips, raked his ass lightly with her nails.

"Oh, yeah. And I have to agree with him on the big part," she said, her hand brushing lightly over his now-freed cock, which jumped at her touch.

"Yeah, you'd better agree," he said, his voice a rasp as she stroked him up and down.

In return, he sucked her nipple though her shirt until the cotton was soaking wet and her nipple was hard and her moans traveled through the yard over the soft rustle of the trees. Her hands ran through his hair as she murmured, "Nice, so nice, Tommy."

It had to have been the first time they'd ever taken it slow during sex, and he planned to make it last as long as he could hold out.

He made short work of her shirt. Leisurely, his tongue ringed the dark pink areola, then swiped her nipple until she was shaking her head from side to side and arching her back toward him.

"Mmmmmm, nice," she murmured. "More...want more."

He suckled her nipple between his teeth and tongue, teasing the tight bud in a way he'd never had time to before this. His other hand trailed down between her legs, where he stroked her leisurely through the shorts, until she began to buck impatiently underneath him.

"Tommy—"

"Yes, baby," he murmured before he could stop himself. He kept his face buried by her breast, because when the hell did he start using terms of endearment?

"*Baby.* I like that," she said. "But I have something to tell you."

"Right now? I'm a little busy," he said, taking her nipple into his mouth again. She moaned, but it didn't deter her.

"Yes, right now."

He propped himself up on his elbow. "Go ahead."

"My heat...it's over."

He stared at her, knowing he should be more angry about the deception, when instead he was oddly comforted. "Yeah, I know."

"Then you know we don't have to..." She pointed between their bodies.

"Yes, I know that. But I want to."

She smiled, her entire face lighting with a soft glow. "I want to too."

He fought a smile at her words, and then he tugged down her shorts impatiently, spread her thighs and moved between them.

He speared his tongue inside of her, until her hips rose off the grass and her sex ground against his face, her thighs locking him there.

A prisoner to her pleasure, he'd gladly give up his freedom for this taste of her, sweet and tangy and so hot. He was buried so deep he could barely breathe and he was going to have marks on his neck where she was clutching him, and he didn't care.

She was wildly out of control, even more so than when she'd been in heat. It was all her now and she wanted him. He'd never been so turned on in his entire life as he swirled his tongue through her hot folds, licking her, making her his.

"God, Tommy...Tommy!" she cried as she came against his mouth, contracting around his tongue.

He waited until her thighs parted and trembled as they rested on his shoulders and she was helpless to stop him.

She tensed as he traced the still-sensitive nub softly, tried to push him away when he pressed harder.

"I can't," she whispered, and oh, yes, he'd make sure she could. His hands held her inner thighs open, his mouth ruthless against her, all for her pleasure. And when her next two orgasms came, one right on the heels of the other, he was almost too hard to move.

He slid up her body, grass tickling his shins and knees as he slid his cock inside her. She was so wet, still spasming. Her mouth parted as if she was trying to breathe and not having much luck as he filled her.

But her eyes, they were wide open and staring up at him—those amber cat eyes he loved seeing. Because ever since the first time she'd gotten up the nerve to show him, she hadn't stopped.

"Your eyes," he said gently.

"What?"

"They change, even now," he said. "Beautiful."

"I didn't know if they only changed during my heat," she whispered. "I never opened my eyes during sex, even during the normal times."

"I don't want you to close them anymore, Kira. You don't have to. You're safe," he said. And dammit, he was going to make sure she stayed that way.

He rocked back and forth, his limbs heavy with pleasure, and Kira wrapped around him as if she'd never, ever let him go. It would be so easy to come now, right this second, let himself drift into that space where nothing else mattered. But no, not yet...

"Has it ever been like this before?" he asked as he held her hips so he could deliver long, slow strokes at just the right angle to make her breathe faster and faster and her eyes roll back in her head.

She couldn't answer, couldn't form a coherent sentence if she tried, and that's just the way he wanted it.

Still, he repeated, "Has it ever been like this before, Kira?" as if his question was a command.

Skin slipped on skin, slippery with sweat, and she was giving him his answer by the way her thighs held him tight and her sex contracted hard around him—by the way she shook her head no because it was the only thing she could do. They were beyond words.

She was all his. It had never been like this—for either of them.

"So you're staying, then?" Dev asked the question he'd been hesitant to ask ever since Oz drove that spirit out of Dev and out of the house.

He glanced over at Oz and was surprised to see him there. He was still having a hard time adjusting to having his sight back, and even though his second sight and CRV powers remained intact—stronger even—Dev hadn't told anyone beyond Creed about his return from the darkness. Or about Oz.

Oz put a black-booted foot up on the desk in Dev's home office and gave him an easy smile. "I'm still here, aren't I?"

"That's not an answer." Still, Dev couldn't help but return his smile.

"Yeah, I'm staying," Oz said quietly. "Hope that's all right with you."

Yes, that was more than all right with Dev—waking up in Oz's arms every morning had only reiterated that desire.

"I don't think I'm going to come back to work at ACRO, though," Oz continued.

"I need you there. I want you there."

"You have plenty of people to watch your back."

"Not like you. Between you and Ender, maybe I can get to the bottom of the leak." Dev was still highly frustrated. Being a son of Itor's leader put Dev in a horribly vulnerable position, especially if Alek knew who and where Dev was.

They'd been fighting about it ever since Oz banished Darius's spirit from his body and Dev got his sight back.

"Even with Darius gone, the mole is still an issue. If I give away my hand too quickly, I don't know if things could get worse," Dev told him.

Oz ran a frustrated hand through his hair. "I get it, Dev, but you've got to get to the bottom of this. You're putting it off, and fuck, I know why . . ."

"I haven't been putting it off. I've been . . ." He closed his eyes, the familiar darkness a sudden comfort. When he opened them, he was staring into Oz's dark ones and he knew he didn't have to explain anything to Oz. Oz just knew.

Dev was still trying to understand what it meant to be Alek's son. ACRO's—and Dev's—sworn enemy. Yet, he had Alek's DNA inside of him.

"You're right. It's time," Dev said. Oz waited on the other side of the desk, his body tense as Dev dialed the contact number obtained from the I-Agent Annika had captured.

He'd wanted to put it on speaker, but Oz told him no. He did agree, however, to stay in the room.

Normally, the number would have connected him to the I-Agent's handler, but Dev had used an unsecure line, ensuring that ACRO's business number would appear on Itor's version of caller ID. He knew the call would be rerouted, and after several rings, someone picked up.

"This is Alek."

Liar. He didn't know how he knew, but he did. "Don't fuck with me."

Silence stretched, and then there was a click, another click, and then a Slavic-accented voice that froze the fluid in Dev's spine.

"Hello, Devlin."

Dev paused, the protocol for speaking for the first time to his evil father escaping him. "Let's skip the bullshit. You know why I'm calling."

"A family reunion?"

"You killed my family."

"The people who raised you? The woman who gave birth to you?" Alek sighed. "You wouldn't be where you are now if they were still alive. There's a reason for everything, you know."

"You sick fuck."

"Really, son, I thought you'd have more class than that."

"You can blame the genetics."

Alek's laughter grated on every one of Dev's nerves. "Devlin, we shouldn't be doing this over the phone. Let's meet. We can bond over a glass of Clynelish."

Dev clenched his teeth before his surprised intake of breath let the other man know he'd hit a mark. There was no way Alek could know Dev's favorite, very rare Scotch whiskey. Sweat broke out on his forehead, and one glance across the desk told him that Oz had become just as uncomfortable. He sat stiffly in his chair, his grip on the armrests scoring the leather.

"I'm not impressed by your psychic parlor tricks, *Dad,* so I think we're done. Just know that I'm on to you."

"I don't think you are," Alek said softly. "But I'm on to you."

Desperate to be rid of the man and wondering what the hell he'd been thinking when he called, Dev reached for the disconnect button but froze at Alek's next words.

"I'll give Ryan your best."

Dev stopped breathing. Oh, Jesus. Oh, *holy Jesus*. No one at ACRO but Dev had known about Ryan's insertion into Itor, a measure Dev had taken to keep the mole from learning about it. But Itor knew. Which meant that either Ryan had fucked up, or ...

"You're a little slow on the uptake, son. You must get that from your whore of a mother." Alek rattled something that sounded like ice cubes in a glass. "A man named Darius put some sort of protective thought-shield on you when you were still in the womb. I finally broke it two years ago. It's been nice to get to know you. And ACRO."

"No," he whispered. He swayed in his chair, feeling like he was bleeding out. And in a way, he supposed he was. His thoughts had been bleeding out, right into Alek's mind. Dear God, he'd been searching for the mole for two years, when all he'd had to do was look in the mirror.

DEV DIDN'T REMEMBER HANGING UP THE PHONE, cutting the connection between himself and his father. He wished it would be that easy to cut off his mind from Alek as well, but no, that was going to take some massive work.

He doubled over and retched into the garbage pail. Oz was next to him in seconds, stroking his hair, wiping his mouth, bringing him water.

He couldn't stop his hands from shaking. And all he could hear was Alek's laugh echo in his ears.

"Oz, I'm ... oh, God, I'm the fucking leak at ACRO," he whispered. "How could this have happened? All this time, I've put my entire staff at risk."

"You didn't know—you couldn't have known," Oz said, and something in his tone made Dev start.

"You knew." Dev's voice shook.

"No ... I suspected, but only since I banished Darius. I'd never put you and ACRO at risk like that. Never," Oz said fiercely. "You have to believe me."

"I do. But shit, he's reading everything ... I have to—"

"I've had a mind-shadow on you ever since Darius left—I've basically been monitoring your mind, so I'd know if Alek tried to break in."

"And did he?"

"He tried. He's trying right now." Oz took a deep breath and Dev knew that a mind-shadow wasn't easy on the person doing the shadowing. No, this would drain all of Oz's energy if he did it for too long.

"This isn't going to work forever," Dev said. "We need plans. Alternate plans."

The muscles along Oz's neck and arms showed his strain. "You'd better do it fast, then. Unless you want Alek to know."

"I'm going to need you, Oz. I know you said you didn't want to come back to ACRO..."

Oz was breathing heavily. Alek was really fucking with him, with both of them, and it was time for Dev to stop giving Oz a choice. For both their sakes. "You're going to take over ACRO for me," he told his lover. "I'm going to sign papers giving you authority until I come back. You're not to tell me anything that happens at ACRO."

"Fuck, Dev, that means I can't even be near you."

"Not for long. I'll get help."

"You need to strengthen your mind—it's not going to be an easy fix. You'll have to learn to recognize the feelings, the signs. Since Alek's your blood relation, that makes it more difficult."

"How can I block him out temporarily? Tell me, Oz," Dev begged.

"We can have a team of ACRO's most powerful psychics surround you with a mind-shield, stronger than what I'm doing," Oz said, the strain evident in his voice.

"The Mystic Research department developed a psychic-numbing drug," Dev said slowly. "Between that and the psychics..."

"You should be safe. You have to be safe," Oz muttered fiercely. He closed his eyes, and Dev noted the sweat beading his brow. And then, the same way it came about, the tension fell from Oz's shoulders and he drew in a deep breath and opened those startlingly dark eyes. "We're clear for right now. But we've got to work fast."

Oz was right—this wasn't the time for Dev to think about the past two years, this was the time for action. Dev could handle this. With Oz by his side, he could handle anything.

CHAPTER
Twenty-two

Borrowing the horse hadn't been the plan, not really, but as Kira stood next to Tom's sleek black Mustang while he locked up, Zorro jumped the fence and trotted up the drive, his shod hooves clacking on the cement.

"Hey, baby," she murmured as he nuzzled her hands. "What are you doing?" From the images she'd gathered from him over the past days, she'd learned he'd been a police horse, retired now and condemned to living out his life in a pasture with no excitement.

His whinny and sharp stomp of one hoof was her answer, and her heart broke for the proud Tennessee Walker. "You want one last hurrah, don't you?"

He tossed his head, and with a sigh, she swung nimbly onto his back. Tom appeared from nowhere, his expression one of concern. "Kira?"

"I need to do this, Tom. He needs it."

For a moment, his silence worried her, but then he nodded, and though he didn't say it, she knew he'd follow.

Zorro carried her swiftly down the country road to the ACRO base, which was pretty much a straight shot and off on a back road of its own. As they approached the gate, Zorro began to get antsy.

"It's okay, boy," she said, but he didn't believe her. Probably because she didn't believe it herself.

This could be a huge mistake, and for a moment she considered taking off in the opposite direction, starting somewhere new, like she always had when the towns turned on her or bad guys tried to shove her into vans.

But she couldn't leave Tom, and if he was right, if these people could find a way to cure her of her yearly heats, she had a shot at an even more normal life with him. Besides, if she joined, they would help her animals. She only hoped it wasn't too late for Luke.

One guard stepped out of the gate shack while another remained inside, and though she didn't spot any weapons, she had no doubt the two men had an arsenal at their disposal.

"Can I help you, ma'am?" the first guard asked, eyeing the stallion with only mild curiosity, as though people rode horses to the fenced compound every day.

She dismounted but kept her hand tangled in Zorro's mane in case she needed to swing back up quickly. "I'm not sure who I need to talk to. Zach Taylor in the Animal Division, I guess."

"And you are?"

"Kira Donovan."

He frowned, and then his eyes shot wide. "Hold on, Ms. Donovan. I'll make the necessary calls."

"Have someone bring a halter and lead for Zorro. He'll need to be taken back to his humans."

The guard entered his shack, but while he made his calls, the other one came outside to watch her warily. She just petted Zorro to keep him calm until the phone call guy stepped out and reached for her.

"Don't touch me," she snarled, and he yanked his hand back like he'd been burned.

Her own violent reaction startled her, but she didn't care. She didn't want any man near her. Not touching her, not looking at her, not breathing her air.

The man looked at her like she'd gone rabid, and extended his hand more slowly. "Ma'am, you need to wear this ID badge."

"Oh. Okay." She took the yellow badge and clipped it to her T-shirt.

A moment later, Zach showed up. He carried the tack she'd requested, and he gave her a friendly smile as he placed the halter and lead on Zorro. "Glad you're back, Kira. You've decided to sign on, I hope."

"That's yet to be determined."

He winced. "I hope your indecision doesn't have anything to do with my behavior before."

"Not at all. My fevers affect all men that way." *Touch me today, however, and you'll have to die.*

Startled once more by her reaction to a man, she stepped back, putting more distance between them. What was wrong with her?

"It's over now, isn't it?" When she nodded, he added, "Well, if you sign on, I can guarantee that once a year you'll be taking a vacation, like it or not."

"Thank you," she said, and almost smiled, because just a few weeks ago she wouldn't have considered the time off a vacation. Now, with Tom, her yearly heats would no longer be a problem.

Bored, Zorro tossed his head, and Zach calmed the horse with words in a language she didn't know. "I'd better get him home." Long fingers stroked Zorro's neck as Zach turned to her. "I wrote up your training program, so we'll be seeing a lot of each other. I hope I can convince you to stay. We need you."

He led Zorro away. Two women waited next to the shack, and how long they'd been there Kira had no idea. The dark-haired Amazonian smiled, but the shorter one, a stunning blonde whose gaze could freeze lava, simply glared.

"Hi, I'm Janice." The statuesque brunette didn't hold out her hand, but did give a brisk nod at the other woman. "That's Annika. We're your trainers. The ones you didn't hang around to meet when Ender brought you in."

"I had some issues with your accommodations."

Annika snorted. "I'd think someone who spent time in a jail cell wouldn't be so picky."

Yeah, this Annika person was going to be a blast. "I'm fine now."

Annika crossed her arms over her ample chest. "Then why is Ender trying to arrange it so you won't have to stay on base for your training like everyone else does?"

Dammit. She hadn't wanted him to do that. Those little rooms wouldn't bother her now that her life wasn't on the line. Still, his concern was sweet, and reminded her of one of the reasons she was here.

He'd said she needed to be, and she trusted him.

"Ender's an asshole," Janice said before Kira could answer Annika.

Annika studied her fingernails, which were long but unpolished. "No argument here."

Kira bristled. Tom might be an asshole, but he was *her* asshole.

"Is that a growl?" Annika asked. "Are you *growling* at me, Kira?"

Startled, she blinked. She hadn't realized what she'd been doing, but something was clearly very wrong.

"Does it bother you that everyone here thinks your lover is an asshole?"

Kira ground her teeth. Tom had warned her not to let Annika catch the scent of weakness, but within moments of meeting the woman, Kira had done exactly that.

"I can't help what people think of Tom."

"Tom?" Annika laughed. "I wonder how many of his other women call him Tom."

Other women. The very idea made her hackles raise.

"What do you think, Janice? Do his one-nighters call him Tom?"

"I doubt they exchange names at all."

"He's not like that," Kira snapped, and instantly regretted her outburst. Not only might they be right, but the spark in Annika's eyes told her she'd walked into a trap.

Red flashes burst in Kira's vision, and a shot of adrenaline sizzled through her veins. Her brain knew Annika was messing with her. But something fierce and primal inside didn't care. It wanted the blood of the woman who dared talk about her mate like that.

Mine.

She lunged as Annika turned away. She hit the other woman in the back, and then suddenly Kira was flat on her back in the grass beside the road, her body twitching and her mind scrambled. Annika's voice drifted down to her.

"What the hell? Why did you attack me?"

Groaning, Kira pushed to her feet, her muscles still contracting with tiny tremors. A bitter burning scent hovered in the air. "What was that?"

"Just a little electric shock. I sometimes respond like that to surprises. You're lucky I didn't fry you like a strip of bacon."

"I don't—" A sharp cramp in Kira's belly sucked her words from her mouth. Another stabbing pain doubled her over and made her cry out. "What... what are you doing to me?"

The two trainers exchanged worried glances.

"Nothing." Annika stepped closer. "Kira?"

Hot liquid gushed between Kira's thighs, and she looked down to see a trickle of crimson running down her leg.

"Shit." Annika caught Kira as another cramp sapped the strength from her legs. "Call the medics. Hurry!"

The world spun. She dimly heard herself shout, "Tommy!" and then all went black.

Three shots of tequila and a beer chaser hadn't made even a small dent in Annika's sour mood. Neither had sitting in ACRO's on-base closet of a bar, listening to hick country music on the juke-box. She stared at the three remaining shots lined up on the table before her, and played eenie-meenie-minie-moe. Some non-Talent supply department dweeb at the pool table eyed her like she was a moron. She flipped him the bird and downed the chosen shot.

The golden liquid burned her throat, but it didn't burn away the bitter taste she hadn't been able to swallow since this morning, when she'd watched ACRO medics whisk an unconscious Kira away in a specialized military ambulance.

But that hadn't been the worst of it. No, what Dev had told Annika later about Kira had knocked her on her ass like no tequila could.

Her pager went off again, and with a flick of her wrist, the de-vice joined her smashed cell phone against the wall of her dark-ened corner booth. Her phones at home hadn't been so lucky. The power surge she'd sent through them had melted them where they sat. At least they'd stopped ringing.

She wondered if Creed had tried to contact her. Not that she cared. Though a couple of rounds of hot sex might take her mind off things. What had he said about that—fuck her problems away? Her usual MO?

She downed the last two shots and stumbled home—converted barracks on base—because she couldn't stand anyone looking at her. She'd give anything to go to Dev's place, but no matter how mad she was, she loved him too much to invade this strange privacy he seemed to need.

But damn, she didn't want to be alone. She'd learned that Kira was fine, and so far, the kid was okay too, but things would be touch and go for the next few days at least. If Annika was responsible for something going wrong with the pregnancy...

Her stomach heaved as she opened her front door. Oh, God, she couldn't handle this. She'd killed a lot of people, had been a weapon for the CIA for years, but none of her victims had been innocents. And never, ever a child.

And still, had she done the same thing five years ago, would it have bothered her?

Would it?

She didn't want to dig too deeply to find the answer.

Lurching, she made it to the bathroom, where she wanted to retch but couldn't. Instead, she stripped and stepped into the shower, hoping to wash away the day's events. But the blistering water couldn't scald the memory from her brain.

Neither could it stop the pain. Or the tears.

Sobbing, she slid down the wall until she was sitting in the corner beneath the hot spray. What was going on with her? What was up with the emotional breakdown over someone else?

Creed had been right when he'd said she didn't care about anyone but herself and Dev. But then, how could anyone expect otherwise, when she'd been raised from the age of two by people whose only goal was to turn her into a merciless, professional killing machine?

Goal accomplished.

Annika had become the CIA's most prized, most successful experiment. They'd congratulated themselves on producing an assassin whose beauty and language abilities allowed her to get close to anyone. Whose fighting skills, killing expertise and lack of remorse allowed her to take out targets with an ease and efficiency they'd never seen.

Add to that her powerful electrical gift, and nothing could touch her.

They'd been so busy celebrating their achievement that they'd neglected to protect themselves from the very weapon they created. And if she felt nothing when she took out assigned targets, she'd felt less when she took out the CIA operatives she'd learned had murdered her birth mother in order to steal her.

She hadn't stopped there. Almost everyone who had played a role in making her into little more than a weapon had paid. Those who'd escaped her wrath, who had put out an order for her termination, didn't get off scot-free. She'd go bloody on them when the opportunity presented itself.

Right now, though, she was content to work for ACRO. For Dev.

She still wasn't sure how he'd become the one person besides herself she could care about, and for a long time she'd resisted letting him in. Just as the CIA had taught her. Feel nothing. Care about no one. Trust no one. But he'd kept trying, long after common sense dictated that he should have left her alone.

And she'd been happy with her life since. Until now. Until Creed weaseled his way into her world and made her feel something other than indifference. Something much more than the decadent orgasms he gave her.

She'd kept the door on her emotions closed to everyone but Dev. Somehow, Creed had opened the door, let them out, and now they didn't want to go back in. They'd flooded her, had overloaded her senses, and she didn't know how to deal with it.

What had happened with Kira shouldn't have bothered her, but now that was all she could think about. She'd even tried to order flowers for the other woman, but when the salesperson asked what to write on the card, Annika had hung up. Was it cool to say,

"Sorry I almost killed you and your kid, and I know you're still in danger, so hey, apologies ahead of time if something bad happens"?

Probably not. And she seriously doubted Kira would appreciate her showing up in person at the hospital.

The water went cold, but she didn't notice. Didn't care. Even as her teeth rattled with the strength of her shivers, the only thing she could think was that maybe, just maybe, the freezing water would numb her, and the pain would go away.

DEV SOUNDED STRANGE. He'd all but ordered Creed to find Annika and help her, but wouldn't give more details.

Creed clicked off his phone before turning his attention to the man stretched out on his couch. He'd been about to call Oz, to see if his returning friend and mentor had any answer, when the doorbell rang. Oz had been waiting on his stoop.

"Quaty contacted me," Oz had said.

Now Oz said, "Go to Annika. Quaty will stay here and keep me company." He looked worn out.

Instead of rushing off, like he wanted to do, Creed sat down heavily in the leather chair next to the fireplace. He'd stopped having the massive chills about five days after Annika ran out on him again, but he still didn't feel right. Kat hadn't been her usual self either. "What the fuck's going on, Oz?"

Oz stared at him, his brown eyes as close to black as Creed's were. The two men could have easily passed for brothers—Creed was slightly bigger and broader, Oz more conventionally handsome and sans tattoos, but their coloring, their movements were eerily similar.

"Creed—"

"I want to know what's going on with me. Why I had that reaction when I left the mansion last year. Why I had the same reaction when the spirit came here, especially if it's not after me."

Oz was silent for a long time, and when he finally spoke again, his voice sounded hoarse. The room had gone deadly cold and Kat was rubbing his back frantically. "Are you sure you're ready to hear this?"

"I need to know. I want to know," he said. He sat there quietly as Kat wailed in his ear.

"Quaty, stop it," Oz commanded, and although the wailing didn't stop, it grew progressively lower. Creed leaned forward in his seat and stared at Oz, waited impatiently.

"There's a way I can free you from Kat," Oz said quietly.

"Forever?"

"Forever," Oz confirmed.

"Shit." Creed covered his ears in a futile attempt to stop Kat's screams from echoing in his ears.

"There's not a big window of time for you to make your decision." Oz spoke calmly, ignored the screeching that Creed knew the man could also hear and told him more about what Creed would need to do to break the bonds with Kat.

Ani. He had to talk with Ani about all of this . . .

"I can't do this right now, Oz," he heard himself say. "I've got to get out of here." He stumbled, half blinded by tears, and Oz didn't try to stop him.

CREED'S THROAT FELT SORE, as if he'd been screaming, when really he'd barely talked at all.

Chills wracked his body again as he knocked on Annika's door gently, then more forcefully when no one answered.

"Annika, open up," he yelled, because he knew something wasn't right. He flashed back to the time he'd kicked open another door, at Dev's family mansion, in order to get to her, and with one heavily booted foot, he did so again.

She hadn't even bothered to set the alarm on her house, and with a quick glance he took in the fried keypad by the door, the melted house phone that looked as if it had caught fire recently.

He heard water running, raced up the stairs and into what must be her bedroom. He opened the door, expected to find himself immersed in a cloud of steam, not the freezing cold blast that accosted his senses. The window was open, and he could tell before he opened the shower door that the water had also run cold.

Through the heavy glass squares that partitioned the shower from the rest of the bathroom, he saw Annika, curled up in a ball on the floor. He stepped in and turned off the water, grabbed a towel and wrapped her in it.

He carried her into the bedroom, shoved her, still dripping wet, under her heavy comforter, and stripped his own clothes off quickly. He got under the covers with her, hugged her chilled skin next to his in an attempt to warm her fast. Even though he felt cold inside, he knew his skin was still much, much warmer than hers.

"Ani," he murmured. "Why the hell did you do this to yourself?"

She stirred, her wet hair sticking to his neck and cheek, and when she turned her head in his direction, he rubbed her lips with his because he wanted them pink and rosy again, not tinged blue as they were.

She was still spooned, her back to his chest. He caressed her belly and breasts with his hands, rubbing them up and down to get her attention. He rolled her nipples between his fingers and thought he heard a small gasp.

"Come on, Ani. Open your eyes," he said. He kissed her shoulder, his cock hardening from the friction of rubbing her—hell, from just *being* near her.

Yes, sex would definitely wake her up—shock her, if nothing else.

He slid down her body, staying under the covers. He shifted her thighs so he could get between them, found himself with them pressing his neck. It didn't matter, as long as he could get his tongue, and his piercing, where it needed to go.

He buried his face in her sex, his tongue stroking her folds, which soon grew hot and wet, and he noted that her hips began to rock slightly. He pressed his tongue deep inside of her, heard her gasp for sure this time. Her hands wandered down to twist in his hair as he probed and licked and sucked. Her thighs squeezed his neck as his piercing connected with the tight nub of nerves, and she shattered against his mouth.

She tasted delicious, like a mix of hot, sweet electricity and sugar, and he pushed his tongue inside her again so he could catch every last bit of her orgasm.

"Creed?" she whispered.

He pulled his head away from her reluctantly. "I hope to hell you weren't expecting someone else," he growled, but she was pulling at him until he was face-to-face with her. She pulled him in for a kiss, her taste still on his lips, and damn, he always found it hot when she did that.

She pulled him on top, so he covered her. Her body was warming nicely, her muscles still tense even as she spread her thighs to welcome him.

"I wasn't expecting you. Not after what happened last time," she murmured. "I fucked up so badly, Creed. Like you knew I would."

"Shhhh, Ani. It's all right," he said.

"Not all right. Won't ever be," she said, but she was still guiding him inside of her. He wanted to pull away, to force her to talk more, but he couldn't. Their bond was too strong when they were close, her energy drawing his until he couldn't do anything but surrender to it, and to her.

He drew a hissing breath between his teeth, because his cock felt so good inside of her, where it was tight and hot and pulsing— all for him. Only for him. She clutched at his shoulders and moaned.

She had tears tracking her cheeks. He kissed them away as he shifted so he could tongue her nipples, and her ankles locked around his lower back. She was everything he never thought he could have, and right now, at moments like this, she was all his.

Her skin was hot now; her cheeks held a pink flush and her heart beat strongly against his chest. He was on his knees and elbows, rutting against her, because she needed him to be deeper, told him that in no uncertain terms by the jut of her hips, by the way she was kissing him.

The sex continued hard and fast, both of them coming within seconds of each other. Creed's orgasm was like a hot burst of

262 • Sydney Croft

white light behind his closed eyelids, like he'd been blown apart and put back together within a second's time.

And then Annika—his tough chick—was crying in his arms. Sobbing as if her heart would break.

"I...hurt...Ender's...girlfriend," she managed. "He's going to kill me."

"Ender will calm down. Kira's all right," he told her. "She doesn't blame you. No one does."

"I've worked so hard to control it," she ground out. "I didn't mean to hurt her."

"I know, honey, I know. Sometimes our gifts don't always co-operate the way we want them to."

"At least yours doesn't make you hurt people accidentally. Doesn't stop you from actually having sex."

"Kat does stop me. And you've never hurt me during sex," he reminded her.

"You're the only one."

"I like being the only one."

"I don't have a choice," she said, her words cutting into him sharper and more effectively than any razor ever could.

"Who knows? Maybe there are more of us out there for you to fuck. Maybe you can take out an ad for willing participants if you're not happy with your current situation."

She didn't answer him. The past months of beating his head against what felt akin to a brick wall came bearing down on him and he rolled off the bed. His feet hit the floor with a solid thump and he sat staring at the wall.

He waited for Annika to storm out, and she surprised him by not doing that. Instead, she reached up and began to massage his shoulders, her hands strong and sure—an apology. As close to one as she'd ever given him.

"I need to know if this is going to work between us, Ani."

"Can't we just keep things the way they are?"

No, not after what Oz told him earlier. His mentor and friend had gripped his arm and foretold a future Creed had never be-lieved could actually happen.

"There's a way for things to be different for me."

"I don't understand." She'd stopped the massage, and when he turned, she was sitting back on her heels, still naked—beautifully, enticingly naked—and he almost scrapped the conversation in favor of making love to her again.

"It's about Kat," he said quietly. "The other day...my tattoos...when they were moving..."

"Something *is* wrong."

"Yeah, it is."

"Have you been to the doctors? I'm sure Dev can find you a specialist if the doctors at ACRO can't help you..."

Creed shook his head. "It's not something any doctor can help me with. It's something I've got to make a decision about before the decision's taken away from me."

"Tell me. Let me help. I can find some way to help you."

God, how he wanted to believe that. The concern in her blue eyes was almost too much for him to take—she'd been through so much shit, and now he was going to ask more of her. Probably more than she was willing to give.

"I've got a certain window of time...it won't be easy, but it's possible that I can live a normal life."

"You mean, without Kat?"

"Right. I wouldn't be tied to her anymore."

"Then what's to think about?"

"My powers. All of them—they'd be gone."

She pushed away from him, half-stunned. "So you'd get your life back, get to be with anyone you wanted to..."

"No!" he shouted. "It wouldn't be with just anyone, dammit. It would be with you. That's the way this deal works. It's you or it's nobody. It's keeping my powers and having women once or twice, or it's staying with you."

"I don't understand."

"That's my choice. My one and only choice, Ani. If it's not something you want, then I'm going to let the opportunity slip by."

"But if it's not me, then you could be with anybody at all."

"I've said it before, I don't want just anybody. I'm not willing to give up everything for just anybody." He ran his hands through his hair, a wave of despair washing over him. Torn between his present and his past, he was breaking in two, literally.

He pushed up from the bed, ignoring Annika's hands trying to pull him back down. He yanked his pants on and grabbed his T-shirt. He almost couldn't look at her, but he forced himself to.

"I'm asking too much, I know."

"Creed—"

"It's all right. I get it. I finally get it," he said. "Some people were just meant to be alone. We're two of those people. It was stupid for me to think otherwise."

He left the room and her house without another word. Kat met him on the outside steps and put her arm around him as he walked home in the rain.

CHAPTER
Twenty-four

"What the hell are you talking about? I followed her here. She was talking to Annika and that other trainer. She was fine." Ender slammed his fists on the desk in front of Dev.

"There was a problem," Dev said. "She attacked Annika."

"Bullshit. Annika's the one with no restraint."

"Annika said something about *you* that hit your animal whisperer the wrong way," Dev said, because Ender's temper didn't scare him the way it did almost every other person on the compound.

"This happened hours ago—why the hell didn't you call me sooner?" Ender asked.

"We wanted to make sure Kira was all right before we called."

"Dev, you'd better start telling me exactly what's going on." Ender's agitation rose to untenable levels, and Dev hoped the man was ready for what he was about to hear.

"Kira's in the infirmary—she's going to be fine. But her body's changed in a way we never anticipated."

Ender got it. Immediately. He sank onto the couch, muttering to himself, "I saw the changes but didn't put it all together."

Then he spoke to Dev. "She said she was on the pill."

"Apparently, Derek switched them out to placebos when he arrived at the refuge. The I-Agent Annika captured in Idaho gave up the intel. We've got Remy on it now to see what else we can extract from the agent."

"They wanted her pregnant."

"Yes, by Derek specifically. With her abilities and Derek's strength..."

"Her child might have a double gift—and with her animal physiology, the strength could be magnified," Ender whispered. "What about our child?"

"Let's just say, that kid isn't someone I'd want to mess with either."

"Does she know?"

"I figured you should be the one to tell her," Dev said, and the familiar tightening in his head began again. Since he and Oz had gotten the psychics to help block his mind from Alek yesterday, he'd been experiencing violent headaches that came out of the blue. A necessary evil while Alek battled the mind-shield for control of Dev's brain.

In a few days, once ACRO's affairs were in order, Dev would take his leave until he could fully protect his mind against Itor. Oz was prepared to take charge, and most of the staff had been notified.

"Dev, you all right?" Ender was asking. Dev looked straight into the man's eyes, and for a second Ender cocked his head and stared at Dev, as if he knew Dev could see again.

"I'm fine. It's just stress. Go now," Dev said.

"Fuck you. Something's up with you. It's that goddamned Oz, isn't it?" Ender continued to stare. "I don't get it, Dev. Letting Oz take over while you go on a vacation doesn't strike me as something you'd do willingly."

"You don't know anything," Dev said.

"I know a hell of a lot more than you give me credit for," Ender countered, but Dev didn't have the time or patience for this. He stood, kicking his chair back behind him.

"Go now, Tom. Get the hell out of my sight. Go to your animal whisperer and figure out whether or not you're ready to play daddy," he said, felt Ender's jerk of surprise.

"Like I said before, fuck you, Dev," Ender whispered, his voice raw. He stormed out with a slam of the main office door, and Dev waited a beat before he slid out the back.

KIRA'S PREGNANT.

The thought hit Ender on a level so deep that he nearly shook as he raced through ACRO at top speed to get to the infirmary. A primal tug to protect her and his baby nearly overwhelmed him, and he didn't give a shit what was happening with Dev. He only wanted to get to Kira. Immediately.

He stormed past both security and the nurses who tried to stop him—and he was pretty sure the nurses were a hell of a lot tougher to get through, but it didn't matter. He pushed past anyone in his way, gently but firmly moving the last nurse—who actually stood in front of Kira's door—by picking her up.

He put her right back in place, and even though his speed was slightly diminished because no food held his interest, he was still a hell of a lot faster than anyone around here.

Kira was sitting up in bed, looking at the door, no doubt having heard the commotion. When the nurse came in after him, Kira called out, "It's all right, Meg. I want to see him. He's mine."

Mine.

"He's yours?" Meg pointed to him. "Good luck with that, honey." The nurse exited, closing the door behind her.

"Hi, Tommy," Kira said.

"Hey," he said. She didn't look any worse for wear—in fact, she looked even more beautiful than usual. Softer, which he'd already mentioned to her days earlier, and glowing. Now he understood why. He walked over to the bed and grabbed her hand. "You look good."

"I'm glad you came," she said. "I'm fine. And please, don't do anything to Annika. None of this was her fault."

He growled again, this time at the mention of Annika's name. "I'll take care of her."

"Tommy, don't you dare. I attacked her first. It was my fault. All I seem to do is cause trouble. I thought maybe it would be different here..." She trailed off absently, pulled the covers around her more tightly.

"I have to ask you something, Kira."

"They don't want me here anymore, right?" she asked, the misery in her tone breaking his heart.

"No, they want you here. You're still safe and this is still the best place for you."

"I don't know what happened, why I reacted that way—"

"Did you have sex with anyone else during this cycle?" he asked quickly, interrupting her before she could go over the entire incident again and again.

She yanked her hand from his. "What the hell is that supposed to mean?"

Ah, yes, hormones. Kira's would probably be much more off the wall than most pregnant women's. Which meant he was screwed. Granted, he could've couched the question a little better, but hell, he'd never promised that he was going to change. Much.

"It's a simple question," he said. "You told me yourself that you've always needed a lot of different men to satisfy you. That you've moved from man to man during your heat before."

"Yes, before," she practically spat. "You know there was only you."

"I won't be mad or anything. I understand. It's just that I need to know." Fuck, he was practically stuttering. "Did you sleep with Derek before I got there?"

"No," she said, with a hard shake of her head. She was staring at him, her brow furrowed in anger.

"You're sure?"

"I think I'd know," she said, and he thought about the time he'd drugged her. Derek could've easily taken her then, and she wouldn't have known.

Derek was out cold. There was no way...

"How are you feeling now?" he asked finally.

"A little more tired than usual, but I think that's probably tied into the heat cycle ending early."

"When did it end exactly?"

"Two weeks ago."

"Before you rearranged my furniture?" he asked gently, got a small smile from her.

"Yes."

"And the heat ending early, that's never happened before?"

She shook her head. "Never. Something's wrong, isn't it? You know something."

"Yeah, I do." He stared up at the ceiling and then back down at her. "I know why it ended."

"Am I all right? Am I sick?"

"No, you're not sick. You're pregnant."

He stood next to her bed and waited for the fallout.

PREGNANT.

Oh, shit.

Shock stole her breath, something she didn't realize until her lungs burned and she had to gasp for air.

"Kira? Are you okay?"

Tom's voice, low and deep, soothed her almost as much as his hand rubbing her back.

"I can't be pregnant. I'm on the pill," she said finally, and then felt herself pale when she remembered the questions he'd had about her sleeping with someone else. "You don't think I did this on purpose, right? To trap you, or something?"

"No." He pulled up a chair and sat beside her. "We know Derek tampered with your pills."

"Why? Why would he do that?"

"To get you pregnant for Itor." He clenched his fist at his side. "I should have caused him a lot more pain."

"But I thought they wanted me dead. To keep me from ACRO."

He exhaled and looked away. "Yeah. I guess we were wrong about that."

Ice-cold terror wracked her body at the idea that she could right now be the property of a supernatural terrorist organization. And that she would be giving them a child to do God-knew-what with.

A child. Joy, shock and fear streamed into a big river of tears that spilled down her face. "This . . . this doesn't change things between us, does it? I mean, I hoped to have your children someday, but—"

"You did? You wanted kids? With me?"

"Of course." Ignoring the tug of the IV line, she laid her hand over his. "I mean, I never thought I'd have them, because no man would want me for a mate. But you know what I am, and you don't care. Why wouldn't I want to have your children?"

"Because of what *I* am," he said quietly.

"An excedo . . . whatever? Meg explained that. Said you and a gob of other people here are perfectly normal, but different. That you have an excess of certain traits, sort of like how greyhounds are built for something completely different from mastiffs, but they're still dogs. She said excedos are like that. Some are superfast, like you. Others can hear better than cats. She said you've even got one guy who has sonar like a bat. So if you're fine with what I do, I'm fine with what you do."

"I wasn't talking about that."

"Then what? Your job? Bringing in people like me? Defending yourself and them when you have to?" When he winced, she experienced a sharp zing of panic. "Oh, God, you don't want this, do you?"

His gaze dropped to where their hands met. "Kira, I'm not going to lie and say I'm thrilled, because right now I'm scared as hell. But we'll handle it." Lifting his head, he stared at her so intently, she had to measure out a long, slow exhale. "And never, ever think I don't want it."

Love, big and mushy and nearly overwhelming, filled her until she couldn't keep it inside or she'd burst. "I love you, Tommy," she whispered. He swallowed like he wasn't sure what to say, but she wouldn't take it back even if she could. "I've loved you since that day in the car, when you threw the hamburger away. No one has ever cared about me enough to respect my feelings like that."

There was a tap at the door, and then Dr. Lavery, ACRO's veterinarian, strode in. The mildly animal-empathic brunette might be a medical professional, but she was still a woman, and she cast an appreciative look at Tom. A low rumble vibrated Kira's chest, but it wasn't until Tom squeezed her hand that she realized everyone else could hear it.

Dr. Lavery smiled. "Is everything okay in here?"

"If by okay you mean that I just found out I'm pregnant and I have these weird reactions to everything, then yep. Everything's okay."

"This is the father, I presume?"

"Yes." Tom's tone left no doubt that he was certain of it, and Kira felt a strange, happy warmth surge through her. "How did you know?"

Dr. Lavery unwrapped her stethoscope from around her neck and prepared to listen to Kira's heart. "Because she's touching you." She went silent for a moment as she moved the bell around Kira's chest, and then she glanced over at Tom. "I'm Dr. Lavery. I'm a veterinarian, but I've taken the lead on this case. Dr. Brown will consult."

"Kira said she'd seen a vet before, for a canine virus, but why does she need a vet now?" Tom asked.

Kira blushed as Dr. Lavery straightened to check her IV and said, "Because Dr. Brown is male, and she bit him."

Tom coughed a little. "*Bit* him?"

Dr. Lavery nodded and made a note on Kira's chart. "Once the sutures are removed, he should regain full use of his hand." The vet cleared her throat, but the amused twinkle in her eye gave her away. "Apparently, you're the only male she's let near her since she arrived at ACRO this morning."

How humiliating. Especially because half the time she didn't realize she was acting out until it was too late. "Doctor, is the pregnancy causing this? Will it stop?"

The veterinarian peered at Kira over the top of her black-rimmed glasses. "Females of some species turn on the males once they conceive, but it's usually temporary, so there's no reason to think this won't be temporary as well."

"Good. Because going out in public could be a little awkward if I'm biting and growling at every man who looks at me."

"I don't mind if you growl at them." Tom flashed her a masculine, possessive smile laced with heat. "But save the bites for me."

Oh, boy. She wanted to bite him right now. In the soft spot between his shoulder and neck, while he took her hard. "I can do that."

Dr. Lavery cleared her throat again, and Kira felt her cheeks grow hot. She'd forgotten she and Tom weren't alone. He did that to her, made her focus her attention so strongly on him that nothing else existed.

"No biting, or anything... else, for a week," Dr. Lavery said, and Tom groaned.

"Easy for you to say," he muttered. "Kira is ruthless when she wants something."

"Oh, thanks."

Dr. Lavery laughed. "Well, you're just going to have to be firm and tell her no."

"When can she go home?"

Home. She'd been a nomad for so many years that she'd forgotten the meaning of the word. It sounded so good coming from Tom.

"Kira suffered light blood loss from what we call a threatened miscarriage. Her ultrasound appeared normal, though, and her hormone levels are high, so barring a traumatic event, she stands a good chance of carrying this child to term. We'd like to keep her overnight, and then she can go home in the morning, but she'll need to take it very easy for a few days." The vet gave Kira a stern look. "Can you do that?"

"It'll be difficult, but I'll manage. I want this baby." She bit her lip and glanced at Tom. "I want a family."

Ender knew he was in the midst of the nightmare, but no matter how hard he struggled to wake up, the scene played out in front of him relentlessly.

"Hey, Ender, want a cigar?" Aces threw him a Cuban, and both men lit up under the darkness of the Afghan sky.

His Delta team had made it to the LZ two hours early, hung back and waited in the foothills of the mountains along the Khyber Pass for their ride. Their successful mission, taking down a small cell of terrorists as per a CIA order, had taken them two weeks to complete. And now Ender and company looked forward to R&R.

Damien grabbed the cigar from Ender's hand and lit it. "You're getting slow in your old age, man," he said.

Ender's twenty-fifth birthday had come and gone during the past week, and he was about to tell Damien to fuck off when he heard the pop of gunfire.

"Ender . . ." Damien wheezed through a mouthful of blood, and everything after that happened in slow motion. More enemy shots rang out from the cover of some scrub on the ridge, and Damien screamed, clutching his chest. Ender pushed Damien down and moved into position

to cover him. *Damien was still screaming—he'd been hit badly, and then suddenly, he was on fire.*

"What the fuck kind of weapon do they have?" Aces shouted as he raced to put out the blaze that had engulfed their teammate. As Aces approached, flames seemed to erupt from Damien's fingertips, and Ender swore the other man actually threw a blast of fire at Aces, who dropped to the ground, shrieking and writhing.

"Damien, no!" Ender shouted, scrambling away even as fiery bolts continued to shoot from the man the team called Devil because of his dark good looks. And God, the enemy insurgents, his own team—they were all burning except for Ender, whose speed allowed him to outrun the flames. Choking on greasy smoke, he crouched behind a rock, M24 sniper rifle in hand, useless against the blazing carnage and suffering.

Ender's mind screamed that this couldn't be happening, but the sounds, the smells, the blistering heat on his skin told him otherwise. Impossible situation or not, men were dead or dying, and Damien was still lighting up anything that moved. Tightening his grip on the rifle so his hands wouldn't shake, Ender killed Damien and then put a bullet into each of his team members as they twitched in the throes of death.

Then they were all dead and he was standing alone. He'd been screaming internally, his own pulse pounding in his ears so loudly it almost drowned out the sounds of the C-130 crashing into the ground below him.

As always, Ender never got farther into the nightmare than hearing the plane crash, never relieved the part where he'd dragged Dev, kicking and screaming, from the burning C-130.

Instead, he woke up drenched, screaming and shaking, standing in the corner of his basement, holding an M16 pointed into the darkness. Ready to kill.

With trembling fingers, he checked to make sure he hadn't fired any rounds, discovered that he hadn't even loaded the gun. He could lock and load in his sleep, but thankfully he hadn't taken his training that far.

He sank to the floor, back to the stone basement wall, ran his hands through his hair and wondered when this would stop.

His chest tightened. He needed to get out of here, go running, burn off all this worry and tension. But his legs were still shaking, and his body wasn't functioning well. This kind of physical weakness had never happened to him, and before he'd gone to bed he'd tried to force down some steak he'd bought on the way home from the hospital.

Every bite made him think of Kira. The woman pregnant with his child, who expected them to make a life together and be one big, happy, special-ability-type family.

How was he supposed to keep them safe when he was sleep-walking with guns, when *he* was the danger? *Hi, kiddo, don't worry—Daddy's a killer, but he won't hurt you.*

No, he couldn't be sure of anything. He had the nightmares for a reason—to remind him that he was, and always would be, better off alone.

THE MOMENT TOM ENTERED KIRA'S ROOM in the morning, she flew into his arms. She must have caught him by surprise, because he rocked back as though she was too heavy.

"Sorry," she said, as she wrapped herself around him. "I'm a little excited to see you."

He held her tight, like he didn't want to let go. She knew the feeling. "Tom?"

"Hmm?"

His hands stroked her back through the scrubs she'd been given to wear home, and she sighed against his neck. "I know you're worried about all of this, but you're going to be an awesome dad."

His body went so taut she could be hugging a board. She backed out of his arms. "You look terrible. I told you something was wrong, that you were getting sick. You should see that doctor I bit." When she felt his forehead for fever, he gently grasped her wrist and moved it away.

"Kira, we need to talk."

"Okay. But let's do it at home." She grinned like an idiot, because she finally had a home, for the first time in her life.

He took her hand and led her out of the clinic and into the cloud-filtered sunlight, his tense silence breaking her mood a little. Obviously, whatever he wanted to talk about was important, and as they walked along the sidewalk toward the little duck pond, she couldn't take the quiet anymore.

"Dr. Lavery said Luke arrived last night. She put him on an IV, and Zach talked to him, got him to eat a little. So it looks like he'll pull through. I can't thank you enough, Tommy. The rest of the animals will be here in the next couple of days."

"That's great."

The odd tone of his voice sent a low-level buzz of worry through her, and then she noticed where they were heading—or, more important, where they weren't heading. "Why are we walking away from the parking lot?"

"Because," he said, staring straight ahead, "I'm not taking you to my house. I'm taking you to an apartment on base."

"But I don't need to be near the clinic."

"I'll explain when we get there."

She planted her feet on the ground and her fists on her hips. "No, you'll explain now. Why are we going to be staying in an apartment?"

He stopped, but didn't turn around. "Kira—"

"Now."

He cursed, but it was a soft, pleading sound, so unlike his usual harsh invective, which worried her even more. "I really think it would be best to do this in private."

"Do what?" A shroud of dread settled over her. "You don't plan to stay there with me, do you?"

"No. You'll only be there until a house on base is set up the way you want it. A nursery and furniture . . . a place for your animals." She didn't have time to think or react, because he swung around to her, his eyes red-rimmed, and she didn't know if they'd been that way since he arrived and she hadn't noticed, or if it had just happened. "I can't do this, Kira. I'm not cut out to be a family man. I'm sorry."

She recoiled, unable to process what he'd said. This had to be a joke. Except the tension in his body, his face, told her he was dead serious. "But you said—"

"I know what I said. I was wrong. I'll make sure you have everything you and the baby need."

"We need *you*." Her voice was so full of tremors that she barely understood her own words. "Why are you doing this?"

"For you. For your own good."

"What? *Are you kidding me?* That's bullshit, and you know it. We're good together. I'm happy for the first time in my life. So how is dumping me like an unwanted dog for my own good? It's not." No, there was something else going on here, and she was going to find out what. She marched up to him and poked him hard in the chest. "I want answers. The truth. Do you think this baby isn't yours?"

"God, no. And even if it wasn't..." He shook his head. "It doesn't matter. I can't raise a kid. I'm a killer, Kira. Not good father material."

Relief flooded her, a heady sensation when mixed with the fear-based adrenaline that had juiced up her body. "Are we back to that again? You're a good man, Tommy. You do what you have to do to protect people and defend yourself. I'm fine with that." She grabbed his hand to lead him toward the parking lot. "Now let's go home."

He didn't budge, forcing her to turn back to him. He kept hold of her hand, gripping tight. "No. Listen to me. My job is more than bringing people like you in to ACRO. Sometimes my missions are based on my speed and shooting skills."

Goose bumps prickled her flesh. "So...What? Are you saying you're an assassin?"

"Something like that."

A breeze ruffled his hair, drawing her thoughts to how many times she'd run her fingers through it, how his breath would catch, almost imperceptibly, when she did so. Little things like that had made her fall for him, and she wasn't about to give up now.

"Well," she said, lifting her chin in resolve, "I don't know how I feel about that, but we can work it all out at home. I'm sure the people you're sent to, um, take care of, are horrible people."

"Dammit, Kira! Stop making excuses for me. I'm not a good person, and the people I have to *take care of* aren't always the devil incarnate." He released her. "I almost killed you, okay? Do you get it now?"

Geez, he had serious guilt issues. Which only proved her point about him being a good person. "You didn't almost kill me. If you hadn't gone after those men in the woods, they would have killed you and done God knows what with me. It wasn't your fault you couldn't get to me right away when I needed sex. In the end, you saved me."

"I'm talking about my orders. They were to bring you back here," he said. "Or kill you if you refused."

Her stunned silence was broken only by the blood pounding in her ears.

If you don't leave with me, you're going to be killed. And that's something I can promise you will happen.

The words he'd spoken back at the refuge the night she'd attacked him for sex roared through her head. He hadn't been talking about Itor. He'd been talking about himself. Itor had never planned to kill her, and he'd known it even then.

But she *had* refused to leave with him—and he hadn't killed her. They'd been talking at the tiger enclosure after they'd made love. He'd stood there, his hand over the bulge in his bag pocket.

The same pocket where he'd kept his gun.

Her heart careened to a stop with such violence that it must have left skid marks on the inside of her rib cage.

"Oh, God," she whispered. "Oh, my God...that night at the big cat pens." Her gut clenched, and trembles wracked her body. "Were you...were you really going to kill me?"

"Yes."

She shook her head so hard, her hair whipped at her eyes, stinging them. "You're lying. I know you are. You wouldn't— couldn't—do that to me."

"The animals knew," he said hoarsely, and she remembered how they'd tried to warn her, how they'd sensed danger. Her gaze snapped to his, to the cold, hard truth in the depths of his eyes.

The ground dropped out from beneath her, leaving her swaying in a vertigo spin. *Ohgod, ohgod, ohgod.*

"Kira—" He reached for her.

She stumbled backward. "Don't touch me," she whispered.

He held his hands up as if in surrender and stayed rooted to his spot. His chest rose and fell in great, shuddering swells, and he looked flushed, feverish, and it struck her that he had no right to be as miserable as she was.

Silence stretched. "So that's it," she said finally, with a calm she didn't feel. "Nice knowing you, nice knocking you up, but you're better off without me, and, oh, by the way, I was going to kill you?"

"I'm so sorry." The way he said it, like he truly felt regret, lit her fuse. How dare he lie like that? If he were telling the truth, he'd be trying to convince her he loved her, that he wouldn't really have killed her, not throwing her away like garbage.

"You're sorry?" Her voice was reedy, shaky, and she hated herself for it. "You're sorry that you were going to shoot me and my baby?" She pressed her hands to her belly, because although she hadn't been pregnant at the time—at least, she didn't think so, but Dr. Lavery hadn't determined that yet—she was now, and the thought that her child would never have had a chance to grow inside her…

"You're upset—"

"No shit. Tell me, *Ender*, when you were inside me, were you thinking about killing me? What were you going to do with my body? Feed me to the tigers to get rid of the evidence? Bury me with Derek?" The harsh reality swirled in the watery depths of his eyes, and she backed up another step, the backs of her knees striking a park bench. "My God," she croaked, "you're a monster."

His throat worked hard on a swallow, and she expected him to try to talk his way out of her accusation, but all he finally said was "Yes."

"That's it? Yes? You planned to murder me while you were

coming inside me and all I get is a *yes?* You son of a bitch. You fucking son of a bitch!"

She lunged. Her palm connected with his face hard enough to knock his head around. With his reflexes, he could have stopped her, but he hadn't. He didn't look at her either.

Hand and eyes stinging, she shoved him. "Get away from me. Get out of my sight. I never want to see you again."

"That's probably for the best. But for what it's worth, you're safe now. No one will ever hurt you again." His voice cracked, and as he walked toward the clinic, so did her heart.

"No one but you," she whispered.

Oh, God, how could this have happened? Sobs stole her breath and tears blurred her vision. Now what? She wasn't stupid enough to think the ACRO people would just let her waltz off the compound; they were no doubt watching her right now. She felt exposed, vulnerable, and her instincts told her to go to ground. After that, she had no idea. She couldn't think about the future or what to do even in the next thirty seconds, because all she wanted to do right now was cry.

ENDER STOOD INSIDE THE INFIRMARY, gazing blankly out the window at the park where he'd left Kira. He could go after her, pull her to him, force her to try to understand. But there was no point to that when the fact remained the same—he was a trained killer, not meant to be a father or a husband, and he'd come to terms with that long before the animal whisperer had walked into this life.

Being shot didn't hurt half as much as having his heart voluntarily ripped out of his chest.

"Ender?"

He turned abruptly, and Annika put her hands up in fight position, ready to shock him if he touched her. He didn't. He stuffed his hands in his pockets and stared at her.

"Dev knows I'm here," she started after he didn't say anything. She still kept her hands poised and ready for attack. "He said Kira went into hiding and won't come out."

"She's over there." He motioned toward the row of bushes across from the medical building he'd watched her run off to.

"Ender, I just want you to know that I never meant to hurt her—"

"I know that," he said fiercely. "I didn't mean to either."

"Okay." She put her hands down. "We've made arrangements for her to stay with Haley and Remy. I'm going to get her."

"Don't corner her, Annika," he said, hating the desperate quality his voice held. "She'll go feral, run or fight if you corner her, and with the baby..."

"I'll be really careful. I promise," she said.

He thought about the promises he'd made to Kira. Made and broken—for her own good. His too, probably.

He turned and walked away, to head back to the emptiness he knew his house would now hold, before he lost his willpower.

ANNIKA WOULD HAVE KNOWN where to find Kira even if Ender hadn't pointed her out.

With the exception of three security guys sent to watch over Kira, the little park was free of people, but ahead, rabbits and squirrels collected around a bush, a woman huddled inside, knees drawn up to her chest. As Annika approached, the creatures scattered.

"Kira?" Annika crouched on her heels and peered into the foliage made darker by the thin morning cloud cover. "It's Annika."

Kira burrowed deeper into the brush, and Annika wondered what she'd been thinking when she'd gone to Dev and begged him to let her try to talk Kira out after several nurses, a psychologist, and a Convincer had failed. Annika had only wanted to try to make up for what she'd done, but it was probably a huge mistake. Annika was, no doubt, the last—well, the second to last—person on earth Kira wanted to see. Everyone said that Kira didn't blame her, but deep down, how could she not?

"I'm not going to hurt you. But we've got to get you out of there and away from ACRO."

"Away?" Kira's thin voice dripped with desperation and hope, and Annika knew she'd struck on the way to get her out of there.

"Yes. I'll take you to a friend's house, and I promise, no one will come near you if you don't want to see them."

"I don't trust you."

"I know. But isn't it better to take a chance on me than to sit under this bush until you starve?" Or until the vet showed up with a tranquilizer.

She felt ridiculous talking to the shrub, but after a few moments of silence, Annika sighed. She *so* wasn't good at this touchy-feely crap. "Look, I'm sorry about what happened when you got here. I'm normally more in control than that. I've just been stressed lately..." She trailed off, because Kira didn't give a shit about her problems with Creed, and Annika didn't want to talk about it anyway. No man was going to turn her into a blithering idiot.

Finally Kira peeked out from between some branches. "You'll really take me away from here?"

"Yeah."

Kira bit her lip, considering, and then she crawled out of the bush, her scrubs smeared with dirt, twigs and leaves tangled in her hair. "I don't want to see...anyone."

Anyone, meaning Ender. Annika chose not to bring up his name as she led Kira toward the parking lot. The way Kira seemed to look everywhere at once, sometimes stopping suddenly and sniffing the air, reminded Annika of a skittish stray cat.

"We won't see anyone but Haley and Remy. Haley's a parameteorologist at ACRO, and Remy is a special operative like En— uh, me. Haley's totally starched, but for a scientist, she's cool. Remy's probably the only person on the planet besides Dev who can stand En—" Crap. She cleared her throat. "Anyway, you'll like them. Nice house." A house where Dev had sent a crack security team to keep Kira safe from intruders—but more likely to prevent her from sneaking away.

"I hope he's the understanding type, because I haven't been behaving well around men lately."

Annika fished her keys out of her BDU leg pocket as they approached her Jeep. "Dev mentioned that." *Don't let Remy near her. She bites.* "Don't worry. They've been briefed. Remy'll keep his distance. Haley's a workaholic, so she'll give you plenty of space as well."

Everyone had been briefed on Kira's issues, and Ender's warnings had hammered them home. He'd looked like hell, had sounded worse.

Annika had never been his biggest fan—oh, hell, who was she kidding, she couldn't stand him—but she respected his Special Forces expertise and combat skills, and if she had to partner-up for a mission, he was always a good one to have at your back. She even identified with his arrogance and I-don't-give-a-fuck attitude that kept everyone away and lent an image of invulnerability. Which was why it had been a shock to see him like he was today, pacing, intense worry creating dark circles around his bloodshot eyes.

Vulnerable.

Seeing him like that made her break out in an itchy sweat, because if *he* could be brought to his knees, anyone could.

Yet another reason that getting close to Creed couldn't happen, and why she couldn't give him the commitment he'd asked for.

Annika eyed Kira as she settled into the front passenger seat of her old green Wrangler. Annika had seen some of Ender's women, and Kira didn't fit the profile. He'd always done the tall, gorgeous, bubbleheaded blondes. Kira, with her dark hair and petite frame, didn't strike her as his type, and while she wasn't a classic beauty, her exotic features and full lips gave her a sleepy kind of sensuality that seemed too subtle for someone as hard as Ender to notice.

What struck Annika the most, though, was Kira's inherent air of innocence. She hadn't believed people like that existed. Certainly, they didn't exist in her world. Maybe Ender had gotten wrapped up in the need to protect Kira, but who would protect her from *him?* Annika couldn't imagine that Ender was all that gentle with her.

And why the hell did she care? Jesus, she was losing it. She needed an assignment—a gritty, bloody one that would give her back some perspective.

"Do Haley and Remy have any animals?" Kira asked, as they headed down the road to Haley's farmhouse five miles away.

"They have a cat."

"Good." Kira wrapped her arms around herself and stared out the window. "Good."

CHAPTER
Twenty-six

Haley's house turned out to be the opposite of Tom's. Ender's. Whatever the heck his name was.

Where his was newer, with modern decor and appliances, Haley's renovated farmhouse could have graced the pages of a country living magazine. The mingled scents of line-dried linens and banana bread permeated the air, and antique furnishings completed the charm.

Annika had been right: Kira had instantly liked Haley, and Remy had been at work when she arrived at the house. Annika had stayed long enough to ask about some kind of weather machine, and then she'd taken off with a brisk nod of good-bye.

Yesterday Kira did nothing but lie in the guest-room bed with Haley's cat, Geordie, curled up behind her knees. Haley brought food and always offered to lend an ear, but Kira didn't feel like talking. Or thinking. Or eating. But she had someone else to consider now, and for the baby, she choked down the vegan meals Haley prepared.

"My parents were vegetarian hippies," Haley explained when Kira asked about the complicated dishes that went well beyond the salads most people believed vegans ate exclusively. "I'm an expert in this kind of cooking."

On the second day, Kira could no longer hang out in bed. Wearing a pair of Haley's blue silk pajamas, she migrated to the living room, where the other woman sat on the couch and plugged away at a monstrous laptop computer. As Kira watched, Haley sighed and dragged her hand through her long, caramel-brown hair.

"Do you always work from home, or are you babysitting?"

Haley looked up and smiled, a sunny contrast to the gloomy, overcast day outside. "Babysitting."

"Well, at least you're honest."

The thump of boots on the stairs startled Kira, and she turned to see a dark-haired man in ACRO BDUs coming down them. "*Bebe*, I can't find my jacket. Oh, there it is—" He froze as he reached for the leather bomber draped over the couch next to Kira, and she realized she'd been growling. Snarling, really.

"Sorry." She scampered to an overstuffed rocking chair across the room. "Dr. Lavery said it's some sort of weird instinct." She smiled weakly. "Who knows what other strange instincts will emerge once the baby gets here."

The baby whose father had been sent to kill its mother.

Raw grief ripped through her insides, and she burst into tears. It was humiliating, crying like this in front of an audience, but she couldn't stop.

"Kira?" Haley moved close, kneeled at her feet, while Remy eased into a chair at the kitchen table. "What is it?"

"I'm going to have to raise this baby alone," she sobbed. "What will happen when my season comes, and I can't take care of the child because every four hours I need, um, you know?"

"That's one of the best things about ACRO. You're never alone. Everyone will help. And I'm a great babysitter."

"ACRO? You can't be serious. They wanted me dead. They sent Tom to kill me." Palming her belly protectively, she shrank back into the recliner, but her mind was already working on a way to get out of there—not that she knew where she'd go. "They aren't getting near my baby."

"No one is going to touch either one of you if you don't want them to. I promise. But I don't think you know the whole story." Haley and Remy exchanged glances, and Haley rested a soothing hand on Kira's knee. "Do you know why Itor wants you?"

"At first, Tom said they wanted me dead. It was a lie." The acid in her tone bled through loud and clear, and Remy cocked a dark eyebrow.

"He told you what he needed to in order to get you out of there and to gain your trust."

"Whatever," she muttered. "In the infirmary, he said they'd wanted to engineer my pregnancy. God only knows what they want my baby for." She wiped her eyes with the back of her hand, and Haley handed her a box of tissue from the end table. "It's all insane and horrible, but not something for ACRO to kill me over."

Remy shifted in his chair, but when she bared her teeth at him, he held up his hands. "Easy there. I'm not moving." He stretched his long legs out in front of him, more slowly this time. "I interrogated the Itor agent Annika captured in Idaho. What I learned . . ." He grimaced. "Kira, I was a Navy SEAL before I came here. My specialty was interrogation. I've seen things, done things, heard things, and shit, I thought I'd experienced it all. But I've never been more sickened than by what that Itor bastard told me."

She was afraid to ask, and didn't have to, because he pierced her with a stare that sent chills ricocheting up and down her spine.

"What ACRO was afraid of turned out to be the case. Itor was going to use you, and possibly your child, as a biological weapon."

Okay, she'd run a lot of scenarios through her head, but that one hadn't come close to crossing her mind. "A biological weapon? How?"

"Something to do with your physiology. They planned to introduce a deadly animal-specific virus into your body in order to mutate into something humans could contract. Something that would take scientists years to develop a vaccine for because they wouldn't recognize the disease or be able to locate the source."

"But why? Why would they want to spread something like that so indiscriminately?"

"Profit. Itor would develop a vaccine, but the rest of the world would be vulnerable. They could have used you to infect huge populations, millions of people. Then they could have sold the vaccine for billions. Or they could have sold you to the highest bidder as a WMD."

"Oh, my God." She was going to be sick.

After a long silence, in which she thought she heard a distant rumble, Remy spoke again, his voice quiet, deep like the thunder. "I know what you're feeling. Itor wanted to do something similar to me."

Shell-shocked and not a little bitter, she cut him a hard look. "And did ACRO send someone to kill you too?"

"They sent someone for another reason." He slid Haley a secret smile, and then he made it disappear. "But that was a different situation. I was military. My background gave me an edge when it came to Itor. And I was willing to do whatever I had to do to make sure they never took me alive. You're a civilian, with a major distrust of the government, if what Ender told me is true. If you wouldn't join ACRO—"

"I couldn't be left for Itor to take."

"Exactly."

Somewhere deep inside she got that. She may never forgive whatever bastard handed down the order, but she also wouldn't have wanted to be responsible for the deaths of millions.

Tom, though...that was a betrayal that drilled into levels of emotion she hadn't known existed.

"You're thinking about him, aren't you?" Haley asked, and Kira dug her fingers into the arms of the chair instead of answering.

The jingle of metal swirling on wood as Remy played with a set of keys on the tabletop startled her. "He didn't know you."

"Oh, he knew me," she ground out. "I assure you of that. And he still planned to kill me. Even after..." She couldn't finish the sentence. *Even after all the intimacy.* "How can I get past that?"

"Kira," Haley said, "he's not my favorite person in the world, but you need to know that to save you, he disobeyed about a thousand orders." She tucked her legs beneath her and got more comfortable on the rug. "He risked his career and his friendship with Dev, who is pretty much the only person at ACRO he calls his friend."

Remy shrugged. "He just won't admit how much he likes me."

"He's sort of stubborn that way," Kira said, her chest constricting because, dammit, she loved Tom so much.

And yeah, okay, he'd done a few things he didn't have to do. Like call the refuge to arrange for her animals to be brought to New York. And he'd saved her from being serviced by strange men at the training facility. He'd risked his life to keep her from the Itor agents who were after them. He'd stopped eating meat for her.

God, she could go on and on, but doing so made her miserable. She couldn't imagine life without Tom, but she didn't know if she could ever look at him without seeing the face of the man people called Ender. The man who had gazed at her with such uncompromising calculation as he held his hand over the gun he would have used to kill her.

Everything about him screamed warrior, from the way he moved to the way he took in the world around him. And she'd been around predators long enough to recognize the deadly focused look in one's eyes before it took down its victim. So how could she have been so naïve?

But she knew. Desperate for love and acceptance, and under the influence of a sexual pull, she'd been blind.

So stupid.

Her stupidity alone made her a danger to herself, to her animals, to the entire damned world.

"Can I get you anything?" Haley gripped Kira's hand, giving it a reassuring squeeze. "Tea? Water? A bottle of Jack Daniel's and a beer chaser?"

That got a smile out of Kira, the first in what felt like forever. She shook her head as the low, rolling sound of thunder rumbled outside, closer than the last time. Inside, a strange pressure built, a tangible thickening of the air. Haley swung around to her husband, her hand absently rubbing her hip. When Kira looked over at Remy, she nearly gasped.

Lightning flashed in his eyes—not the reflection of lighting, but actual lightning. And he was fixated on Haley. Leaning forward in his chair, he dropped his head low to stare at his wife, utterly captivated in a way that took Kira's breath away. Holy cow, she'd known he was a handsome man, but now she saw more than that, saw the animal intensity, the single-minded focus of a predator that hungered, and hungered *now*. But what did he…? Oh.

Oh.

Then he was up, taking the stair steps two at a time. Haley stood. "Will you be okay for a few minutes?" she asked, sounding breathless.

"Yes, fine. Thank you."

Haley hurried up the stairs, and thirty seconds later, the muffled noises that drifted from above left no doubt as to what was going on up there.

The storm picked up, mercifully masking the sounds from upstairs—and what had the crashing noises been? She and Tom hadn't broken anything during even their most vigorous lovemaking, though a couple of bathroom sinks had been in danger.

Tom.

She couldn't stop thinking about him. Heck, she still smelled him on her skin, even though she'd showered. Twice. It was like he was a part of her now, inside her.

She touched her belly. Yes, he was inside her.

Damn him. She hated him for how easily he could have followed his orders. Even after having sex with her, he could have done it.

Sure, he'd eventually changed his mind, and she supposed she should be concentrating on what he *had* done, rather than what he *could have* done. But she wasn't ready to do that yet.

Didn't know if she'd ever be ready, no matter how much she loved him.

Time drifted away with the thunderstorm, and eventually

Haley appeared, wearing a different outfit than she'd worn earlier, and Kira suspected that Remy's enthusiasm might be as hazardous to clothing as Tom's.

The phone rang, but Remy must have picked it up, because it stopped after two rings.

"Sorry about disappearing on you like that," Haley said. "I don't know what Ender told you about Remy, but—"

"Bebe?" He clomped down the stairs and grabbed the keys off the table. "The ACRO jet's on approach with Akbar and Sheila coming in off a mission. Sheila's hurt, but there's a storm over the runway and the plane can't land. ATC wants me to move it."

"Have fun."

He winked at her. "I already did." With a nod at Kira, he sauntered out the door.

"What does he have to move?"

"The storm." Haley sank onto the couch. "He can control the weather. And sometimes, like you just saw, it controls him."

"I can understand that."

"I know. Just think about what we said about Ender and ACRO. Both are demanding and tough, but there's a lot of good there too."

Before the tears began again, Kira stood. "Thank you, Haley. I'm going to try to get some sleep." She headed toward the stairs, but before she mounted them, she said over her shoulder, "Oh, and Geordie promised not to scratch the furniture anymore."

KIRA COULDN'T SLEEP. Her mind reeled with the new information and old memories, and fear for her future kept butting in. And she knew it was a bad idea, but she wanted to talk to Tom. She loved him, hated him, wanted him to suffer like she was, wanted him to be okay. Basically, she was one big mess.

He, on the other hand, had probably already moved on, could even now be rolling around with someone new.

Sitting up in bed, she reached for a tissue on the nightstand, but her hand went to the phone.

Not a good idea.

But once again, her heart overruled her head, and with trembling fingers, she dialed the number for Tom's cell phone, the one he'd given her when he'd cuffed her to his bed. She nearly hung up on the second ring, but when she heard a gruff "What?" on the other end, she froze.

"Goddammit, *what?*" Silence, and then a soft "Kira? Kira, is that you?"

"Yes," she croaked.

"Are you okay? Where's Haley?"

"Haley's downstairs. Everything's fine." If the fact that she was dying inside was fine. "I just...I guess I just wanted to know... when did I become more than a job? Was I ever more than a job?"

For the longest time, she heard only the sound of his breathing, and her heart sank lower in her chest with every passing second. Then she heard a strange sound on the other end, almost like a sob, and when Tom spoke, his voice was gravelly.

"You were special from the beginning."

"And yet, you could have—"

"I'd have paid for it, Kira. I'm paying for it anyway."

God, she actually felt sorry for him, which pissed her off. "You aren't the only one, Tommy." She squeezed her lids tight to keep from crying again. Her eyes were already aching and swollen, and she didn't want to make it worse. "Do you even miss me?" The question was out of her mouth before she could stop it.

"More than you know."

"But you still don't want me." She let out a strangled sound of horror at the way her mouth kept falling open and saying stupid things. Even if he wanted her, could she get past her issues? Or was she clinging to them like a shield because it would be too painful to know that the only reason they weren't together was because he didn't want her and his child?

When he said nothing, she had her answer. Furious, hurt and shaking, she hung up the phone without another word.

Now she could sleep, and with any luck, she'd wake up and find out that this was all one big nightmare.

CHAPTER
Twenty-seven

Ender had been severely light-headed for two days. He'd blamed the stress of the situation with Kira and his lack of protein but hadn't rectified either situation. When he collapsed on his kitchen floor, he wasn't surprised as much as he was pissed at suddenly being rendered helpless. He was even more pissed to be discovered lying there by Remy.

"What the hell is up with you?" Remy drawled, having walked in like he owned the damned house.

Rescued by a motherfucking SEAL. What a way to go.

"You do realize you said that out loud, asshole." Remy's drawl floated somewhere above Ender.

"I can't get up," he murmured. God, his eyes were heavy.

He stared up at the ceiling, which he knew was white but now looked like a hazy shade of dark gray. He blinked twice and wondered if the lights were on or off and then realized that it didn't matter.

"Are you shot or did you break something?" Remy asked, standing over him. Ender felt the SEAL's fingers on his pulse.

"No," he managed.

"You need a doctor."

"Just leave me alone, SEAL. I'm fine."

"Yeah, you're about as fine as Kira is," Remy said, and Ender grunted as he struggled to sit up.

"Is she all right? Is the baby—"

"The baby's fine, man. She's miserable without you . . . she just hasn't come to terms with everything yet."

"Doesn't matter." Ender thought back to the phone call—his chance, probably the last chance, to tell her that they could make things all right somehow.

"You didn't do something to yourself because of Kira, did you?" Remy asked, a note of concern tingeing his thick Southern drawl.

"Yes. Not what you're thinking, though," Ender muttered. "Long story."

"Well, you can tell it to the doctor."

"Private," Ender said.

"Yeah, yeah, I wasn't going to parade you through the halls, even though I know that's what you'd do to me."

Well, yeah, that was definitely true. Good thing Remy was a hell of a lot nicer than Ender could ever be. Fucking frogman.

"You said that out loud too, asshole," Remy said. "But don't worry—I always knew you liked me a lot more than you let on."

Ender wanted to give him the finger, but didn't have the energy for even that small task. "Just tell Kira . . ." he started.

"Tell her what?"

Ender shut his eyes. "Nothing."

Instead of helping him up, Remy slid down to the floor next to him. "It's all right to have baggage, you know."

Ender cut his eyes toward the dark-haired man. "Now you're a shrink? I thought all you were good for was creating thunderstorms."

"How the hell were you ever a team player?" Remy asked him.

"It wasn't as hard for me to be one back then," Ender said, more to himself than to Remy.

Ender had joined the Army, spent two years as a mechanic before being selected for Ranger school. Thirty days into the training, he'd been pulled aside and told about a very special group they thought he'd be an excellent addition to.

He didn't know much about special abilities at that point, hadn't really considered that there were others out there like him. He just knew he was faster than anyone he'd ever known, that his eyesight was way better than the twenty-twenty needed to be an effective sniper and that the training for Delta Force had been a fucking breeze.

He'd loved it—every single minute of backbreaking, mind-bending training that stretched every normal limit he ever had.

He was always careful not to let on that he was superhuman fast, hard as that was to tamp down. His eyesight was a benefit to the entire team, even though scientists wanted to study it and his body and everything else about him.

He'd blown it off and done his best to make a career for himself. A life.

His unit had been tight-knit. He traveled mainly with the same four men, worked under a general who commanded a large number of Deltas housed on the Fort Bragg base, and no one but his men and their wives knew what he was. To the rest of the world, he was a mechanic working in the motor pool.

John "Digger" Kramer, Ferdinand "Aces" Ramirez, Chase Holden, Damien "Devil" Canter and him, Tom "Ender" Knight, made a hell of a good team. For five good years, they ruled the world, wiping out terrorism and all its evils.

At the end of those five years, he killed his best friends in the world. In those brief moments, one of their own had become their worst enemy, and Ender would later learn that this was a conse-quence of not understanding—or being able to control the gift.

Damien had been a pyrokinetic. And even if Ender had known at the time, it wouldn't have made his decision any easier. He took credit for Dev's plane crash too, since he knew he'd be spending the rest of his life in jail, and the man he'd found in the cockpit claimed he'd been blinded. Claimed he was haunted.

Ender knew now that what Dev told him was no joke. All

special-ability types were haunted, no matter how well adjusted they were.

You're a monster.

Yes, he was. And he'd lost Kira and his chance at a life with her forever with that admission. Better for her and their child, but it still hurt like hell.

"My team stopped trusting me toward the end," Remy said, and *Christ*. Ender realized he'd spilled that whole fucking story out loud. *Dammit.* "It hurt like hell not to be with them anymore, but I've got a new team now. One that you're a part of."

"I don't want you watching my back," Ender said, which was ironic since he was still flat on his. "I'm fine on my own."

"Yes, fine," Remy said dryly. "You might not want me watching your back, but I've got yours anyway."

"Great—want me to tell you that makes me feel all warm and fuzzy inside?"

"You're an asshole."

"Everyone says that like they're surprised."

"You love her, you know."

"It doesn't matter," Ender managed quietly.

"That's the only thing that matters," Remy said. "I'm going to help you up now." But Ender was too unsteady even for that. Remy slammed Ender over his shoulder, and *fuck*, that knocked the wind out of him. "You're fucking heavy as hell. I'd better get some kind of hazard pay for this one."

KIRA SLEPT FOR FOUR HOURS. When she woke, she showered and dressed in a sweatshirt and a pair of sweat shorts Haley had loaned her. The clothes were too big, but they were soft and comfy and the floral fabric softener smell temporarily masked the earthy scent of Tom that wouldn't scrub off her skin.

The nap and shower had breathed life back into her, and for the first time since Tom dumped her, she was ready to make some decisions.

What Remy had told her about Itor's plans terrified her to the marrow. Even if she was willing to take a risk with her life, she wouldn't risk her child's. She might not like it, but ACRO could protect them. She had to stay.

But what about Tom? The phone call had put some things in perspective. Namely, that her feelings regarding what he'd been sent to do to her were moot, because he didn't want her anyway. The call had also brought up questions. Did he plan to be involved in their baby's life at all? Did he expect her to lie about paternity so he could weasel out of involvement? How would she react when they ran into each other on base?

Stop it. She had to stop thinking about it. She had bigger things to worry about, like the fact that hunger pangs were gnawing at her stomach and if she didn't eat, she'd probably pass out.

Stomach growling, she padded toward the kitchen, slowing at the sound of Haley and Remy speaking in hushed voices.

"...I don't know, Remy."

"We have to tell her."

"I just think we should wait until we know for sure."

Kira stepped into the hall as Remy said, "The doctor is sure."

"The doctor is sure of what?" she asked, a knot of unease forming in her gut, replacing the hunger there.

Haley chewed her bottom lip and stared at the hardwood floor, but Remy turned to her, those beautiful eyes brimming with concern. "How do you feel about Ender?"

"What do you mean?"

"Do you love him?"

"Of course I do. But that's not—"

"Are you willing to fight for him?"

"What's this about?"

Remy scrubbed a hand over his face. "He loves you." She snorted, but before she could say anything, he held up his hand. "He does. He's got this crazy idea that he's too screwed up and dangerous for family life, but with you out of his life..."

"With me out of his life, what? What's happened?"

"He's sick, and he just doesn't care."

Ender had suspected what was happening, but Dr. Brown confirmed it quickly enough after that damned SEAL had carried him in and set him down on the hard metal table.

"He's all kinds of fucked up, Doc. You'd better help him quickly," Remy had said, then insisted on staying until the tests came back.

When the doc told them the prognosis, that Ender's health was being severely compromised, Remy had cursed softly in Cajun French under his breath and left the room, and *dammit*, Ender knew where he was going and couldn't do anything to stop him.

He felt slightly stronger than before, wondered what the doctor was feeding into his vein via the IV.

He tugged at it, and the doc said, "It's just glucose. The energy you're going to get from it will be temporary. I also dosed you with taurine and arginine, as well as some other amino acids your body is missing because of your diet. Again, a temporary fix."

He didn't want it, temporary or otherwise. He reached down and yanked the needle out of his arm.

"Dammit, Ender!" the doctor yelled. "You need to eat your normal diet."

"Protein bars," Ender managed as the doctor bandaged his arm to stop the bleeding.

"Protein bars are meant to get you through in a pinch, Ender. But your unique body chemistry won't allow you to survive on those alone. You need to go back to being a carnivore."

"No."

"You're killing yourself, Tom. And not slowly either."

In a sudden burst of strength, Ender reached out and grabbed the doc by the throat. "You don't get to call me Tom. Only Kira gets to call me—"

"Tommy!"

Of course Kira had to show up right now, when he had a death grip on the doctor's windpipe. At least his growl had come back.

Until he realized that the low, menacing growl wasn't coming from his throat, but rather, was emanating from Kira's as she held Dr. Brown's forearm in her teeth.

"Shit. Kira, honey, you shouldn't bite the doctor," he said, and opened his own hand as Kira moved away from Dr. Brown. Ender laid his head back on the pillow as the doc wheezed a breath and rubbed the bite mark on his arm.

"Then the doctor shouldn't be touching you," Kira said to him, and told the doctor, "He's mine."

"He attacked *me*," Dr. Brown protested, but finally backed off—and out of the room, as Kira moved next to the bed.

"Tommy," she said.

"Go away."

"I'm not going anywhere."

"You should. I'm not safe for you to be around. A killer."

"For the good of this agency. For the good of the world," she said quietly, and he stared at her.

"How could killing you have been good?"

"You didn't kill me. You saved me—from Itor and from myself," she said. "And you gave me a child. Something I never thought—"

"You'll be a great mom," he said.

"Oh, no, Tom Knight, don't you even act like you won't be here."

"I'm not meant to be a father," he said. "How would I explain what I do to a kid?"

"We'd do it together. We'd explain that you save the world from the bad guys. And you're not one of the bad guys. You never were."

"No, he never was," Dev's voice rang out in the tiny room from behind Kira. "Are you going to tell her, Tom, or should I?"

"Dev, don't do this."

"He saved my life, you know," Dev told Kira. "Saved my life and then took a punishment that was meant for me."

"Is that true, Tommy?" she asked quietly.

"It didn't matter. I was going to spend the rest of my life in jail anyway. For killing my Delta team," he said—didn't feel as satisfied as he thought he would when he saw the look of shock on her face.

"Jesus Christ, Tom, do you want to explain that one a little more, before you start taking the damned weight of the world on your shoulders again?"

"Look who's talking," he muttered, but Dev was already explaining to Kira about the hurt pyrokinetic.

"His men were dying—horrible, terrible deaths. It was just a matter of time, excruciating time, before they died. There was no way to help them," Dev said, and Ender saw Kira swallow hard.

"He killed them to help them," she said.

"They were begging him," Dev said softly.

"Who are you again?" Kira finally asked the man who was doling out Tom's violent history a piece at a time.

"Dev. Devlin O'Malley."

The man responsible for the order to kill her. She'd wondered what he would look like, had prepared herself for an ugly, Jimmy Hoffa–ish brute, but the attractive man with unseeing brown eyes and spiky, dark hair caught her completely off guard.

She cleared her throat. "Mr. O'Malley, would you mind waiting outside for a moment?"

He inclined his head and then moved silently and unerringly out of the room.

"Tom," she said, taking his hand, which was too cool in hers. "The teammate thing... is that what your nightmares have been about?"

His jaw tightened, and he turned his head away. Smoothing her other hand over his jaw, rough with stubble, she tipped his face toward her. He looked at her, his normally bright, blue-eyed gaze washed out, and it hit her just how miserable he was.

"No more secrets. Not now. Not after everything." She pushed his hair off his forehead. "The nightmares are about what happened to your team, right?"

"Yes."

"Have you always had them as frequently as you've been having them lately?"

Again, he looked like he didn't want to answer, but she kept stroking his face, his cheek, his forehead, and finally he said, "No. I'd have them sometimes when Dev dreams of it, but I think... I think these started up because of you. I let you in. And then there was the guilt..."

"Because you were supposed to kill me?"

What little color he had in his face flushed out. "God, Kira, I'm so sorry."

She had no idea what to say, because she hadn't completely worked out her feelings on the subject yet, but his anguish was genuine, especially if the situation had stirred up nightmares.

Finally, she settled on a simple "I know."

"I don't think you do." He nuzzled her hand, pressed a kiss into her palm. "I love you. Did you know that?"

"Yes," she said, smiling. "And that's why you're going to do what it takes to get better. Tommy Junior and I need you to keep us safe."

"I'm the danger, Kira. That's what I've been trying to tell you. The nightmares—"

"May very well be over. You don't need to feel guilty anymore. I forgive you," she said fiercely, because she did. The idea that he would let himself be so miserable that he'd waste away rather than hurt her or their child was enough to break through any barrier that remained. "You were doing your job, and you have nothing to feel guilty about. You had the opportunity to follow orders a hundred times over, and instead, you protected me and kept me alive."

"I'm a killer," he said.

Dammit, why was he fighting her on this? "Yes, you are. But you know what? I can't judge you for that. I've lived with animals for so many years, and not all of them are gentle sheep and ducks. Tigers are killers, but they have to be in order to eat and to protect their young. And Tommy, if someone was threatening you or this baby, I'd turn into a tiger real fast."

A weak smile turned up his mouth. "Yeah, I know you would."

"Good. Don't make me turn into one now. You need to get better."

"That's not the only issue."

"I know. Remy filled me in on the way over here."

"I can't eat meat, Kira. Not knowing what it does to you."

God, she loved him. "What were we just talking about? Big cats. You're a big cat, Tommy, a cheetah. And cheetahs, like all cats, are true carnivores. Which means that unlike dogs or bears or people, they will die without meat. *Die.* Apparently, your excedosapien gift comes from the same type of genetic makeup. So for you, it's not a matter of choice. It's a matter of necessity. I get that. I don't want you to die." She ran her palm over his chest, trying to ignore that it felt caved in. "I need you, Tommy. *We* need you."

He drew the back of his hand over her abdomen, and she felt a wonderful fluttering inside. "I need you too."

Grinning, she moved to the door. Outside, Haley, Remy, the doctor, and Mr. O'Malley were talking. "Would someone please get Tom a burger?"

"It's about freakin' time," Remy said, and headed down the hall.

Kira went back inside to wait. Tom promised to do his carnivore thing while at lunch and away from the house so she wouldn't have it near her, and he even swore he didn't mind her vegan meals for dinner. He was lying, of course, but she loved him that much more for it.

When Remy returned with a foul-smelling bag of food, she left

Tom to eat and slipped out of the room to talk with the head of ACRO, who paced in the hall. The doctor had gone, and Haley was pouring coffee at the machine near the end of the corridor.

"Mr. O'Malley," she said, being careful not to get too close. She was still on edge with men, men who *hadn't* ordered her execution, so she wasn't ready to trust herself with him yet.

"It's Devlin. And thank you for getting Tom to eat."

"It wasn't much, considering he saved my life, Mr. O'Malley. More than once."

His eyebrows shot up half an inch before his expression settled into one of acceptance, and yeah, he might be physically blind, but that was as far as it went—he got why she wasn't ready to call him by his first name. "You understand the reason behind the orders that brought you here."

It wasn't a question. "I do. And I wouldn't want your job and the decisions you have to make. You've obviously done a great thing here...everyone I've talked to seems happy, including the animals. This is an amazing agency. But given my hormonal state and everything that's happened, don't expect me to be your number one fan right away."

One corner of his mouth turned up in amusement. "What if I told you that if you sign on, we'll make generous contributions to the animal charity of your choice? And I'll let you head up an animal rescue program that will allow you to travel to disaster zones and gather animals that need help?"

Her breath lodged in her lungs. She'd already decided to sign on with ACRO, but what he was offering...she could help animals on a global scale, something she'd dreamed about. "Why? Why would you do this for me?"

"A happy agent is a good agent." He shrugged. "Besides, everyone asks for something special when they sign on."

Haley walked up behind Devlin. "I got the house of my dreams." She sipped her coffee. "And a bike."

"We'll have to alter our training program because of your pregnancy. Light day-training only, and we'll give you an apartment on base instead of making you stay in the dorm—"

"Fuck that," came Tom's voice from behind her. "She comes home with me."

Devlin rubbed the back of his neck. "Yeah, I figured that's the way it would go."

"Tom! Get back in bed." Kira hurried to where he was propped against the door frame.

Remy stood behind Tom, muttering something about *"stubborn fucking Deltas,"* but he backed out of the way as she wrapped her arm around Tom's waist and guided him back to bed.

"What were you thinking?" she said, as she pulled the sheet up over him.

"I was thinking I didn't want you to be that far away."

"I was standing in the hallway."

"Too far."

Her heart flipped, and not caring if anyone else was in the room, she kissed him. He'd brushed his teeth—Remy must have brought toiletries with the hamburgers—and he tasted like mint and man, and before she knew it, she was stretched out beside him on the bed, his face framed in her hands, his tongue sucking gently on hers.

"Ah...uh...excuse me?" Dr. Lavery's voice pierced the haze Kira had gone into as she lay half on, half off of Tom.

"Thank God, ma'am," Remy said from near the door, where he was holding Haley's hand. "I was about to turn a hose on them."

Heat seared Kira's cheeks, but Tom just grinned like the cat that ate the canary. Clearly, the food was already working.

The veterinarian sighed. "Remember what I said about waiting a week?"

"Don't worry," Kira said. "I can restrain myself."

Tom looked at her like she was a big, fat liar, and if he weren't lying in a hospital bed she'd have hit him.

"Good." The vet glanced at Haley and Remy. "I have some news, but it might be best to have some privacy."

Before Remy and Haley could back out of the room, Kira shook her head. "No. They're friends. Family. They can stay."

Tom groaned, and she could have sworn he mumbled the words *"So screwed."*

Dr. Lavery nodded. "If you're sure. I've been working with the research department and the lab, and we think we can help ease your spring fevers. Before you get your hopes up, you need to know that the cure could take time, as in years. But in the meantime, we can make them more manageable. We'll create prepared applicators—backup in case Tom gets sick, injured or just needs a break." She shifted her weight and steeled herself with a deep breath, and Kira knew this was going to be interesting.

"We'll have Tom bank his—"

"Ah, wait." Tom struggled to sit up. "What? No. Whatever you're going to say, no. A couple of weeks is not a problem."

Kira bit her lip. "Um, it's four."

"Four what?"

"Four weeks."

Tom slid back down in the bed. "Christ."

She patted his shoulder. "It'll be fine. Since I'm on abstinence orders this week and you're not, we can get started with the bank thing right away. Fun!"

For the first time ever, Tom's cheeks flamed, and Remy wasn't helping things, not with the way he was laughing so hard he was in danger of busting something. Like his ribs, which had Haley's elbow in them. Over and over.

"There's more," Dr. Lavery said, and Haley took the opportunity to drag Remy out, apparently deciding that Tom could handle only so much family.

Dr. Lavery drew a photo from the folder she'd brought with her and clipped it to a lighted board on the wall. "This is your ultrasound. See these circles?"

Kira's lungs seized, and Tom went taut. "Is something wrong? Is Kira okay? What about the baby?"

"Everything's fine," the vet said in a low, reassuring tone, and Kira felt the breath she'd been holding blow out in a rush of relief. "It's just that we think, based on your estimated window of conception and the size of the fetuses, that your gestation period might be accelerated."

"Fetuses?" Tom sounded a little strangled.

"Yes. Each circle represents one fetus."

"But there're three." Kira frowned. Tom's hand tightened around her waist. "Oh, my God. Three."

"It appears you have a lot more in common with the animal world than we thought," Dr. Lavery said. "Litters."

Two days after Ender was discharged from the infirmary and Kira had moved out of Haley's house, Haley hurried into the reception area of Dev's office, to find a scowling Marlena. The woman must not like working for a new boss.

"I need to see Mr. Oswald," Haley said. "It's an emergency."

Marlena buzzed Haley in, and she stepped into Dev's office to find a man she'd never seen before, though he looked familiar. "Mr. Oswald, I'm Haley Holmes."

"Call me Oz." He threw a foot up on the desk. "So what's up?"

What a strange man. Definitely not military. Once again, Haley wondered why Dev had turned ACRO's reins over to him, but really, it wasn't any of her business as long as this guy knew what he was doing. Which, at the moment, she had her doubts about.

"I don't think we've met. I'm the head of the Meteorology department. Did Dev fill you in on the weather-machine situation?"

"Itor supposedly has some monstrous thing capable of creating massive tornadoes and hurricanes?"

"Yes. I've been looking for it since September." She opened her briefcase with shaking hands. "I think I've found it."

She slid a computer printout across the desk to him. "It took this long because I had to compile known data from the mini-machine's weather patterns—I'd encountered it last fall, and then had to search the world for similar patterns, as well as determine—"

"I trust your research. Skip to what I'm looking at."

"The coordinates." She strode to the giant map of the world on Dev's far wall, her stomach queasy with excitement. "It's here."

One dark eyebrow crawled up his forehead. "That's the middle of the Atlantic. That's impossible."

She nodded. "That's what I thought. Then I got some satellite photos." She hurried back to her briefcase and pulled out a stack of papers. "At first, all I saw was water."

She handed him the photos, and he sifted through them, seeing nothing of significance.

"But then I got a close-up with this one." When she pushed the last photo in front of him, he glanced at it and then looked up again.

"It's more water."

"Look closer."

What he did was look at her like she was insane, but he finally peered down at the picture. After a moment, his eyes went wide, and she knew he'd seen it.

The fuzzy, nearly invisible outline of a monstrous oil platform.

"Holy shit," he breathed. "They have a light-bender."

"A what?"

Tracing the oil rig with his finger, he breathed deeply. "Someone who can bend light to create an invisible shield. ACRO used to have one. Maybe he's still here. But he could only do this to himself. I've heard rumors of a guy who can do it and take small things like chairs with him, and *that* is extraordinary." He stabbed the photo with his finger. "This...this is un-fucking-believable. And an oil platform..."

Before she could say anything, he slammed his fist on the desk. "Mother. Fuck."

"That's kinda what I was thinking."

He pierced her with a hard stare. "We'd have an easier time breaking into Fort Knox than we would getting onto this. They'll know our methods, and this thing will be a fortress. Not to mention they have the world's biggest moat around it. We're screwed."

She snapped her briefcase closed. "Welcome to ACRO."

Epilogue

Whenever Ender came home from a mission, he was on edge. He thought about taking a hotel room or staying at ACRO for the night, just to decompress. This was the first time he'd ever come home from an ACRO job to *someone*. And not just someone—his *mate*.

Except, fuck, he missed Kira like crazy and with the babies due in just a few months, he wanted all the alone time with her he could get.

He walked into the house carefully. He'd already put the safeties on his weapons and now he placed them into the steel-doored closet he'd had built the second he'd realized he was going to be living in a fucking menagerie.

He'd put his foot down when Kira told him that Spazzy had requested to live inside the house. Because a man had to put his fucking foot down at some point.

He tripped and cursed, because she'd rearranged the living room furniture while he'd been gone—no doubt, to balance his chi or something crazy like that.

He shook it off and moved on.

They attacked him when he was halfway through the kitchen, took him down hard on the ceramic-tile floor.

"Dammit, Babs!" he yelled at the Weim, who'd Velcroed herself to his side. She merely raised her ears and wagged her tail, while Rafi was fucking sitting on his chest, staring down at him. And there was Spazzy, standing over him and so *not* outside the house.

So. Screwed. And that was without the three little monsters, three girls, who were going to be running loose around this place and running roughshod on him.

Kira was watching him from the doorway, and God, she looked even more beautiful than she did last week when he'd left. She was round and curvy and he was going to make love to her tonight—she'd left him a message a few days earlier that Dr. Lavery had given her a clean bill of health at her August checkup.

"I'd like to have some time alone with Tommy," she said now, and immediately the animals dispersed, though they hung around in the distance. He stood and embraced her gently.

"Hey," he whispered.

"Hey yourself." She ran a hand along his cheek. "Are you okay? Need some time alone?"

He looked around at the animals surrounding them, and at Kira's belly, and finally at her. "No," he said. "Not right now."

She tugged his shirt and began to walk up the stairs, him trailing closely behind. "Remy said that you tried to strangle the pilot tonight when you landed."

"He had a shitty touchdown," Ender said. "And Remy has a big mouth."

They were on the landing, right outside the bedroom, and she turned toward him, shaking her head.

"Wait a minute... You don't expect me to be... nice, all of a sudden, do you?" he asked.

She laughed at what must've been the look of horror on his face. "No, Tommy—I want you just the way I fell in love with you."

"Well, good. But that guy's an asshole."

"Yes."

"Moody."

"Of course."

"Not a nice guy," he said. "Never going to be a nice guy."

"I don't like nice guys," she said, and he growled deep in his throat. She growled right back at him before she ripped his shirt open, and he knew he'd found the not-nice woman for him.

About the Authors

SYDNEY CROFT is the pseudonym of two authors who each write under their own names. This is their second novel together; their first was *Riding the Storm*. Visit their website at www.sydney croft.com.

Read on
for a sneak peek
of

SEDUCED
by the
STORM

by Sydney Croft

Coming from Delta in Summer 2008

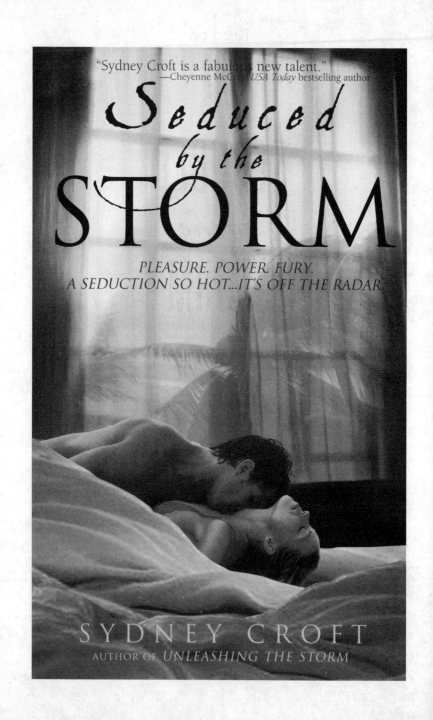

Seduced
by the
STORM

PLEASURE. POWER. FURY.
A SEDUCTION SO HOT...IT'S OFF THE RADAR.

SYDNEY CROFT

AUTHOR OF *UNLEASHING THE STORM*

SEDUCED *by the* STORM

On sale Summer 2008

Faith Black had been beaten, drugged, and imprisoned, but none of that scared her. No, what frightened her to the core was the man confined with her. Chained to an improvised medieval rack and bare from the waist up, he lay on his back, arms over his head, his incredible chest marred by bruises and a deep laceration that extended from his left pec to his right hip.

He might have been rendered immobile, but he was in no way helpless.

His weapon, far more dangerous than the telekinesis—to her, at least—was his overpowering sexuality, a force that tugged her toward him, made her burn with need despite their grave situation.

Head pounding from the blow she'd taken to the cheek, she pushed to her feet and padded close, her nudity barely registering. She'd been stripped naked while unconscious, her clothes tossed into one corner of the windowless, steel-walled room. The weak yellow light from the single bulb emphasized the deep amber of Wyatt's eyes, no longer green, as he settled into the transitional period many telekinetics experienced when their powers flared up. The air in the room stilled, and the chain around his right ankle began to rattle.

"Don't," she said quietly, and he shifted his head to look at her as though he hadn't realized she'd regained consciousness.

"Faith." His voice was rough, as haunted as his gaze. "I didn't tell him. I swear."

"Tell who what?"

"Your boyfriend. I didn't tell him about us. He knew."

"Sean's not my boyfriend," she said, and Wyatt cocked a dark eyebrow like he didn't believe her. "And I know you didn't say anything."

She knew, because she'd been the one to confirm Sean's suspicions that she and Wyatt had slept together.

Wyatt's head lolled back so he was staring up at the steel beams crisscrossing the ceiling. The corded tendons in his neck strained and tightened as he swallowed. "I'm sorry I got you into this."

"You didn't."

A growl rumbled in his throat. "I seduced you. I shouldn't have. Not here. Not on the rig where he could find out."

She inhaled him into her, the masculine scent that threw her off balance whenever he came near. No, she couldn't blame him for anything, least of all her out-of-control desire for him. He was here to do a job, just like she was, which meant getting the assignment done by any means necessary.

"I'm not here because Sean is jealous." Though Sean was, furiously so, but Wyatt didn't need to know that.

"Then why?"

Dragging her gaze from the strong, brutally handsome features of his face, she let her mind focus on a realm of existence most people never saw. Instantly, Wyatt's aura became visible, a shifting, undulating layer of light around his body. And God, something was wrong, so wrong she nearly gasped.

Wyatt radiated power, so his aura should reflect the same. Instead, it stretched thin around his body like an ill-fitting, secondhand coat, ridden with weak spots and holes, like he'd suffered repeated supernatural attacks. She could repair the damage, but her efforts would amount to little more than a patch job on his psychic garment. Replenishing his aura, renewing it... that, only he could do.

For now, she concentrated on the cut on his chest, worked her power into beam of energy that knit the wound together. The muscles in his abs rippled, carved so deeply that they cast shadows on each other. She knew how they felt beneath her touch, how they flexed when they rubbed against her belly, and she had to clench her hands to keep from reaching for him.

The wound closed in a whisper of sound, and Wyatt sucked in a harsh breath. "Jesus. You're a fucking agent."

His eyes glowed amber again, and the chains binding him rattled.

"Please don't," she said, letting her psychic fingers slide south on his body. "Let me. Follow my lead."

He moaned and then grit his teeth against the sensations she sent streaming into his groin.

"I'm going to need you to scream, Wyatt. Scream like I'm killing you."

The bulge in his pants began to grow with each of her virtual caresses deep inside his body, and his eyes flashed green fire. "You are, Faith." His voice rumbled, dark, dangerous. "I've been through the gates of hell and survived, but somehow, I think you're going to be the devil who takes me down."

Chapter
Two

Wyatt Kennedy was a dead man, and other than a few problems like being unable to use his credit cards, it hadn't been so bad.

Of course, he'd already been declared dead once before, a long time ago, so he knew the drill. Lay low, use cash, watch your back.

When he'd dropped off the face of the earth years earlier, he'd had ACRO—the Agency for Covert Rare Operatives, of which he was one—on his side. ACRO had recruited him, changed his name, and killed him off so he wouldn't face a murder rap for the death of his half brother.

Which, for the record, he still wasn't sure whether or not he was responsible for, thanks to a slight memory lapse that lasted for five years, despite ACRO's best efforts otherwise.

This time, he got to keep the same first name, at least. The most important part of being dead this go around was letting everyone at ACRO think he'd been killed—for reasons he didn't quite understand but when orders were given, orders were followed. The rest of the world, and Itor Corp—ACRO's major rival, had never known Wyatt had existed anyway, and he knew the mission he was dealing with—finding the weather machine that Itor Corp had built and hidden on an offshore oil rig, was some serious *we plan on destroying the world* shit.

It's not like he looked like he had special powers, anyway. But he was tall enough that most of the men in his general vicinity gave him a wide berth, which was cool with him. He tended to live mostly inside his own head anyway and preferred his own space, big-time.

The bar crowd tonight was rough, made up mostly of roustabouts who wanted to be roughnecks and roughnecks who wanted to be drillers, all either preparing to rejoin their offshore rig or just coming off their two-week workweek. Wyatt was just coming off his own fourteen days off, prepared to go back in and finish up the job he'd started for ACRO.

Wyatt had grown up in this life under the name of James Jasper—his father owned his own drilling company by the time Wyatt had been born, and he'd already had three sons from his first wife.

Ten years had separated Wyatt and the next youngest sons—twins—and a twenty year difference separated him and the oldest. That oldest half brother had been killed the week Wyatt was born—bringing Wyatt onto the earth during major family chaos. One of the twins lost an arm and a leg in a rigging accident a week later—the other twin helped his father run his rigs—mostly in the Indian Ocean. The twin with missing limbs worked the business angle until he was found murdered, his neck broken in a mysterious accident they blamed Wyatt for since he'd been in the military at the time and more than capable of snapping a man's neck.

His hand wrapped around the neck of the beer bottle and he shifted on the barstool, hating *that* particular uncertainty with a passion. He'd dealt with everything else concerning his special abilities, but the idea that they might've had something to do with murdering his half brother in cold blood left a lingering unease that never fully allowed him to come to grips with his destiny.

Wyatt's mother died when he'd been thirteen, just around the time all the other crazy shit had started happening all around him full force.

For as long as he could remember, he'd always had what he'd thought of as secret powers. He remembered moving an object with his mind when he was just two years old, but it had gotten worse when he'd hit puberty. Out of control, until every time he lost his temper even slightly, shit would fly.

At first, the doctors were concerned, and then they became downright fed up with him. Especially because he became really good at ripping up their offices, all while sitting in a chair looking innocent.

One minute, he'd been drilling, the next, learning how to hide medication he didn't want to take by hiding it in his mouth at a certain angle. He never did tell anyone about the semi-psychic thing he had going on, and the sex thing, a power no one, not even the ACRO scientists, had been able to figure out, hadn't begun full-force until he'd been around fifteen. Even then, everyone assumed he was getting laid on a regular basis because he was good-looking.

Yeah, totally *One Flew Over The Cuckoo's Nest,* only not as fun, and he'd escaped before the electroshock therapy by seducing all the female nurses and pretending to be normal.

Pretending. Wyatt did that a lot. Pretend to not be telekinetic. Pretend to be dead...

So far, pretending to be dead this time around was pretty cool. He'd always wanted to come back as a ghost, thought that would be the coolest part of actually being dead. Creed, another operative at ACRO—a ghost hunter—had assured him that most ghosts were on the up and up, even though Oz, a medium who spoke to ghosts who were the worst of the worst, disagreed.

Oz was taking over temporarily for Devlin O'Malley, the head of ACRO. Oz was the one responsible for Wyatt's death and his current assignment, which placed him back on the job as a roughneck.

Like being fucking reincarnated.

Just concentrate on getting your shit together, man.

When his concentration went elsewhere, his gifts began to scatter like loose marbles on a slick, hardwood floor.

So right now, he was trying an image, an offshoot some of the psychics at ACRO told him was an anomaly. He didn't have to touch anything to actually see what looked like a blurred snapshot in his mind, of people, of things, their past, present, or future. And even though it wasn't his strongest gift, using it meant seriously draining his telekinetic skills. Not that he'd need them tonight—if anyone started a fight, with or without weapons, he could take them down with his bare hands. Just like the military taught him.

When he'd been released from the mental ward at sixteen—he'd worked on the oil rig until he was nineteen and then he went the military route. Learning to drill had been cool, and in his blood—learning to destroy had been equally so. Fuck the middle of the road bullshit. As someone as bent on extremes as he was, he went straight for the roughest route possible.

Special Forces. SEALs, specifically. The drill sergeant at boot camp had taken one look at Wyatt's lanky six-foot-four-inch frame and laughed. Wyatt had knocked him out cold with one punch, spent the night in the brig and found himself in BUDs two days later. As punishment.

He loved it—every single brutal minute.

He'd passed his psych evals for the Navy with no problem. He'd faked it, the way he'd faked a lot of things, but the Special Forces community wanted its men to be a little bit on the crazy side, even if they didn't outright admit it.

Fuckin' A-Right.

But the sex thing, *oh yeah,* he'd let his handle on that slip, especially this past week. Mainly because it was fun as hell letting it go out of control and he'd known he wasn't going to get laid at all during the next phase of his mission.

He'd been tamping it down hard when he'd been rigging for three weeks straight—so hard that it made his head hurt.

When you could have any woman—or man, if he'd swung that way—sex got old fast. If his libido wasn't in constant overdrive, he'd have given up sex all together long ago, shaved his head, and become a monk.

He'd tried the monk thing once, when he was seventeen. His apprenticeship lasted exactly three weeks, until he couldn't stand the other men trying to break into his room and have him. The head of the abbey finally asked him to leave. Not before trying to screw him, though.

Wyatt had learned to control his pheromones so that now they only worked on who he wanted them to work on, unless he'd let himself go too long without. In that case, everyone and their mothers—literally—needed to watch out.

He didn't need the sex thing to get laid, had put it to rest yesterday after a round with two women in a ménage that lasted all night and into most of the afternoon. It wasn't a severe drain on his powers, but it did mess with his head.

When a man's fucking, his walls crumble, Dev always said. And yeah, that was the truth in plain English.

English. Like the accent purring against his ear "got any plans for tonight, luv?"

FAITH BLACK'S PLANS for the night hadn't included a tall, dark, and handsome man, but with someone trying to kill her, she'd had to make some adjustments.

The stranger she'd propositioned wrapped his arm around her waist. Before she could so much as blink, he tucked her between his long legs. The bar stool bit into the front of her thighs and his fingers bit into her hip, and for some reason, all she could think about was biting into *him*.

"I can always make room in my schedule for a beautiful woman," he said, in a rich, whisky-smooth southern drawl that made her want to drink him in. And those eyes...even in the hazy, dim light from the beer signs, they glowed clear green. She'd never seen anything like it.

And as a telekinetic who had grown up alongside people with gifts even more incredible than hers, she'd seen a lot.

"I'm not usually so forward," she said, tearing her gaze away from his when the pub door opened. "But see that man walking in?"

The stranger inclined his head almost imperceptibly, as though he hadn't looked, and she gave him points for his in astute assessment of the situation.

"He's my ex-lover," she lied. "He's a loon. Completely mad, and he's stalking me. I told him I have a new lover—"

"And I was the first guy you saw?"

"Yes." No, but when she'd detected a tail as she strolled along the shadowed boardwalk, she'd slipped into the nearest public place that would be full of men, and as luck would have it, these weren't just men. They were bikers, oil drillers, and roughnecks, and the man who now held her had stood out as the toughest of the tough.

Marco watched from near the entrance, not bothering to hide his annoyance.

"Well," the stranger said, threading one hand through her hair to pull her face close to his, "I can either take care of you, or I can take care of him."

A sweet offer, but no matter how capable this guy looked—and he did look capable, all steel-strapped muscle and broad shoulders beneath his black AC/DC T-shirt—Marco was a trained killer, an excedosapien with reflexes a hundred times faster than the average person's. She knew because she'd gone head-to-head with him a year ago, and though her combat skills couldn't be better, his speed and fondness of the wire garrote had nearly spelled her doom.

She fingered the black lace choker that hid the thin scar circling her neck, before catching herself and dropping her hand to his shoulder. "I'd love it if you'd play along, for just a bit."

One corner of his made-to-please-a-woman mouth turned up like she'd picked the right answer, and then suddenly she was experiencing just how much that mouth was made to please.

The contact was gentle, more a brush of lips than anything, but her body's response was immediate and alarming. A blast of heat that had nothing to do with the Florida summer temperatures licked at her breasts, her belly, her inner thighs. When the expert sweep of his tongue opened her mouth, her legs opened, too. At least, as much as they could open with her caged between his jean-clad thighs.

This was not good.

Mustering all her self-control, she concentrated on Marco, using her unique form of telekinesis to probe his aura with her mind, searching for a weakness, a chink in his armor. On average, it took her thirty seconds to penetrate the protective weave of energy around a human, but in the heat of battle, thirty seconds was about twenty-nine and a half seconds too long—and which was why she'd honed her hand-to-hand combat skills to a machete edge. Fortunately, she had time now, but this wasn't going to be a thirty-second jobber. It figured that Marco's aura would be the psychic equivalent to Kevlar.

"What's your name?" the stranger murmured against her lips, and for a moment, she forgot about Marco.

"Faith Black. Yours?"

"Wyatt." He dragged his mouth across her cheek to her ear. "What did he do to you?"

Marco sauntered toward them, his khaki business casual out of place in a rough crowd like this. Men jeered ... until Marco shot them a dark look that shut them up in an instant. Even predators recognized when they were in the presence of something higher on the food chain.

His flat, black eyes remained trained on her as he took a seat at a nearby table.

"Nothing I want to talk about," she said finally.

Wyatt pulled back like he wanted to say something, but the bartender, a bulldog of a man with gray hair pulled into a low ponytail, interrupted.

"Can I get you anything, lady?"

Taking the opportunity to peel herself off Wyatt, she sank down onto a bar stool. "I'll have what he's having."

The bartender palmed a highball glass. "Jack on the rocks, coming up."

"So, Faith," Wyatt said after the bartender slid her drink to her, "where in England are you from?"

She sent out another probing pulse toward Marco, and thank God, found the chink. "All over, really."

Standard answer. She'd spent a lifetime cultivating an accent that wouldn't reveal a background from any particular region, especially Devonshire where she was born, or Yorkshire where she grew up after her parents were killed. In order to confuse people even more, she threw German inflections and American phrasing into her speech.

Blending in helped keep a secret agent alive.

One of Wyatt's hands came down on her knee, but she felt it to her core. Moisture drenched her panties, and her head felt light, her breasts heavy. The sensations breaking over her body were strangely intoxicating, and she had to give a little shake of her head to clear it. No man had ever affected her like this. Not even Sean, the one and only man she'd ever loved.

It had been a year since she'd last seen him, since they'd played cat and mouse, pain and pleasure. He couldn't resist her even when his job was to kill her.

She was counting on his predictability once more, because this mission could get her very dead if Sean's love for her had finally taken second place to his job with Itor.

"It's a little hot to be wearing leather." Wyatt's gaze took in her Goth attire, her black leather pants, the crimson silk and lace corset top and leather jacket, his appreciation obvious in the way his lids grew heavy.

"The heat doesn't bother me." Neither did the cold. She'd always been able to regulate her own body temperature, though that was the extent of her powers over her own bodily functions. She could, however, do anything she wanted to anyone else.

Sliding a glance at Marco, Wyatt downed the whiskey in his glass. The fine muscles in his throat worked beneath the golden, whisker-roughened skin there, holding her gaze for a moment. When he finished, he spun the glass across the polished bar top and nodded to the bartender for another.

"Think the heat will bother Khaki Boy?" he asked.

She grinned. "It might," she said, knowing full well that nothing would deter Marco from his goal but needing time to finish breaking through his aura.

"Let's find out, because the way he's looking at you is bugging the shit out of me." He cupped his palm around the back of her neck and slanted his mouth over hers once more.

Even though she'd anticipated the kiss, her breath caught. The way he maneuvered his lips, teeth, and tongue with gentle, dominant skill... Christ, the man could probably make her orgasm from kissing alone.

"We've got be convincing, right?" he whispered, and then licked the swell of her bottom lip so a ragged moan escaped her. "Open for me."

She didn't hesitate, welcomed the slide of his wet tongue against hers. He tasted like whiskey, smelled like earth and man, a potent combination that made her loosen up more effectively than if she'd poured the entire fifth of Jack Daniels down her throat— her throat that throbbed in a grim reminder that Marco wanted to slit it.

Doing her best to ignore what Wyatt's hand was doing to her thigh, she used her mind to pluck at the weak strings in the weave of Marco's aura. Finally, with Wyatt trailing kisses along her jaw, visions of the internal workings of Marco's body filled her brain.

He still watched, but had leaned forward, elbows propped on knees, enjoying the show. The dozen or so patrons in the pub could care less, were too fascinated by the two scantily clad women near the pool table who were doing a lot more than kissing the four guys they were with.

Marco's heartbeat gave nothing away. Slow, steady, strong. She could stop it in an instant, give him an aneurysm, or boil his blood.

But all of those things would attract attention. Besides, killing one of Itor's men when she would be meeting with a top Itor operative tomorrow was not conducive to a good working relationship. Even if—or especially because—she was going to be faking the relationship.

In the back of her mind, she knew Wyatt was nuzzling her ear, knew he'd pulled her nearly into his lap and that he had a monster erection nudging her hip. She knew her fingers were gliding over his hard, bunched biceps, and that her sex had flooded with silken cream.

If Marco weren't a threat, she'd drag Wyatt No Last Name to her hotel room and take him over and over.

But she wouldn't put it past Marco to try and take them both out before they made it to her bed.

A psychic flare of awareness drew her to Marco's stomach, full after a meal, and in her mind, she reached for his pylorus, the ring of muscle that separated the stomach from the small intestine. With a mental nudge, she opened it, allowing unprocessed food to spill through.

Marco winced, rubbed his belly. He'd cramp up soon, but she needed something more immediate to distract him until the cramps started.

"Wyatt, God," she gasped, when she felt the slide of his palm beneath her corset-like top.

His tongue swirled against her neck. "Do you think he's convinced?"

"I don't know, luv, but I certainly am."

His smile tickled her skin, and before she became distracted again, she dropped south inside Marco's body, located his bladder, and gave a mental squeeze.

The expression of horror on Marco's face as his pants darkened with urine brought immense satisfaction. He looked around wildly for the toilet and, then, clutching his gut, he ran for the men's sign near the back of the pub.

"Brilliant," Faith said, pulling away from Wyatt and ignoring her body's protests. She drew a ten from her pocket and tossed it on the bar top. "I've got to go. Cheers."